ALSO BY SIERRA SIMONE

Co-Written with Julie Murphy
A Merry Little Meet Cute

Priest
Priest
Midnight Mass: A Priest Novella
Sinner
Saint

Thornchapel
A Lesson in Thorns
Feast of Sparks
Harvest of Sighs
Door of Bruises

Misadventures
Misadventures with a Professor
Misadventures of a Curvy Girl
Misadventures in Blue

AMERICAN QUEEN

SIERRA SIMONE

Bloom *books*

Published by Bloom Books, an imprint of Sourcebooks
P.O. Box 4410, Naperville, Illinois 60567-4410
(630) 961-3900
sourcebooks.com

Originally self-published in 2016 by Sierra Simone.

Cataloging-in-Publication Data is on file with the Library of Congress.

Printed and bound in the United States of America.
VP 10 9 8 7 6 5 4 3 2 1

PROLOGUE

THE WEDDING DAY

Love is patient.
Love is kind.
Love is not envious or boastful or arrogant or rude.
It does not insist on its own way; it is not irritable or
resentful; it does not rejoice in wrongdoing, but
rejoices in truth.
It bears all things,
it believes all things,
it hopes all things,
it endures all things.

It endures all things.

I stare at the last line of the Bible verse as my cousin Abilene and her mother continue to fuss with the edges of my veil. The entire passage from I Corinthians is etched into a marble block in the church's narthex, and any other bride standing here might have seen these words as a comfort and an encouragement. Perhaps I'm the only bride ever to stand in front of these massive sanctuary doors and wonder if God is trying to give me a warning.

But when I think of what awaits me at the end of the aisle, of *who* awaits me, I straighten my shoulders and blink away from the verses. From the moment I met Ash, I knew I was destined to love him. I knew I was destined to be his. There's no place he can go that I won't follow, no sacrifice he can demand of me that I won't give, no part of myself that I won't offer willingly and completely to him.

I will bear, believe in, hope for, and endure Ash's love until the day I die, even if that means robbing my own soul.

And it *will* mean robbing my own soul.

My only comfort is that I won't be alone in my suffering.

With a deep breath, I step in front of the doors just as they open, the airy notes of Pachelbel's Canon in D drifting through the stone nave. My grandfather takes my arm to guide me down the aisle. The guests are standing; the candles are flickering; my veil is perfect.

And then I catch sight of Ash.

My pulse catches, races, trips over itself as it rushes to my lips and face and heart. He wears his tuxedo as if he were born wearing one, his wide shoulders and narrow hips filling out the tailored lines perfectly. Even if he didn't stand at the top of the stairs leading up to the altar, he would still seem taller than everyone else around him because that's just Ash. He doesn't have to exude power and strength; he simply *is* power and strength made manifest. And right now all of that power and strength is bent toward me as we lock eyes and, even across the distance of the nave, begin to breathe as one.

Shock seems to ripple through him as he fully sees me—the dress, the veil, the tremulous smile—and pleasure kindles and glows in my chest at this. He wanted to wait to see each other until the ceremony; he wanted this moment.

And I have to admit that watching his handsome face struggle to contain his emotions, feeling my own blood heat at the sight of him in his tuxedo—it was worth it. No matter how outdated the tradition is, no matter how much it inconvenienced our guests, no matter how long those hours were this morning without him, it was worth it.

And then as my grandfather and I move closer, I see *him*.

Right next to Ash, dark-haired and slender, with ice-blue eyes and a mouth made for sin and apologies, sometimes even in that order. Embry Moore—Ash's best friend, his best man, his running mate…

Because of course, I'm not just walking down the aisle to the man I've been in love with since I was sixteen. I'm walking down the aisle to marry the president of the United States.

The hundreds of guests fade away, the massive stands of flowers and candles vanish. And for a moment, it's only the bride and the groom and the best man. It's only me, Ash, and Embry. There's no presidency or vice presidency or freshly painted First Lady's office awaiting me after the honeymoon. There aren't hordes of cameras inside and outside the cathedral, and the pews aren't filled with ambassadors and senators and celebrities.

It's the three of us: Ash, stern and powerful; Embry, haunted and pale; and me, with bite marks on the inside of my thighs and a hammering heart.

It's when I'm almost to the front that I see the best man has a bite mark of his own peeping above the collar of his tuxedo, large and red and fresh.

It's when I'm almost to the front that I see that the small white square in Ash's tuxedo pocket isn't a silk handkerchief—it's undeniably the familiar lace of my panties. No one who hasn't seen my panties before would know, but he's so blatantly displaying them, like a trophy. The last time I saw them they were clutched in Embry's strong fist…

My grandfather lifts my veil and kisses my cheek, putting the veil back down over my face. Ash extends his hand and I slide my fingers into his, and we step up to the priest together, one of my bridesmaids straightening my dress after we find our places and stand still.

I don't realize I'm crying until Ash lets go of my hand, reaches under my veil, and swipes his thumb across my cheek. He lifts his thumb to his lips, licking the taste of my tears off his skin. His dark green eyes smolder with promise, and behind him, Embry's hand unconsciously goes up to touch the bite mark I'm certain Ash left on his neck.

I shiver.

The priest begins, the guests sit, and I wonder one last time if God wants me to stop this, if God can barely stand to look at the three of us, if God wasn't trying to warn me before, because what did I really think I could endure? What did I really think the two most powerful men in the world would be willing to endure from me?

But then I catch sight of Ash's eyes, still flared with unmistakable heat, and Embry's long fingers, still probing the mark on his neck, and I decide now that this fairy tale couldn't have ended any other way.

I mean, God can warn me all he wants, but that doesn't mean I have to listen.

THE PRINCESS

CHAPTER 1

EIGHTEEN YEARS AGO

I WAS CURSED BY A WIZARD WHEN I WAS SEVEN YEARS OLD.

It was at a charity gala, I think. Save for the wizard, it wouldn't have stood out from any other event my grandfather took me to. Ball gowns and tuxedos, chandeliers glittering in opulent hotel ballrooms while string octets played in discreet corners. Ostensibly, these events raised money for the various foundations and causes championed by the rich and bored, but in reality, they were business meetings. Political allegiances for this candidate or that were sounded out; potential donors were identified and wooed. Business deals began here, and marriages in the upper reaches of society began here as well—because among the wealthy, what were marriages but lifelong business deals?

I understood some of this, even as a young girl, but it never troubled me. It was life—or at least Grandpa Leo's life—and it didn't occur to me to question it.

Besides, I enjoyed dressing up in the expensive flouncing

dresses Grandpa Leo bought for me. I enjoyed having adults ask my opinion, I enjoyed seeing all the beautiful women and handsome men, and most of all, I enjoyed dancing with Grandpa Leo, who always let me stand on his shoes and who never forgot to spin me around and around so that I could pretend I was a princess in a fairy tale.

And late at night, when the big black car would pick us up and take us back to the Manhattan penthouse, he would let me chatter happily about everything I'd seen and heard, asking me questions about who had said what, about how they said it, if they had looked happy or sad or mad as they said it. He would ask me who looked tired, who looked distracted, who grumbled under their breath during the keynote speeches. It wasn't until a few years later that I realized Grandpa relied on me as a kind of spy, a watcher of sorts, because people will behave around children in ways they won't around adults. They let their guard down; they mutter to their friends, certain that a child won't notice or understand.

But I did notice. I was naturally observant, naturally curious, and naturally ready to read deeply into small comments or gestures. And at Grandpa Leo's side, I spent years honing that natural weapon into something sharp and useful, something he used for The Party, but that I used for him because I wanted to help him, wanted him to be proud of me, and also because there was something addictive in it. Something addictive in watching people, in figuring them out, like reading a book and deciphering the big twist before the end.

But the night I met the wizard, all of that was still in the future. At that moment, I was giddy and wound up from spinning in circles and sneaking extra plates of dessert from the winking waitresses. I was still spinning when my grandfather beckoned me to join him near the doors of the ballroom. I skipped over, expecting another of his usual friends—the Beltway wheelers and dealers or the snappish, bored businessmen.

It was someone different. Some*thing* different. A tall man, only in his midtwenties, but with crow-dark eyes and a thin mouth that reminded me of the illustrations of evil enchanters in my fairy-tale books. Unlike the evil enchanters, he didn't appear in a cloud of smoke or wear long, trailing robes. He was dressed in a crisp tuxedo, his face clean-shaven, his dark hair short and perfectly combed.

My grandfather beamed down at me as he introduced us. "Mr. Merlin Rhys, I'd like you to meet my granddaughter, Greer. Greer, this young man is moving here from England, and coming in as a consultant to The Party."

The Party. Even at seven, The Party was a force in my life as strong as any other. A risk, I suppose, that came with having a former vice president for a grandfather. Especially when that former vice president had served in the White House with the late Penley Luther, the dead and revered demigod of The Party. It was President Luther who was referenced in all the speeches and op-eds; it was Luther's name that was invoked whenever a crisis happened. What would Luther do? *What would Luther do?!*

Mr. Merlin Rhys looked down at me, his black eyes unreadable in the golden glow of the ballroom. "This seems a bit dull for a girl your age," he said, softly but also not softly. There was a challenge in his words, lodged somewhere in those neatly folded consonants and lilting vowels, but I couldn't puzzle it out, couldn't sift it away from his words. I kept my eyes on his face as my grandfather spoke.

"She's my date," Grandpa Leo said affectionately, ruffling my hair. "My son and daughter-in-law are traveling out of the country for humanitarian work, so she's staying with me for a few months. She's so well-behaved. Isn't that right, Greer?"

"Yes, Grandpa," I chirped obediently, but when I caught the frown on Merlin's face, something chilled in me, as if a cold fog had wrapped itself around me and only me, and was slowly leaching away my warmth.

I dropped my eyes to my shoes, shivering and trying not to show it. The glossy patent leather reflected the shimmers and glitters of the gilded ceiling, and I watched those shimmers as Merlin and my grandfather began discussing midterm election strategy, trying to reconcile what I felt with what I knew.

I *felt* fear, the kind of creeping, neck-prickling fear I had when I woke up at night to see my closet door open. But I *knew* that I was safe, that Grandpa Leo would keep me safe, that this stranger couldn't hurt me in a room full of people. Except I wasn't afraid of him hurting me or stealing me away, necessarily. No, it was the way his eyes had bored into mine, the way his disapproval of me had enveloped me so completely, that frightened me. I felt like he knew me, understood me, could see inside of me to all of the times I'd lied or cheated or fought on the playground. That he could see all the nights I'd been unable to sleep, my closet door open and me too afraid to get up and close it. All the mornings my father and I went walking in the woods behind our house, all the evenings my mother patiently taught me tai chi. All the fairy-tale books I so adored, all of the objects I'd gathered in the little treasure box stored under my bed, all of my secret childish dreams and fears—everything. This man could see it all.

And to be seen—really *seen*—was the most terrifying thing I'd ever felt.

"Leo!" a man called from a few feet away. He was also with The Party, and Grandpa gave my hair a final ruffle as he gestured to the man to approach him. "One moment, Mr. Rhys."

Merlin inclined his head gravely as my grandfather

turned to speak to the other man. I willed myself to meet his eyes again and then immediately wished I hadn't. His eyes, I now realized, had been shuttered when speaking to Grandpa, and they were un-shuttered now, burning with something that seemed a lot like dislike.

"Greer Galloway," he said in that soft-not-soft voice. Something like a Welsh lilt emerged in his words, as if he'd lost control of his voice as well as his eyes.

I swallowed. I didn't know what to say—I was a child, and always my girlish demeanor had been enough to charm Grandpa Leo's friends, but I sensed that it would do no good here. I could not endear myself to Merlin Rhys, not with smiles or dimples or twirls or childlike questions.

And then he knelt down in front of me. It was rare for the adults in Leo's world to do that—even the women with children of their own preferred to stand over me and caress my blond curls as if I were a pet. But Merlin knelt so that I could look him in the eye without craning my neck, and I knew, despite my fear, this was a sign of respect. Merlin was treating me as if I were worthy of his time and attention, and even though it was tainted with disapproval, I was grateful for it in my own young way.

He reached out and took my chin in his long, slender fingers, holding my face still for inspection. "Not ambitious," he said, dark eyes searching my face. "But often careless. Not cold but sometimes distant. Passionate, intelligent, dreamy…and too easily hurt." He shook his head. "It's as I thought."

I knew from the stacks of books beside my bed that the words of an enchanter were dangerous things. I knew I shouldn't speak. I shouldn't promise him anything, agree to anything, concede or lie or evade. But I couldn't help it.

"What's as you thought?"

Merlin dropped his hand, and an expression of real

regret creased his face. "It cannot be you. I'm sorry, but it simply can't."

Confusion seeped past the fear. "What can't be me?"

Merlin stood up, smoothing his tuxedo jacket, his mind made up about whatever it was. "Keep your kisses to yourself when the time comes," he said.

I didn't understand. "I don't kiss anyone except Grandpa Leo and my mommy and daddy."

"That's your world now. But when you are older, you will inherit *this* world," Merlin said, gesturing around the room, "the world your grandfather helped create. And this world hangs on a thread, balanced between trust and power. Powerful people have to decide when to trust each other and when to fight each other, and those decisions aren't always made with the mind. They're made with the heart. Do you understand this?"

"I think so…" I said slowly.

"Greer, one kiss from you would swing this world from friendship to anger. From peace to war. It will destroy everything your grandfather has worked so hard to build, and many, many people will be hurt. You don't want to hurt people, do you? Hurt your grandfather? Undo all the work he's done?"

I shook my head vehemently.

"I didn't think so. Because that's what will happen if your lips touch another's. Mark my words."

I nodded because this was logic that spoke to me. Kisses were magic—everyone knew this. They turned frogs into princes, they woke princesses from deadly sleep, and they decided the fates of kingdoms and empires. It never once crossed my mind that Merlin could be wrong, that a kiss might be harmless.

Or that a kiss might be worth all the harm it caused.

The regret in his eyes turned into sadness. "And I am

sorry about your parents," he said softly. "Despite everything, you are a sweet girl. You deserve only happiness, and maybe one day you'll learn that's what I'm trying to give to you. Hold tight to the things that make you happy, and never doubt that you are loved." He nodded toward Grandpa Leo, who was now walking back toward us.

"Don't be sorry for my parents," I said, puzzled. "They're just fine."

Merlin said nothing, but he reached down and touched my shoulder. Not a pull into a hug, not a pat or a caress, just a touch. A moment's worth of weight, and then nothing but the feeling of air on my skin and worry settling into my small bones.

Grandpa Leo scooped me into his arms as he reached us, planting a big mustached kiss on my cheek as he did. "Isn't my granddaughter something special, Merlin?" he asked, grinning at me. "What were you two talking about?"

I opened my mouth to answer, but Merlin cut in smoothly. "She was telling me how much she enjoys staying with you."

Grandpa looked pleased. "Yes. I love Oregon as much as anyone, but there's nothing like New York City, is there, Greer?"

I must have answered. There must have been more conversation after that, more words about politics and money and demographics, but all I could hear were Merlin's words from earlier.

I am sorry for your parents.

In my overactive imagination, it wasn't hard to conjure the worst. It was what always happened in the stories—tragedy, omens, heartache. What if my parents had been killed? What if their plane had crashed, their hotel caught on fire, their bodies beaten and robbed and left to die?

I am sorry for your parents.

7

It was all I could think of, all I could hear, and when Grandpa Leo tucked me into bed later that night, I burst into tears.

"What's wrong, sweetie?" he asked, thick eyebrows drawn together in concern.

I knew enough to know he wouldn't believe me when I told him that Merlin was an enchanter, maybe a bad one, or that he could somehow sense my parents' deaths before they happened. I knew enough to lie and say simply, "I miss Mommy and Daddy."

"Oh, sweetie," Grandpa Leo said. "We'll call them right now, okay?"

He pulled out his phone and dialed, and within a few seconds, I heard Mommy's light voice and Daddy's deep one coming through the speaker. They were in Bucharest, getting ready to board a train bound for Warsaw, and they were happy and safe and full of promises for when they returned home. For a short while, I believed them. I believed that they would come back. That there'd be more long forest hikes with my father, more tai chi in the evenings with my mother, more nights when I fell asleep to the sound of them reading poetry to each other with logs crackling in the fireplace nearby. That the warm sunshine and tree-green days of my childhood still stretched out before me, safe in the cozy nest of books and nature that my parents had built.

But that night as I tried to fall asleep, Merlin's words crept back into my mind along with the fear.

I am sorry about your parents.

I barely slept that night, jolting awake at every honk and siren on the Manhattan streets below Grandpa's penthouse, shivering at every creak of the wind-buffeted windows. Dreams threaded my sleep, dreams of tree-covered mountains in a place I'd never seen, broad-shouldered men crawling through mud and dead pine needles, my parents dancing in the living room after they thought I was asleep. A train steaming across a bridge, and the bridge collapsing.

My parents danced, the wind blew through the trees, men crawled through mud. The train plunged to the valley floor.

Dance, trees, mud, death.

Over and over again.

Dance, trees, mud, death.

And when I sat up in the weak sunlight of morning to see my grandfather standing in the doorway, his eyes blank with shock and horror, his phone dangling from his hand, I already knew what he was there to tell me.

Like King Hezekiah, I turned my face to the wall and prayed.

I prayed for God to kill me too.

CHAPTER 2

ELEVEN YEARS AGO

GOD, AS HE OFTEN DOES, CHOSE NOT TO ANSWER MY PRAYER. Or at the very least, chose not to answer yes.

Instead, my life went on.

My mother's parents were aging and frail, and while I had an aunt and uncle in Boston, they already had a daughter my age and they made it quite clear that they weren't willing to take on another child.

But it hardly mattered. From the moment Grandpa Leo got the phone call, from the very second the reality settled over us, it was never in question that I would live with him. He was only in his fifties, healthy and energetic, with plenty of room in his house for another person. He was a busy man, busy with The Party and his thriving green-energy empire, but Grandpa Leo was the kind of person who never said no to anything except sleep.

He moved my things into his penthouse, enrolled me in a small but academically rigorous private school on the Upper West Side, and folded me into his life as best a widowed grandfather could.

I remember crying before and after the funeral, but not during. I remember hiding inside myself at the new school, so different from the airy Montessori classroom back in Oregon. I remember Grandpa Leo buying me stacks of books to cheer me up, and I remember reading late into the night. I remember missing my parents so much it felt like someone had scooped something vital out of my chest with a giant spoon. I remember hearing Merlin's words about my parents.

Merlin's prophecy.

If he'd been right about their deaths, was he also right about the other things? He'd told me to keep my kisses to myself—was it a warning I had to follow?

I was certain it was. I was certain now that Merlin could see the future, that he could predict doom, and in my grief and terror, I promised myself at seven years old that, no matter what, I would never kiss a man or woman so long as I lived.

Never ever, ever.

———

When I was fourteen, Grandpa Leo asked me whether I'd like to continue going to school in Manhattan or if I'd like to enroll in a boarding school overseas. My cousin Abilene was being sent there in the hopes that she would settle down and focus on her schoolwork, and Grandpa thought I might like to go as well. I was already an excellent student—there were no worries there—but I think Grandpa worried that I was too isolated, living alone with him, only going to environmental fundraisers and party events, spending my evenings immersed in gossip and speculation about politicians and businessmen, and spending my weekends as Grandpa's secret weapon, observing and reporting back to him.

"You're young," he said, sitting at the dinner table as he handed me the booklet for the school. The pictures seemed almost calculated to lure me into saying yes—thick fog, old wooden doors, gold and green English summers. "You should see the world. Be around other young people. Get into a little bit of trouble."

Then he laughed. "Or at the very least, keep your cousin out of trouble."

And that was how Abilene and I ended up at the Cadbury Academy for Girls the autumn of my fourteenth year.

Cadbury was an impressive place, a large and sprawling complex of stone and stained glass, with towers and multiple libraries and an honest-to-God Iron Age hill fort right in its backyard. I loved it immediately. Abilene loved only its proximity to the boys' school a mile down the lane. Almost every night, she would crawl out of our ground-floor window and creep across the soft green lawn to the road. Almost every night, I would go with her, not because I wanted to see the boys, but because I felt protective of her. Protective of her safety, of her future at Cadbury, of her reputation.

We crept into dorm rooms, met in the back gardens of pubs that didn't bother to kick us out, joined illicit parties on the massive flat-topped hill where the Iron Age fort once stood. We weren't the only girls most of the time, but Abilene was the constant, the leader, the instigator.

By fifteen, she had the tall, willowy body of a model, with soft budded breasts and long red hair. She was loud and vivacious and pretty; she drank more than the boys, played lacrosse like her life depended on it, and always, always had a circle of people around her.

In contrast, I was a thing of shadows and corners. I spent most of my free time in the library. I often ate alone on the grounds with a book resting against my knees. I ignored sports but chose dance and creative writing as my extracurriculars instead. I was shorter than I wanted to be, my body lagging behind Abilene's in the things boys liked to see, strong enough for dance but not quite slender enough to look good in the leotard. My chin had the slightest hint of a cleft, which Abilene and I would spend hours trying to hide with makeup, and I had a beauty mark on my cheek that I loathed. My eyes were gray and felt flat compared to Abilene's lively blue ones, and all of this would have been fine if I had even one ounce of the charisma Abilene so effortlessly exuded, but I didn't. I was quiet and spacey and dreamy, terrified of conflict but sometimes thoughtless enough that I accidentally caused it, fascinated with things that my peers cared nothing for—American politics and old books and coral reef bleaching and wars fought so long ago that even their names had all but turned to dust.

The one thing I liked about myself at that age was my hair. Long and thick and blond—golden in the winter and nearly white in the summer—it was the thing people noticed first about me, the way they described me to others, the thing my friends idly played with when we sat and watched TV in the common room. Abilene hated it, hated that there was any one thing about my appearance that showed her up, and I learned within a few weeks at Cadbury that her sharp tugs of my ponytail weren't signs of affection but of barely controlled jealousy.

Despite the hair, Abilene was still the monarch and I still the lady-in-waiting. She held court and I anxiously kept a lookout for teachers. She shirked her homework, and I stayed up late typing out assignments for her so she wouldn't fail. She partied and I walked her home, balancing her on my shoulder and using my phone for light as we stumbled down from the hill, her hair smelling like spilled cider and cheap cologne.

"You never kiss the boys," she said one night when we were fifteen, as I guided her down the narrow lane back to the school.

"Maybe it's because I want to kiss girls," I said, stepping over a patch of mud. "Ever think of that?"

"I have," Abilene drunkenly confirmed, "and I know that's not it because there's lots of girls at Cadbury who would kiss you. And still you never kiss anyone."

Keep your kisses to yourself.

Eight years later, and I could still see Merlin's dark eyes, hear his cold, disapproving voice. Could still remember the eerie feeling of portent that came over me when he predicted the death of my parents. If he believed people would suffer if I kissed someone, surely there was a good reason.

An important reason.

And besides, it was such a small thing to give up. It's not like I had boys knocking down my door to kiss me anyway.

"I just don't feel like kissing anyone," I said firmly. "That's the only reason there is."

Abilene lifted her head from my shoulder and hiccupped into the chilly night air. Somewhere nearby a sheep bleated. "Just you wait, Greer Galloway. One of these days, you're going to be just as wild as me."

I guided her around a pile of sheep shit as she hiccupped again. "I doubt it."

"You're wrong. When you finally cut loose, you're going to be the kinkiest slut at Cadbury."

For some reason, this made me flush—and not with indignation but with shame. How could she know the thoughts that flitted through my mind sometimes? The dreams where I woke up throbbing and clenching around nothing?

No, she couldn't know. I hadn't breathed a word of those things to anyone, and I never would.

Like my kisses, I would keep those things to myself. After all, I was happy like this. Happy to take care of Abilene and dream of college.

Happy to pretend that this was enough.

CHAPTER 3

THE PRESENT

"AND SO IF WE TURN BACK FURTHER THAN GEOFFREY OF Monmouth, back to the *Annales Cambriae*—that's the Annals of Wales for those of you not up on your medieval Latin—we see the earliest mention of the Mordred figure, here called 'Medraut.'"

The clack of keys on laptop keyboards echoes through the small classroom as the students furiously type out notes. The bulk of the undergrads here are actually pre-med or poli-sci, only taking my Arthurian Lit course to tackle a humanities credit, but that doesn't stop them from striving for the highest scores. Georgetown isn't cheap, after all, and a lot of the students here need to keep their grades up to retain scholarships and grants. And I empathize completely; only a couple months into this lecturing gig, I can still vividly remember the late nights and coffee-fueled mornings as I finished up my master's in medieval literature at Oxford. Sometimes it's still hard to believe I'm actually done, actually back in the States, actually doing a grown-up job with a nice leather briefcase and everything.

"Mordred is only mentioned as dying alongside King Arthur here," I continue, moving from behind the podium over to the whiteboard, "and we are given no information as to his role in the battle, whether he was fighting against or alongside Arthur, whether he was Arthur's son or nephew or simply just another warrior."

I uncap a dry erase marker and start editing the family tree we've been working on as a class throughout the fall semester, writing a question mark next to Mordred's name.

"The King Arthur legend is famous for many things—the Holy Grail and the Round Table, of course—but maybe it's most famous for the epic love story between Lancelot and Guinevere." I draw a heart between their two names on the board, and giggles ripple through the class. "But as we saw moving backward from Chrétien de Troyes to Geoffrey of Monmouth, Lancelot was a character invented by the French to satisfy their need for courtly romance. He's not in the earliest mentions of the legends at all."

I cross out Lancelot's name on the board, writing *made up by the French* above his name. More keys clacking.

"But there is the hint of another romance, older than the Lancelot story and even more dangerous." I draw a new heart, this time between Mordred and Guinevere. "After the Annals, the next mentions we get of Mordred almost always depict him kidnapping the queen or trying to marry her. This is usually pointed to as the source of the strife between him and King Arthur—who long before being depicted as Mordred's father or uncle may have simply been a romantic rival."

I cap the marker and turn back to the podium. "I think Mordred, more than Lancelot, highlights the central problem of King Arthur's court…which is that trust, love, and family don't always come packaged together."

I can hear the old wall clock behind me tick over, and the students slowly begin closing laptops and opening bags, trying to appear attentive but their minds already out the door.

"That's all for today," I announce. "Next week, we'll start into the Welsh Triads. And don't forget to submit your final project proposals!"

They finish packing up as I walk back to my desk to pack up my own things. A few students stop by with questions and to pick up graded assignments, and then I'm alone in the room.

For a few minutes after they've left, I stare out over the vacant seats, as if trying to remember something I've forgotten. I haven't forgotten anything, of course, and nothing is wrong, but an empty restlessness chases after my mind all the same.

You have everything you need, I remind myself. *A good job, a nice house, a grandfather who loves you, a cousin who's your best friend.*

I don't need anything else. What I have is enough.

But then why do I feel so lost all the time?

————

My office at Georgetown is small and shared with two other lecturers, so it's crammed with desks and file folders and books and stacks of neatly stapled handouts. I love it. I love it so much that I've been known to sleep here instead of my small town house near the university (which of course, I can only afford to live in because it belongs to Grandpa Leo and he refuses to hear anything about me paying rent). It's something about being in the old stone building, alone in the hallway of mostly empty offices, the darkness falling through the office window… It makes it easy to remember why I sought out this life. A life of books instead of kisses. A life where Merlin's warning doesn't feel like a curse but a choice.

I'm used to working late into the night, to being the last

one left in the English department, and tonight's no differ-ent. I grade a few papers and then move on to the book I'm trying to write—a literary examination of kingship as chronicled through the multiplicity of Arthurian legends throughout the ages.

I know it sounds boring, but really, I promise it's not. At least not to me. After all, I met a real wizard once, my very own Merlin…even though as an adult I can laugh down the idea of magic and tell myself that his warning was nothing more than nonsense.

After all, I ignored it twice and nothing happened.

Other than my heart breaking both times, nothing happened.

I'm buried deep in my own mind, trying to recreate a line of thought I had last night about leadership in the Dark Ages, when the back of my neck prickles with awareness, as if someone is standing behind me.

Someone is.

I turn in my chair to see a man leaning against the doorway, arms crossed over a muscular chest, his bright blue suit stretching across his shoulders. Even with the jacket buttoned, I can see the way his tailored pants hug his hips and thighs, the way his white silk tie lies flat against the tight button-down underneath.

I tilt my face up to his, swallowing.

Ice-blue eyes and day-old stubble. High cheekbones and a straight nose, full lips and a tall, aristocratic brow. A face made for brooding on a moor somewhere, a face made for Victorian novels or Regency period dramas, the face of the prototypical elitist stranger at a ball in a Jane Austen book.

Except this man's no stranger to me.

Embry Moore.

Vice President Embry Moore.

I scramble to my feet. "Mr. Vice President," I manage. "I didn't—"

His eyes crinkle at the edges. He's actually a year younger than President Colchester, who took office only six months before turning thirty-six, but years of sunshine and four tours of duty have given him the tiniest lines around his eyes, visible only when he smiles.

Like right now.

I swallow again. "How can I help you, Mr. Vice President?"

"Please don't call me that."

"Okay. How can I help you, Mr. Moore?"

He steps forward into the office, and I can smell him. Something with bite—pepper maybe. Or citrus.

"Well, *Ms. Galloway*, I wondered if you were free for dinner tonight."

Oh God.

I peer around him, and he waves a hand. "My security detail is waiting for me at the end of the hall. They can't hear us."

I should ask him why he's here, why he's at Georgetown, in my office, at nearly midnight. I should ask why he didn't call or email or have some secretary chase me down. Instead, I ask, "Isn't it a little late for dinner?"

He glances at his watch without uncrossing his arms. "Maybe, but I'm confident that any restaurant you'd pick would be happy to open up for me. Or open up for *you*—I'm pretty sure there isn't anyone in this town that doesn't still owe Leo Galloway a favor or two."

"I don't throw my grandfather's name around," I say, a little reproachfully. "I don't like the way it makes me feel."

"Just because you want to forget who you are doesn't mean the rest of us can forget you." His voice is soft.

I take a step back. I swallow. A subdued and dignified anger, sculpted into a careful, quiet shape after five years, rises from its slumber. Because, of course, Embry had once been very good at forgetting me.

"Why are you hiding away here?" he asks, uncrossing his arms and taking a step forward. His voice is still soft—too soft, the kind of soft that croons promises in your ear and then breaks them.

I should know.

"I'm not hiding," I say, tilting my head at my desk, stacked high with papers and books and Moleskine journals. "I'm working. I'm teaching. I'm writing a book. I'm happy."

Embry takes another step forward, swallowing up the space in my office with one long stride. He's close enough that I can smell him again, a smell that hasn't changed after all this time.

I close my eyes for a minute, trying to reorient myself.

"You never were a good liar," he murmurs, and when I open my eyes, he's so close to me that I could reach out and run my fingers along his jaw. I don't, turning my head away and looking out the window instead.

"I'm not lying," I lie.

"Come to dinner with me," he says, changing tactics. "We've got a lot to catch up on."

"Five years." The words are pointed, and to his credit, he doesn't parry them away.

"Five years," he acknowledges.

Strange that such a long time can sound so short.

I sigh. "I can't have dinner with you. If I'm seen out with you, then my face will end up all over social media, and I can't handle that."

Embry is listening to me, but he's also reaching out to touch a strand of white-gold hair that's fallen free from my bun. "That's why we're going late. To an unannounced place. No one will know but me and you and the chef."

"And the Secret Service."

20

Embry shrugs, his eyes starting to crinkle again. "They won't write their tell-all memoirs until after they've retired. Until then, our dinner is safe."

I can say no. I know I can, although I've never been able to say it to Embry. But I don't want to say no. I don't want to go to the pristine town house, impeccably furnished and impossibly soulless, and spend another night alone in my bed. I don't want to be staring up at the ceiling of my bedroom, replaying every moment, every glance, my hand stealing under the sheets as I remember the citrus-pepper scent and the way the shadows fell across Embry's cheeks. I don't want to be whipping myself for another wasted night, another missed chance…especially with him.

Just for one night, I can pretend I'm someone else.

"Dinner," I say, finally conceding, and he grins. "But that's it."

He holds up his hands. "I'll be as chaste as a priest. I promise."

"I hear not all priests are that chaste these days."

"Chaste as a nun then."

I reach for my trench coat by the rack near my desk, and he grabs it for me, holding it open for me to step into. It's attentive and intimate and charming while being dangerous—all the things I remember Embry being, and I can't make eye contact as I step into the coat and belt it closed over my blouse and pencil skirt. For a moment—just a tiny, brief moment—I imagine I feel his lips on my hair. I step and turn, facing him and trying to keep my distance all at the same time.

Embry notices, and his smile fades a little. "I'll take care of you, Greer. You don't have to be afraid of me."

Oh, but I am. And not a little afraid of myself.

———

Teller's is a small Italian restaurant a few blocks away from campus, and it's one of those delicious, tiny places that's been around forever. Embry doesn't seem surprised when I suggest it, and after a few phone calls and a very short trip in a black Cadillac, we are inside the old bank building being seated. We're the only ones there, the waiter's footsteps echoing on the cold marble floor and the lights dimmed except for those around our table, but the chef and the servers are nothing but polite and happy to feed us. The Secret Service find discreet and distant points in the dining room to stand, and for a moment, without them in sight, with Embry's suit jacket thrown carelessly over the back of a nearby chair, I can pretend that this is normal. A normal dinner, a normal conversation.

I take a small drink of the cocktail on the table, trying to wash away history, drown it in gin. My history with Embry is hopelessly tangled up in my history with someone else, and as long as I let that someone else cast a shadow over our dinner, there's no way I can hope to have a conversation that isn't strained with pain and regret. The only answer is to put everything in a box and shovel gravel on top and bury it until it suffocates.

"How have you been?" Embry finally asks, sitting back in his chair. I try not to notice the way his shirt strains around his muscular shoulders, the way the lines of his neck disappear into the bleach-white collar of his shirt, but it's impossible. He's impossible not to notice, he's impossible not to crave; even now, my fingers twitch with the imagined feeling of running them along his neck, of slowly unbuttoning his shirt.

"I've been fine," I finally manage. "Settling into my new job."

He nods, the candlelight at the table catching on his eyelashes and casting shadows along his cheekbones. "So it seems. I bet you're an amazing teacher."

I think of my lonely classroom, my silent office, my pervasive restlessness.

I change the subject. "And your job? Being vice president? There's more to it than being photographed with a different woman every night, I'm sure."

The old Embry would have laughed at this, grinned or winked or started bragging. This Embry sits forward and stares at me over his cocktail glass, his hands coming together in his lap. "Yes," he says quietly. "There is more to it than that."

"Mr. Moore—"

"Call me that one more time, and I'll have you arrested for sedition."

"Fine. *Embry*...what am I doing here?"

He takes a deep breath.

"The president wants you to meet with him."

Off all the things he could have said...of all the reasons I thought I might be sitting across the table from a man I haven't spoken with in five years...

"President Colchester," I say. "Maxen Colchester. That president?"

"As far as I know, there's only the one," he replies.

I take a drink from my cocktail, trying to keep my motions controlled and my expressions blank, although I know how pointless that is with Embry Moore. When I first met him, he was a servant to his emotions, impulsive and moody. But in the last five years, he's become the master of deliberate, studied behavior, and I know by the way his eyes flicker across my face that I'm not fooling him at all.

I set down my drink with a sigh, abandoning all pretense of calm. Like he said before, I've never been a good liar and I hate lying anyway.

"I'm a little confused," I admit. "Unless the president wants to talk about the influence of Anglo-Saxon poetry on

Norman literary traditions, I don't see why he'd want to talk to me."

Embry raises an eyebrow. "You don't?"

I glance down at my hands. On my right pointer finger, there is the world's smallest scar—so small it can't be seen. It can only be discerned in the way it disrupts the looping whorls of my fingerprint, a tiny white notch in a tiny white ridge.

A needle of a scar, a hot knife of a memory.

The smell of fire and leather.

Firm lips on my skin.

The warm crimson of blood.

"I don't," I confirm. I have hopes, I have fantasies, I have a memory so powerful it punishes me nightly, but none of those things are *real*. And this is real life right now. This is the vice president, that is the Secret Service over there, and I have a stack of papers waiting to be graded at home.

I'm not sixteen anymore, and anyway, I told myself that I was putting that other man in a box and burying him.

"He saw you at your church last week," Embry finally says. "Did you see him?"

"Of course I saw him," I sigh. "It's hard to miss it when the president of the United States attends Mass at your church."

"And you didn't say hello?"

I throw up my hands. "Hello, Mr. President, I met you once ten years ago. Peace be with you, and also the left communion line is the fastest?"

"You know it's not like that."

"Do I?" I demand, leaning forward. Embry's eyes fall to my chest, where my blouse has gaped open. I straighten, smoothing the fabric back into place, trying to ignore the heat in my belly at Embry's stare. "He was surrounded by Secret Service anyway. I wouldn't have been able to say hello even if I wanted to."

"He wants to see you," Embry repeats.

"I can't believe he even remembers me."

"There you go again, assuming people forget about you. It would be sweet if it wasn't so frustrating."

"Tell me why he wants to see me."

Embry's blue eyes glitter in the dim light as he reaches for my hand. And then he lifts it to his lips, kissing the scarred fingertip with a careful, premeditated slowness. Kissing a scar that he should know nothing about.

My chest threatens to crack open.

"Why you?" I ask, my voice breaking. "Why are you here instead of him?"

"He sent me. He wants to be here so badly, but you know how watched he is. Especially with Jenny—"

Darkness falls like a curtain over the table.

Jenny.

President Colchester's wife.

Late wife.

"It's only been a year since the funeral, and Merlin thinks it's too soon for Max to step out of the 'tragic widower' role. So there can't be any emails or phone calls," Embry says. "Not yet. You understand."

I do. I do understand. I grew up in this world, and even though I never wanted to be part of it, I understand scandal and PR and crisis management as well as I understand medieval literature.

"And so he sent you."

"He sent me."

I look down at my hand, still held tightly by Embry's. How did I end up tangled with these two men? The two most powerful men in the free world?

This is real life, Greer. Say no. Say no to Embry, and for God's sake, say no to the president.

I breathe in.

25

Fire and leather. Blood and kisses.

I breathe out.

"I'll see him. Tell him I'll see him."

I don't miss the pain that flares in Embry's eyes, pain that he quickly hides.

"Consider it done," he says.

CHAPTER 4

TEN YEARS AGO

"YOU HAVE TO HOLD STILL," ABILENE FUSSED AT ME. "I KEEP messing this one up."

I sighed and forced my body to stay still, even though I was so excited I could barely breathe. In just a few minutes, a hired car would pull in front of the London hotel Grandpa Leo had put us up in and take us to a large party in Chelsea, a party with adults and champagne. There would be diplomats and businessmen and maybe even a celebrity or two—a world away from the stale beer and crackling speakers of the hill parties back at school.

It was my sixteenth birthday, and as a special treat, he'd allowed us to tag along with him to the party. Or rather, he'd invited me and only reluctantly allowed Abilene to tag along—he could hardly invite one granddaughter and not the other, but we both knew (even if we didn't say it aloud) that bringing Abilene to something like this carried a significant risk of embarrassment. She'd nearly been thrown out of Cadbury multiple times for a host of crimes—drinking on the premises, breaking curfew, a nasty incident that led to another lacrosse player with a black eye—and every time, Grandpa Leo had quietly paid the right money and pulled the right strings to keep her installed there.

The last thing he wanted was for her to disgrace him at a party full of his friends, but I promised him that I'd keep her on her best behavior. I promised him that I'd keep her from drinking too much, from talking too much, from flirting too much, just as long as he'd let her go, because she would be so hurt if I was able to come along and she wasn't.

And Grandpa Leo, who used to terrorize senators and petroleum executives, who helped shape the strongest environmental legislation on record and publicly excoriated his enemies on a daily basis, relented to my pleading with a gruff smile and let Abilene come along.

And that's why Abilene and I had spent our evening in an expensive hotel getting ready, why I was currently trying not to squirm in a chair as Abilene carefully pinned my final curl in place.

When she finished and I stood up to give myself a final once-over before strapping on my high heels and going downstairs, she made a noise behind me.

Worried, I spun around to the mirror. "What is it? Is my bra showing?" I tried to turn this way and that, positive that Abilene had seen something potentially disastrous.

"No. It's…it's fine." Her voice sounded choked. "Let's go. Grandpa's waiting."

I shrugged and sat down to pull on the strappy heels that matched the blush-pink gown Grandpa had bought me earlier that week. The tulle and organza dress had a narrow waist and form-fitting bodice, a delicate sash in back, and a skirt that erupted from sedate layers into luxurious drapes and loops. With a matching tulle flower set into my hair and metallic pink heels, I felt like a princess, even though I knew I wouldn't look like one compared to Abilene.

Tonight, she wore a tight dress of electric blue, with a keyhole in the center of the bodice displaying a swath of creamy-pale skin, and her glossy red hair was down in loose waves. She looked years older than she was, mature and sophisticated, and I stifled the usual pang of weary resignation that came along with seeing Abilene dressed up.

I was used to being in her shadow, after all, the companion to her Doctor, the Spock to her Kirk, and so it shouldn't bother me tonight. Even if it was my birthday. Even if I was in the most beautiful dress I'd ever worn. But after looking at her, so polished and alluring, it was impossible to look at my reflection and see anything other than the faint cleft in my chin, the ridiculous beauty mark that refused to be covered up, the flatness of my eyes even after the most strategic uses of mascara and eyeliner.

So I did one final check to make sure my strapless bra wasn't showing, that I hadn't accidentally smeared pink lipstick across my face or sat on Abilene's half-eaten chocolate bar, and then opened the door. Abilene pushed past me without a word and refused to speak to me on the ride down to the lobby.

The mirrored doors opened, and she strode out of the lift, her heels clicking on the marble floor. "Are you angry with me?" I asked.

I racked my brain trying to think of anything I could have done to make her mad and came up with nothing. But sometimes that didn't matter with Abilene. For all the times she hugged me out of nowhere, made sure I was invited to a party, or defended me to her friends, there were other times when she'd plunge suddenly into a dark, sullen mood, when her stare would burn like acid and her words char my skin like fire. I'd learned not to negotiate with these moods or try to appease them, even though they seemed to happen more and more frequently. There was no point—you couldn't argue with a storm cloud; you could only wait for it to blow past.

"I'm not angry with you," she said, still walking fast. I could make out the stout shape of Grandpa Leo through the front doors and, overlaid on top of him, our reflections: Abilene all scarlet and sapphire, and me shell-pink and gold.

She must have seen it too because she froze, staring at the door. Then she turned to me. "Just stay out of my way tonight," she mumbled. "Just stay away from me."

Stung, I watched her walk through the doors as the doorman opened them for her and give Grandpa Leo a big hug, a fake smile plastered onto her face. I wanted to yell at her, tell her that I was the only reason she was going to the party in the first place. I wanted to scream and kick because couldn't I have *one* night, just *one*, that wasn't all about her, that she didn't upstage or steal or poison with her drama?

And most of all, I wanted to cry because Abilene was my best friend, maybe my only friend, and the whole world felt off-kilter when she was like this with me.

But what could I do? What could I say or scream or beg that would make her understand?

So I did what Greer Galloway usually did.

I quietly followed in her footsteps.

I went through the doors and into Grandpa's arms and then climbed into the car with her. We sat shoulder to shoulder, my skirt overflowing onto hers, her soft hair brushing against the skin of my arm, and we didn't say a word to each other the entire drive.

———

Within minutes of arriving at the party, Abilene disappeared. I made to go find her, but Grandpa Leo held me back with a hand on my arm and a shake of his head. "She'll be fine after

30

a few minutes," he promised. "Some space to cool down will do her good, and besides, I'd like to introduce you to a few of my friends." I knew *introduce* was Grandpa Leo–speak for planting me as his spy, that he would want me to circulate and listen, or stand by his side and observe people while he talked, and I wanted to do that, I really did, but I also wanted to fix whatever was wrong with Abilene and me before the night grew any older.

I bit my lip, scanning the crowd for any sign of dark red hair, but I saw nothing. She was long vanished into a sea of tuxedos and circulating cocktail trays. I reluctantly allowed Grandpa to pull me deeper into the party.

Women cooed over me and men complimented me, their eyes trailing along my body in a way that I wasn't used to, and I knew it was all because Abilene wasn't next to me. They couldn't see how marred my face was, how boring my body, without a gorgeous redhead the same age standing beside me for comparison. This thought should have made me happy, that without Abilene's radiant charm, I could finally bask in the kinds of compliments she gathered so effortlessly, but it didn't. I only felt more miserably aware of her absence. After an hour of this, I excused myself from Grandpa and a circle of guests to go find her, and that's when I ran—literally—into Merlin Rhys.

He reached down to steady me by the elbow, keeping the amber drink in his other hand from sloshing as he did so. "Pardon me," he apologized, even though it was my fault.

"No, it was my mistake," I said. "I'm sorry."

He peered down into my face and something shifted in his expression. "You're Leo Galloway's granddaughter," he said. No inflection, no follow-up. Just that one fact, the one fact that identified me wherever I went, as if the ghost of President Penley Luther was standing right behind me.

"Yes," I said. "We met once, you and I, but I was a little girl."

You predicted my parents' deaths.
You warned me never to kiss anyone.

"I remember," Merlin replied, and the way he looked at me almost made me feel as if he could read my thoughts. Like he'd heard them as clearly as if I'd spoken them aloud.

"Merlin!" A man in military attire appeared next to us and clapped a hand on Merlin's shoulder. Merlin smiled tightly at him. "I was wondering when I'd catch up to you. How have you been?"

Merlin turned to answer the general, and I took the opportunity to vanish, my heart pounding in my chest.

Merlin unsettled and frightened me, and through all these years, I'd thought it was because I'd met him as a little girl, at an age when almost anything can seem scary. But he still scared me at sixteen. There was something about him…not hostile necessarily, but aggressive. You felt his mind pushing at yours, challenging the walls around your thoughts, slithering through the defenses you kept around your feelings. It made me feel exposed and vulnerable, and I'd had enough of that from Abilene tonight.

I found my cousin in the town house's library—a large lovely room with open french doors leading to a wide patio outside—with an empty champagne flute dangling from her fingers as she let a man older than her father kiss a trail of sloppy kisses down her neck. I cleared my throat and he straightened up, embarrassed. He beat a hasty retreat with a muttered apology in Italian, leaving Abilene against the wall looking livid.

"Who the fuck do you think you are?" she demanded once he left the room. "I told you to leave me alone, not barge in here and ruin my life!"

"I'm not trying to ruin your life!" I exclaimed. "I just wanted to make sure you were okay."

She snorted in disgust. "Yeah right."

"What is going on with you tonight?" I asked. "You've been angry with me since the hotel."

"I'm not angry," she maintained, her nostrils flaring. "I just don't want to be around you right now. God, why is that so fucking hard to understand?"

"It's not—"

"And you know what, you always do this," she went on, her eyes starting to shine with unshed tears. "You always push and push and push, like you have to know fucking everything, and one of these days, you're not going to like the answer."

I raised my hands, as if to show I meant no harm. "I don't want to push you. But I know you're angry. And I know it has something to do with me. I want to fix it, Abilene, let me fix it, please."

"You can't fix it," she hissed. "Just stay away—"

"I'm not going to do that. I *can't* do that—"

"Just leave me alone!" Her shrill voice rebounded through the room, and as if to punctuate her statement, she threw the champagne glass to the floor, where it shattered like ice on the polished parquet.

"Abilene," I whispered, because I had never ever seen her like this, so angry that she would act like this in someone else's house, and there seemed to be a moment where it caught up with her too, where her eyes widened and her pale skin went even paler.

And then she stormed out of the room.

For a long minute, I stared at the mess on the floor. It glittered and flashed in the oppressive silence that followed her exit, and it filled my vision, filled my mind and my throat and my chest, until it shrank back to normal size and I could breathe again.

My eyes burned with tears and my throat itched with all the things I wanted to scream at my supposed best friend, but

33

I didn't do any of that. I didn't cry and I didn't yell. I dropped to my knees and began picking up the shards of glass, sliver by tiny sliver, picking up after Abilene like I always did.

"You'll cut yourself if you're not careful," an unfamiliar voice said from the patio door.

Chapter 5

Ten Years Ago

The voice was American, which at this very London party was enough to make me pause and look up. He was in his midtwenties, wearing an army dress uniform, and as he strode toward me, it felt like all the air left the room, like I couldn't breathe, like I would suffocate, but suffocate in the kind of way where visions dance before your eyes as you die. Broad, powerful shoulders tapered into trim and narrow hips, and his face… It was a hero's face. Chiseled jaw, strong nose, full mouth. Emerald eyes and raven hair.

He walked over, close enough that I could read his nameplate now. *Colchester.* A name that sounded strong and solid and a little chilly.

He squatted down next to me, his pants pulling tight over his muscled thighs. "Let me help."

Say something, my brain demanded. *Say anything!*

But I couldn't. I didn't know how to make the words come out. I had never seen a man so handsome, so overtly masculine, and for the first time in my life, I felt overwhelmingly and painfully *female*. I felt slender and soft, yielding and pliant, and when he looked up from the glass to smile kindly at me, I wondered if I would fall apart, like a blown rose caught in a strong wind.

He stood and deposited some of the broken flute in a nearby wastebasket, and then he brought the basket over to me. He knelt down again to pick up more glass.

"She's jealous of you, you know." Colchester said it quietly, while keeping his gaze on the floor.

I thought I'd misheard him. "Jealous?"

He cleared his throat. "I hope you don't mind, but I was standing outside when you first came in the room. I heard you exchange words."

I frantically searched my brain, trying to remember if I'd behaved immaturely. This man was so much older than me, so contained, so *fucking hot*, and the desire to impress him was as sharp as the shards of glass in my hand.

He shook his head as if reading my thoughts. "Don't be embarrassed. I was impressed with how calm you stayed, considering how angry she was with you. Of course, when I saw you, I understood immediately."

"Understood what?"

"That she's jealous."

It took me a beat to understand what he meant. "Of me?" I let out an incredulous laugh.

I wasn't in the habit of being falsely modest. This wasn't me begging for compliments or trying to patch my insecurities with flattery because two years with Abilene had trained me to accept her greater worth on nearly every level—save for the academic and in earning Grandpa Leo's love. There, I excelled. But everywhere else—beauty, friends, personality—Abilene surpassed me. And any other girl at Cadbury would have agreed.

"Abilene's not jealous of me," I said with a smile. "She's *Abilene*. I'm just me... I'm not *like* her. If you saw her, you'd understand."

"I did see her," he replied dryly. "She and her acquaintance took occupancy of the room while I was on the patio, which left me stuck outside. Red hair, blue dress, right?"

"Yes," I said, my smile fading. "So you did see her. You do understand."

"I did and I do. Let me see your hand."

I gave him my hand without thinking, extending it out and offering him the small pile of broken glass I'd collected. With deft fingers, he plucked the shards out of my palm and dropped them one by one into the wastebasket. "I thought I told you to be careful," he said.

I was staring at his face, mesmerized, and I had to tear my eyes away and look down at my hand. I'd cut myself somehow, driven a needle-thin point of glass into my fingertip while trying to clean up, and now blood welled around it, wet and sticky.

"Oh," I whispered.

And I don't know if it was the sight of the blood or the icy prick of pain or my sudden proximity to him, but my vision shifted and my perception sharpened, and for a minute, I saw *him*, the real him behind that striking face and decorated jacket. I saw him like I would have if we'd met in the stuffy clusters of the party, if we'd met while Grandpa Leo stood beside me, waiting for me to deliver my observations and deductions.

I saw the small cut along his jaw.

I saw his hand cradling mine, sure and strong, his skin rough and nicked from war.

I saw the dull glint of the Distinguished Service Cross pinned near his heart.

I saw the faint smudges under his eyes.

I saw it all, and the pieces pulled together and wove into a picture.

"They say meditation helps," I said quietly. "With the insomnia."

His gaze snapped up from my finger to my face, and his eyes—already the dark, clear green of a glass bottle—seemed to grow both darker and clearer.

"What did you say?"

"Meditation. It's supposed to help."

"What makes you think I have trouble sleeping?"

How could I explain the way I knew things? The way I'd been trained for years to hold up a magnifying glass to everyone? I searched for the easiest answer. "It looks like you cut yourself shaving this morning. Like you were too tired to keep your hand steady." And without thinking and without hesitation, I reached up with the hand he wasn't holding and touched his jaw, lightly grazing my fingertips over the cut.

His eyes fluttered closed while his other hand came up against mine, holding it tight to his face. The long sweep of his black eyelashes nearly covered up the sleepless bruises under his eyes. The moment froze—the feeling of his smooth face warm against my palm, the blood still dripping from my finger, the muffled noise of the party through the closed door to the hallway.

"I'm sorry," I offered gently. "If I could help you sleep, I would."

He smiled, his eyes opening, and the moment unfroze, although I still felt it hanging between us. A palpable pressure, a prickling awareness.

A thawed energy.

Scared of its strength, I started to pull my hand away from his face, but he kept it there for a moment longer, looking me in the eyes. "I've never told anyone I have trouble sleeping," he said. "I can't believe you just knew."

"Lots of soldiers struggle with it after difficult missions," I said, looking down. He released my hand and I let it drop, keeping my gaze on the sparkling glass in my palm. "I just wanted to help. I'm sorry if I overstepped."

"Not at all." His voice was warm and filled with wonder. I risked a glance up at him and saw him staring down at me with an awed gratitude so intense it made me flush. "Actually, I should thank you," he said. "It's almost a relief to have someone know. To be able to quit pretending, just for a minute, that everything's okay. That I'm still strong."

"You are strong," I whispered. "I don't know what happened to you, I don't know what you did, but I know that if you can stand in front of me tonight and still be kind, that makes you strong."

He took in a deep breath at my words, those green eyes like emeralds in the dark, and then let it out. "Thank you," he said.

"You're welcome," I said back.

And this time it was his turn to break our connection and look down, turning his attention back to my injured hand.

"This will hurt a little," he warned, gently tugging the glass splinter loose. Another teardrop of blood oozed out, and without a word, he bent his head over my hand and drew the pad of my finger into his mouth, sucking the blood off my skin.

I could feel every flicker of his tongue, every soft scrape of his teeth. And every thrum of my pulse and every beat of my heart cried out for more, for something, for I didn't know what, but parts of me knew. My skin erupted in goose bumps, and I wanted to press my thighs together to soothe an ache that seemed everywhere and nowhere all at once.

When Colchester lifted his head, a small drop of blood clung to his lower lip and he tasted it with his tongue, his eyes locked on mine. I couldn't breathe, couldn't speak, couldn't think. I could only feel—feel and then obey when he said, "Stand up."

We both stood.

It was as if my blood and his gratitude had woven a spell around him. His pupils were dilated and dark, his lips parted—and it was those lips that captivated me now. A perfect mouth, not too lush or too pink, just full and ruddy enough to contrast with the hypermasculine square of his jaw and the strong line of his nose. The sharp angles of the cupid's bow on his upper lip begged to be traced, and for a minute, I imagined doing just that. I imagined reaching out with the finger he'd just kissed and running it along the firm swells of his mouth.

"That's the last time you are allowed to hurt yourself for her, do you understand?" His voice was almost disciplinary.

It's not his business, a wayward thought intruded, but I pushed it away. The moment I'd mentioned his insomnia, the moment I'd touched his face, he and I had gone beyond what could be called a normal interaction. And there was something so knowing in the way he said it, so caring, and I realized how I felt now must have been how he felt when I told him I knew he couldn't sleep.

"Yes," I said, meeting his gaze. "I understand."

He nodded. "Good girl."

I flushed again, pleasure curling deep in my chest for reasons I didn't understand, and he let out another long breath, his eyes on my pinkened cheeks.

I felt like a live wire, like a hot beam of light, all energy and vibration with no direction or outlet. A few minutes before, I'd felt female, but now, I felt *young*. He was a man, and I was still very much a girl, and that difference was so deeply erotic to me, so delicious, and I just wanted to melt into it. Dissolve into him.

Perhaps he felt it too because he murmured, "You're trembling. Are you scared of me?"

"I don't know," I whispered. It was the truth.

He liked that answer, it seemed, because he smiled. "I'd like to touch you again, if that's okay."

I thought of his lips on my finger, the bruises under his eyes, the heavy ache somewhere deep in my body. "Yes, please," I said.

His hands came up under my elbows, cradling them as he searched my face. He must have seen what I felt, the echo of my words stamped all over my face:

yes please

yes please

yes please

And then he pulled me closer, those large, warm hands sliding behind me, one planted firmly between my shoulder blades and the other against the small of my back, and I could feel every curve of my body pressed against the wide, hard expanse of his chest. My head tilted back of its own accord, and his eyes dropped to the long arch of my throat.

"Stay there," he breathed. "Don't move until I tell you." And then he bent down to press his lips against my neck.

I shivered—no one had ever done that before. Everything he was doing to me, every command and touch and caress—it was all new.

Virgin territory.

"What's your name, angel?" he asked. I was still frozen like he'd asked, and he was clearly enjoying it, running his lips down to my collarbone.

"Greer."

"Greer," he echoed, nuzzling into me. "Tell me, Greer, do you like my lips on your skin?"

"Yes," I responded, a little breathlessly. "And—"

"And what?"

"You telling me to do things. Ordering me. Moving my body."

He groaned at that, lifting his head from my neck and pressing me closer to him. Even through the uniform jacket and my own dress, I could feel the firm lines of his chest and stomach. And for the first time, I could smell him. He smelled like leather and woodsmoke. He smelled like a fire burning.

Burn me, I thought, a little wildly. *Consume me.*

His gaze fell down to my mouth, and his eyelids hooded. "You're so young…" he whispered.

Somehow, I knew what was coming next, I knew what he'd say. In the same way he'd asked for permission to touch me, he'd need to know it was okay to do more. He'd need reassurance that I was old enough, that I was an adult, that my consent would have legal weight.

I wanted to lie. I *needed* to lie. Because if I told him what he wanted to hear, I knew he'd kiss me. And nothing seemed more important than that right now, nothing seemed more urgent and necessary. I needed him to kiss me; if he didn't, my body would curl into ash like kindled paper and disappear, please please please—

Except I wasn't a liar.

Except I wasn't supposed to kiss *anybody*, that was the promise I made to myself nine years ago after all, and *anybody* included handsome American military officers.

Except I was certain that—somehow—he'd know I was lying. I knew those green eyes would blaze into mine and illuminate the outline of every lie and half-truth I'd ever told.

"Tell me you're eighteen," he whispered.

"I'm not."

He swore.

And then he tilted my face back up to his, and his mouth came down over mine anyway.

I'd never kissed a boy or a girl, never even tried, and now I had a man's lips firm and warm over mine, insistent and demanding. If I had been thinking clearly, I might have worried that I would be bad at kissing, that I would be laughably awkward and a disappointment to this beautiful stranger. But I wasn't thinking clearly. The only thoughts I had were single words—*fire* and *leather* and *more*—and I didn't need to know what to do.

He knew. And that was how it was supposed to be.

One warm hand cupped the nape of my neck while the other pressed against the small of my back, and his lips parted my own. I gasped the moment I felt him lick inside my mouth—it tickled.

It was soft—dangerously soft—silken, and warm. Every nerve ending I had came frighteningly alive, crackling with need.

And all from one lick of his tongue.

I opened my mouth more to him, sighing as he pressed me closer, so close that I would have lost my balance if he let go of me. It felt so right to open to him, to mold against his body, and I wanted to offer him every inch of my skin. The column of my neck, the space between my breasts, my inner thighs…everywhere.

The thought made me bold, and I realized I wanted to kiss him back. He groaned as I tentatively licked inside his mouth, and I felt his entire body shudder as I did it again.

He tasted sweet and clean, like mint and gin, and the more I kissed him, the more I could taste the lingering salt-tang of my blood. My finger stung from the cut, and I wanted him to suck on it again, I wanted it so badly, and so I pressed it against his lips and into his mouth.

His eyes burned as he closed his lips around my finger and sucked, and everything felt throbbing and swollen—especially the space between my legs. And then his lips were hot on my neck, covering the dip of my clavicle, nibbling on the lobe of my ear.

"Greer," he breathed. "God, where did you come from?"

I don't know, but I feel like I've always been waiting for you.

And then his forehead fell against my neck. "And why aren't you eighteen?" he mumbled into my skin.

"How old are you?" I asked.

He lifted his head, resignation and regret in his eyes. "Twenty-six."

His grip on me loosened, his hands sliding away from my body. I made a noise as he let me go, a noise of pure pain and loss, and he gave a breath like he'd been punched in the gut.

"Please," I begged. "Please."

He inhaled raggedly. "You don't even know what you're asking for."

"I don't care. Anything—I'll let you do anything to me."

"I believe you. That's why you're so dangerous."

We stared at each other, and I lifted my fingers to probe at my lips, which thrummed with blood and heat, swollen and soft. "That was my first kiss," I said, more to myself than to him.

His own lips parted in surprise. "It was?"

"I haven't..." *He doesn't need to know you're a virgin, Greer. It's embarrassing enough that you've never been kissed.* "Yes. You gave me my first kiss."

His eyes blazed a deep green, a summer forest about to catch fire, and there was a moment that I thought he was going to reach for me again. As if the idea of being the first man for me ignited a sense of possession in him. But at that moment, the door to the library opened and Merlin Rhys came in from the hallway.

Keep your kisses to yourself.

Tell me you're eighteen.

Oh my God, what have I done?

We both froze, and then Colchester stepped back and cleared his throat, slipping back into cocktail party mode. "Merlin, hello. Ah, this is Greer...um..."

44

"Greer *Galloway*," Merlin supplied, and his friend swiveled his head to look at me.

"As in Vice President Galloway, Greer Galloway?" Colchester asked me, his strong face both interested and vulnerable.

"*Former* Vice President," I mumbled, not for the first time in my life and certainly not for the last.

"Ah, okay. And, Greer, this is Merlin Rhys. He's a family friend and invited me here tonight. I'm in between assignments, but I didn't want to go home, so he graciously let me tag along."

"Much good it did if you spent the night hiding on the patio," Merlin said mildly.

Not the whole night, I wanted to say, but then Merlin's dark eyes raked over my lips, and somehow—*somehow*—he knew. He knew that I'd kissed his friend. He knew that I wanted to do it again. He knew that I wouldn't have stopped, would have surrendered every bit of myself right here in the library.

"We should go," Merlin said shortly, his eyes still on me as he addressed Colchester. "It's getting late."

Colchester stepped away and then looked back at me, biting his lip. It made him look almost boyish, almost my age, until I looked closer and could see that he bit his lip not out of uncertainty but to control himself.

Merlin sighed and left the room. There was a second when I was certain Colchester would follow him right away, catching the closing door in his large hand and ducking out without a word of goodbye, but then the door closed. And my stranger was still in the room with me.

He was on me in a second, pressing me against the wall, stoking my body to flames once more. "I don't want to leave," he told me, tracing his nose along my jaw.

"Then don't," I practically pleaded, and he swallowed

my pleas with his mouth, kissing me and kissing me and kissing me until there was nothing but his hot mouth and the blood pounding deep in my core.

He stepped back with a heavy breath. "I have to go," he said with genuine regret, after running a hand through his short hair. He looked as put together and collected as when he'd first strolled in from the patio, as if the kissing hadn't even happened. As if *I* hadn't even happened.

"Wait!" I called out as he reached the door to the hallway that Merlin had walked through moments earlier. "I just realized...I don't know your first name."

He paused with his hand on the doorknob and looked down at it. "Captain Maxen Ashley Colchester." He bowed his head. "At your service."

"Maxen," I echoed.

He glanced up and a shy smile crossed his face. "I think I'd like it if you called me Ash."

And then he was gone.

CHAPTER 6

Dear Captain Colchester,

I hope it's not too forward of me to email you—or too awkward. But I asked my grandfather if he could find your email address for me, since Merlin is a mutual friend, and I wanted to tell you that it was really nice to meet you last Saturday. I know we didn't talk about it very much, and it's probably nosy of me, but I was thinking more about your insomnia and I thought you might like a couple of the attachments about meditation I have at the bottom of the email.

I hope you're enjoying London!

Sincerely yours,
Greer Galloway

Dear Ash,

Is it okay if I call you Ash? You said so the night we met, and I would like to, but it also feels strange to call a near-stranger by their first name. Especially a military stranger, because Grandpa Leo has so many military friends that I'm pretty much trained to salute whenever I see a uniform. I also hope I didn't bother you by not mentioning my last name while we were talking. Sometimes at parties like that the Galloway name means certain things—usually that people want me to pass on messages to Grandpa or ask for favors. Sometimes it means they don't want to talk to me at all because they hate my grandfather and his political party. Or sometimes it just means that I can't start from scratch when I meet someone new. I know that seems like a silly thing to care about, but my whole childhood I was introduced to the world as Leo Galloway's granddaughter. Here at Cadbury, I'm always "Abilene's cousin" or "Abilene's roommate." I'm never just Greer, and I got to be that with you, and that was special for me. I hope you don't feel like I was trying to hide something from you?

Anyway, if you're still in London, I hope you're having a good time.

Sincerely yours,
Greer Galloway

Dear Ash,

I wasn't going to bother you any more since it's been almost three weeks since I sent my first email (and I

48

was certain that I was annoying you) but when I was watching the news about the Krakow bombing last night, Grandpa Leo called. We talked about what the bombing meant for Europe and NATO and America, and then he mentioned that you'd been reassigned back to the Carpathian region the week after the party. I feel so terrible for emailing you such trivial stuff when you were back on duty, and I just wanted you to know that I had no idea. I'll make sure to light a prayer candle in church for you and pray a rosary for you every night.

Be safe please.

Sincerely yours,
Greer Galloway

Dear Ash,

It's a real war now. Officially. The Carpathian problem has been around for so long that I'm not sure even Grandpa Leo ever thought it would really come to a head like this. But the Krakow bombing last week— over nine hundred dead—there's no way war wouldn't be declared. At least that's what Grandfather said.

Did you know that my parents were killed by Carpathian separatists? Almost ten years ago now. They blew up a train bridge and killed almost a hundred people, my parents included. All that death, my childhood completely torn apart with God only knows how many other children's, and for what? A small chunk of land squashed between Ukraine and Poland and Slovakia? It makes no sense to me.

Except, in a weird way, it does. I have every reason to hate the Carpathians, but I can't. I can't actually transpose my own pain and grief over the images of the war I'm seeing. Instead, I keep thinking of the Carpathian children who might lose their own parents. I keep thinking about how peaceful and quiet I feel when I remember my childhood in Oregon, when I remember what home feels like. There's no doubt that a handful of the militant separatists have done terrible things, and I understand why there is war now. But part of me wishes that we could simply sit down and grant them what they want—their home. Sovereignty is a complicated thing, and creating a new nation is a fraught prospect in a region already as carved up as Eastern Europe, but what if there could be a way forward without war? I've been raised in politics and I'm not naive enough to believe that we can erase killing and violence, but even if we could reduce it just a little…wouldn't that still be worth trying?

I've been praying for you every night like I said I would. I hope wherever you are that you can feel that. Somehow.

Sincerely yours,
Greer

Dear Ash,

You're famous now. Imagine my surprise yesterday at waking up to your face all over the news. My horror when I found out what you lived through, my relief that you were unharmed. It's unthinkable to me that you were able to fight your way out of a building surrounded by separatists, all while carrying that wounded soldier. I can't fathom what kind of courage it took for you to stay with your friend when the rest of your squad escaped. What kind of skill it took for you to fight off your attackers and eventually save yourself and him. But after reading and watching all the profile pieces on you, I shouldn't have been surprised. You have a history of being a hero, don't you? And I'm not trying to tease you or make you uncomfortable. I've been around every sitting president, vice president, and first lady since I was a baby, and I have seen how tiring it can be to have people fixate on your accomplishments. But I can't write this letter without telling you that I'm in awe of how many times you've risked your life for your fellow soldiers. "No greater love than this" is what Jesus says about men like you, and I'm honored to say that I've met you in person, and that you're even kinder and more humble than all the profile pieces and journalists say.

That being said, to me you are still Ash. Our acquaintance lasted only an hour, but the things that I remember about you—the cut on your jaw, the way your hands felt as they worked the glass splinter out of my finger—are more than your battles. You are a hero to me, but you are a man too. Maybe even more man than hero.

Yours,
Greer

Dear Ash,

It's been six months since we met, and part of me is embarrassed to look at this chain of emails—a chain with only me in it. I tell myself it's because you're at

51

war, because you've been saving lives—last week, that high school building where so many civilians were taking shelter!—but I guess I'm also not foolish enough to believe that a twenty-six-year-old war hero wants unsolicited emails from a boarding school student. So I should stop bothering you, I know I should, but it feels as if I have taken you up as a sort of hobby. Reading about you, thinking about what I should write to you. The girls at school are obsessed with the fact that Abilene and I were at the same party as you this summer, and even though it's one of the only times anyone has been interested in actually talking to me, I hold what happened between us as my own private secret. I don't want anyone else to know what it felt like to be in your arms. I don't want anyone else to know about the little groan you made when we kissed for the first time. I'm greedy for you, or at least for those memories of you. I'm not stupid—I know that you must have a girlfriend or that you've had them—I know I'm not the only person who's heard that little groan or felt the heat of your hands on their back. But I like to pretend. I like to feel possessive of these small parts of you, the parts that don't belong to the public imagination, and maybe that's the real reason I can't stop writing.

Yours,
Greer

Dear Ash,

It's my seventeenth birthday today. It's been exactly one year since we met, and while you've fought in several crucial battles and saved countless lives, I've completed a year of high school. The two don't really compare, do they? I told myself after my last email that I wouldn't bother you again, both for your sake and for my pride, but tonight I feel strange. Restless, I guess. It's hot for England, even for May, and muggy. I have the windows thrown open and a fan blowing, but I can't seem to cool down. Every part of me feels flushed. And Abilene is gone from our dorm room and I found a bottle of Prosecco stashed in her mini fridge, and so I'm tipsy and alone, on top of being restless and hot.

It feels like the kind of night to make a bad decision. I think normally girls my age find boys my age to make their bad decisions with—at least that's what Abilene is out doing right now—but I don't want that. There's something really pedestrian about the kind of fun Abilene seeks out, and this is not me trying to force morality onto her, because I don't think there's anything immoral about having sex, but it's more of an…aesthetic…thing, I guess. I don't want boring, common ways of being bad. I want ways that rattle me to my bones, that send me to my knees in repentance, I want to be the kind of bad that leaves me wrung out with bite marks blooming purple on my body. I want to go to the brink of not knowing myself. I want someone to take me there and hold me by the neck and make me stare at an entire reckless realm of possibility. What's the point of sex if you don't feel like every dark crevice of your soul has been exposed to the light? If someone doesn't take your lust and your shameful thoughts, and twist them into a spell that leaves you panting like a dog for more? I think I want that for myself. I want a normal life too—I want an education and career and my own house and to make all of my own decisions— but whenever I think about sex, about what sex would be like when I'm older, I don't ever imagine the Titanic *hand-hitting-the-car-window thing. I want to feel like my veins are being sliced open by the sheer desire of someone powerful. I want to be handled and cherished and used and worshipped. I want a man or woman to claim me as their equal partner in every way—until we're alone. Then I want to crawl to them. I can have that someday, right?*

Right now, as I type, I've got one leg slung over the arm of my computer chair because it's so hot, but also because it makes it easy to tease myself in between writing sentences to you. I do this a lot when I'm thinking about you. (I am guessing you probably don't know that, and tonight, for some reason, it just feels like I should tell you.) I started by running a fingertip under the lace of my panties, imagining it was you. Imagining that we are back in the library and we were never interrupted by Merlin. I imagine you pulling up my skirt after I tell you that you were my first kiss, because you want to know if I'm a virgin. You want to feel if I'm still intact, if I'm wet for you, you want to know what I'd feel like wrapped around your dick.

God, I'm so wet right now. I wish it were your fingers inside me, your thumb on my clit. You'd be so good at that. I can't stop thinking about your hands, how big and strong they are. I bet your eyes would burn green as you rubbed me. I bet you would lick your lips at the thought of tasting me, of being the first man to ever taste me. I think about what it would have been like if you'd fucked me that night, right there against the wall maybe, or on the large desk in the corner. Abilene says boys should always wear condoms, but I wouldn't have wanted you to. I would have wanted to feel your skin, if it was hot and if it was smooth and silky. I would have wanted you to feel me. I would have wanted you to whisper in my ear how good I felt, what a gift I was giving you, how you could stay inside me forever and ever if only I'd let you.

What noises do you make when you come? Do you gasp? Groan? Whisper names? I think I'd like you to whisper my name. Sometimes I imagine you in your cot on base, your hand beneath the blankets trying to be quiet, and then when you come, you have to bite your lip so you don't say my name aloud. I imagine you fucking your fist in the shower, wishing it was me instead of your hand. I imagine you imagining me in every different way a man can be with a woman, sweet and rough and slow and angry and loving. And right now, I'm going to stop typing and finger myself until I come, and when I come, it will be your name I say.

I don't know if this will ever be read. If it will go straight to spam or into some folder marked "Silly Girls with Vice Presidents for Grandfathers." I almost hope you never see this, but it couldn't go unwritten. Not tonight. But this will definitely be the last time I write to you. Tomorrow, I'll wake up hungover and ashamed, although hopefully with that dark excitement that comes with making the best kinds of bad choices. You won't hear from me again, and I'm sorry if any part of this made you uncomfortable or irritated. But you should know that even if I'm not writing you emails any longer, I'll still be thinking of you every time I dig my fingers into my pussy.

Be safe.

Yours,
Greer

CHAPTER 7

THE PRESENT

TEN YEARS SEPARATE ME AND THAT MOMENT IN THE LIBRARY. Ten years encompassing wars and illness and the entirety of my adult experience, and yet somehow it all shrinks to a pinprick point and disappears as I walk into St. Thomas Becket Church. It's erased and there's nothing between me and the man kneeling near the front of the sanctuary, his head bowed. There's no air, no time, no different versions of ourselves... I could be sixteen right now, walking up this aisle, and he could be twenty-six.

Maybe it's because of this that I hesitate as I get closer to him, my feet slowing as my pulse speeds up. When Embry suggested my church as a meeting place, I leapt at the idea. The church is where I feel safe, the church is where I feel watched over by God, and most importantly, the church is neutral territory. I can't bear the thought of waiting in line to see him in the West Wing, a hastily penciled-in visitor, and I even less could bear the thought of being smuggled into the Residence. I understand discretion, but I also don't want to feel like contraband. Like the living embodiment of a lie.

Stop flipping out. You still don't know for sure why he wants to meet you. Embry had hinted—intimately—at the reason, but I've been burned by hope before. And besides, how could there be any room for hope at all? After Jenny, after that long, sweaty night in Chicago, *after ten years between our first kiss and now*, for fuck's sake. I should keep this box buried. I should save myself while I still can.

But I don't stop walking. I send a quick prayer—a blank prayer, a silent plea, because I don't even know what to pray for at this point—toward the tabernacle as I genuflect and slide into the pew behind the president. I carefully set down the kneeler and get to my knees, lacing my hands together and bowing my head, as if to pray, but I never get around to actually forming the words.

I study the president instead.

He's praying as well, kneeling like me, his dark head hanging down over his hands. He's shucked his jacket, leaving him in a white button-down shirt. His sleeves are rolled up, exposing tan, muscular forearms, and I can tell from the loose way the shirt collar lies against his neck that he's unbuttoned his top button and loosened his tie. The shirt stretches and pulls over the wide shoulders and broad muscles of his back as he keeps his head bowed.

And because I can't help it, I let my eyes trail down to the narrow lines of his hips. His pants are excruciatingly tailored, *excruciatingly*, the fabric hugging a firm ass and hard, thick thighs. Heat floods me everywhere, sending sparks and electric flashes dancing across my skin. How could I have forgotten how powerful he is in person? That there is still a soldier's body under those dark suits and requisite flag pins?

And then when he speaks, the sparks dancing across

my skin ignite into true fire as I remember the words he murmured against my lips that night a decade ago—*tell me you're eighteen* and *do you like my lips on your skin* and *God, where did you come from?*

"I've prayed for the free world, the less-than-free world, my enemies, my allies, my staff, and my mom's favorite dog," the president says without looking back at me, his voice rich and burred around the edges. "Am I missing anything?"

"The babies trapped in limbo, maybe."

"How could I forget about them?" He leans his head farther down for a brief second. "And please watch over the babies trapped in limbo. In the name of the Father, Son, and the Holy Spirit, amen."

He crosses himself, and I get a glimpse of those large, square hands that once cradled mine. "Thank you for meeting me," Ash says. "I know it was presumptive to send Embry—especially as you haven't ever met him—to do something so personal, but I couldn't wait another minute after seeing you here on Sunday. And I also couldn't get away to do it myself. I mentioned it to him and he volunteered to help right away." He smiles. "He's an amazing friend."

Especially as you haven't ever met him…

Ash doesn't know that Embry and I know each other? A quiet worry starts tugging at my heart, but I push it aside. "Vice President Moore is a very persuasive messenger."

"I know. That's why I sent him. Trust me—the things he's persuaded *me* to do can't be spoken aloud in a church." The president stands and comes around to the side of my pew, extending a hand. I take it and look up, and all worries about Embry fade into nothing. There is only Ash.

Since the night we kissed, I've seen thousands of pictures of Maxen Ashley Colchester, I've watched all his televised rallies and debates and press conferences, but it in no way prepared me for seeing him right now. Even though he's perfection personified in any medium, no picture or video can do him justice. Nothing can compare to seeing him in person, face-to-face.

Still the same chiseled planes and full mouth, the bottle-green eyes—still the most handsome man I've ever seen, aside from Embry Moore. But what the president has is more than good looks. There's a certain nobility to his face, an honesty and openness, and even more than that, a sense of purpose. Like he knows exactly who he is, and within seconds, he can tell you exactly who you are. It's electrifying.

I allow him to help me to my feet. I'm shaking, and he notices.

"Do I scare you?" he asks, his brow furrowing. Like Embry, there are lines around his eyes and mouth that weren't there a decade ago, and I see a few silver strands peeking through his jet-black hair. If anything, it makes him even sexier now than when we first met.

"Will you be angry if I say yes?" I manage.

His hand slides from mine up to my elbow, and I realize how close we're standing. "Angry is not even close to the kinds of feelings you stir up, Greer."

Oh God.

I can't handle how intense this is, how fiercely my body is reacting to his mere proximity when all we shared was an hour a decade ago and another hour five years after that. I fumble for a way to defuse the sudden weight of the conversation. "Mr. President—"

He sighs. "Please don't call me that. Not here. Not now."

I try to force myself to say his name aloud—the name that I wrote a thousand times in looping cursive during my high school classes, the name that I sighed to myself in my shower with my hand between my legs—but my decorum was forged in the crucible of The Party and it's so hard not to use the title I know I should use.

He leans in, and I smell the fire and leather smell of him. It makes me dizzy.

"You can call me sir, if you like," he murmurs. "But only when we're alone."

I have to close my eyes.

He guides me into the aisle, and then we're walking past the altar to a door at the side of the church. We walk by stone-faced Secret Service agents and go out into the church garden, his hand moving from my arm to the small of my back, steering me where he wants us to go. The gesture is possessive, peremptory, as if he assumes he has prerogative over my body.

I want him to. I want him to have every prerogative over my body.

I don't see any agents in the garden, even though I know they must be there, but for the moment, it feels as if we're alone among the rustling red and gold trees and wilted fall flowers, and he stops us in the middle of a flagstone-paved clearing, next to a bleached-white statue of the Virgin.

"I won't waste your time. God knows I have little enough of my own. But I couldn't—" He pauses, the famously eloquent soldier at a loss for words. "I couldn't wait any longer," he finally says in a low voice.

He is so close, and all I can smell is leather and leaves, and I force myself to take a step back. I have to think. I have to use my brain, because my body and my heart are screaming so loudly that I can't hear anything else, and what they're screaming is *yes please yes please yes please* even though a question hasn't been asked yet.

The president—*Ash*, I mentally correct myself—lets me step back, but his eyes are on me like hands, still possessing me, still steering me.

"I don't think I understand," I say. "I don't understand why you wanted to meet with me."

He runs a hand through his hair, a gesture I recognize from that night. "That's fair, I suppose," he says, his eyes on the leaf-covered ground as he frames his next statement. "And I don't want to scare you away by being too...direct."

"I mean, I'm still shocked that you remember me. We met only the once."

"Twice," he corrects me. "Chicago, five years ago. Remember?"

Flames lick my cheeks and I take a deep breath. "I remember." It was the night I lost my virginity, after all. Girls usually remember that sort of thing. "Twice then. We've talked twice."

And then I bite my lip, remembering something I've managed to forget for several years because it's not exactly true that we've only talked twice. *I* have talked to Ash more than that, though he never talked back.

The emails.

My face flushes even hotter, this time with humiliation.

God, the emails. Why was I so young and stupid? So ready to attach meaning to the things adults do without thinking twice about it?

"They were very memorable," he says. "Two times in ten years might not sound like a lot, but it was to me..." He trails off, and my heart squeezes.

But I breathe a silent sigh of relief that he doesn't mention the emails. I never did get a response to any of my messages, and I had assumed for years that he'd never received them, since he had been actually fighting a war at the time. The younger Greer spent too many hours brooding in the dark about those unread messages, but now as an adult, I pray he's never even seen them.

"Something's wrong," he says, reaching out to tilt my face up to his. I realize that I was staring off into nothing.

Lie. Just lie.

But I hate lying. I try to find an answer that isn't the whole shameful truth. "I'm embarrassed. Of how I acted when I was younger."

A smile, surprisingly tender. "Is that all this is? Why you're acting like you don't understand why I want to see you?"

"I just...I thought about that kiss so much," I whisper. "But I knew there was no way you would remember it. Why would you? You were an adult, a man, and I was just a child. And you've gone on to live this incredible life, to be a hero and now a leader, and you had your beautiful wife—"

Fuck! I swallow the rest of my words, wishing I could swallow up my own stupidity along with them. Of all the things I shouldn't bring up, the late Jennifer Colchester was at the top of the list. And sure enough, Ash winces at the word *wife*. Just the tiniest bit.

"I loved Jenny," he says quietly, letting go of my chin. And it's then I notice the dark smudges under his eyes, the telltale signs of exhaustion in his face. He still has trouble sleeping, even after all this time. "And I miss her. It hurts me still that she died so young and in so much pain. But, Greer, I won't pretend that I ever stopped thinking about you. I can't pretend that."

"It was one kiss," I say, shaking my head. "Why would you—"

He holds up a hand to stop me, and I fall silent. "I'm not going to let you do that," he tells me. "You're not allowed to dismiss what happened or tell me that it wasn't worth remembering. I *did* remember. I *do* remember. And I won't forget any second of that night."

"It's just so impossible to believe. That *you*—Maxen Colchester—remembered me. Thought about me."

A noise leaves him, half heavy breath, half incredulous laugh. "We are meeting after all these years," he says, "and you believe I haven't been thinking about you?" He takes a step closer, so close that I could lean in and press my lips against his icy-blue tie if I wanted. It's nearly the same color as Embry's eyes.

"Look up at me, Greer," the president orders me. I do as he says. It almost hurts to look him full in the face, he's so perfect, but it hurts more not to look.

"All the words that men use about women—enchanted, charmed, addicted—they don't even begin to cover what I felt for you and your handful of shattered glass. I thought about you that night, and the next and the next, and when I was deployed to Carpathia, you were *all* I thought about. I built these fantasies in my mind where I would come home after the war and find you at whatever university you were at. I would kiss you until you were like you were that night at the party, begging me to do whatever I wanted." His green eyes are dark, stormy, his pupils wide. "Years later when I finally came home, all I wanted was to find you. But things happened…the war started up again and I was promoted and Merlin needed my time and then I met Jenny…" He lets out a breath. "I had just proposed to her the night before I saw you in Chicago."

Chicago. Also known as the night I met Embry. The night I lost my virginity.

"Ash, you don't have to—"

"I do," he cuts me off. "Because I don't think you believe me. And it makes me a terrible man, wanting you after all this time, *through* all these years. Because I did want you, even while I was married to Jenny. I sought out your grandfather every chance I could, just to listen to whatever scraps of news he had about you. Whatever academic honor you'd been given, what you decided to major in, whether you wanted to move back to America or stay in England. And late at night, while Jenny slept next to me in bed, I'd replay

63

our kiss over and over again. What it felt like to pin you against the wall. What your voice sounded like in my ear, all breathless and full of wonder, like I'd just given you a gift. And I would hate myself for it, but I couldn't stop."

His eyes search mine. "So why did I want to meet you today? Because I haven't been able to stop wanting to meet you for ten years. Because I want you. I want to kiss you again. I want to learn everything about you, everything about what you love and hate, what you study, what you want for your future." He reaches up, his thumb brushing against my lower lip. "I want you to be mine."

I try to hide my shiver. He can't know, he can't possibly know, how those words roll through me, punch through my skin and crawl into my veins.

Be mine.

Not *let's date*, not *be my girlfriend.* This would be more than anything that trivial, and Ash knew it.

But the exhilaration is chased by a quick, cruel voice.

Remember the times you've been hurt before?

There's no way this can be true.

This is absurd.

Say no.

Leave.

I shake my head, but his thumb stays against my lip. I fight the urge to bite it or lick it. Instead, I meet his eyes and say firmly, "You don't know anything about me, other than what I kissed like once. That's not enough to build on."

"Does it scare you that I thought about you as much as I did?"

I think for a moment. It doesn't, actually, especially given how much *I* thought about *him*. Much more than thought—I wrote to him. I touched myself to the memory of him.

"No. Just, it's so unexpected. I had no idea how you felt…"

His thumb sweeps across my lip a final time and then moves to the line of my jaw. "I was at war, Greer. And then I was married. It wasn't something I could act on."

I nod. "I get that." But I don't say anything else because my mind is racing faster than my pulse, stacking what I know against what I feel.

I now know that Ash has been as preoccupied with me as I was with him—for all these years. So preoccupied he wants to be with me now, and I can't pretend this doesn't make me dizzy. Like my blood is carbonated, like my body is fizzing over with feelings. Excitement, lust, relief. But those ten years didn't just sail by—they left an indelible mark on me. I fell in love with Ash only to watch him marry another woman. I slept with a different man only to never hear from him again.

In short, this last decade has been a harsh lesson in guarding my heart, and I have been a very, very apt pupil. I have built walls around my feelings, barriers and bridges and moats, all to protect me from the possibility of getting wounded again.

So how can I honestly be thinking about saying yes to Ash? How can I—cautious, closed-off Greer—concede to being his? What if he hurts me again? What if he's disappointed in me or falls in love with someone else?

And the largest question of all, how can I try to date Ash with Embry in the background?

For the first time, Ash looks uncertain. "You're thinking of reasons to say no, aren't you?" he asks quietly. "Did that night not mean to you what it meant to me?"

I shake my head vigorously. "No, no. That night meant absolutely everything to me. And that's why this is a bad idea. Aside from you being the president and having no time or space for some girlfriend, I'm scared that I'll get hurt. I'm scared that we'll find that we don't have anything in common, that our kiss was just a fluke, and even after all that, that it won't matter because I'll still fall in love with you. I'll fall in love with you even as we find out we're all wrong for each other and I'll be left brokenhearted over you again—"

"Again?" he asks.

I try to look away, but he won't let me. He keeps my face tilted toward his, lowering his own until our noses touch.

"God, if you only knew what it does to me to hear that you felt that way." His voice is hoarse. "Tell me what I have to do to earn it back. Tell me what I have to do to make you as twisted up over me as I am over you. I'll do anything. Anything."

I can feel his breath against my lips. Warm and intimate. I should make him promise something. I should demand his fidelity or honesty or utmost care. But that would be too close to lying, and instead I admit the terrible truth.

"You don't have to do anything, Ash. I'm already yours."

He breathes out, a shudder going through him, and then he presses his lips to mine.

It's nothing like our first kiss, and yet everything like it at the same time. I still feel soft and young and female as he pulls me close against his body. I still feel like I want to melt into him, dissolve into nothing and everything at once. And he still makes that low, quiet groan in the bottom of his throat, as if he can't help himself, as if I've irrevocably weakened him by letting him touch my lips with his.

Our first kiss was impulsive, exhilarating, and stunning, but unplanned, a kiss between strangers with no past or future. This time Ash kisses me with intent, with the promise of more, with the promise of a future and his affection and care. And I kiss him back as a woman, not as a girl, just as eager as I was then, but more experienced. All the more ready to surrender.

We break lips just for a moment, and I look up into his eyes. "Wow," I whisper.

"Wow," he laughs back at me.

"This is my first kiss in five years." I don't know why the confession is dragged out of me, but it is. I want him to know how much he meant to me, how much he means to me now.

I see the way his eyebrows pull together at my revelation, see the way he mentally tucks that information back to ask me about later, but for the moment, he only murmurs, "Then let's make it count," and lowers his mouth back down to mine. I smell the leaves and leather, feel the firm warmth of his mouth and the strength of his arms, and then I'm drowning in him. His certainty and his strength, his desire and his need. And then beyond a shadow of a doubt, I feel *him* drowning in *me*, feel him giving over every atom of himself to my keeping. We are consumed and rebuilt all within the same moment of lips and hands fisting tightly in clothes.

A clearing throat interrupts us, and Ash reluctantly pulls away. I see a Secret Service agent waiting by the entrance to the garden.

"Mr. President, it's time."

Ash closes his eyes a moment and then opens them with a sigh. "I have a meeting with the Polish ambassador at four."

"About Carpathia?" I ask. The war has been theoretically over for two years, but there's no doubt that the region is still deeply volatile.

"Always about Carpathia," he says with a rueful smile. "I'd rather spend the evening with you though."

I want to ask when I can see him again—or more honestly, when I can kiss him again—but he beats me to it.

"Greer, my job—and the kind of man I am—I tend to ask a lot of the people I care for. My schedule is…well, it's fucked. Constantly. I want to promise that I can see you right away, but that may not be the case."

"I understand," I say softly. "You forget that I know what it's like for you better than most people."

"I hate this," he says suddenly, fiercely. "I want to take you home with me tonight, and I don't want to wait to see you again."

"Ash, really, I understand—"

"No," he interjects. "*No.* I've waited ten years, and I refuse to wait any longer. If I send a car for you tonight, will you get in it?"

I think back to earlier, to my relief at not being smuggled into the White House like a mistress, like a dirty secret. Discretion is one thing, but is that what I want for myself? To be a late-night visitor? To be the hidden plaything of a man in power? I've stayed away from politics for years, built myself a nest in an ivory tower so I wouldn't ever have to think about politics again, and I'm willing to surrender myself to the most famous politician in the world after one kiss?

But then I look again at Ash, at those green eyes burning down at me, and I realize that all this debating is pointless. Of course I'll get in the car. Of course I'll go to him. It almost feels like I don't have a choice, like my choice was made when I was sixteen and pinned between the wall and an eager army captain.

"Yes, of course," I tell him. "I'll go anywhere you want me to."

CHAPTER 8

THE PRESENT

WHEN THE CAR PULLS UP, I'M READY. I'M SO READY THAT I'M trembling, part of me wanting to run and hide and the other part of me wanting to run straight to the White House so I don't have to wait a second longer. I've showered, shaved my legs, put on makeup, taken off the makeup because it felt like too much, then put a little makeup back on…and still there's so much time to kill. I change outfits at least three times, settling for a short blue dress of embroidered cotton with a flared skirt and cap sleeves. The short hemline and the nude high heels I pair with it are just sexy enough to signal how I'd like the evening to go, but the high neckline and sweet blue color are enough to claim innocence in case I'm wrong about what he wants with me.

Wants *from* me.

I pray with every cell in my body that I'm not wrong.

But at the same time, I find myself hoping the car doesn't show. Because if it shows, if I get in it, then it's all over.

I'll go from being Greer Galloway the academic to Greer Galloway, presidential mistress. And the Beltway will smell the Galloway in me and finally suck me down into its swamp once and for all.

Headlights sweep across the living room, and for a moment, I consider locking the door from the inside and refusing to go out. Sending a message to Ash saying, "Sorry, but I can't be part of your world." Continuing my life of solitude and study.

But then I look around my living room—clean wood floors and loaded bookshelves and the well-used fireplace—and I see the decades stretching out before me. The new Greer with her scars and all her reserve living lonely and empty, while the old Greer—a girl who wrote a soldier halfway across the world her darkest thoughts—suffocates silently and dies slowly under a veil of dust and term papers.

I go outside to the car.

The Secret Service agent has a faint smile on his face as he opens the door for me. "Good evening, Ms. Galloway."

"Good evening," I say a bit breathlessly.

And that's the last we speak for the entire drive.

Growing up as Leo Galloway's granddaughter, I'm not intimidated by Secret Service agents necessarily, but I do wonder what this one thinks of me, since it must be painfully obvious what's going on. But he acts as if there's nothing abnormal about a young blond being summoned to the president's side this late at night.

And then I have a terrible thought, a thought that twists my stomach. What if it's not abnormal? What if I'm just another in a long line of women secreted into the Residence, like some kind of modern-day concubine? What if all of Ash's talk about *being mine*, about wanting me, is just the game he plays to get women into his bed? He hasn't publicly dated anyone since Jenny's death, but that doesn't mean that he hasn't been seeing women privately. I mean, how likely is it that a man like Ash—sexy and powerful—would be celibate for more than a year?

I have no right to be upset about it, but I find that I am. It was hard enough knowing he was with Jenny when she was alive, that she got to be the one next to him, the one kissing him, the one who heard his murmurs and moans late into the night. But that there might have been any number of women since then...

Suddenly feeling very lonely, I pull my legs up onto the car seat, careful to keep everything covered, and rest my chin on my knees, an old habit from when I was a girl riding with Grandpa Leo back and forth across Manhattan. But as much as I'd like to pretend I'm still a little girl safe with her grandfather, I can't. Not with where I'm going. Not with who I will see when I get there. Even the city outside wants to remind me I'm not a child anymore, the sedate streets and stately parks a world away from the busy, messy capitalism of Manhattan.

It *is* beautiful, though, and I find myself lulled by the passing of gold and red trees, lamps wreathed by fog, sternly noble buildings rising together as we approach Pennsylvania Avenue.

And then the car is rolling through the gates, through the various security checks, and we come to a stop. I'm helped out by the taciturn agent and delivered to a young man with light bronze skin wearing a tweed jacket and horn-rimmed glasses waiting by the door.

There's something about his boyish, bookish face that makes me trust him immediately. But even though he looks kind, capable, and discreet, my stomach still clenches at yet another person being involved. Another person who thinks that I'm—what? A mistress? A whore? A weak, lonely woman?

"Ms. Galloway?" he asks.

It's only the memory of Ash's lips on mine that nudge me forward. "Hello," I say. "It's nice of you to meet me."

He waves my words away. "I'm here all the time anyway. This is the first time I get to do something fun for the president."

His words give me the tiniest edge of relief; maybe Ash isn't secretly fucking his way through Washington's eligible women after all.

"I'm Ryan Belvedere, but everyone calls me Belvedere because there's like four Ryans on staff," he says, his words coming out in the fast, pattered rush of the chronically busy. He sticks out a hand, which I shake. "I'm President Colchester's personal aide," he continues. "He wanted to be the one to greet you, but his meeting with his foreign policy staff has gone late. He sends his apologies, but it was necessary business after his meeting with the ambassador, I'm afraid."

Carpathia, I think. *He's had serious news about Carpathia from the Polish ambassador.*

"I completely understand," I say.

"I knew you would. You're Leo Galloway's granddaughter, huh? What was that like?"

"What's it like working here?"

Belvedere glances around the nondescript entrance we're standing in. "Less glamorous than the brochure."

"Then you've got your answer."

He laughs and starts walking, gesturing for me to follow. "It can't be all that bad. And it made it really easy for them to do your background check tonight—you've had so many already over the years."

"I'm still not sure they didn't do one on me before I was born," I say and he laughs again. He seems quick to laugh… I could see why Ash would have chosen him to be his right-hand man.

We walk down a hallway, and then down another hallway, up and around a maze of stairs and doors and into a room lit with a handful of soft, low lamps and studded with sofas, end tables, and bookshelves, with a desk at one end. The wall color and furniture have changed since the last time I was here with Grandpa Leo, but I know exactly where I am. My stomach twists and all my doubts rise again. Do I really want to be here in the Residence? Practically throwing myself at the mercy of the dead-eyed, forever glad-handing gods of political life?

"President Colchester has invited you to make yourself at home," Belvedere says, interrupting my unhappy thoughts. "I would suggest in the living room here or…in his bedroom." Belvedere's eyes twinkle. "It's just through those doors."

I can't stop the rush of blood from going to my cheeks. What am I doing? I'm *inviting* trouble. I'm inviting the inevitable internet storm once it gets out that I'm here.

"I'm sorry," Belvedere says, his eyes still sparkling. "I shouldn't tease. It's just, we're all really excited."

"Excited?" I ask warily.

"About the president having a date with you tonight. We've been trying to coax him into moving on for months. It's time for him to have some sort of companionship, and frankly, he needs to get laid *bad*."

I let out a shocked laugh. "You can't talk about the president that way."

"The hell I can't. You haven't seen him like I have, and I'm telling you with all the nonexistent authority I have, he needs to let off some steam."

I hate myself for asking such a leading question, but I can't help it. "Surely he doesn't need a date for that to happen? To be with someone?" *Please tell me what I want to hear, please please please.*

Belvedere shrugs as he walks toward the entrance to the

hallway that will lead him back to the West Wing. "Maybe not, but it hasn't happened. At least that I know of, and I'm around him constantly."

"So I'm...the first? Since Jenny?"

Belvedere pauses and looks at me. The smile on his face is less gleeful now and more understanding. "He's not the kind of guy who does casual sex, and it's too risky in his position anyway. Add that to his grief over Jenny and his drive for this job...well. We all understand why he's waited. But we're also excited that you're here. He needs someone for him, someone who can be there only for him, and I really hope you can be that someone. Even if it's just for one night."

The aide's words touch me, and underneath all my misgivings, I find the truth. "I think I hope I can be that someone too," I say, and I mean it.

It takes another hour for Ash to return to the Residence, an hour which I've spent exploring and fiddling with my phone and checking my hair in the bathroom every ten minutes. The sitting room is generously decorated in pale creams and minty greens, the antique furniture giving the room a very traditional, very postcard-from-the-White-House feel, making me think that an interior designer did most of the choosing.

But when I get brave enough to crack the bedroom door and look inside, I see only Ash's hand. Lots of muted grays and deep charcoals, a small array of understated furniture and a rigid adherence to geometry. No soft angles, no unnecessarily decorated furniture. Everything is deeply functional, solidly built, and free of ostentation. A room for a soldier.

My eyes light on the large four-poster bed, and my breath catches. Will I lie on that bed tonight? Will I wake up there tomorrow morning? Or will I be packed off while it's still dark, sent away under the cover of night to avoid the press?

The thought makes me anxious, and I go back to the bathroom to smooth my hair one more time, staring blankly at the woman in the mirror.

I see a slender neck and a delicate jaw. Breasts that are high and firm, a narrow waist, and slender hips. In the low light coming from the sitting room, the shallow cleft in my chin and the beauty mark on my cheek seem exotic and striking, my lips full and pink, and my eyelashes long and dark. The mass of white hair—which is slowly darkening to gold in the chilly fall weather—currently pinned back into a sleek knot.

She's jealous of you, you know.

All those years ago, that's what Ash had said to me. I hadn't known what he meant, was unable to conceive of any universe where Abilene had anything to be jealous of. It took a few years for me to finally realize what everyone else saw the night of my sixteenth birthday, but even I eventually had to admit that I was no longer the ugly duckling I'd branded myself. I'm maybe not the sensual, exuberant swan that Abilene was and still is, but I do have a beauty all my own.

To kill time, I wander to the far edge of the sitting room, looking out over the dark stretch of the South Lawn. In the distance, the Washington Monument pierces the midnight air, the squatly elegant dome of the Jefferson Memorial close by. I've never seen this particular view at night, and it hits me, really hits me, that I'm standing in the White House waiting a few feet away from the president's bedroom door. Waiting for exactly what, I don't know, but I'm so ready. So very ready.

I turn away from the window and walk a perimeter around the room, feeling my high heels press deep into the thick carpet, and I'm stopped by a large framed photograph on the wall, the subjects initially difficult to make out in the dim light. But my pulse speeds up as I realize who's in the picture.

It's Ash and Embry, somewhere deep in the mountains of Carpathia, wearing their Army fatigues with guns and helmets and armor. They have their arms slung around each other's shoulders, and the way they smile at the camera makes it seem like they have some kind of secret, like they'd just gotten away with something. There's so much friendship in the picture, so much brotherhood and trust, and I remember that it was Embry whom Ash saved that day in a Carpathian ambush, Embry that he faced down an entire squad of enemy soldiers to save. But of course there were more battles after that, four or five more, where Embry and Ash both emerged as heroes—Ash the brilliant tactician and Embry the reckless brawler who flung himself heedlessly into every storm of bullets he encountered. I may have stopped writing to Ash the year I turned seventeen, but it didn't mean that I stopped searching for his name in the news, which meant that I also searched for Embry's. My intense feelings for Ash never went away, but they had been joined by new feelings for the handsome, rakish face that joined his in every newscast and online article.

What girl wouldn't have fallen in love with those two?

I touch my fingertips to the glass, as if I could touch both of those men at the same time, and even just the thought of that, of touching Embry and Ash at the same time, makes me light-headed.

Be careful, I caution myself. *If you do this thing with Ash, there will be no escaping Embry either. You'll be playing with fire.*

"That was after the village of Caledonia," Ash says from behind me. "The one where Embry was injured and I had to carry him out."

Trying not to act startled, I drop my hand, still feeling the cool glass against my fingertips. "Were you friends before then?"

"Yes. But after that, we became much more than friends. Like brothers."

I turn just as Ash's hands slide up my bare arms, warm and large and slightly rough.

"I'm glad you got in that car," he says, ducking his head to meet my eyes. "I was a little worried you'd change your mind."

"I was worried *you'd* change your mind," I tell him. "This is still so surreal to me."

"That I want to spend time with you?"

"That you remember me at all."

He gives me one of his smiles, the kind where his eyes crinkle up and his face opens into an expression of unimaginable warmth and joy. I'm reminded forcefully of Embry. Maybe the pair are only brothers in the emotional sense and not the biological, but they share the same weather-beaten, mischievous smile, and that smile is enough to get me to agree to anything.

"Don't move," Ash says, and he disappears into his bedroom. He returns with a small wooden box. "Have a seat." He gestures toward the end of the room.

Thinking he means the sofa by the window, I move toward it, but he corrects me, and when he does, there's a change in his voice. It gets sterner somehow, and the effect on my body is immediate. "Sit on the desk, facing the chair."

It's a strange request, and there's a moment when I want to ask why. But then I see the fire in his green eyes, the same fire I saw when I told him once upon a time that I liked the way he told me what to do with my body.

It's a test, I realize. And what's more, it's a test I want to pass, a test I want to do. Listening to Ash feels as natural as breathing, and after only a breath of hesitation, I walk over to the desk and slide myself onto it, careful to keep my skirt from riding too far up my thighs.

I'm not sure what exactly I expect him to do, but when he comes and sits in the chair in front of me, it feels right. The way it's supposed to be.

"Thank you for listening to me," he says. He keeps his gaze on my face.

"I like listening," I whisper.

"Do you?" he asks, setting the box in his lap and leaning back. "How much?"

"A lot," I admit quietly. "It feels…natural…with you."

A small smile. "I'll tell you a secret: I like it when you listen. That feels natural to me too."

I glance down at the box, wondering what could be inside. It's about the right size for cigars, but Ash doesn't strike me as much of a smoker. What else then? Something sexual? Condoms, maybe, or lube? Nipple clamps?

Ash notices my wary look. "Nothing in there will bite, I promise."

So no nipple clamps then.

"Do you remember at the church?" he asks, changing the subject. "When I told you that I ask a lot from the people I care for?"

"I do."

"I meant that in more ways than one. I'm busy, for one thing, often traveling and always stressed, and I—" He stops himself, searching for the right words.

I nudge his knee with my foot. "You won't scare me away by being too direct. I promise."

"'To answer before listening is folly,'" Ash quotes, shaking his head, and then sighs. "It took a long time for us to be alone in a room together. Part of me thinks I should enjoy it before I ruin it."

"And the other part?"

His eyes darken. "The other part of me thinks you should be more nervous."

I shiver. A good shiver, but a shiver nonetheless, and he doesn't miss it, his eyes trailing from the pulse pounding in my throat to the goose bumps on my thighs. He looks at the wooden box a moment and then seems to make up his mind.

"We are going to have a conversation now," he says, "among other things. And we can stop at any time."

"I don't want to stop."

"It's hard to want to stop," he says, running his fingers along the edge of the box. "It's even harder to say the word when you know you should. Have you ever used a safe word?"

For that one whole time I had sex? I laugh out loud. "No."

He doesn't seem offended by my laughter. "Perhaps we should find one for you."

"I don't think I need a safe word for a conversation. Even a conversation with unspecified *other things*. And especially not with you."

"You especially need one when you're with me." He says it calmly, evenly.

And then suddenly I believe him.

Despite that open, handsome face, despite the historic building I'm standing in and the elegant antique furniture all around us, I believe him. I can't tell if it's something in the cool way he says it or something in the flare of light in his eyes, or if it's the remembered shards of that night, of the way he said *good girl* to me when I obeyed his order or the way he licked the blood from my fingertip…

"All those times you've asked me if I was scared of you, you were serious?"

"It was with good reason." He leans forward. "I'm not trying to tease you or frighten you unnecessarily. But I'm hard on the people I love. It took me a long time to learn that, and you are too important to me for me to treat that lightly. You have to know that you can stop anything about me—my words or my body—at any time. You have to know that you can leave me at any time."

I'll never want to leave. The thought appears unbidden and I shove it aside. But it's harder for me to shove aside the word *love*, as if I'm one of the people he loves, because to be loved by Ash…I've wanted that since I was sixteen.

"If you don't have a word in mind, you can use my name—my first name."

"Maxen?"

He nods. "You say that when we're alone together and everything stops. For a break—if you need one—or completely, if that's what you need instead."

I think for a moment. The kind of pornography I watch and the kind of books I read—well, I'm definitely no stranger to this kind of thing. In fact, certain facets of this lifestyle have been the subject of my fantasies since I was old enough to have fantasies. But faced with the reality of a relationship like this, I find myself shy. Not out of fear necessarily—although there is a little fear and I'd be foolish not to be at least a little wary—but out of an acute awareness of how little I know. Of how meager my experience with any kind of romance or sexuality is. When I speak next, my voice is hesitant. "Does all this make you…the kind of person who dominates people?"

Another nod. "Yes."

"Are you going to whip me or something?" I ask, suddenly nervous.

"Not all dominants are sadists, Greer. I won't always want pain or humiliation, but I will always want control."

"But you will want pain and humiliation sometimes?"

He leans back again, his face thoughtful. "I'm approaching this wrong. You'll have to forgive me… It's been six years since I last initiated a relationship with someone, and I'm out of practice. And in any case," he says, rubbing his forehead with his thumb, "I didn't know enough about myself then to warn Jenny."

It's Jenny's name that galvanizes me. It's a sick urge, to want to show up a dead woman, to prove I'm as good as she was, but it's an urge I can't fight in time to control myself.

"Show me," I say. "Show me what you need to warn me about."

CHAPTER 9

"SHOW ME," I REPEAT.

His eyes lift to mine.

"You said we were going to have a conversation among other things, right? Let's do it. I know what to say to make you stop. I trust you."

"You barely know me," he points out.

"You're a war hero and the president of the United States. If I can't trust you, I can't trust anybody."

He smiles again at that. "You make a specious case, given how many manipulative presidents there have been, but I want to be convinced, so I'll allow it." He reaches down and slips a high heel off one of my feet, repeating the action on the other foot, rubbing gently at the red line left above my toes. "Why you act afraid of pain when you already wear these is a mystery to me."

I giggle a little, and the look on his face at the sound of my laughter is electrifying. Belvedere, Embry, me…the president seems to love the laughter of others. The realization strikes me with a chord of melancholy. What loneliness and darkness does he carry in his heart that he needs such people around him?

He places my left foot on the arm of the chair he's sitting in, and as soon as I see that he's going to do the same with my other foot, I instinctively pull it back, since that would entail me spreading my legs in this short skirt. He doesn't react, other than to look up at my face, and I realize that he's waiting to see if I'll say his name. My new safe word. I bite my lip and force my body to relax.

I place my foot back in his hands, and he sets it on the other arm of the chair. I'm grateful that our relative heights mean that he's at eye level with my chest and not my pelvis, but that gratitude disappears when he says, "Pull your skirt back for me."

My hands shake when I obey, partly from excitement and partly from nervousness. I wasn't lying when I told him it felt natural to obey him, but I've also never exposed myself so brazenly, so intimately and deliberately. Despite the impassive look on Ash's face, I can see that he's fascinated, aroused by bossing me around like this, and that bolsters me.

"I've never done this before," I admit as I finish pulling my skirt up. Cool air wafts around my inner thighs and against my lace-covered pussy.

"Which part?" Ash asks, keeping his eyes on my legs, on the sliver of lace between them.

"Listening to someone. Showing myself off. I've only ever had sex once," I confess.

His head snaps up. "Only once?"

I nod, swallowing. "When I was twenty."

He groans, resting his head against my knee. "You mean I'm going to be the second man who's ever been inside you?"

"You sound so certain that you're going to take me to

83

bed," I tease, but my teasing comes out breathier than I mean for it to. It's the way his dark head looks as it leans against my bare thigh, the way his legs are spread all strong and casual in the chair…yes, he should be certain that he's going to take me to bed. I'll take myself there if he doesn't.

"It's my job to be certain of things, Greer." I feel the movement of his lips against my thigh as he speaks, and it makes it impossible to sit still. "Tell me—why haven't you been with more men? Or women?"

"I've been asked out a lot," I say. "Men and, yes, a couple of women. But I've said no to them all."

"Did someone hurt you the first time you had sex? Or was it otherwise unpleasant somehow?"

I think of Embry's long, muscled body moving over mine, of his strong hands digging into my hips. "It was amazing. But it was the second time I had kissed someone and then had my heart broken, so I decided not to repeat that pattern."

"And that's why you haven't kissed anyone since then," Ash says, a question in his voice. "You're worried if you kiss a new person, that new person will also break your heart?"

"That's right."

"I won't break your heart," Ash promises.

"Again."

Another groan. He seems to like being reminded that he had that power over me. He lifts his head. "Pull your panties aside. I want to see your pussy."

"Okay," I whisper, and I do as he says. It's almost frightening how easy it is to listen to him, how easy it is to do something as unlike myself as spreading my legs on a desk for a man I barely know, but dammit, it feels right. It feels good. It feels like another Greer—a Greer I put to sleep and buried in the backyard of my mind—is slowly waking up. The Greer who wrote those emails to Ash, the Greer who bit

Embry's shoulder and trailed scratches down his back as he moved between her bloody thighs. She is loving waking up to this; she wants to preen like a cat as Ash draws in a long breath once he sees the already-wet flesh of her pussy.

His hands slide up the outside of my calves, the rough skin tickling my knees and then my inner thighs as he braces his hands there and pushes me wider apart. I feel myself opening, feel his eyes on the part of me only one other man has seen. One other man who happens to be his best friend. And the vice president of the United States.

"Beautiful," Ash says, a hint of awe in his voice. "Just… beautiful."

I'm chewing hard on my lip, my thighs quivering, because as excited as the old Greer is about this, I can't help the new Greer's litany of worries—if I look too wet or not wet enough, if he can smell me, what I'll taste like if he wants to taste me.

"Look up at the ceiling and breathe in and out in counts of four," Ash tells me. "It will help calm you down."

I'm surprised he can read my body so easily, but then maybe I shouldn't be. He can perceive the meanings behind the faces of dignitaries and the words of politicians—why not a woman's body? I tilt my head back and breathe like he told me to, in and out.

One two three four…
one two three four…
one two three four.

"Some dominants don't like to sit with their head below the head of their partner," Ash says conversationally below me, his fingertips beginning to trace circles and loops on the inside of my thighs. "Because it's demeaning. But look at us right now. Who is the demeaned one?"

I look down from the ceiling and right into the mirror hanging behind the desk. I see a young woman with

85

flushed cheeks and wide eyes, the tops of her naked thighs visible within the frame. And Ash's silhouette in the chair, those powerful shoulders and that strong neck. And then I look down at him, with his sleeves rolled up and his tie still perfectly straight and clipped to his shirt with a slim silver bar.

"Me," I say, swallowing. "I'm the demeaned one."

"And how does that make you feel?" His tone is still casual, still distantly curious, as if he's asking me about a book I'm reading.

"A little excited. A little ashamed."

"Why ashamed?"

I close my eyes. "I like this more than I should."

"There are no *shoulds* when you're with me," Ash says. "The only things you worry about are the things I tell you to worry about. Understood?"

"Yes."

Fingers skate up to the place where my legs join my hips, and I bite my lip again. "Now," Ash says, leaning down to press his lips to the inside of my thigh, "would be a good time to call me *sir*."

"Yes, sir," I breathe.

"And since I'm in charge of you while we are alone together, I also want you to know that you're not allowed to worry about pleasing me. It might seem like there's a lot to learn, a lot to know, but there's not. I'll tell you everything you need to know, and you will only have two responsibilities—surrendering to me and saying my name aloud when it would hurt you physically or emotionally to continue. Understood?"

"Yes, sir," I say again, and who *am* I right now? Agreeing to something so extreme with a man I've only been in the same room with a handful of times? But I don't care. I want this, I want this, I want this. I don't care how dangerous or how demeaning it might seem. Right now, it only feels quiveringly, perfectly right.

"Good," he says, a smile in his voice. "You have no idea how much it pleases me to have you here. I've fantasized about this moment for so long."

"You have?"

He sits up and reaches for the box balancing on his thigh. "Here. Open this."

Curious, I wrap my fingers around the proffered box and pull it closer. Ash leans back as I examine it, smoothing his tie and looking faintly amused. "There's nothing dangerous in there," he tells me.

Still, I take my time opening it, wondering what could be so important that he had it in his bedroom, at the ready. I have no idea what to expect—bullets or military badges or mementos of his dead wife even—but it's none of those things. I swing the lid all the way open and pull out a stack of papers folded into quarters, papers that are dirty and soft from repeated handling.

I glance at Ash with a confused look, and he inclines his head toward the papers in a silent invitation. He wants me to read them.

With hesitant fingers, I unfold the paper. It's computer-printer size, looks like it had once been bright white with fresh black printer ink. But the black of the words has faded and dulled, and the paper is smudged with what looks like oil and dirt and blood.

Dear Ash,

It's my seventeenth birthday today. It's been exactly one year since we met...

My eyes snap to his. "My emails," I say a little numbly. "I thought you never got them."

"I got them," he replies. "I got them and I read them a thousand times and then I printed them out so I could read them wherever I went."

"But you never wrote back, never even once. Not even to tell me to stop writing to you."

"You were seventeen, Greer. Was I supposed to write back and tell you that yes, I did fuck my fist every night thinking of you? That every time I read your emails I had to jack off, that even the mere sight of your name on my computer screen got me hard? I hated myself enough for having those feelings for a girl that age. I couldn't make it worse by reaching out to you." He gives me a rueful smile. "But I also couldn't bring myself to tell you to stop. To block your emails. God, I wanted you so much and it was the only way I could have even this little piece of you. So I kept reading. Kept coming to fantasies of you fingering yourself at your desk as you wrote to me."

"Ash," I say, stunned.

"I have them memorized, you know. Word for word. 'I don't want boring, common ways of being bad,'" he recites, his hands once again warm and rough on my inner thighs. "'I want to be the kind of bad that leaves me wrung out with bite marks blooming purple on my body. I want someone to hold me by the neck and make me stare at an entire reckless realm of possibility. I want to crawl to them.'"

My cheeks are flushed as he says my own words back to me. I'm so embarrassed and yet…that he memorized my words, touched himself thinking of them, that he carried my words with him wherever he traveled…

"Greer," Ash says, his hands sliding up to my hips and holding me tight, "I have to know you meant what you said. It's been ten years since you wrote me that email, and while I've spent those ten years wishing to God that you were mine, I know things might have changed for you."

Everything *has* changed. So much has changed. And yet nothing at all, because here I am just as breathless and squirmy as I was kissing him when I was sixteen. As infatuated and obsessed as when I wrote those emails.

"I want to know if I can be the man to hold you by the neck," he says. "I need to know how much you'll let me do to you, how far you'll let me go, because you are the only woman who's ever said those words to me. The only woman who's wanted that from me."

His fingers dig into my hips, and I nod, vigorously, desperately. "Yes," I plead. "Yes, please."

A certain tension leaves his shoulders, and the smile he gives me is luminous. "I've waited so long for this. Wanted this so hard, so painfully, and now..." He takes a breath, moving his hands down so that his palms rest on the top of my legs and his thumbs brush against the crease of my thighs. "Now you are here, and you are actually telling me you want to be mine."

"I've wanted to be yours since I was old enough to want it," I tell him. I can feel the warmth from his thumbs, the faintest movement of them as they gently rub closer and closer to my cunt, and it makes me ache so fiercely I can't handle it. I try to subtly move my hips so that I get the touch where I need it, but he merely presses his palms against my thighs to stop me.

"What do you want?" I ask him in a whisper. "Let me give it to you."

The words are like water to a parched man, and he presses his eyes closed for a moment. Then he opens them. "Don't move," he orders, pressing my legs wider apart. I'm so exposed to him, and his thumbs are so very, very close to the place where I throb and need.

"Yes, sir," I murmur.

And then the first press of his touch. His thumbs brush

against my folds, up and down, up and down, until I'm fighting the urge to squirm, and then he spreads my pussy open. He can see every fold, curve and slick line of me, and the way he's looking at my cunt, as if it's something for sale, a thing for his pleasure and his possession, it makes it impossible to stay still now. I wriggle a little on the desk.

Thwack!

A sharp slap on the inside of my thigh.

I'm surprised by the hot flash of pain, and even more surprised at the way my pussy tightens at it, the way goose bumps pepper my flesh and the way my nipples harden. I can't stop the whimper that leaves my mouth.

"I'm the first man to look at your pussy this way, aren't I? The first to spread you open and just look."

"Yes, sir," I confirm, heat flushing in my stomach as I remember Embry that night. There had been no looking then, no deliberate teasing. Just hands and mouths and need. There's something that's so inherently, deeply right about the way Ash takes his time and exerts his control. Embry treated me like a treasure he couldn't stop himself from plundering. Ash is treating me like a jewel to be polished and then shattered and then polished again. Like I'm all the more beautiful for the ways he'd like to wreck me.

"I want you to show me what you did when you wrote to me," he says. "I want to see what it looks like when you fuck yourself."

I let out a ragged breath. "Right now?"

"Yes. Right now."

All at once, my bravery leaves me. "I'm just... I've never done that in front of anyone. I'm worried I'll look stupid."

"For ten years, I've been dreaming about you," Ash reassures me, his thumbs back to rubbing their sweetly teasing rubs. "Just having you here, on my desk and spread open for

90

my pleasure, is more than I ever hoped to have. There's no earthly way you can disappoint me."

But sensing my hesitation, he wraps his strong hand around my own and gives it a squeeze. "I'll help you get started," he informs me, guiding my hand to my waiting pussy. I'm bare, and the outer skin there is so soft, so deliciously soft. "Don't think of it like anything other than what it is. I'm making you do this. You don't have a choice. It doesn't matter that it feels strange or embarrassing because the only things you have to worry about are listening and remembering your safe word. Say *yes, sir* if you understand."

His words relax me, soothe me. There's no way in hell I want this to stop, and he's right—the minute I relinquish all control and surrender my body to his wants and commands, the fear of embarrassment slips away. "Yes, sir."

"Good girl. Now show me what you did in that computer chair all those years ago. I want to see you come."

I do as he says, letting my eyes fall shut as he moves my hand so that my fingers graze the wet folds and then move up higher to my swollen clit. The moment my fingers touch it, I nearly jolt off the table. I'm starved for this, needy, because even though I get myself off nearly every night, having Ash here changes it fundamentally. It's no longer me and my blurry memories merging with my darkest fantasies; it's me and Ash and Ash's hands moving back down to grip my hips and Ash's pulse thudding above his collar and Ash's silver tie bar glinting in the dim light of the White House living room. It's both of us together, and it feels just as intimate as sex, even though we are both fully clothed, even though the hand slowly rubbing my clit is my own.

It only takes a minute for me to find my rhythm, to find that perfect pace and pressure to send my body slowly spiraling upward. I bite my lip to muffle the tiny moans coming from deep in my throat, but I can't stop the rocking of my hips as my body wakes up and begins demanding more. I spread my thighs wider, Ash's pleased hiss rocketing through me like a meteoroid, and I severely underestimated how much I needed this because I'm so close, so impossibly close, and it's only been a couple of minutes.

"You're going to come for me, aren't you?" Ash asks in a low voice.

I nod, panting. I'm wet everywhere, my body hot, my thighs tight, my clit feeling firm and puffy all at once. My other hand, still pulling my panties aside so I can work myself for Ash, begins to cramp, and as if Ash can tell, he hooks the fabric with his thumb, freeing my hand from its task. I place that hand behind me so I can tilt my head up and lean back farther, relishing the feeling of Ash's hands on me, his hungry eyes on my pussy, and that thought alone is enough to push me right to the cliff's edge.

"Tell me when," he orders. "I want to know when."

"Now," I manage. "Right now."

Without hesitation, he plunges two of his fingers inside me. The rough intrusion sends my body convulsing, the orgasm suddenly infinitely more intense for those large, unfamiliar fingers inside me, and I clamp down on them, shuddering out my release.

"Look at me," he tells me, and I do, meeting his eyes as my climax continues to pull at my stomach and thighs. As I continue to squirm down onto his hand and ride out my first non-solo release in years.

"Oh, that's good," he murmurs, glancing down to where I'm still trying to fuck his fingers. "That's so good. That's exactly what I need."

He says it almost like feeling my pussy come around his fingers was some sort of audition and that I passed with flying colors, and the thought prolongs the shuddering contractions until finally several seconds—or hours—later,

I'm left loose and tingling on the desk. And then I give a little laugh—incredulous, exhilarated.

I can't believe I just did that.

I can't believe it at all.

"Did that feel good?" Ash asks, fingers inside me still.

"Yes," I breathe.

The fingers twist cruelly, pain flaring up and bringing with it a wave of deep, itchy desire. "Don't be ungrateful," the president chides. "What do you say?"

It's so hard to think with his fingers inside me and pleasure still leaking through my limbs. "Yes, *sir*?"

Another twist and I have to fight the urge to start fucking his fingers again. "Try again."

Twist go the fingers, moan goes Greer.

"What. Do. You. Say." *Twist twist twist.* "When. I've. Made. You. Feel. Good."

"Thank you, sir," I gasp, not fighting myself anymore and rocking into his thrusts.

A small smile like a comma at the corner of his mouth. "Good girl." He presses his thumb to my clit and starts working it, building me up to a second orgasm so fast that I barely have time to register that it's about to crest, and then it's on me, and I'm shivering apart into bliss, contracting around the president's hand, and gasping *thank you thank you thank you* as his eyes blaze with heat.

With gratitude.

"No, thank *you*, angel," he murmurs, eyes on my face, fingers still gently working. "Thank you so much more than you can ever know."

CHAPTER 10

THE PRESENT

ASH'S FINGERS PROBE ME ONCE OR TWICE MORE, PRESSING against my G-spot and testing my responsiveness, and then he slides them out, using my dress to dry his hand. The gesture is at once degrading and unbelievably sexy, and before I can again plunge into a *who am I* mental soliloquy, he says, "Snap your fingers instead of saying my name if you need to."

I blink at him, confused, and then all of a sudden his large hand is fisted in the hair at the back of my neck, literally dragging me off the desk and to my knees. I tumble past his legs, his hand in my hair preventing me from using my hands to balance myself, and I land hard on the carpet, my dress catching between my body and Ash's legs and baring my ass.

Ash's hand is already on his belt buckle, deft and sure, and then his pants are open and I catch a glimpse of him. Male and hard and thick and so much more beautiful than

I ever could have imagined—all smooth ridges and a wide flared tip, every part of him flushed a dusky red. It's hard for me, throbbing for me, and like a greedy girl, I reach for it with both hands.

A sharp tug of my hair. "Just your mouth," Ash says.

I have next to no practice doing this, but I remember Ash's comforting words from earlier and put that out of my mind. He wants me to try, I want to try—that's all that matters. And so I lean forward and run the flat of my tongue up the underside of his cock, feeling every curve and swell of his shaft, relishing the shaky breath I hear him take above me. I repeat the action, faster this time, and start flickering my tongue experimentally around his tip, finding all the spots that make him pull my hair harder, the places that make his stomach tighten and his breath catch. Without my hands, it's hard to apply the right kind of pressure, and so I lean forward even more, pinning his cock against his muscled stomach, which is still mostly covered by his expensive white button-down. There's the scratch of Italian cotton on my cheek and the glide of his silk tie, a contrast to the heat of his skin, and then his hand is at his root and his other hand yanking at my hair, and my mouth is forced down onto his dick.

His crown is so wide, and I choke as he holds my head down onto him. The minute he hits the back of my throat—still far from all the way in—he yanks my head up and I gasp for breath, the stinging in my eyes manifesting into tears that smudge my mascara. My heart is racing, my blood flooded with adrenaline, and I realize I'm squirming the tiniest bit, my pussy already demanding more. I'm aroused and exhilarated and ashamed all at once.

Ash doesn't speak, doesn't loosen his hold on my hair or move the hand currently controlling his erection, and I realize he's waiting. He gave me a small taste of what this would be like, and he's waiting to see if I'll snap my fingers or say his name to stop it. But I do neither.

I lick my lips instead.

He smiles then, a quick smile that doesn't seem like it's necessarily for me. Like he's smiling at himself, smiling in satisfaction. Like he knows he made the right choice.

His cock is forced past my lips again, but this time I'm ready for it, opening my lips and taking a deep breath through my nose.

"Relax your tongue," he murmurs from above me, and then lets out an, "Ahhhh, yes, like that," when I comply. He moves a little slower than the first time, pulling me off and back onto his erection with a steady but not unkind pace, going a little deeper each time, until there's finally the moment he pushes deep into my throat. My body rebels, my throat convulsing and threatening to gag, but then I realize the hand in my hair is caressing my scalp and that he's crooning something to me. I can't hear what he's actually saying over the panic in my mind and the blood in my ears, but just hearing his voice grounds me. I breathe through my nose, more tears leaking over the edge of my lower lids, and reflexively swallow against the urge to gag.

"*Holy shit*," Ash swears as I swallow around him, his hips bucking up into me. "*Fuck.*"

I do it again, with much the same response, the swearing and the jerky thrust into the tight vise of my throat, and at the same time I feel a rush of triumph, I also see my mascara-stained tears begin to drip onto his white shirt. He must see them too, because he gives a groan—half regret, half sheer cruel desire. I can feel his reluctance as he lifts my head and his dick leaves my mouth, but all I feel is a rush of overwhelming gratitude and also a kind of indescribable pride that I made him react that way.

I suck in several desperate breaths while he stares down

at my face and gently wipes at the black tears on my cheeks with his thumb. "More," he says, "I need more," and then he's shoving up inside me again, this time without mercy. I don't snap my fingers, I don't struggle—because God help me, I love this too much—but I can't help the way my fingers claw at his thighs and my bare feet kick at the carpet as I let him fuck my throat. It's invasive and brutal and fucking intoxicating. I'm the one being used, but in the dirty, airless heat of it all, he's the one weakened and at the mercy of my mouth. He's the one unraveling, thrusting and swearing and sweating, the one who's more beast than human, and all because of something I'm doing. And doing well.

"Need to come," he mutters raggedly. "I'm going to come."

I get a quick break for air and then I'm back down, and I feel both of his hands on my head, pushing me down as far as I'll go, to the point where my nose is buried against the clean, shortly trimmed hair at the base of his cock. Now that I know the swallowing trick, I do it repeatedly, driving him into a frenzy, and soon his forearms are clamped on my head and his body curled over mine, holding me fast as he pumps several hard, short thrusts into my throat. The silk tie rasps against my cheek, and my hands are desperate and everywhere, pulling at his pants, his belt, the expensive leather upholstery of his chair.

He finally erupts with a breathy grunt that makes my toes curl. I'll be hearing that grunt in my dreams, in my fantasies, how helpless and yet strong it was, how very, very male. The sound of it lodges in my gut, and when the hot warmth of his climax finally hits my throat, I know I'm a lost cause. Nothing—not literature, not teaching, not traveling or looking out over Manhattan at night—nothing compares to this. Having the powerful body of a powerful man pressed against me, owning me and taking pleasure from me. Having his most intimate, unguarded self unveiled, and only to me.

Because this night, this moment? I could be the only woman in the world, the only mouth and the only body, and that isn't love exactly, but it feels like it, and maybe that's what counts in the end.

He lifts my head off his cock and says simply, "Lick me clean," which I do. Thoroughly. So thoroughly that he starts to get hard again and pushes me off.

"Enough," he says sternly, but when I look up, his eyes are sparkling with amusement. "You're too good."

Despite my raw throat, despite the wet tears on my cheeks, his words make me want to purr and stretch like a kitten. I don't think I've ever felt so close to another person, so admired and, yes, despite the brutal face-fucking, respected. I've never been this happy and content, save for that handful of moments under Embry's body all those years ago. I rub my face against Ash's knee, like a cat indeed, and he indulges me, stroking my hair and praising me for how good I made him feel.

After a few minutes of this, he straightens up, tucking himself back into his pants. "Stay like that, on your knees, and put your hands behind your back."

I do as he says, watching him stand up and walk into his bedroom again, thinking there will be more to the night. My cunt rejoices because I am so incredibly worked up after making Ash come, but when he comes out of the bedroom, he's not holding any kinky sexy toys or condoms. He holds only a soft-looking washcloth and a hairbrush.

He sits back down in his chair and tilts my chin up, cleaning my face slowly and gently, wiping away every last black mascara trail and cooling what I know must be flushed cheeks. Then he tells me to turn around, still kneeling, and I feel him begin to pluck the hairpins out of my ruined chignon one by one.

"Your hair," he says in a low voice. I hear the pins hitting the desk one at a time, *clink clink clink*, as if he kept them all in his fist and then dropped them onto the desk in a steady rain. "There's no end to the things I've thought about doing with your hair. It was the first thing I noticed about you that night, you kneeling among all that glittering glass, your hair like sunshine. Like white gold." I can practically hear him shake his head. "I suppose I'll never know if it was your hair or seeing you on your knees that captivated me at first. I'll also never know if it was you noticing my sleeplessness or watching you bleed for someone you loved that made you unforgettable to me."

His words are rolling through my veins, a spell of fire and heat.

"But that hair. I used to think about it incessantly, what it would look like wrapped around my fist as I fucked you from behind. How it would feel wrapped around my cock, like so much loose silk. There were times when it was all I could think about, what your hair would smell like and what it would feel like against my lips..." I feel his lips against my hair now, dropping kisses onto the crown of my head.

We've just been so intimate, his fingers in my cunt and his cock in my mouth, but for some reason the kiss on my hair reverberates through me like a church bell. It's gentleness and desire all at once, and after what we just did together, that kind of warm affection seems more precious for all the abuse that came before it. Tears smart at my eyes again, this time for a very different reason than physical pain.

He picks up the brush and starts to pull it through my hair with even, soothing strokes. I only have a few tangles, and Ash works through them with care, so that I barely feel any tugging or stinging. "But of all the things I thought about," he continues, "it was brushing your hair that I thought about the most. Just watching it glint in the light, hearing the brush move through it. There would be nights in Carpathia where we'd be out on patrol in the mountains, freezing in the darkest hours of the night when it was too dangerous to light a fire, and to pass the time, I'd imagine brushing your hair. Sometimes you were the age you would have been at the time—seventeen or eighteen—and other times I'd imagine you older. Pregnant and at my feet, with my ring on your finger."

The image gives me a moment's pause. In my loneliest hours, I have imagined something very close to his little fantasy, and hearing him admit it sends another church-bell-style shiver through me.

The brush pauses in my hair. "Does that make you uncomfortable?" Ash asks. "I know that I'm basically confessing to a history of obsession. And I don't want that combined with my position as president to make you feel coerced or threatened."

"I don't feel that way at all," I murmur, and the brush starts back through my hair again.

The brush is replaced by his fingers, running through the tresses over and over again, smoothing and separating and smoothing them again, like a hand moving through running water. It's impossible to describe being touched like this when no man or woman has ever touched me this way before. When I was a child, I was touched with a parent's or grandparent's love, and when I was a teenager, there had been the inevitable tickles and snuggles with my best friend and cousin. But I've never been touched as a woman by another adult this way—with reverence and care. With sex still hovering in the air. It thrills me and unnerves me at the same time because what if it ends? I'm not a woman of low self-esteem, but how can I possibly be worthy of the love of a man like Ash? What will happen if he realizes this?

"I know I probably haven't earned this privilege," Ash says after several long moments of stroking my hair, "and that it will mean that things will change, but I would love it if you spent the night with me. If you slept—and I mean that literally—in my bed with me."

"How will things change?" I ask.

"There's a chance the press will see you leave. There's a chance a staffer will recognize you as you exit the Residence. There's a chance I'll be doodling your name on every bill I sign tomorrow."

I can't stifle my girlish grin at that, and I'm glad he can't see my face. I take a minute to think. After what we shared, after learning about the emails—it hasn't shrunk my fears about delving back into this life, but the fears are put in perspective. Ash is worth it. The Greer I used to be is worth it.

As my answer, I turn to face him. "We could do more than literally sleep, you know."

A reproachful tap of the brush on my upper arm. "Don't tempt me. I think we've committed enough sins for one night."

Vulnerability must have flashed in my eyes, because before I know it, I'm being raised to my feet and kissed deeply. Ash's tongue slides against my own, his lips firm, and his hands are sliding up my back to find my zipper. He tugs it down, and soon I'm standing in a pool of blue cotton, wearing nothing but my panties and bra. Ash pulls back with a smile and takes my hand to press against the front of his still-unbuckled pants.

"See?" he asks as I wrap my fingers around the thick erection I find there. "Trust me, Greer, there's hardly anything I want more than to throw you onto my bed and rut into you until I'm too tired to move. But I've waited so long to have you here…" He reaches out and twines a strand of gold hair around his finger. "I want to take my time. I know that sounds horribly old-fashioned, but we only get to have these first times together once. I want to savor them."

That touches me, strangely. I want to savor these times

too, although the idea of waiting for them is almost unbearable. "I guess when you put it like that, it's hard to argue with."

"*I'm* hard to argue with," he informs me. "That's why I'm the president."

He scoops me up into his arms with a sudden movement, carrying me to his bedroom, and I let out a stream of giggles like bubbles underwater. Each one seems to light up his face more and more until he's practically glowing as he sets me down on the bed. "You have the most incredible laugh," he says, dropping a kiss onto my waiting lips. He walks over to his dresser and retrieves a plain white T-shirt for me to put on. "Has anybody ever told you that?"

"Only you."

He sighs at that, the idea of being an *only* or a *first* for me seeming to please something deep inside of him, and when our fingers brush as he hands me the T-shirt, I resist the urge to grab his tie and pull him to me so we can get started on some other firsts.

He returns to the dresser and removes his tie bar and cuff links, dropping them slowly into a dish inside his top drawer. His handsome face turns uncertain. "Greer...if this—if us spending the night together is too much, I want you to tell me. I know I can be controlling, and sometimes I forget to ask people how they feel before I demand to have my way. It's probably a good quality for a soldier or president, but it's not necessarily a good one for a lover. That's one of the reasons your emails had such an impact on me—even before I knew who I was and what I wanted, you seemed to know exactly what you wanted. You wanted to have done to you the kinds of things I wanted to do to you, and it made me feel like...maybe..." He pauses, does the thing where he rubs at his forehead with his thumb. It's sweet, somehow, seeing this famous orator, the president famed for his certainty and surety, at a loss for words. For me.

I stand up, still in my bra and panties, clutching the shirt in my hand. I go to him and hand him the shirt and then turn back to face the bed. He understands immediately, his strong hands unfastening my bra hook by hook.

"I still want those things," I tell him. I look at him over my shoulder. "I want you to do them to me. Do you remember what I asked you in my last email?"

He lets out the kind of breath that tells me he knows exactly what I'm talking about. "'I want a man or woman to claim me as their equal partner in every way—until we're alone. Then I want to crawl to them.'"

The bra is loose, and I turn to face him again, letting it fall from my shoulders and onto the floor. His eyes darken into the deepest green at the sight of my naked breasts. "That hasn't changed," I whisper. "If anything, it's truer today than it was then. I promise to tell you everything—even when I think you won't like what I have to say—but I want you to know that it's not too much. I know it's fast right now, but we've also had ten years leading up to this. And even though I told myself I was over you, past that time in my life, I think without knowing it that I've been waiting for you all along." I brush my fingers along his jaw, and he closes his eyes for a moment. "I'm ready to stop waiting."

He opens his eyes and smiles. "Me too. Arms up."

I don't miss the way his gaze sweeps hungrily over my breasts as I raise my arms, and I hope that he'll change his mind about having sex tonight, but despite the erection bulging the front of his slacks, his self-control is ironclad. He pulls the T-shirt over my arms and head, and then gives me a little smack on the bottom. "There's a spare toothbrush in the bathroom cabinet. Brush your teeth and then get in the bed."

I obey, walking through his dressing room and into the bathroom. As I brush my teeth, I can't help but gaze around, trying to wrangle the surreal feeling of brushing my teeth in the president's bathroom. The bathroom is as modern as the dressing room is traditional—clean lines of black marble and white tile, clearly recently renovated. But the dressing room still retains its antique feeling, with an ornate fireplace in the corner and richly red drapes hanging around the windows. An unused vanity sits against the wall next to a tall window, its mirror spotless and its surface clean, except for one picture frame. I remember seeing pictures of First Ladies sitting in here, at this very vanity, and my chest feels hot. I never wanted this, never pictured myself living here, either as a president or the First Lady, yet for a moment, I see it. I see it and I don't hate it. Not for the fame or power or even the beautiful old house, but for Ash. For Ash, I think I might be able to live here.

I wander a little closer, looking at the picture. It's Ash with two women, both black, one old and one young. I recognize the young one right away—Kay Colchester, Ash's foster sister and current chief of staff. The older woman must be Ash's foster mother. I scan the picture for every single detail, as if it contains a biography of Ash's life, but all it shows me is love and warmth. All three of them grin at the camera as the sun shines on a tidy little bungalow behind them, and even though the media always painted Ash's orphan backstory as nobly tragic, there's nothing sad or tragic about this picture at all. Ash had a happy childhood. That touches me in a very deep place, so deep that I almost want to cry, but I don't.

Instead, I turn abruptly from the vanity and go back into the bathroom to finish up. Ash joins me, and while I want to stay and watch him brush his teeth, he waves me away with a look that tells me he hasn't forgotten that he gave me particular instructions. With a stifled pout, I go to the large four-poster bed and crawl under the soft, gray blankets.

When Ash enters, he's only wearing his slacks, the white shirt and tie abandoned somewhere along the way. My mouth gapes a little at the sight: those powerful muscles shifting under all that warm skin, the lines of his hips tapering in from his wide shoulders, the V that disappears into the low waist of his tailored slacks. Smiling at the way I'm gawking, he unzips his pants and steps out of them, draping them over a low sofa, and stalks toward the bed.

I can't believe this is happening. That this is real life right now. The president—the Ash of my dreams for ten years—wearing tight boxer briefs and walking toward me with a hungry look in his eyes. Maybe I'm dreaming. Maybe I'm hallucinating.

But no. He clicks off the light and slides into the bed, his iron arm snaking around my waist and then pulling me tight into him, my back to his chest. I let out a happy sigh at the feeling of his long, big body curled protectively around mine, and then I wriggle my hips suggestively when I feel the thick rod of his erection nestle against my ass. He gives me a light pinch. "Don't be naughty," he breathes in my ear. "I've had ten years to dream up punishments for you, and I can't wait to try them out."

"Neither can I."

"I think you really mean that. And it pleases me more than you can know." He pulls me a little tighter and kisses the back of my neck. "Have you ever slept in a bed with a man before? Just slept?"

As much as he loves knowing he's my first at things, I can't lie. I nod my head against the pillow. "Yes. The night I lost my virginity."

He stiffens a little, and I can practically feel his jealousy roiling through him.

"You're not…mad…that I'm not a virgin, are you?"

"Oh, Greer, of course not. How could I be when I was

married to someone else? I begrudge you nothing. But him—whoever he was—I begrudge him fucking everything."

There's a kind of dark bitterness to his words that thrills me, with my craving to be possessed. But they also scare me. Because for some reason, just now, it hits in a real and concrete way.

Ash doesn't know I slept with Embry.

Ash doesn't know that the man he wants to begrudge everything is also his best friend.

The quiet worry I pushed aside this afternoon comes back, no longer quiet but shrill and keening. I no longer feel as if Ash is holding me by the neck, forcing me to face some reckless, unknowable fate, but that I am holding him. That we are both on the precipice of some terrible and beautiful and inevitable destiny, and that if I don't stop us, we'll both go tumbling headlong into its welcoming teeth.

I shift, suddenly restless, at odds with my own thoughts, and Ash is there with a kiss to my shoulder. "Keep still for me, angel," he murmurs. "Let me hold you for a few minutes longer."

How can I deny him—or myself—that? I still my limbs and relax back into him, deciding to muffle my thoughts about Embry until tomorrow. My body folds into Ash's as if it was made for it.

"I have to tell you that I'm still not a great sleeper," he says after a couple of quiet minutes, and I remember noticing the smudges under his eyes this afternoon.

"I've heard meditation helps," I say a little dryly.

"You know, I've heard that too," he says just as dryly.

"I shared a bed with my cousin for years, and she kicks and grunts in her sleep. I can handle you."

He laughs a little laugh. "I wish I could get to the point where I can sleep long enough to talk in my sleep. But probably I'll end up going over to the office to work at some point in the night. I just don't want you to feel abandoned or worried if you wake up and don't find me next to you."

I rub my ass against his cock again. "I've heard of something other than meditation that puts men to sleep."

That earns me a real pinch, and I let out a little yelp.

"Go to sleep, Greer" comes his voice in the dark.

"Yes, sir."

And I do.

CHAPTER 11

FIVE YEARS AGO

WHEN I WAS SIXTEEN, I LIED BY OMISSION TWICE. BOTH LIES landed with cat's-paw softness, light and silent, and for many years I thought that both were harmless.

I thought wrong.

The first lie was to Ash. I wrote to him that the girls at my school were obsessed with him, obsessed with the fact that Abilene and I had been at the same party mere weeks before his heroic act launched him into fame. I didn't tell him that *Abilene* herself was the most obsessed with this fact.

And the second lie was to Abilene.

It wasn't abnormal for me to keep things to myself for a few days before I confided in her, and so I didn't tell her about Ash and the kiss for a week after it happened. And then the story broke about the village of Caledonia. The news showed a formal picture of Ash in his uniform, and his face was strong and noble on the screen in our dorm common room.

Abilene, who had refused to speak to me since the night of my birthday, forgot her anger and turned to me with her dark blue eyes alight. "I remember him!" she exclaimed. "He was at the party in Chelsea!"

Which is when I should have said *I know, I made out with him in the library.*

What I said instead was, "I remember seeing him there too."

And then Abilene went and told every girl she could find about our brush with the famous.

As the news and internet outlets began churning out detailed profiles of Ash, Abilene's fascination only grew. She printed out his military photo and carried it in her binder. She obsessively memorized every fact about his life: his absent parents, his early life in a foster home, becoming valedictorian at his high school. She started telling anyone who would listen that she would marry him some day. She joined groups online dedicated to Colchester fan worship. And I knew, with all the perception that Grandpa Leo had drilled into me, that the truth would wound her instantly and fracture whatever peace we'd managed to restore after the night of my birthday.

Anyway, it had only been a kiss, and as the weeks wore on and my emails to Ash went unanswered, I decided that a kiss wasn't worth destroying our friendship over. In the heat of her adoration for the newly famous war hero, she had once again welcomed me into her confidence, and things were finally back to how they'd been before the party. I couldn't bear to give that up. Not again.

And aside from our repaired trust, I also assumed she would get over Ash as quickly as she got over most things. Abilene wasn't flighty by any means, but she was passionate, and one passion could easily drive out another. After a few months she would meet a new boy or start a new sport and she would forget all about Maxen Colchester.

How wrong I was.

———

The years passed. I turned seventeen and stopped writing to Ash, although my chest never stopped squeezing when I heard his name. I turned eighteen and graduated from Cadbury Academy. Abilene left for college back home; I applied to Oxford and got in. I turned nineteen and picked a major that definitely wasn't politics or business, much to Grandpa Leo's disappointment. I turned twenty, glanced around at my bare-bones flat with its beat-up teakettle and air mattress, and bought a plane ticket home for the summer.

I'd been home frequently to visit Grandpa, but something about that summer felt different. Maybe it was the ten solid weeks in America looming ahead of me or maybe it was the fact that Grandpa was traveling for work and I had the Manhattan penthouse mostly to myself, but I felt displaced and lonely. So when Grandpa invited Abilene and me out to Chicago to stay with him while he worked on his latest green-energy acquisition, I jumped at the chance, finding a flight the very next day.

My plane landed at the same time as Abilene's, and when we met each other, we fairly collided into an embrace, jumping up and down.

"My God," Abilene said, pulling back, "you finally figured out how to do your own makeup."

"Nice to see you too," I teased.

She smiled, her eyes flicking from my hair to my bright pink dress, but there was a new shadow in her smile.

She's jealous of you.

I shook the thought away. She looked gorgeous in her short shorts and halter top, hair glossy and red, and her pale shoulders smattered with freckles. That old fight couldn't reach us here, now, not when we hadn't seen each other in so long and had an entire week to spend together. I slung my arm around her shoulders, having to reach up as I did so since she was a few inches taller than me, and squeezed her into my side. "I missed you, Abi," I said. "I wish we were going to the same school."

Abilene rolled her eyes but put her arm over my shoulders too. "If you want that, you're going to have to come to Vanderbilt. There's no way I can handle another rainy summer in England."

"Girls." Grandpa Leo greeted us fondly as we walked into the penthouse suite after a sweltering drive from the airport to the hotel.

We ran to him and hugged him like we were seven years old instead of twenty, exclaiming over his bald head and bushy beard and thin face.

"You need to eat more, Grandpa!"

"You need to shave!"

He waved us off like we were fussy saleswomen. "I'm fine. And I hear that the beard thing is in for women right now. Is that not true?"

Abilene and I wrinkled our noses and he laughed. "Well, never mind then. Consider it shaved. I have to head out for lunch with some old friends—do you girls want to tag along?"

"I'm going to take a nap," Abilene declared. She flopped dramatically onto the hotel suite's couch, as if she'd been traveling all day instead of riding on a plane for an hour.

Grandpa looked over at me. "Well, Greer? You know I always like to have you and your eyes with me at these kinds of things."

I was tempted to stay at the hotel too, but I knew Abilene would make good on her threat to nap, and I had no desire to knock around more empty rooms alone. It's why I came to America for the summer, after all, for conversation and connection, and as much as I wanted to spend time with my cousin, I wanted to escape my thoughts more.

"Of course I'll come," I said.

Grandpa beamed at me. "I'll grab my briefcase and then we can go."

Abilene pretended to snore, and when I went over to give her a hug goodbye, she kept her eyes closed in fake sleep. "Don't get into any trouble without me," she said. Her long dark eyelashes rested prettily on her freckled cheeks, a ginger Sleeping Beauty.

I poked at her side. "You are pretty much the only reason I've ever been in trouble."

She smiled then, a cat's smile, eyes still closed. "That's what I'm saying—I want to be there for any trouble you find."

"At a lunch with Grandpa? Hardly likely."

She yawned for real, settling on her side. "Still, though. Share any cute boys you meet."

———

Lunch was at a well-lit, modern café inside the Art Institute of Chicago, and it was the usual handful of politicians and businesspeople discussing election cycles and policy. Grandpa Leo, sober for thirty years, automatically slid me the wine the waiter poured for him without asking.

I listened politely, white wine bright and crisp on my tongue, watching everyone's faces and gauging their tones, dutifully recording mental notes to report to Grandpa later. Half my mind had already drifted back to Oxford, back to the classes I'd enrolled in for the next session, back to the beaten, dog-eared books stacked next to my air mattress in my grimy little flat.

Until I heard Merlin's name from someone at the table.

My head snapped up in alarm, and sure enough, Merlin

Rhys himself was strolling up to the table, tall and dark eyed and clean-shaven, his expression open and more amiable than I'd ever seen it. Until his gaze slid over to me, that is, and then the openness faded, leaving something tiredly resigned in the lines of his face. I could see it clear as day: he hadn't known I'd be here and he didn't want me here, for whatever reason.

I ducked my head with embarrassment, even though I'd done nothing wrong.

Why didn't I stay at the hotel? I berated myself. If I'd known for one second that Merlin would show up…

"Sorry we're late" came an easy, deep voice from behind Merlin. My heart stopped.

The world bled away.

And there was only Maxen Colchester.

Four years older and painfully more good-looking, post-tour-of-duty scruff highlighting the strong lines of his cheeks and jaw, wearing a long-sleeve T-shirt and a pair of low-waisted slacks that emphasized how ridiculously trim and lean his body was. He folded his soldier's frame into a chair next to Merlin, the elegant table setting in front of him doing nothing to diminish the sense of raw power and strength radiating from his body. I'd forgotten, somehow, what that power and strength felt like in person.

It felt like drowning.

Tell me, Greer, do you like my lips on your skin?

Yes.

I believe you. That's why you're so dangerous.

My fingers curled around the stem of my wineglass, and I forced myself to focus on it, on the way the glass felt on my skin. Smooth and whole, not at all like the jagged shards and splinters I'd cradled in my hands the night I met Ash. All these years, I'd told myself I didn't care about Ash, wasn't haunted by our kiss. I'd wanted to be sophisticated, the kind of aloof girl who kissed men like Ash and then forgot all about it. I wanted to be different than Abilene, with her fan forums and obsessive fantasizing. I wanted to be wise and worldly and apart from such schoolgirl crushes.

But I couldn't pretend that any longer. Not when faced with the warm-blooded, green-eyed reality of him.

Right now, I was the Greer who'd written those embarrassingly honest emails, the Greer who'd melted into his touch, who'd shivered as he licked her blood from her skin. Right now, I was a vessel of pooling want. I was ready to be whatever he wanted me to be, ready to crawl into his veins and make him mine. I was eager and humiliated and yearning and mortified, and I knew the absolute truth in that moment—I was in love with Maxen Colchester. It was foolish and silly and absurd—nothing could be more unworldly and unsophisticated—but somehow, terribly and incredibly, it was true.

"…and my granddaughter Greer."

I lifted my gaze, realizing Grandpa Leo had been talking this whole time, introducing the others at the table to Ash and Merlin. I suddenly wished I was in something less girlish than this pink knee-length dress with its neatly folded bow at the back. I wished I had put my hair up or reapplied my lip gloss, or anything to feel fresher and prettier and *more* than I was in that moment. Instead, I felt incredibly naked and young as I met Ash's stare across the table.

He'd frozen in place—just for a second—his eyes flaring into a green fire before settling back into their usual emerald. Then he gave me a genuinely happy smile and said in that easy, confident voice, "Greer. So good to see you again."

Again.

He remembers.

I took a breath and smiled too, a smile that felt too shaky and too excited and too hopeful. "Yes. So nice to see you too."

114

And then I lifted my wineglass to my lips, hoping no one saw the trembling of my hand as I did.

The lunch went on as normal—Merlin was having a party tonight for his fortieth birthday, and everyone at the table was going—and the conversation turned back to politics, although with Merlin there, the conversation finally drifted away from the minutia of elections and numbers and into slightly more interesting territory. Merlin was asking my grandfather if he'd ever support a third-party presidential candidate, and the table stirred with the natural antipathy establishment politicians have to such talk.

But even that couldn't hold my attention when Ash was so near. He talked very little, choosing mostly to listen, but when he did speak, it was so concisely elegant and perceptive that even these people, who spent their lives talking over everyone else, had trouble finding a response that matched his insight.

Every word he said, I stored away, as if his opinions on the viability of a third-party candidate were secret revelations about himself. I watched his every movement from under my eyelashes, the way his hand looked as he twirled the stem of his wineglass between his fingers, the way he held himself perfectly still as he was listening to someone else—perfectly still except for the occasional nod of understanding—a stillness not learned in a courtroom or a legislator's chamber but in battle. A stillness that could have been curled over a sniper's rifle, it was so deliberate and immovable. A stillness that accounted for the movements of wind and the fluttering of leaves and careful intakes of breath. A stillness that was patient.

Predatory.

If Ash ever became a politician, he would clear through these people like a stick beats a path through weeds. They'd be bent and broken before they ever saw it coming.

I didn't have that stillness. Perception, yes. Patience, no.

And so it was agony to be so close to Ash, able to soak up every lift of his shoulders, every flex of those fingers, every rich, deep word, and to know that there was nothing to be done about the tempest inside me. There was no outlet for this restless ache, this almost-pain, this fidgety, giddy feeling twisting inside my chest. At any moment, my control would break, and it would all come spilling out of me.

Do you really remember me? I would blurt, leaning forward. *Do you remember our kiss? I do. I remember how you took care of my cut, I remember how you told me not to move, I remember how you pinned me against the wall. I dreamed of it for years after; I still dream of it. I thought I didn't care, I tried to shove down that girl, I tried to be someone else, but now that I'm with you, I don't think I can. I don't think I can want anyone else, and I don't think I want to be any other version of myself than the girl you boss around.*

I can bleed for you again.

Let me bleed for you again.

And then, as if he'd heard me, as if my thoughts had reached out to him, he turned his head and met my stare head-on. His fingers tightened almost imperceptibly on the wineglass, and I imagined them tightening in my hair, fisting my white-gold locks and snapping my head backward so he could bite my throat.

I caught my breath at the thought, tearing my gaze away from his. I had to go. I couldn't be wet and panting and miserable at this table—not with these people, not with my grandfather, not with the source of my torture so breathtakingly close.

I leaned into my grandfather. "Is it okay with you if I go poke around the museum a bit?" I asked quietly.

"Yes, sweetie. I imagine you must be bored to death. I'll text you when we're done."

Gratitude flooded through me, and I gave him a quick peck on the cheek. "Thanks, Grandpa."

I pushed my chair back and excused myself with a hurried murmur, careful not to make eye contact with Ash as I did. Even so, I could feel his eyes on my back as I left, and I wanted to look back so badly, I wanted to see for sure if he was watching me leave, if he was watching my legs or my hips or my hair, but I didn't. I strode quickly out of the restaurant, only breathing once I was out the doors and on my way to the museum proper. There was something inside my body that kicked and struggled at being separated from Ash, just as there was something that kicked and struggled while in his unbearable presence.

As I paid for a museum ticket and took a small folded brochure with a gallery map, I ran back through everything I had done and said. Had I humiliated myself in any way? Had I looked too much at him? Spoken too breathlessly? I couldn't bear anyone at that table thinking I was ridiculous—especially Merlin, who already seemed to dislike me for some unaccountable reason—but I didn't want Ash in particular to think I was besotted. No doubt he would find it as ridiculous as I found it myself.

I saw nothing as I walked through the galleries, absorbed nothing, thinking only of Ash. I didn't even bother glancing at the map in my hand, so I had no idea where I was when I found myself in an enclosed courtyard surrounded by statues. I was alone and the sunlight on the stone gave the room a holy glow, like a church. The silence was so profound that I could almost hear the statues themselves, marble so lifelike you watched for it to breathe, collecting dust, their creators long dead.

My mind quieted.

I stopped in front of one statue, arrested by the delicate stonework—a young woman veiled and dressed in robes—a tambourine hanging limply from one hand. There was something about her face—downcast and a little stunned—or maybe it was the instrument dangling listlessly from her fingertips, that made it look like she'd forgotten how to be inside her own body. Like she'd fall apart if she tried to stand or speak.

I could empathize.

"That's Jephthah's daughter" came Ash's voice from behind me.

I'd been so absorbed in the sculpture that I hadn't heard his footsteps, and I spun around to hide my surprise.

"What?" I asked, hoping I sounded normal and not the strange version of panic-excited I felt like.

"Jephthah," he said, nodding toward the statue as he took a step toward me. The light glinted off the face of the large watch on his wrist as he put his hands in his pockets. "He was a judge in ancient Israel, a war leader who fought against the Ammonites, and he made a vow to God. If he won his fight against his enemies, he would offer the first thing that came out of his house when he returned home… he'd make it a sacrifice, a burnt offering. I'll give you one guess what he found coming to meet him."

"His daughter," I said, sadness and disgust sticking heavy on my tongue.

"His daughter," Ash confirmed. "She came out dancing, ready to make music with her instruments. When he saw her, he despaired and tore his clothes, but when he told her what he had vowed, she refused to let him renege on his word to the Lord. She asked for two months in the mountains with her women so that she could 'bewail her virginity.'"

"So she could bewail her virginity," I repeated. "I know how that feels."

His mouth twitched at that, but I couldn't tell if it was with a smile or a frown. "And then she returned to her

118

father. The Bible only says that he made good on his vow…
It doesn't go into detail—almost as if the priests writing it
knew how awful it was even then. And after she was sacrificed, there was a festival of women every year, who gathered
together for four days to lament her death."

"And that's it?" I asked incredulously. "He was allowed to
murder his own daughter and burn her corpse? Just because
of some promise he made about a battle she had no part in?"

Ash nodded. "Awful, isn't it? You can see why she seems
so shocked. So sad."

He stepped closer again, this time standing next to me
and looking up into the downturned face of the statue.
"Some people say that it was a rash vow, a vow made in haste
without much thought, and that may be true. But I think
some people haven't ever been in a war. You don't know what
you'll promise yourself or God until you're facing down that
moment yourself. Until the lives of countless others rest on
your shoulders and yours alone."

I turned to look at him, meaning to examine his face,
to question him, but it took me a second to regain my train
of thought because fuck, he was good-looking. *Hot* wasn't
the right word, neither really was *handsome*. They didn't
capture the raw masculinity that barely seemed contained in
his wide, lean frame. They didn't capture the potency of his
muscular body, the keen flash of his eyes, the unexpectedly
generous lines of his mouth. "So are you saying you approve
of him sacrificing his daughter?"

"Fuck no," Ash said, and something about seeing a man
so in command of himself use a word like *fuck* was undeniably erotic. "Even taking into account the fact that human
sacrifice was a norm in the Levant, it wasn't supposed to be
a norm for the Israelites, certainly not during the period of
the Judges. Rabbis from as far back as a thousand years ago
have contended that Jephthah never actually murdered his

daughter, that he instead 'sacrificed' her to a life of religious servitude. Some people think it never happened at all, but it was a story retrofitted to explain the ritual of women gathering to lament a maiden's death."

"What do you think?"

Ash's eyes narrowed ever so slightly at the statue, as if he could persuade her to spill her secrets. After a beat or two, he shrugged and sighed. "I think what actually happened is less important than the story we want it to be. Is this a morality tale, cautioning against impudent vows? A different morality tale, showing the righteousness of upholding a vow even when it's hard? Is this a narrative showing where a pagan tradition was shoehorned into the well-ordered history of the Levite authors? The first step to understanding anything—whether it's the Bible or *Fifty Shades of Grey*—is acknowledging that we come to it with agendas of our own. We want it to mean something, we are biased whether we know it or not, and usually what we walk away with is what we want to walk away with."

"What do you want to walk away with? What do you want it to mean?"

For the first time, he looked down at the floor, and for a moment, just for a moment, I could see the weight of every death, every battle, every cold night spent in the fens of Eastern Europe pulling on him. And then he turned to me and it all vanished, leaving only a regretful smile. "I guess I want it to mean that the Lord forgives soldiers for unacceptable sacrifices. For decisions made in the heat of the moment, when there was no good choice, there was only what would save the most people, even if it meant leaving someone to burn." A deep breath. "Metaphorically, I mean."

I pulled him into a hug.

I don't know why I did it, how I overcame that twisting, awkward agony that came with being near him, but he sounded so pained, so burdened and haunted, and my heart had known no other way to tell him *It's okay. I'm here and I know and it's okay.*

So I wrapped my arms around his waist, turned my face against his broad chest, and pulled him close. There was a moment, an exhale that sounded like a breathless groan, and then his arms were around me too. I felt his lips against the crown of my head, lips and then his nose and his cheeks, as if he were rubbing his entire face against my hair. As if he was marking himself on me or I was marking myself on him, as if he wanted to make a life for himself in the tousled waves.

"It seems you are always meant to be comforting me somehow," he said, lips moving against the golden tresses.

"I like making you feel good," I whispered. *Better*, some distant part of my mind said, *you meant to say that you like making him feel* better. But that wasn't entirely true, maybe not at all true, because making Ash feel good conjured all sorts of lip-biting images in my mind. And whatever images it conjured for Ash seemed to be lip-biting as well because I could feel a thick erection beginning to press into my lower belly.

I pushed against it, eliciting a real groan from Ash this time, and then his hand was in my hair, fisting at the nape and yanking my head back, just like I'd imagined at the restaurant. He didn't say anything, simply stared down at my parted lips and exposed neck, breathing hard, his erection now like steel against me.

He didn't ask me anything, didn't say a word, but his whole face seemed like a question, his whole body, his hard cock and his rough hands. *Do you like this?* his face seemed to ask. *Do you want more? Would you crawl for me? Bleed for me?*

He didn't say the question out loud, but I said the answer out loud.

"Yes, please."

His hand tightened in my hair, his pupils widened, and for one perfect moment, I thought he was going to kiss me. I thought he was going to toss me to my hands and knees in the middle of the sculpture courtyard and give me a reason to stop bewailing my virginity. I thought he was going to drag me by the hair back to his hotel room and show me every single shadow that flickered in those forest eyes.

And then the moment crested and broke, like a wave. The energy dissipated; his hand loosened in my hair and then was gone, he stepped back and ran a shaking hand over his face.

"That was inappropriate," he said unsteadily, his thumb moving to rub against his forehead. "That was wrong. I'm so sorry."

I stepped forward, my heart in my hands. "It wasn't wrong. I said yes, Ash—"

But what I would have said next—what he would have done—became nothing more than a barely legible entry in the diary of what might have been because at that moment my grandfather strolled into the courtyard, beaming at us both, totally oblivious to what had just happened between Ash and me mere moments before.

"Major Colchester! I wondered if you'd vanished to take in the art too. A shame to come here and eat in a place meant for looking."

I let my grandfather pull me into a side hug and give me a whiskery kiss on the temple. "Ash—I mean, the major— was explaining this statue to me. It's a very sad story."

Ash stopped rubbing his forehead, and it seemed to take great effort for him to pull himself together. "It's a story from the Hebrew Bible," he said, almost absently.

"Ah, say no more," Grandpa said. "All those Old Testament stories are too grisly for my tired bones. That's the part of Mass when I usually dart off to use the bathroom."

"Oh, Grandpa, you do not," I said.

"But wouldn't it be funny if I did?" he asked, eyes crinkling. "Anyway, I am stealing Greer away for the time being, but I won't apologize because you'll have her back tonight for more Old Testament horror stories."

"Tonight?" Ash and I both asked at the same time.

"Merlin's fortieth birthday party, of course," Grandpa boomed. "I'm bringing my granddaughters, and I know you're coming and bringing that excellent Captain Moore with you. You'll have even more time to talk then."

Ash's lips parted and pressed together. And then parted again. "Yes. Greer and I need to talk."

The look he gave me was nothing less than urging, pleading almost, and I could feel the ghost of his fingers in my hair. God, I wanted him to urge me to do anything, plead with me for anything, and I wanted it so much that I almost felt ready to make my own rash vows.

"I'm looking forward to talking," I said, somewhat pointlessly.

But Ash didn't look satisfied at that. He looked miserable.

"Goodbye, son," my grandfather said, and I gave Ash a wave as Grandpa and I started for the doors. Ash waved back, once again wrapped in his unreadable stillness, and I gave a little shiver as I turned around and walked out of the courtyard.

What exactly had just happened?

CHAPTER 12

FIVE YEARS AGO

ABILENE SQUEALED AND THREW HER ARMS AROUND MY NECK, strangling me into a hug. "A party with Maxen Colchester!"

I had just told her about Merlin's party tonight and how Grandpa wanted us both to go. Her dark blue eyes had simmered with excitement, had taken all of three seconds to boil over, and then she was shrieking and hugging me, jumping up and down as she did.

"Oh my God, just you wait and see how fantastic this going to be!" she exclaimed. "This is so perfect, it's too perfect. *Maxen Colchester*. I've been dying to meet him for so long." And then she added, as if realizing that I was still there with her, "And maybe he'll bring his cute friend, the one they have on the news all the time."

"Embry Moore," I supplied, the sudden rush of adrenaline making my head spin. I felt outside of myself, like I was floating, like I was drifting backward in time, back to Ash and our kiss four years ago. Back to the courtyard this afternoon, his hand in my hair and his eyes on my throat, like a hungry vampire. God, I couldn't stop seeing his face in that moment, couldn't stop feeling his body pressed against mine.

"Right," Abilene said, letting go of me and clapping her hands together, "Embry Moore. And then you can meet Embry and I'll meet Maxen, and everybody will fall in love and live happily ever after." She said it with a laugh that could have been self-deprecating, as if she understood how ridiculous the whole idea was, but all the same, her eyes shone with the kind of dangerous Abilene energy that meant she was about to get her way. I'd seen that energy before every lacrosse game, before every meeting with the headmaster, every night before she'd swung her leg out of the dorm room window to sneak out.

And for the first time in four years, my little lie of omission suddenly seemed a lot less little.

I almost opened my mouth to tell her—well, I don't know what exactly I planned on saying—but she interrupted me by shoving my purse into my hands.

"We're going shopping," she declared. "And we aren't stopping until we find the perfect outfit."

And as usual, I let myself get swept up in her plans. Who knew what the night might bring? Ash might change his mind about going, or he might change his mind about talking to me at all. Dread soured my stomach, even as a part of me realized it might be for the best. It would hurt awfully, but it wouldn't hurt as much as losing Abilene's friendship.

Would it?

———

Merlin's party was on the rooftop of an upscale hotel overlooking the Chicago River, and by the time Abilene and I arrived, it was well underway. While Grandpa went early because he planned on leaving early to catch a late meeting, Abilene had insisted we get there an hour after the party's start time, so that we didn't look desperate or, worse, get forced into making small talk with inconsequential people. I rolled my eyes at that, but I didn't argue. I was still twisted up in knots about going—about Ash—and it didn't take much to convince me to hide in my room for another hour.

But when we got there, I had to agree that Abilene had made the right decision. It was so much easier to step off the elevator and melt into a crowd of boozy chatter than it was to stand around awkwardly and stare at the newcomers walking in. I offered to get Abilene and I each a drink and slipped away from her, tugging self-consciously at the short hem of the raspberry minidress Abilene had somehow talked me into buying.

"Miss Galloway" came a voice from behind me.

Startled, I turned to see Merlin himself standing behind me in line, elegant as always in a three-piece suit. Even the strong breeze ruffling his black hair looked refined. But all that elegance couldn't hide the dislike that glittered in his onyx eyes or the displeasure pulling at the corners of his thin mouth.

"Mr. Rhys," I said politely, making to turn back around, my chest thudding with nervousness.

He caught my arm before I could turn away and steered me away from the line, toward the far corner of the patio. "I know you are here because of your grandfather," he said once no one could hear us, "and because of the love I bear him, I won't ask you to leave. But you should."

"You want me to leave?" I asked, stunned. Of all the things to worry about tonight, that had never occurred to me. That I actually wouldn't be welcome.

"Of course."

"Of course?" I repeated. "I'm sorry. I don't understand. Did I do something wrong? Do you…hate me…or something?"

"*Hate* is a word used by the young," he said, looking at me with an exasperated, chastising look. "I have no reason to hate you. Surely it must occur to you that I don't act or speak without a good reason to do so."

"And there's a good reason why you don't want me here tonight?"

At that, Merlin's face softened, and when it did, I saw that underneath his sharp, predatory gaze, he was a handsome man. Handsome and tired, like Ash had been when I met him. "There is a good reason. And it's that I don't want to see you or someone else I care about hurt. But I suppose it might be too late for that." He sighed and stretched his neck. "Do you remember that night in London, when you kissed Maxen?"

Heat rose to my cheeks. "Yes. Not that it's any of your business."

Another sigh. "It *is* my business. I don't like that it is, but I can't help a lot of things I don't like. You see, I care a lot about Maxen. I believe someday very soon, he's going to be more than a hero. I think he's going to be a leader. But a leader is only as powerful as the people around him, and it matters which people he surrounds himself with."

I bristled at that. "I'm not a bad person, Mr. Rhys. And I'm not a weak or stupid person either."

"Oh, no," Merlin said, shaking his head, "you misunderstand me. You are absolutely none of those things. You are too much of the opposite."

I had no idea whether that was a compliment or a warning, but I did know that I wasn't willing to let go of Ash, not for Merlin. "I'm not convinced."

Merlin gave me a sad smile. "The thing is, Miss Galloway,

you don't need to be convinced. It's over now, for better or for worse." And then he took my shoulders and turned me to face the other guests, and the noise of the party faded until there was only the sound of my sharp, staccato breath and the wind blowing off the lake.

Ash. Ash was here.

My chest expanded.

And then Ash turned and I saw that his arm was wrapped around a pretty brunette. She smiled up at him, and he leaned down and kissed her nose, and they both laughed. The sun glinted off a dazzling ring on her left hand.

Ash was here with another woman. The same Ash who'd almost kissed me this afternoon, who'd pressed his hard-on against me, who'd smelled and kissed my hair as if it were the only thing he wanted to smell and kiss ever again. A flash of rage—hot and bright—and then I remembered the way he'd stepped away from me in the courtyard, the unsteady, troubled way he'd said *That was wrong, I'm so sorry.* How miserable he'd looked when he said that we needed to talk tonight.

Of course. It all made sense now—the aborted kiss, the misery, the *talk*.

My chest contracted, and somewhere inside myself, a valiant, flickering little hope was snuffed out, leaving only smoke and the faint whiff of what could have been.

"He asked her to marry him yesterday," Merlin said, his polished voice cutting through the wind. "So you see how things are."

It felt like I couldn't breathe. Couldn't think.

But yes, I could see how things were. I certainly could do that.

"This is what I would have protected you from," he continued quietly. "Discovering this so, *ah*, publicly."

I made myself turn away from the happy couple, feeling

disoriented, feeling weak. "Of course he would have met someone else," I mumbled, mostly to myself. "It makes sense. He's not a priest. Why wouldn't he be with someone?"

But I had honestly never thought of Ash with another woman, it had never occurred to me to imagine such a thing, and the reality of it felt almost cruel in its obviousness. He was handsome and famous and kind and delightful, and why wouldn't he fall in love with a beautiful woman? Why hadn't I thought of this?

Whatever my reasons had been, I felt terribly and horribly ashamed. Ashamed of falling in love with a man I didn't know, ashamed of hoping he'd remember something that happened in another country four years ago, ashamed of being young and clueless and helpless and so utterly stupid.

"I should go," I said suddenly, feeling a familiar ache at my throat. "I need to go."

Merlin didn't say anything to convince me otherwise; he merely nodded. "You're a good person, Greer. And you deserve happiness. I only ask that you keep your kisses to yourself awhile longer. And someday, there will be a happily ever after for you too."

I didn't want to keep my kisses to myself, though, and I certainly didn't want a thin promise of *someday*. I wanted Ash, and this afternoon in the courtyard had sealed my fate. I was doomed to want him and not have him, and like the Lady of Shalott, I'd be weaving pictures of my pain and devotion for years to come.

"Goodbye," I muttered, swallowing past the knot in my throat and turning away. Merlin stayed in the corner, his gaze like iron chains weighing me down as I tried to flee, linking me to him and his awful words. I had this miserable portent that I would be dragging these chains for years. My curse, my punishment for a crime I couldn't have stopped myself from committing, even now.

129

A curse for a kiss. That's how wizards worked, wasn't it?

There would be tears, I knew, and soon. I kept my head down as I walked, trying to hurry without actually seeing what was in front of me, navigating around tipsy businessman and lobbyists and state senators, trying not to run into the low sofas and glass tables, remembering vaguely that the elevator had been in the center of the patio.

And of course, since I wasn't watching where I was going, since my mind was so busy with Merlin's words and my heart was too preoccupied with its mortal wound, I tripped over a step I hadn't seen and stumbled right into Ash's hard body.

I hadn't known he was there, had been trying to avoid coming anywhere near him, in fact, but the moment I put my hands against his solid chest, the moment he grabbed my elbows to catch me, I knew it was him. That body and those hands…the memory of them had been etched into my brain forever. More than etched—*branded*.

My cheeks flamed red with humiliation, my pulse spiking and my chest caving in from the weight of this embarrassing moment. Being held by the only man I ever wanted to hold me…and at the same moment that fantasy had to be euthanized. At the same moment I realized he was going to be married to another woman.

Get away get away get away, my mind screamed in a rabbit shriek of panic, but my body keened for his touch, begging me to press closer to him, melt into this moment forever.

I found a breath but I couldn't find my voice. He'd stolen it.

"Greer," he exhaled. His pupils had shrunk and then dilated into wide black pools, as if he'd stepped through an invisible doorway into some sort of darkness no one else could see. He flicked his tongue across his lower lip, as if unconsciously remembering our kiss, remembering this

130

afternoon, and I let out a tiny helpless noise that only he could hear. His grip tightened on my elbows.

I could feel Merlin watching me, his elegant hands inside his elegant pockets, waiting to see what I would do. Waiting to see if I still carried his chains and his warnings in my heart.

"I'm so sorry," I mumbled to Ash's chest, ducking my head down. "Excuse me."

I tried to take a step back, but his hands stayed firm on my arms, his eyes searing into the top of my head. He wasn't letting me go, and I didn't want him to let me go, but I couldn't do whatever this was. I couldn't do the fake acquaintance, catching-up small-talk thing. I couldn't do the pretending and the smiling and the polite questions when I knew that he'd be going home with his someday wife tonight.

I jerked myself out of his hold, stepping back and twisting away, and I ended up twisting right into Ash's fiancée, who seemed to be returning from the bar, a martini in each hand. We collided and cold gin splashed onto the front of my dress, soaking the raspberry fabric and turning it into a deep maroon.

"Oh my God, I'm such a klutz!" she exclaimed as I blinked, unable to process this new development as fast as I needed to. "I'm so sorry, oh my God, here, here." And she set the glasses on the ground and started trying to mop at my dress with her own, fussing over me with that big sister behavior that all women nearing thirty have toward younger women.

I know now that her name was Jenny—Jennifer Gonzalez, soon to be Jennifer Gonzalez-Colchester, a family law lawyer and amateur sharpshooter—but in that moment, I only knew what I saw. I saw that she was lovely, with large brown eyes and skin the color of rich amber. I saw that she was kind, with the way she apologized and worriedly sponged at my bodice with the hem of her own fluttering dress. I saw that she was happy, and it was Ash that made her so.

I saw that you can be hurt—mortally wounded, in fact—and it doesn't have to be anyone's fault. Sometimes the world is just cruel that way, and it wasn't fair to begrudge them their happiness even as it tore down my own.

Tears burned hot at the back of my eyelids, and I pushed Jenny's hands away. "Thank you, I'm fine," I said thickly. "I have to go, though. Excuse me."

And I pushed past her to get to the elevator. My only thought was of escape, my only feeling was the desperate, clawing need to be alone, and so I ignored her concerned voice, the hesitant murmurs of the people around us.

But I could not ignore Ash's voice. I was almost to the elevator, almost to freedom, when I heard him call my name. "Greer?"

I didn't want to look back and yet it was the only thing in the world I wanted. My head swiveled of its own accord, and I glanced at him over my shoulder. He was looking back toward Merlin in the far corner, and as he turned back to face me, confusion and a dawning realization were written all over his face. He took a step toward me, his eyes begging me to stop, but I couldn't. Not even for him would I draw out this public gutting.

I turned around and stabbed at the elevator button several times in quick succession. Luckily, it opened for me right away, and I stepped inside. I refused to look up, kept my eyes only on the door-close button, and jammed it in so hard that the knuckle on my thumb turned white. Out of my periphery, I could see him say something to Jenny and then walk toward me, and panic flared in my chest.

By the grace of God, the elevator doors slid shut then, leaving me all by myself. With a gentle lurch, the elevator started going down, and I slumped against the mirrored wall and finally allowed myself to cry.

132

When the elevator doors opened to the hotel lobby, I was still crying. In fact, my tears had escalated into very loud, very embarrassing sobs, the kind that leave you sucking for air, the kind that contort your face into something ugly and wrung out. And my phone was buzzing insistently in my coat pocket, and I was fumbling for it as I exited the elevator, trying to hold in my sobs and failing, trying not to make eye contact with any of the hotel guests in the lobby, and then I pulled out my phone and saw texts from Abilene on the screen, coming in almost too fast to read.

> Abilene: r u okay?
> Abilene: did you just leave the party
> Abilene: like, it looked like you were running for the door
> Abilene: maxen *is* here but fuck he's with some girl
> Abilene: some lawyer
> Abilene: r u coming back up? come back up so we can figure out what do about this lawyer girl with max

Goddammit, Abilene. I tried to wipe at my eyes so I could see the phone's screen to type an answer, but there were too many tears, and then I was jostling against a stream of people walking into the lobby, and for the third time tonight, I walked right into another person.

"Fuck," I swore, already swerving to push past him and reach the door.

"My favorite word," said a smoothly pleasant voice, and that voice was hypnotic in its charm. Almost against my will, I looked up into the face of one of the handsomest men I'd ever seen. Maybe *the* handsomest on purely looks alone, since so much of Ash's attractiveness came from who he was as a person. But this man, with his ice-blue eyes and cheek-bones even God would be jealous of, he'd be stunning no matter what kind of person he was.

I was halfway to smiling at him through my tears when I realized I'd seen those blue eyes and those cheekbones before, and my smile froze in place.

He was Embry Moore, and he was Ash's best friend. And that association was enough to jump-start my body again, if not my mind, because the last thing I could handle was a protracted interaction with someone close to Ash.

"Pardon," I mumbled, the tears coming out thick and hot and garbling the word. I moved around him and reached the wide revolving door that led to the sidewalk outside, and then I was free to breathe the warm evening air and hear the impatient honks of taxis and the sound of sirens somewhere in the distance.

I took a deep breath, trying to stave off the tears for long enough that I could come up with a cogent plan. There was Abilene to think about, of course, and also questions from my grandfather I wanted to avoid, which he would certainly ask if he came home from his meeting and found me home early, crying into a pillow.

I could fake sleep, though. And there was no way I could stay here.

I would just have to tell Abilene I was going home, and then I would hide until I could find a way to lie about what happened tonight, or at least hide it. But when I reached for my phone, I couldn't find it anywhere—not in either of my pockets or the inner pocket of my jacket—and that's when I heard the footsteps.

I turned around to see Embry Moore walking to me, my phone held in his outstretched hand. Like Ash, he wore a fitted button-down shirt, but unlike Ash, he'd layered a gray vest and gray blazer on top—both the shirt and jacket sleeves rolled up to the elbow. With the cuffed sky-blue pants and loafers, he looked like a playboy let loose from his yacht, and even in my current emotional state, I couldn't help but appreciate his graceful and lanky male form as he strode confidently toward me.

"You dropped this," he said in that sophisticated purr, a purr that belied money and education and privilege.

"Thanks," I muttered, taking the phone with one hand as I tried to wipe my face with the other.

"Are you okay?" he asked, ducking his head a little so he could look into my downturned face.

"I'm fine," I snapped, turning and starting to walk again. It was unbelievably rude to leave him like that, I knew, but I couldn't help it. It was just a testament to how fucked up tonight had become.

After a few steps, my tears finally started to slow. I had a plan—I had my phone back—and if I could just make it back to Grandpa's hotel, I could cry until my pain dried up and my body went limp. I just had to make it there was all, and that started with getting a cab.

I swung toward the road, and to my utter shock, Embry Moore was right behind me, his hands jammed into the pockets of his ridiculously blue pants. "Are you sure you're okay?" he asked, concerned. "I feel constitutionally unable to leave you alone like this."

"I'm fine," I said through gritted teeth. "Not that it's any of your business."

"But what is anyone's business, really?" Embry mused philosophically. "That's the first question man ever asked God, you know. 'Am I my brother's keeper?'"

I snorted, the derision somewhat undercut by the tears and snot that accompanied it. "It was a rhetorical question asked by a murderer to stall a missing persons investigation. I wouldn't start with Cain as your entry point into the fundamentals of humanity."

"John Steinbeck did. Are you saying *Of Mice and Men* is a bad book?"

"I'm saying that the parallels to be drawn from the world's first murder to migrant farm brotherhood to us standing on a Chicago curb right now are nonexistent." But despite myself, I found my lips tugging up into a smile.

"Well, now you're just being deliberately uncreative." He pouted. It was an unfairly sexy look on him.

"Also, Steinbeck once ended a book with an adult breast-feeding scene," I pointed out, needing to say something before I started staring at his perfect, full mouth.

"To illustrate the *human condition*!" he exclaimed with mock frustration. "Who hasn't breastfed a little bit to understand the dehumanizing depths of poverty and displacement?"

"Me. I haven't done that."

"Well, me either, but maybe if I buy you a couple drinks tonight we could change that for each other." He waggled his eyebrows, and the whole thing was so ridiculous that I giggled.

"I'm not letting you breastfeed from me," I said, wondering how this conversation got so strange and funny, and also wondering when I'd stopped crying, because I realized I had.

"Get your mind out of the gutter," he said with a pitying shake of his head. "I obviously meant that you would breast-feed from *me*."

I giggled again. "I didn't peg you for the kinky type."

"You aren't pegging me at all. That's our current problem."

And it was a joke, and he said it with that crooked dimpled grin, but suddenly my mind was filled with the image of Embry underneath me, moaning and panting, and heat filled my cheeks.

He was still talking. "Can I tell you about my actual kink?"

I nodded a little uncertainly, realizing that I'd stepped away from the curb and was facing him completely now.

"Well, the kink that really gets me off is taking gorgeous strangers to get hot dogs on Navy Pier. Sometimes if I'm really kinky, we ride the Ferris wheel too."

Was he saying that he wanted to do those things with me? "I imagine the porn for that particular kink is woefully lacking."

"It is. I only get my fix in real life." He stepped closer to me and offered his arm, and even through the shirt and blazer, I could see the firm swells of muscle. "What do you say? You, me, hot dogs, and more Steinbeck bashing?"

Yes.

It was incredible that as much as I wanted to hide away, as much as I wanted to cry and wail and gnash my teeth, as much as Ash filled every breath and thought with his face, I wanted to say yes. Embry was so funny and smart and effortlessly charming, and I felt better just for these last five minutes with him. Not to mention how flattering it was after everything that someone as famous and interesting as Embry wanted to spend time with me.

Also, he was *so fucking hot*.

But—"Don't you have a birthday party to be at?"

His eyebrows pulled together, puzzlement sliding into understanding. "Ah. I'm guessing if you know who I am and what party I should be at, you came from there yourself?"

I looked back toward the street, not wanting to talk about it. "Yes."

"Ah." And then he thankfully, thankfully left it at that. "So what do you say? I mean, if you can play hooky from the party, so can I."

"I don't know…" I kept my eyes on the road because I knew if I looked at him, it would be all over. "I had planned on going back to my hotel. Calling it an early night."

"What a waste that would be," he said softly, taking a step toward me.

I allowed myself to glance at his feet, the cuffed pants showing the barest glimpse of dark brown hair just above his ankles. I wondered what that dark hair looked like on his calves and thighs, if it looked dusted on or if it grew thick and manly. If it matched the hair stretching from his navel to his cock. I wondered what it would feel like under my fingertips or rubbing against my own legs.

"You don't even know my name," I said, stalling.

"I know that you're beautiful. I know that you know your twentieth-century American lit. I know that you've been crying and I would do anything to see you smile instead. I'd say that's enough for a hot dog and a Ferris wheel ride, wouldn't you?"

My resistance, already crumbling, caved completely, a pile of hesitation and good intentions now resting at my feet. I looked up into those glacially blue eyes and knew that something was about to change. Maybe it had already started to change.

"My name is Greer," I said.

"Sweet Greer." My name sounded so heavenly on his lips. I wished he would say it over and over again. "Let me take you out for bad food and neon lights. I don't know what happened to make you leave Merlin's party in tears, but I don't want it to have the final say in tonight. I think *we* should have the final say, don't you?"

"Yes," I whispered, and I slid my hand onto Embry's arm.

He grinned down at me, and the world was never the same.

CHAPTER 13

FIVE YEARS AGO

Two hours later, Embry and I were swinging high above the ground in an enclosed car, alone, our mouths sweet from cotton candy and our bodies warm from wanting each other. I could smell him now, something with citrus and heat, like pepper, a smell that made my toes curl in my shoes, a smell that made me restless with the urge to kiss him.

On one side of us there was the relentless glow of the city, and on the other the relentless black of Lake Michigan, and Embry and I were two twilight figures in the middle, half in shadow and half in the heady light of the city and carnival rides below us. We sat on the same side of the car, our bodies near but not near enough, and just a minute before, Embry had taken my hand in his. There had been some accidentally-on-purpose brushes of fingers and shoulders throughout the night, a moment where he'd smilingly wiped a pink smear of candy from the corner of my mouth, but there was something so deliberate and intentional about the way he reached for my hand and placed it firmly against his own. Then our fingers interlaced, and my heart flipped over.

The only other man I'd held hands with had been Ash, and that had been four years ago. I'd forgotten what it felt like, palms sliding against palms, large male fingers stretching and squeezing against my slender ones. I'd avoided romance and sex in any form since Ash, for reasons I didn't entirely understand myself, and now because of a moment of weakness, I found myself alone with a man who seemed to be romance and sex personified. Even his flaws were attractive: the occasional scowl and frown as we talked about our pasts—me staying studiously away from the topic of Ash or my grandfather and him even more studiously avoiding talk of battles and Carpathia; the somewhat presumptuous way he flirted so filthily and with such confidence; the fleeting giddy grin when we talked about the future and the places we wanted to go and see.

He felt like a *real* person, a person who exuded confidence but had moments of insecurity, a person who laughed because he knew no other way to drive out the darkness, a person who craved connection but couldn't let go of something inside of himself in order to reach for it.

In other words, with all of my gifts of perception and analysis, I couldn't escape the feeling that he felt a lot like me.

And the entire night, through all our wandering talks about Oxford and literature and the beautiful corner of the Olympic Peninsula where he'd grown up, he hadn't once asked me about the party. Hadn't asked why he'd found me crying and gin-soaked and trying to hail a cab. And for that I was eternally thankful. So thankful that I found it possible to confess the events of the party to him, even if only in vague terms.

I looked down to where our hands were linked, up to his face, which was watching mine with an expression of interested but reserved hunger, the way a cat looks when you toss a toy their way but before they pounce to get it.

I took a breath. "There was someone at the party tonight."

He nodded, as he'd been waiting for me to speak these words all night. "A man someone?"

"A someone I had feelings for. And yes, it happened to be a man."

I could tell from the amused quirk of his lips that he was fighting back the urge to banter about heteronormativity with me, and I appreciated it. I liked bantering with Embry, but I wanted to get this off my chest more.

"It's been years since he and I...well, we weren't together in any real sense. But I still had feelings. We met unexpectedly this afternoon, and there was a moment where I thought maybe he felt the same way. But then I saw him at the party tonight with someone else, and it hurt. It hurt and I was so furious with myself for feeling hurt, because I had no right. No normal person would have feelings for four years with no encouragement, no interaction to bolster them, and then feel wounded at the actual proof that there was no hope of a relationship."

I leaned my head back against headrest of the seat and concluded, "I'm disgusted with myself."

Embry's hand left mine, and for a painful second I wondered if I'd disgusted him too, if something about my story conveyed neediness or clinginess or delusion, but then he was on the floor of the car kneeling in between my legs and taking both my hands in his. The car had a glass floor, and beneath Embry's blue-clad knees, I could see the dizzying spin of the carousel far below, the tiny toy-people moving and shopping and eating like miniature dolls in a miniature dollhouse.

Embry moved my hands to his face, and I needed no encouragement to slide my hands over the carved lines of his jaw and cheekbones, to run my fingers over the strong ridge of his straight nose and up the swell of his proud forehead. My hands roamed through his sandy-brown hair, thick and soft, almost curly, and then down to his neck, where I stroked the warm skin along his collar.

"Sweet Greer," he murmured, closing his eyes and leaning his head against my knee. "I'm disgusted with myself too."

My hands paused as I absorbed his words.

"I know exactly how you feel. There's a someone for me—they've been a someone for me for years—but they aren't *my* someone. No matter how much I plead, no matter how much"—his breath caught—"how much I give of myself. I'm wrecked with it, so much that I think it's never possible I'll find another someone and I'm doomed to be miserable forever."

My fingers resumed their stroking, my heart breaking for him and for me and for both of us, and then he caught my wrists and gave the inside of each one a gentle kiss. On the second one, I felt the faintest flicker of his tongue, right over the blueish veins, and something deep inside my body clenched. I was the girl who'd written those emails once again, the girl who wanted *bad*, who wanted *wrong*, and wanted it in the most soul-thrumming, reckless ways possible.

"I don't want to be miserable tonight," I whispered, and Embry lifted his head, his blue eyes unreadable in the shadows. "I don't want to feel doomed or disgusted. I don't want to think about him."

"I can do that for you," he said, his voice low. "If you ask me."

Everything smelled like him in that moment. Pepper and lemon and promise.

The brave Greer spoke for me. "Then do it."

Ash would have hesitated, not out of disinterest, but out of caution, out of a need to establish consent and boundaries, because Ash was—*is*—a self-aware monster. Acutely aware of the marks he would leave on his lovers' souls and bodies, of exactly how dangerous he was.

Embry didn't hesitate. He didn't ask for clarification, for hard limits, for a safe word. He didn't ask what I needed in bed or what I wanted, how many people I'd been with, whether I wanted him with a condom or bare. He left all of those questions unanswered, unasked, and with a searing kiss, showed me the thrilling joy of abandoning safety and leaping feet-first into passion. I kissed him back, not forgetting Merlin's chains, but intentionally throwing them off, intentionally abandoning them.

I wouldn't keep my kisses to myself; I'd give them to Embry instead.

And damn the consequences.

———

When the Ferris wheel landed, we were already rumpled and breathless, and when we finally got a cab, there was no keeping our hands off each other. I had never made out with someone, and at any rate, my last kiss had been over four years ago, and so the experience was intoxicating. The way Embry breathed against my mouth, those tiny stitches of breath when my hands found someplace new, the tiny growls when I opened for him—my lips and arms and legs— heedless of the cabbie in the front seat.

We hurriedly paid the driver, and then Embry fairly yanked me out of the cab, pulling me through his hotel lobby so fast that my feet unexpectedly skipped into tiny jogs to keep up. And then the elevator doors closed and I was pinned against the wall, my legs around his waist and his erection right against my center, his mouth open and hot against my neck and collarbone. All the times I'd fingered myself, gotten myself off with vibrators, none of it could compare to the actual sensation of having a willing, eager male between my legs. The sensation of narrow hips shoving against me mindlessly seeking relief, hands cruelly yanking down my dress and bra cup, the sight of a man's head ducked against my breast, nuzzling and biting and sucking.

And then the doors opened.

Once again, I was yanked along, and since the hallway was empty, I didn't bother pulling down my dress, didn't bother readjusting my bra. Instead, I stood behind him as he fumbled for his hotel keycard, skirt rucked up, hair tousled, breast exposed, begging him in a wild, impatient chant, "Hurry, hurry, hurry…" And when he looked back and saw me exposed and whining with need, he gave an almighty groan. The door snicked and unlocked, and he turned the handle and pulled me inside the dark room, lit only by the skyline outside the window.

He'd pulled so hard that I stumbled as I crossed the threshold, but it didn't matter, because he caught me and swung me into his arms, carrying me straight to the bed. He stood over me, stripping off his blazer and vest and shirt, not even waiting to toe off his shoes before he lowered his body over mine. I heard the shoes clunk, one by one, onto the floor, heard the slow creak of my leather jacket as he bracketed my body with his forearms, heard the hitch in his breath as our bodies met, heard my answering moan as he roughly kneed my legs apart and ground his erection against me.

His mouth crashed down over mine, and I was lost once more. He kissed me like a man who was facing down death, kissed me like he would never see me—or any other woman—ever again. He kissed me like he knew me and knew my pain, something I'd never felt from anyone ever before.

I scratched my nails down Embry's bare chest, catching those flat nipples and making him hiss, reaching for his belt. He knelt up, and I sat up with him, my shaking hands struggling with the belt, the task made all the harder by Embry's insistent hands tugging at my jacket. There was fumbling and pulling and frustrated moans punctuated by leaning, awkward kisses, and then suddenly his belt was gone and his pants unfastened and my jacket was somewhere in the shadowed depths of the room. He was back over me and I arched underneath him, needing the contact, needing the pressure, which he was all too happy to give. I kicked off my heels and used the balls of my feet to work the waistband of his pants down past his firm, muscled ass, and then his cock and my pussy were separated only by the silk jersey of his boxer briefs and the demure cotton of my panties. He swiveled his hips against my cunt, and I cried out with pleasure, my nails digging into his back.

"Fuck," he grunted into my neck, giving another trial thrust. "I'm going to come just like this. Humping you like a teenager."

I could come too, just like this, with the rough grind of his cock against my clit, with the thin fabric between us adding an angry sort of friction. But it wasn't enough for Embry, wasn't enough for me either, because we'd both unlocked the worst kind of desperation in each other, the kind of desperation that wouldn't be satisfied until it had cannibalized itself, caught flame and burned itself to ashes.

Too impatient to pull my dress off properly, Embry tugged on the straps and yanked it down so that it was bunched around my middle.

"Your tits," he murmured. "I want to see them."

I managed to squirm out of my bra, and then he was on my breasts with his mouth and his rough fingers, making me whimper, and suddenly our breastfeeding conversation from earlier didn't seem so ridiculous. In a weird way, it was almost like he was nursing from me; in a metaphorical, vampiric sense, he was seeking succor from my body. Seeking nourishment and release and life, and I wanted to offer it to him.

He licked and sucked and bit with abandon, completely lost to himself and his need. Unlike Ash, who had touched and kissed with such deliberate intention and skill, who awoke my soul with a single brush of his lips, who would later awake the submissive animal within me, Embry kissed with nothing but mindless fire and passion. He awoke the female in me, the woman, and only underneath him could I have found this writhing, assertive version of myself.

Without thought, without anything but thoughtless need, I pushed Embry's head farther down, past the bunched raspberry fabric, past my navel, my fingers fisting in his hair when he pressed his mouth and nose against the damp white cotton that covered my cunt. He inhaled and his ensuing groan seemed to thrum inside my very bones.

He wrapped his fingers around the sides of the panties and pulled them down, tossed aside to join the leather jacket on the floor. And then he was back at my secret place, one arm sliding underneath my hips to lift me to his mouth, the other positioned so he could easily stroke my belly. A kiss on my mound, a kiss to each inner thigh, and then his mouth was there, *there*, and my hips jerked involuntarily at the sensation.

It was too much, too much, even though he'd just started, but I'd never felt this before, never felt what a silky wet mouth could do to silky wet flesh. Never known how the gentle nip of teeth would feel on my clit, the sucking of lips on the same, never guessed what having my hole circled and then fucked with a strong tongue would be like. If I had known—Jesus, if I had known, I would have never turned down those myriad offers of dates and drinks at Oxford.

"You taste so good," Embry growled from between my legs. "You going to come for me now? Going to make me taste you as you do it?"

I nodded even though he couldn't see me, nodded against the pillow, writhing and panting, holding his head in place while I rubbed against him. While I fucked his mouth and face, taking my pleasure with each grind of my clit, with each masterful stroke of his tongue. And my body built and built and built its pleasure from that, like a castle of tightly strung tension, each block taking me higher and higher, each buck of my hips and fluttering suck of his mouth sending me soaring.

I raised my head, looking down my bared breasts and dress-covered stomach to my hips, which were still lifted to his mouth. He looked beautiful just then, the light from the window showing his eyelashes dark on his cheeks, the sensual curve of his muscular shoulders and arms, the slight curl of his thick hair. And—*oh*—his hips moving against the mattress as he ate me, as he mindlessly fucked the bed with his face in my pussy, so needy, so desperate for contact and friction.

That sight—of this powerful, gorgeous man driven to rutting against anything by the taste of my cunt—was what finally did it. I clenched against his mouth and released with something like a scream, my first ever orgasm from someone other than myself, rolling and thrusting and quivering. He pinned my hips in place to hold me still and lapped it all up, licking me until the waves finally stopped cresting, and then he was up on his knees again, wiping his mouth with his forearm. His cock was so hard that the dark tip had pushed its way out of the waistband of his boxers, standing up almost past his navel, the dim city light catching the bead of moisture at his slit.

And his eyes—he was gone. He was raw now, a hard

147

body of speechless need. He stood and shucked his pants and boxer briefs and went into the bathroom, emerging a moment later with a small foil packet in his hand. He handed it to me wordlessly, his hands shaking.

"I need," he said in a trembling voice. That was all.

Not *I need you*, not even *I need to fuck*.

Just *I need*.

The honest primal nature of it took my breath away. I needed too. Just for tonight.

But as I slid to the edge of the bed and tore the foil packet open, I remembered the uncomfortable hurdle of my virginity. I was Catholic, yes, some would even say a devout one, but I wasn't particularly traditional when it came to premarital sex. It was merely that Ash had ruined me for any other touch…at least until tonight.

Should I tell Embry? Should I slow this down?

I don't want to slow down.

I wanted to be fucked, hard. I wanted to come again. I wanted the cruel, vicious knowledge that I'd had a man's cock inside me so that whenever I saw Ash again, I could guard myself with my own experience. He wouldn't be the only one who didn't wait; he would no longer be the only one who'd moved on. I would have fucked his best friend, cried out another man's name, and I wanted that satisfaction so much I could taste it.

Yes, I needed. Yes, in any universe I would be right here, right now, doing this very thing, but in *this* universe, the jealousy and pain fueled the fire, and from the way Embry's eyes hooded at the sight of my hand grasping his erection, I guessed that I wasn't the only one wanting to fuck away my demons tonight.

I had never rolled on a condom before, but Embry helped me, holding his dick steady as I slowly worked the latex down his length. He had a beautiful cock, eight thick inches, straight and proud with a purple-dark tip and close-cropped curls at his base. Even the heavy sac underneath his dick was beautiful, looking so full and ready for release, and I laid back on the bed and beckoned for him to join me, ready for him to spill himself inside me. Ready for him to relieve the ache there.

He followed me, his body still trembling with the effort of holding back, and settled on top of me.

"Open up," he demanded through clenched teeth. "Open yourself for me."

There was no question in his tone. No permission. I might have been any woman underneath him, any warm pussy he'd found for the night, and that thought was freeing and exhilarating in how dirty and impersonal it was.

I spread my legs, and he was right there, the huge head of him pushing against my entrance. It was so big, so wide, so much more than my fingers had ever been, and I cried out in real pain. I wanted this, I knew I did, but my body was at war with itself. My nerve endings shrieked in pain at the same time something much deeper and much more unknowable whispered to me to take it, to move into him, to be penetrated.

"Jesus, Greer," Embry muttered, shoving in another forceful inch. Sweat gleamed on his shoulders and chest, and his lips trembled. "You're too tight. I can't—"

Another shove, another inch. I cried out again, tears spilling from my eyes.

"I'm a virgin," I blurted.

He froze.

"I don't want to stop," I said hurriedly. "I just—I felt like you should know."

"You felt like I should know," Embry echoed, his blue eyes searching my face.

Ash would have stopped, checked in with me. He would

have asked if I really wanted this, to lose my virginity to him, in some anonymous hotel room. It was because Ash would have wanted so badly to be cruel to me, to take my virginity in the most crude and rough way possible, he would have forced himself to be circumspect until he knew it was what I really wanted. Then and only then, would he have let the beast out, the real monster.

Embry was not Ash.

His eyebrows drew together, his lips parted with an exhale so strong I knew that whatever control he'd had was finished, and then the ridged muscles of his flat stomach bunched together and he thrust all the way home.

A sound tore from my throat—raw, real pain—but Embry was heedless above me, fucking into me like a man possessed. It felt like I was being wedged in two, like I was being split apart, and the invasion was brutal and absolute. I scratched at his back and at his ass, and one moment I scratched in anger and pain, the next in desperation to have him deeper and harder. I didn't know my own body in that moment—my own body didn't know itself—that there could be so much pain from such a natural act and yet so much desire. Not that there was pleasure right away. I don't mean that, but that there was something deeper than both the pleasure and the pain, a deep, deep itch that was finally and blissfully being scratched.

"You're with me," he grunted in my ear as he continued to force his way in and out of my virgin cunt. "You're not with him. You're giving this to *me*."

His words made me moan. They were possessive and dark and rude and fetishizing and *I didn't care*. It turned me on to hear and see him so aroused by breaking my hymen, and it piled more fuel onto my jealous, bleeding heart. I *was* giving this to someone else. Ash would never have it, and I let myself imagine that made me satisfied. That it covered up the pain I felt tonight at seeing him with Jenny.

Embry rose up on his knees, keeping his tip lodged in me, and his fingers dug hard into my hips as he swept his gaze over the place where we joined. I looked too, and it gave me some kind of strange delight to see the blood wet and dark on my thighs, smeared across his thighs and hips, glistening in streaks on the condom.

"Yeah," Embry said to himself. "That's it. All mine."

He slid back inside me again, this time laying his whole body over mine. Our naked chests pressed together, sweaty and slick, our bloody thighs sliding easily past each other's, and he wrapped his arms tight around me. His face was in my neck, my chin tucked in his shoulder, and all of his weight was on me. It didn't feel heavy at all, or at least it felt like the right kind of heavy, especially when he began grinding in and out of me with short, rolling thrusts.

And that's when the deep, deep itch finally flared into true pleasure; the drag of his large helmet against my sensitive front wall, the friction at my clit from the base of his cock, the biological urge to be stretched and filled—all of it winding my body like a clock, whirring tighter and tighter.

"You're going to come for me, aren't you?" Embry said in my ear. "You're going to come on my dick. And when you do, when you're shuddering underneath me with blood on your thighs, it's *my* name you say, got it?"

I was in no place to disagree. All I could feel was the hard male body above me, all I could think about was the hard maleness *inside* me, and there was no room between our sweaty, eager bodies for Ash. In this moment, it was only Embry, Embry, Embry, and as he pressed down even harder against my clit, I dug my fingernails into his back and held on for dear life as my body finally wound itself so tight that it broke apart.

"Embry," I chanted, "Embry, *Embry*," as my pussy clutched at him, pulsing in tight, hot, painful waves. The thick length inside of me made all the difference, shifting the locus of my pleasure to deep inside my core, and I found myself bucking against him instinctively, trying to drive him deeper into the seizing, clenching heart of my orgasm.

And all the while he was muttering into my neck, words I couldn't catch but that sounded raw and urgent, and at the same time that he caught my lips in a scorching kiss, he drove himself deeper than ever before and held himself there, grunting into my mouth as he pulsed his own pleasure deep inside me. It went on and on, for both of us, his release so strong that I could feel the throb of his dick as he filled the condom with his orgasm, and I had a surreal moment of regret, wishing that there hadn't been a condom, wishing that it would have been bare, hard flesh buried deep into the soft. That there would have been the uncivilized mingling of my virgin blood with his seed.

Embry lingered a minute more, dropping kisses on my forehead and cheeks and lips as my body gradually stopped quivering, kisses that were as tender as his fucking was rough, and then he circled the condom with his fingers and pulled out. He was gentle and easy with it, but it still stung, and I let out a wounded hiss.

"I'm sorry," he said distantly, climbing off the bed, and the sudden absence of his warmth and the reservation in his voice made me shiver. I felt extremely vulnerable, like my skin had been peeled away, like my chest had been cracked open and my heart was beating in the open air. My throat tightened, those tears from hours ago threatening to return.

Did I just make a gigantic mistake?

He got rid of the condom and then came back and stood over me at the edge of the bed in the near darkness. I had a sudden moment of fear—real, blaring fear—that he was about to ask me if I wanted a cab or an Uber. That he was about to hand me my clothes and wish me a safe ride home.

152

But he didn't do either of those things. He leaned down and lifted me effortlessly into his arms and carried me into the brightly lit bathroom. I was deposited on the cold granite counter while he turned on the shower, me blinking owlishly in the light, and he stepped in between my legs while he waited for the water to warm up.

"Are you okay?" he asked quietly.

"I don't know," I answered, also quietly.

He looked down at my thighs, where lines of dried blood had crusted into thin smears. There wasn't that much blood, actually, it had felt like so much more at the time, but seeing it now without the heady sex hormones and in the bright light of a strange hotel bathroom, it seemed so much more barbaric. It looked violent and regrettable, even though it was neither of those things.

Embry ran a long finger up my leg, stopping well short of my pussy. "I'm sorry," he said, and there was nothing distant about his apology this time. His blue eyes were filled with guilt and his mouth was twisted with a bitter self-recrimination. "I was…I don't know what I was. You deserved better for your first time than me."

I caught his hand and brought it to my lips, kissing his knuckles gently. He let out a low exhale and his sleepy cock gave a stiffening jerk.

"It was amazing," I said. It wasn't my job to assure him or massage away whatever he was feeling right now, but I did want to be honest about myself and how I felt. "The way I felt when I came—the way it felt to have someone else inside me—I loved it. But I also feel really flayed open right now. Like I want to cry, but I don't think I'm sad necessarily. Just aware. Or maybe unaware. I don't know what the right word is. Happy or sad feel too far apart from this."

He leaned forward, resting his forehead against mine. "It was too rough, Greer. First times are supposed to be tender. Slow."

I shook my head against his, squeezing his hand. "I wouldn't have had it any other way."

The truth must have been clear in my voice because he straightened up and looked at me warily as he helped me wriggle out of the dress that was still bunched around my waist. "You're a dangerous girl."

"Dangerous for whom?"

"Me," he muttered, helping me down from the counter and leading me into the shower, but I caught a crooked flash of a smile when he turned away from me to close the glass shower door. My heart fluttered, and I realized he was the dangerous one. I would fall in love if I wasn't careful.

"I meant what I said," I told him, closing the distance between us. "I wouldn't do anything differently. I'm glad it was you. I'm glad you did it the way you did."

"And what is the way I take care of you now?" he asked. "Tell me what you need. Anything. After what you gave me, after what you let me take from you, anything."

That vulnerable feeling again, that heart beating in the open air. "Can I stay with you tonight?"

The way his face looked after I said that, as if I'd broken his heart. "Jesus, Greer. You can stay with me for the rest of my life." His hands found my ass, my waist, my hair, his face in an expression of combined awe and compassion. "Do you really think I'd kick you out into the night? Do you think that this evening meant so little to me that as soon as I came inside you, I'd want you gone?" He shook his head in disbelief. "And I'm over here wondering how much time I can steal away from you this week, wondering when it's okay for me to ask for your number, meet your family, visit you at college. Yes, of course you can spend the night. I want you in my arms until it's time to feed you breakfast in bed, and then I want you in my arms some more."

He leaned his head down to brush his nose against

mine, and I melted. "You are the most extraordinary woman I've ever met," he murmured with a smile. "I'm not stupid enough to let you leave my sight."

———

I suppose now it's easy enough to guess the end of this particular story. Embry and I fooled around in the shower until I was a wild woman in his arms, and then he took me back to bed, where he made love to me as slowly and softly as the first time was rough and hard. It still stung and hurt, the tears came again, but the pleasure found me faster this time, and soon I was coming apart under his expert touch, shuddering in quiet release. He came inside me, and then we cleaned up and fell asleep, me wrapped tightly in his arms. We woke up once more and I was too sore for sex, but Embry slid down my body and tongued me to a vicious, exhausted orgasm, and when I reached for him afterward, he pushed my hand away and knelt up over my stomach. Within six or seven strokes, he was shooting a painful, long release onto my belly, and the sight of him climaxing over me was so beautiful I wanted to memorize it forever.

What a man.

What a heartbroken, funny, charming, moody man.

And the eight-inch dick and muscled stomach and war hero past didn't hurt at all.

I'd texted Abilene from the Ferris wheel to tell her I was out with a guy and planning to spend the night at his hotel—which I gave her the name and the address for, a girl can't be too careful—but when I woke up early the next morning, Embry's naked hairy legs entwined with mine and his warm breath ruffling the hair at the back of my neck, I figured I should go home and show my face to Grandpa and Abilene and find a fresh change of clothes. But after that...well, Embry had mentioned he'd be in Chicago for another week, and my pussy blushed at the thought of all that time together. Funny how the wound created by Ash didn't hurt any less, didn't feel any less jagged or deep, but somehow there was this new space for joy and excitement carved out in my chest. For the first time in so long, I looked forward to the future. Had someone to make each minute feel exotic and newly washed, simply because his memory was stamped upon it.

I extricated myself from Embry's arms, biting my lip to still my huge smile as I looked down at him. He slept like a child, full lips parted ever so slightly, covers all kicked up and tangled around his long, muscular legs. I wondered if I would get to see him again like this, morning after morning after morning, my pussy aching from his attention and my heart thudding with nervous happiness.

God, I hoped so.

I left him a quick note on the hotel stationary—my number and hotel name and room number and promised I was just leaving to reassure my relatives that I wasn't bobbing facedown in the river. I told him I wanted to see him today as soon as he woke up, and I'd be waiting for his call.

I signed my name and added:

ps. I wouldn't do any of it differently. Any of it. I can't wait to see you again.

But I didn't see him again.

He didn't call, didn't come to my hotel, didn't write. Didn't try to contact me or find me. I spent the week curled up in bed while Abilene brought me ice cream and counseled me through what she thought was a normal post-one-night-stand heartbreak. My grandfather flew back to Manhattan with me and tried to cheer me up by taking me to my favorite restaurants, my favorite Broadway shows, and for him I tried to fake smiles and happiness, but the moment I boarded the plane to London eight weeks later, I let the mask fall from my face and shatter at my feet.

For the first time, I considered that Merlin's admonition against kissing was meant for my own well-being. Perhaps he knew, with whatever foresight he seemed to possess, that I was simply doomed to heartbreak. That no matter how isolated I tried to make myself, the men I would invariably trust with my body and my heart would treat those gifts carelessly.

Well, I wouldn't make that same mistake again, I vowed. No more kisses, no more men. No more trusting and giving and hoping. No more of that girl who craved rough and wrong and reckless, no more wanting to crawl or be held by the neck and dominated. That Greer was over, through, suffocated and dead and buried. There would be books and libraries and manuscripts—things that I could trust—and I would build a life all by myself, without anyone else, without the chance of getting used up and brokenhearted again.

I never stopped waiting though. For Embry to call. For Embry to show up with his crooked smile and colorful pants and the best excuse for not coming after me that week in Chicago.

He never did.

Except, of course, five years later when he strolled into my office at Georgetown and asked to take me to dinner.

CHAPTER 14

THE PRESENT

I WAKE UP EXPECTING ASH TO BE LONG GONE, FOR THE BED to be cold and empty next to me, but that's not what happens. Instead, I wake up nestled into a warm chest, a heavy arm draped over my side. For a moment, I forget where I am—*when* I am—and squint at the tall windows at the edge of the room, expecting to see the looming outline of Chicago skyscrapers. But no, it's the weakening fall sunshine overlooking the South Lawn, and I'm not in a hotel room with Embry. I'm in the White House. In bed with the president.

I roll over to look at him, taking care not to wake him up. He stays fast asleep, his breathing deep and even, his face relaxed and vulnerable. I stroke the thick black hair brushing against his forehead and finally indulge my urge from ten years ago and trace his mouth with my fingertips. Against my belly, I feel his sleepy erection, impressive and thick even at half-mast.

My fingertips on his face wake him.

His eyes blink open, finding my face immediately. "Greer," he says, his voice sleep-rough and warm.

I snuggle into him, kissing the warm space below his collarbone. "Good morning, Mr. President," I say.

"I fell asleep," he says, sounding surprised. "I fell asleep with you."

"Wasn't that the idea?"

He kisses the top of my head. "The idea was for *you* to sleep in my bed. I haven't had a full night's sleep since my first tour of duty."

I pull back to look up at his face. The thought sends a pleasant warmth to my chest, that I was able to give him something, that he had something with me that he hasn't had in fourteen years. "Maybe I'm your sleeping lucky charm."

"In that case," he says with a smile and a sudden move so that he's on top of me, "I might have to keep you in my bed forever."

He pins me with his arms and kisses me, and my sighs turn into moans as he rocks his hips against me.

"I want to stay in your bed forever," I breathe. "Please."

And with the pert rap of awful timing, a knock sounds at the door, followed by Belvedere's exasperated voice. "Mr. President, please. I've called every phone you own, and I more than anyone am happy you're still in bed, but you have a meeting in your office in thirty minutes. It's time to peel yourself away from Ms. Galloway and get in the shower."

I burst into giggles, and Ash grins down at me. "I should fire him," he says, leaning down to bite my earlobe.

I run my hands up the wide, muscled lines of his back, trailing my nails back down to his ass, regrettably covered up by his boxer briefs. "You should go," I whisper.

He nods, giving my earlobe a final nibble and then rolling off me. He goes to the door, opening it to an impatient but

159

amused Belvedere. "I'm up, I'm up," he says. "I'll be down in twenty-five minutes."

"Sure," drawls Belvedere. "You won't have any temptation to linger while there's a warm, sleepy blond in your bed. Maybe I should stay."

"Goodbye," Ash says firmly, closing the door on him and turning back to face me.

I'm already up, searching for my clothes to get dressed and leave, but Ash walks over and pulls the dress out of my hands, tossing it on the bed. "Shower. Now."

My body tingles at his words, and I scramble to obey, shedding his T-shirt and my panties as I go. I step into the glass-walled shower just as he enters the bathroom, stripping off his boxer briefs as he does, and I have to force myself to breathe. Even though I had his cock in my mouth last night, this is the first time I'm confronted with his body completely naked, and there's almost too much to take in all at once. Those vast expanses of warm skin, the irresistible curves of muscles and delectable lines of tendons, those angled lines of muscle coming down from his hips to his penis. And that part of him is mesmerizing all on its own, thick and proud even at rest, the crown wide and flared.

"I'm up here," Ash says amusedly as he steps into the shower with me, walking past the knobs without turning the water on.

I drag my eyes up from his cock, barely making it to his face for all the distracting ridges of muscle and flat, brown nipples and wide, powerful shoulders. "You're beautiful," I tell him honestly. "I want to stare at you forever."

"We don't have forever," Ash says. "We have about ten minutes. And those ten minutes are going to be for me."

"For you?" I ask to clarify. I don't understand, even though I can't think of anything he'd do that I would object to. And I have my safe word if he does.

"Turn around," he orders. "Hands on the wall, legs spread. This is the first time I get to see you naked too, don't forget, and I'm not going to miss a thing."

With a happy shiver racing down my spine, I do as he asks, trying not to feel self-conscious as I feel his hands on my ass, squeezing and separating so that the most basic parts of me are exposed for his viewing. He squats down behind me, to look at my cunt more closely. "Perfect," he says in a whisper, kissing me there. I moan and shove my hips back, wanting more, and he stands up with a laugh and slaps my ass. "Turn around, angel."

I turn and he catches my wrists in his strong hands, moving both above my head. "Keep those there," he says as he lets go and takes a step back to look at me. The posture has my chest jutting forward, my breasts pert and high, and my stomach stretched taut, and his gorgeous cock thickens and stirs. He doesn't take it in his hand though, and neither does he touch me. He simply takes in every shadow and curve of my body, every inch, every secret and public place.

Finally, when my nipples are hard under his gaze and my cunt wet and swollen from wanting him, he comes close to me. He fingers the ends of my hair, idly, almost like a horse buyer does with a horse's mane. "This is all mine now, isn't it?"

"Yes," I pant.

"This hair and these tits and that pussy—all mine."

"Yes, Ash, all yours. Please—"

He gives me a stern look. "When I want you to beg, I'll tell you."

My cunt is so tight it hurts. "Yes, sir."

"Good." He nods, looking back down at my hair between his fingertips. "On your knees."

I kneel, the cold tile hard on my knees, but I ignore it, enraptured by the man in front of me. His hands are running through my hair, smoothing and stroking it, and then it's only his left hand while his right slowly fists his cock. Slowly moves from the root to the crown, as surely and deliberately as Ash does anything. I'm lit on fire by the sight of that hand, strong and big and scarred. There is the faintest dusting of dark hair on the back, only near the wrist, hair a shade lighter than the black hair leading like an arrow down from his navel. Everything about him—legs shoulder-width apart, muscles in his arm flexing as he strokes himself, that insatiable dick ridged with veins—is so male and rough and greedy.

"That hair," he says, wrapping it tighter around his hand. I begin to feel the tug on my scalp, but I don't mind. I want my hair pulled, I want my eyes to water, and more than anything I want to see Ash come.

He wastes no time, his hand working hard and fast, his eyes searing trails from my face to my tits to my bare knees on the tile and finally landing on the skein of blond hair circling his hand. He lets out a low exhale, the furrowed lines of his stomach tensing, and then those dark eyelashes flutter as he comes, aiming not for my tits or my face, but for the hair he's so obsessed with. I watch in hungry fascination as he erupts, thick and hot and long, my gold hair now seeded with the white pearls of his climax.

I could stay like this forever, I think dizzily. On my knees, marked by him, beside him.

But we don't have forever. I have to fight off a serrated bite of frustration as I remember how limited his time is and will be for years to come. There will be no days where I'm his only focus. No long lazy mornings in bed, no time spent without an eye on the clock. I'll never be anything more than a ten-minute mistress when he's married to a nation.

I reach for his legs and bury my face in his hip, trying to hide my thoughts, and he lets me for a moment, stroking my head and allowing me to nuzzle against him. My wet desire has receded in the wake of this desperate need to be close to him, to reassure myself that he's real, that right now, in this moment, he is mine to press against and I am his to use and pet as he sees fit.

After a long minute like this, he tugs my head back by my hair—gently this time—and searches my face. He doesn't say anything, doesn't ask me what's wrong, and he doesn't need to. He gives a small nod to himself, as if he saw what he expected, and then reaches for my elbows to guide me to my feet.

"Stay there," he says. In a few seconds' work, the water is on and warm and he's guiding my head under the spray. He doesn't let me do anything myself—he wets my hair and then massages in the shampoo. Rinses it and then massages in the conditioner. I relax and let his strong fingers do all the work, washing away the traces of his orgasm.

The shampoo and conditioner are for women's hair, brand-new, and I wonder if he had them sent for as early as yesterday afternoon. As early as a few days ago, when I told Embry I'd meet him. And I'm about to remark about how skilled he is at washing a woman's hair when I remember that he's a widower. He was married for years. Of course he's done this before.

And of course I'm not jealous of a dead woman. Of course not.

In any case, he's as efficient as he is gentle, and within a few minutes, we are both washed and clean and wrapped in towels. I sit down on the bed and watch him get dressed, the act of fastening cuff links and knotting his tie almost as erotic as anything else we've done in the last twelve hours.

I've almost worked up the courage to ask when I can see him again when he turns to face me, fixing a silver tie bar into place. "I hate this as much as you do, you know," he says, looking at me. "I hate squeezing you into the margins. I hate that I can't give you all of my time. All of myself."

163

He walks over to the bed, tugging at my towel, rendering me naked and damp. Goose bumps erupt everywhere, my nipples hardening into stiff furls. "You deserve more than me. You deserve a whole man, not a man who can only give you scraps of himself."

"I'll take whatever you can give me," I say, shuddering with pleasure when he runs a pensive finger down my neck to my nipple.

"I know," he says, and his voice sounds almost sad. "But it isn't kind to you. Lie down and spread your legs."

I shift on the bed, opening myself to him, the act of such wanton obedience still triggering a wave of modesty and shame. But I cling to the shame, delight in it, and let it guide me.

His fingers caress my pussy, parting the petals to find the wetness within. "I want to give you everything it's possible for me to give. I want to give you everything I can. And I don't want you to be a secret." His long middle finger slides inside me, and my back arches off the bed. He sits next to me and then there are two fingers, crooking expertly against my sensitive front wall as the heel of his palm grinds against my clit. My body takes to his touch like dry tinder, sparking immediately.

"I know you've stayed away from this world for a reason. I know it might be asking a lot of you." He looks up from where he's touching me to meet my eyes. "But I don't just want you at my feet. I want you by my side."

It's so hard to think with his hand moving like that, fucking me so perfectly. "I don't want to be a secret either," I manage, my thighs tensing and my belly clenching. I'm so close to the edge already, and it's ridiculous that it should take so little, but nevertheless here I am clenching around his fingers. Any second now I'm going to come, any second now, any second now…

"Good, then you'll come to the state dinner next week," Ash says, pulling his fingers out of me and standing up.

My pussy wants to sob. *So close.* Without even thinking about it, I snake a hand down to my clit, ready to finish myself off. And then, with a movement so quick I don't even see it, Ash is on the bed kneeling over me, one knee planted firmly on each side of my rib cage and my hands both trapped over my head. He circles my wrists with his left hand and then shoves the fingers of his right hand into my mouth—not gagging me exactly, but keeping me from talking. I remember what he said last night—that I could snap my fingers to safe out if I couldn't speak—but I don't want to. I'm instantly, deliriously wet, my whole body trembling with burning need as the president kneels over me and pins me to his bed.

I smell leather. I smell fire. I smell and taste myself on his skin. I could die right now and be happy.

"You don't get to come unless I say so," Ash says. "I don't care if you're alone, if you're with me, if I'm holding a Hitachi to your clit while I fuck you—your orgasms are mine and if you have one without my permission, then you're a thief. You're not a thief, are you?"

I shake my head, his fingers still deep in my mouth. I can still taste myself on them—a lot sweet, a touch of sour, that rich smell that only seems to come from a cunt.

"Good," Ash says. Kneeling above me like this, he looks more like the soldier I know he is, and with a frisson of electric fear, I can suddenly imagine him fighting someone. Killing someone. I can't explain how I can know this and also still feel completely safe; I can't explain the deep thrill of having a dangerous man mounted on top of me like I'm a lamb about to be tied up and carted off to slaughter. But it's there. Undeniable and addictive.

I can feel the tension in his thighs as he keeps me

restrained underneath him, see the turgid outline of his erection pushing against his expensive slacks. "Do you know what they used to do to thieves?" he asks.

I do, actually. Incidental to studying medieval literature is some familiarity with medieval law. But that's not part of the game right now, so I shake my head again.

"I'm not going to cut off your hands, of course," he murmurs, his eyes now on my hands. His grip on my wrists tightens. "But I think I could devise my own version of the stocks. Or I could punish you according to biblical law, and make you return what's mine but again sevenfold. That would be seven orgasms you would have to give me for each one you stole. But either way, angel, there's going to be punishment."

His fingers leave my mouth and then he's back on his feet beside the bed, wiping his hands on his handkerchief and carefully adjusting his slacks before he finds his suit jacket.

"Why are you leaving me like this?" I whimper in frustration. "You could have finished me."

"Because," he answers, swinging on his jacket and buttoning the middle button, "I want you to say yes to the state dinner."

I groan, searching the ceiling as if there's an answer written there. "If I attend that dinner, then there's no going back. You and I will be…real."

"We're already real," he says, bending down to brush his lips on my forehead. "And I don't want to go back. I want you to be mine in here, and I want to be yours out there. And besides, if you go to the state dinner, I'll let you come afterward."

"That's not until next week," I squeak.

He shrugs, tucking his phone into his inside pocket and walking over to the door. "Then I know you'll really, really want to be there."

"You aren't playing fair," I accuse, rolling up on one elbow to glare at him more directly. I'm not really playing fair either, since I know that I'm displaying my tits and hips to their greatest advantage here, and sure enough, his eyes blaze at the sight of me when he turns around.

But his control is absolute. He simply smiles and says, "I never said this would be fair. But if we do it right, it may just end up being fun." He opens the door and pauses. "It's what we both need, Greer. Isn't it?"

I bite my lip. I nod.

I'm rewarded with a lion's smile, and then the door closes and he's gone. I flop miserably back down on the bed, my cunt awake and pulsing and my chest threatening to crack with happiness.

He's right.

The bastard is right.

CHAPTER 15

THE PRESENT

THAT DAY BELVEDERE ARRANGED FOR ME TO GET HOME, AND somehow I had to pretend life was normal. I taught class, I went to faculty meetings, I tried to work on the book. But I couldn't pretend, not when every time I closed my eyes, I could see Ash sitting in that chair in front of me, powerful legs sprawled out, eyes hungry as he watched me touch myself. Not when I could still smell smoke and leather and not when I could still feel the weight of his arm as we slept together in his bed.

No, there was too much to pretend, not to mention that I didn't *want* to pretend things were normal. I wanted that flutter in my chest as I remembered that Ash wanted me, and wanted me in every way. I wanted the nervous trembling in my hands as I thought about seeing him again. I wanted that deep, itchy frustration as I remembered I couldn't touch myself, couldn't come without his explicit permission.

But with the wanting came doubt. I'd had this feeling,

this *wanting*, three times before—after meeting Ash in London, after our afternoon in the sculpture courtyard, and after I'd slept with Embry. Three times, I'd felt the dizzying pull of falling in love, only to have the embers of my heart stamped out on the cold ground.

Could I really trust this feeling again? Or did it even matter? Even if I decided I wasn't going to fall in love with Ash again—if I'd ever even stopped loving him—could I really stay away from him? Was I doing what I *wanted* to do or was I listening to parts of myself that didn't need to be listened to?

I spent the next two days going around in circles with myself. I loved Ash, I wanted him, but I also doubted Ash, I doubted our happiness.

It was this doubt that made my happiness feel sharp and brittle, as if it would shatter and cut me at the slightest touch. Well, the doubt plus two other reasons. One reason was Embry.

The other was Abilene.

A few days after my night with Ash, I'm walking into a trendy NoMa office building in search of my cousin. I'm jittery, both with the anticipation of talking to Abilene and also with three days of pent-up lust knotting in my cunt. Though we haven't been able to meet again, Ash has called me every night, sometimes ordering me to finger myself but not come, sometimes ordering me to listen to him as he strokes himself. Sometimes just to talk, and after we hang up, I realize with a pang how lonely I've actually been all these years that I've avoided romance.

And I hear it in his voice—he's been lonely too.

Corbenic Events is on the fifth floor, a striking office of glass walls and bright colors, and it's Abilene's very own.

169

After she graduated from Vanderbilt, she used seed money from Grandpa to start her own event-planning firm in the heart of DC. Weddings, cocktail parties, galas—you name it. Her calendar was full after two weeks in business, and she was able to pay Grandpa back after only six months. That Abilene was able to build such success in such a short time surprised Grandpa and her parents, but it didn't surprise me. She always was passionate, and when she wanted something, she went after it with a single-minded zeal that would shame a saint. It was more surprising that she kept the venture going after three years, since her interest in things usually fizzled out long before that. But there were—and are—exceptions.

Which is why I'm here today. I'm here to undo my silence about Ash from ten years ago. I'm here to confess.

I walk through the busy office, crowded with harried young interns and planners snapping at people on speaker-phone as they leaf through stationery books. Abilene's office is in the very back, with an impressive view of the shiny new condos that have sprung up here recently, and I find her inside, bent over a glass desk spread with papers.

I take a moment just to watch her without me knowing. She really is beautiful, and there's something undeniably sexy about the way she holds herself, every movement and gesture so graceful and deliberate it looks like she's performing for some unseen audience. In fact, I know she is—she used to spend hours in our dorm room watching movie clips and mimicking the most mundane things. The way Zoe Saldaña stretched her neck. The way Scarlett Johansson glanced up from under her eyelashes. The way Keira Knightley held a teacup. It was hypnotic to watch, the way that watching a 3D printer is hypnotic; I watched Abilene create herself, form herself into a predetermined image to her liking. And this is the result, a woman whose movements are sensual and studied, so rehearsed that they're ingrained, and even though it should make her seem distant or forced, it doesn't. It only makes her more intriguing, more mysterious.

I shove down a resigned sigh—that old, familiar jealousy—and push the glass door open. "Hey."

Abilene looks up and smiles at me, her long red hair moving against her slim black dress. Abilene always makes black look classic and stylish. On me, it always looks like funeral wear. "Greer," she says, glancing back down at her work, "is it our lunch day? I must have totally forgotten. This malaria benefit next week is scrambling my brains, seriously."

"No, it's not our lunch day," I say, taking a seat in front of her desk. I see a pair of Louboutins in the corner of the room, a sparkly clutch perched on a credenza nearby. "Date tonight?"

Abilene sighs dramatically, throwing her head back. "Yes, though I'd rather break my ankle than go. Some Hill staffer I met at the gym. He didn't have his shirt on when he asked me to dinner, and I couldn't stop staring at his abs long enough to figure out how to say no."

"Maybe he'll be good in bed?" I suggest.

She looks at me with a smirk. "With all those muscles, he better be, although it's usually the pretty ones who are the worst lays." She pauses. "I take that back. It's the *senators* who are the worst lays. Three pumps and a gasp, and then you've got a sweaty fifty-year-old on top of you who's already feeling guilty about lying to his wife."

I laugh. "It only happened that one time, Abi. Hardly a real data set."

"One time was enough," she mutters, back to the papers.

"Maybe try an ambassador next. At least they have accents."

"How do you know I haven't tried them already?" she challenges playfully.

She's always been like this about sex, regaling her friends with her exploits over cocktails, casually referencing men she's slept with or expensive hotel rooms she didn't have to pay for. Only I out of all her friends know the truth—that Abi has never taken a man to bed that she didn't respect or who didn't respect her. That the hilarious blind dates and furtive one-night stands with politicians are few and far between, and most of her lovers have been men she felt genuine affection for, or at least genuine attraction. To Abi, sex is something to be taken or consumed, and then mostly forgotten, like a good cup of coffee. But like most coffee connoisseurs, Abi is still choosy about what she drinks.

I sigh. "I wish I were like you."

She tosses her hair in that joking, faux-smug way of hers—a move perfected from watching Emma Stone interviews—and shrugs. "Of course you do. What is it today that's made you realize the obvious?"

I lean back in the chair, running a finger along the dark wood of the armrest. I think about waking up with Ash, his words as he left the room: *It's what we both need, isn't it?* "I wish I could be as comfortable with sex as you are. As confident and, well, casual isn't the right word. But I guess it's the closest word I can think of."

"Honey, you can have all the casual sex you want. Any bar in the District—I can find you a lawyer in less than two minutes. A rich one in less than five."

I shake my head, smiling. "I know I can do that, but it's not what I *need*. I need it to be..." God, how can I describe this in a way that won't make me sound like I'm into tentacle porn or something? *Just use the right words, Greer. If you do it in bed, you should be able to say the words.* "...I need it to be, um, controlling. Dominating and submitting. That kind of thing."

Her blue eyes light up. "I knew it!" she crows. "I knew

172

you were secretly kinky. You are totally in the right city, my freaky cousin. I mean, it's not my scene, but I know everyone in this town and I can get you anything you like. Congressmen who like being whipped, pegged, electrocuted, you name it."

I can't help the small giggle that escapes, and I'm waving my hand for her to stop. "No, no, I don't need someone—" I was going to say, *I don't need someone who wants to be whipped, I want to be the whip-ee,* because I know that Abilene wouldn't immediately guess I'm submissive. She may not be into kink, but she'd be a domme for sure if she were, and she would assume I'd be too, simply because that's how her mind works.

But maybe it's something in my tone or my face, because she misinterprets my sentence and by doing so, correctly interprets everything else. "Because you've met someone already?" Her eyes go wide and she scans my body, from my knee-high boots to my sweater to my face. "You *have,* haven't you? You have that glow! Oh my God. Have you had sex? Is it someone powerful? Why didn't you tell me the minute it happened?"

My stomach flips with nervousness, and I smooth my skirt over my gray tights. "It just happened this week. It's really new…or I guess, it's kind of old too. And we haven't had sex yet. We agreed we would take our time with it."

Abilene smirked. "What is he, religious?"

"Sort of. I mean, yes, but I don't think he's a monk or anything. He lost his wife recently."

She leans forward. "A widower? Greer, is this an *older* man?"

Tell her. You have to tell her now. My stomach flips again, and I want to lie. I detest lying, and yet telling the truth seems so unnecessarily awkward and provocative…

But then I remember the state dinner this week. If I

don't tell her myself, she'll hear about it anyway, and that will be so much worse.

I take a breath. "Do you remember that party in London, the one Maxen Colchester was at?"

She looks a little thrown by the change in subject. "Yes, but what does that—"

"I kissed him," I interrupt. "In the library. After you and I fought, he came in from the balcony, and we talked and then we…kissed."

Abilene's eyebrows rise and her mouth gapes. "What?"

"We kissed, and then after that, I was going to tell you, I swear, but you seemed so taken with him and I didn't want you to be angry with me, especially when I thought I'd never see him again. It wasn't worth it. So I didn't tell you."

She blinks. I've never seen her this stunned, this slow in gathering an emotional response. The vacuum of anger— anger I know will explode out of her at any second—gives me the courage to finish.

"And in Chicago I saw him again, and we had a moment…but it didn't matter because then we all saw that he was with Jenny. That night, the man I slept with who never called me back? It wasn't some random guy I met at the party. It was Embry Moore."

"Holy shit," Abilene says, still blinking.

"And so Embry Moore came to me a week and a half ago, and told me Maxen wanted to see me. And we met and kissed and it was just as magical as the first time, and we—" Once again, I struggle for the right word. Dating sounds too informal, and it's too early to claim love, at least anywhere outside my own head. "He's asked me to go to the state dinner this week with him," I say, and I planned on being soft, being giving, because I'm the giving one in our friendship, always, always, but instead, I find my voice getting stronger and my chin lifting defiantly. "And I've agreed to go."

She doesn't respond, and I see signs of that Abilene rage fluttering under the surface of her skin: a dangerous flush on her neck, a brightness in her eyes, a tightness in her lips.

"Abi," I say. Plead. *Don't do this. Don't make this into a fight.*

But then she swallows and gives me a forced smile. "Well, I'm happy for you. My crush on Maxen Colchester was so long ago, I barely remember it. And if anyone is going to be with him, it should be you."

I want to believe her. I want it so badly. "Are you sure?"

This smile comes a little easier, although there's still that same strange brightness in her eyes. "Yes, Greer. It would be ridiculous for me to carry a torch for someone I've only seen in person once. I'm glad you told me."

"I was so scared to tell you because I knew how much you adored him when we were younger," I say on a relieved breath. "Thank God you don't hate me now."

"Of course I don't hate you." She sits back, tapping a fingertip on the glass desk. "So the president and the vice president too, huh?"

"No, no," I rush to clarify. "What happened between Embry and me was a very long time ago. And I was upset about Ash and Jenny, and obviously Embry didn't enjoy it that much, since I never heard from him again."

Abilene's head cocks at my casual use of Maxen's middle name, but she doesn't comment on it. Instead she says, "Are you sure there isn't something between you and Embry still? You're blushing."

I press a hand to my cheek, and sure enough, the skin is warm and flushed. I try not to think about that night in Chicago. I try not to think how handsome he looked in the candlelight at our dinner last week, how that citrus and pepper smell of him seemed to follow me home and taunt me while I tried to sleep.

Just because you want to forget who you are doesn't mean the rest of us can forget you.

"There's nothing between Embry and me," I repeat, but my response took too long and my face betrays too much. I never was a good liar.

Abilene's smile curls into something sharp. "Whatever you say, cousin mine. Just be careful. This city is full of wolves, and they are always hungry."

"There's nothing for them to be hungry for," I say again. "Embry isn't a problem."

The smile curls sharper. "I think he's very much a problem for you. And for the president too."

I frown. "What's that supposed to mean?"

"Just this, Greer, that men like them have secrets. You don't get to be that powerful that young without some big skeletons in your closet, and I guarantee you that the president and Merlin Rhys would be willing to do anything to keep those secrets contained. Anything."

"I feel like you know something I don't."

"If you're dating the president, you'll find out soon enough," she says and there's something cruelly gleeful about her voice. "And I think some women might be able to live with his past, but you're not one of them, honey."

I flick my mind over my mental log, trying to scan Ash's past for any whisper of scandal, but I come up short. Before I can say anything else, Abilene waves off my words. "Don't worry about it. Seriously. I'd hate to scare you off of a romance you just started. Now, I have a meeting in about five minutes. You're welcome to wait in here until I get back and then we can grab lunch or…?"

The meaning is clear. *It's time for you to leave.*

Grateful for the exit strategy, I stand up. "I've got to get back to work. A new batch of projects have come in for grading."

Abilene stands too and comes around her desk. She gives me a hug that isn't any lighter or shorter than any other hug she's given me, but all the same, I can tell there's something new between us. Something ugly. And while half of it is her jealousy, the other half is this new doubt she's sown in my mind, this new fear.

You'll find out soon enough.

I shiver as I leave her office and step out into the chilly November air.

What does that even mean?

And what if I don't want to find out?

CHAPTER 16

THE PRESENT

WHEN I OPEN THE DOOR TO MY TOWN HOUSE, I'M SO distracted by my conversation with Abilene that I don't even notice the tall man standing in the living room. I throw my purse onto a nearby chair and get ready to walk into the kitchen to forage for some coffee—coffee with a hefty amount of bourbon thrown in—and get the shock of my life when I see Merlin Rhys out of the corner of my eye.

"Jesus Christ," I gasp, stepping back and slumping against a bookshelf. He steps out of the November afternoon murk gathering in the corners of my living room, putting his hands up to indicate he means no harm.

"Ms. Galloway," he says, inclining his head.

"How the hell did you get in here?" I say—well, sputter, really—trying to cover over the adrenaline with outrage.

"I used to live here," Merlin says calmly, producing a key from his pocket and setting it on the coffee table. "Years ago, when I was just moving to Washington, your grandfather was kind of enough to let me stay here until I found a place of my own. I promise I won't intrude again, but I did think it was time that you and I have a talk."

The bookshelf presses into my back. A cloud passes over the sun. The room is cold shadows as Merlin takes a seat on the armchair, crossing his legs. The movement is graceful but not sensual, elegant but overly deliberate. There is something almost non-corporeal about the way he carries himself, just as there's something ageless in the sharp lines of his face.

It's been five years since I last saw him in person, although it was impossible to avoid seeing him on television or hearing his name on the news in the time since. He was the campaign manager for Ash's run, and now he's Ash's senior advisor—one of those roles that seems as ubiquitous as it is mysterious—and I know the timing of this encounter isn't a coincidence.

"A talk," I repeat. My throat's dry, and I clear it. "Five years ago, I came to your birthday party and you told me—again—-to keep my kisses to myself. Are you going to tell me a third time? Am I in trouble?"

And in the gloom of the shadows, the man I've been afraid of since I was seven laughs.

Laughs.

Not a sinister laugh, not a cruel laugh. A happy laugh. A friendly laugh. And through the shadows and years of fear, I see that he's just a man. Not a wizard, not a psychic, not the kissing police. Just a well-bred, perceptive man who is capable of laughing loudly enough to fill a room.

Ash does love to surround himself with laughter, I think, peeling myself away from the bookshelf to go sit down across from Merlin.

"You're not in trouble," he says finally, a smile still on his face. There's warmth in his eyes—real warmth—although I still detect the same wariness from our past encounters.

But I'm not seven or sixteen or twenty anymore. The wariness doesn't upset me like it used to. "Then what do you want to talk about?"

"I want to tell you a story," he says, folding his hands in his lap. "It won't take very long to tell, and you may not care that much about it, but I think it's an important story for you to hear."

I consider this for a minute. I would be well within my rights to demand that he leave. I could even leave myself. I don't have to sit here and listen to a man who's been nothing but rude and terrifying to me since I was a child. But I can't help it, I am intrigued by the idea of Merlin telling me a story. I teach literature, after all; stories are what I deal with, what I think in.

"Okay," I finally concede. "Tell me." As if on cue, the clouds move across the sun again and the room brightens with weak sunshine.

"Once upon a time"—Merlin starts slowly, irony twisting his mouth a little—"there was a man who fell in love with a married woman."

"That's a little different than the usual beginning," I cut in.

"It's more common than you'd think," he replies. "David and Bathsheba? Tristan and Isolde? Arthur Dimmesdale and Hester Prynne?"

"Those are not very happy stories," I point out.

"I never said this would be a happy story. Only a common one," Merlin responds, leaning back a little in his chair. "Now, back to our man and woman. This is a common story, and so this man tried all the common ways of getting the woman to notice him. He flirted, he pleaded, he tried to impress her daily. They worked in the same place, you see, and so he could be relentless in wooing her, just as his own love for her felt unmercifully relentless to him. But she

180

loved her husband, and even if she didn't, she was the kind of person who didn't believe in breaking marriage vows."

"Good for her."

He nods. "I agree. It was difficult to resist this man, though, especially as the years dragged on. He was handsome and powerful and he wanted her, even when she was pregnant with her husband's child. It's a flattering feeling to be desired by the president of the United States, which I'm sure you know."

I can't hide my surprise. "The man was a president?"

Merlin looks me straight in the face. "A president your family knows very well. President Penley Luther. Your grandfather's running mate."

I must look like a mask of shock, but I can't help it. Grandfather only had glowing things to say about President Luther—really, everyone only had glowing things to say about him. It's hard to imagine the hero of the American economy and international diplomacy chasing after a married woman.

"You have to remember," Merlin says, "that Luther was a bit of a playboy. And he was divorced. To him it seemed natural that she would want him, and Luther never ignored nature for morality's sake, at least in his personal life."

"So what happened?"

Merlin looks down at his hands for a moment. "What usually happens in these cases, although it didn't happen in the usual way. There was an economic summit hosted by the United Kingdom at a secluded estate in Wales. Luther brought this woman along, since she was his senior advisor, just as I am to Maxen now. The summit was brief but busy, and on the last night, the people gathered there had a small party. Lots of drinks. Warm fires in the chilly spring night. You get the picture.

"The night grew late, and everyone went to bed but

Luther, who stayed up by the fireplace in the central hall, drinking and looking into the flames. He was so absorbed that he didn't notice the caretaker and his wife clearing away the empty glasses, or their little boy helping them. Finally, the little boy walked up to him and touched his arm. 'Do you want help back to your room?' the boy asked.

"'I do want to go to bed, but not to my own,' Luther said. He was too drunk to care that he was talking to a child. But this child was more observant than other children. 'I can take you to her room,' the boy offered quietly. The man didn't answer, but it was obvious he was gripped with some kind of indecision.

"'I can take you around the outside and through the balcony door,' the boy said. 'No one would see you then.' Luther looked up, his eyes growing clearer, and then he stood and followed the boy."

I find I'm leaning forward in my chair. I make myself sit back. "What happened then? Did he go to her room? Did she kick him out?"

"No. She welcomed him inside and locked the balcony door behind him."

"But she resisted him for *years*! Why give in now?"

Merlin shrugs. "The human heart is a mystery. Perhaps she loved him as ardently as he loved her and couldn't bear to hold herself back any longer. Perhaps it was the alcohol or the seclusion. Perhaps he wore her down. I do know that she and her husband separated shortly after—perhaps they'd already agreed to the separation and she didn't see her marriage as an obstacle anymore. But what is certain is that they spent the night together—and several more after that. And that winter, she had a baby."

I search all my memories of President Luther, all of the stories I've heard from Grandpa. "I don't remember Luther having any children though."

"No children that he claimed." There's a fleeting look of sadness in Merlin's eyes. "The woman, she died in childbirth. It's rare in this day and age, but it happened. An amniotic embolism. At the time of her death, she and her husband were in the middle of divorce proceedings and the husband knew the child wasn't his. Luther, for all his public peccadillos, knew it would be politically dicey to claim the baby as his when the child's conception was shrouded in a cloud of adultery and unseemliness. So the baby was absorbed into the system and put into foster care. Her husband kept their little girl—still a toddler—and Luther went on living his life, although I've heard he was never quite the same after her death."

I think of that woman, perishing before she could hold her own child. Was she alone? Was there anyone to comfort her as she labored, to hold her as she died? "This is awful."

"Greer, can you think of anyone you know who was raised in the foster care system? Any famous orphans that you know of?"

It takes a second for his words to tumble over in my mind, to find purchase in what I already know. "You can't mean…"

"I do mean. Maxen Colchester is Penley Luther's son. Abandoned at birth to be raised by strangers for the sake of political expediency."

I think of that picture in Ash's dressing room, arms wrapped around Kay and his foster mother. "Maybe it was for the best," I say slowly.

"That he was raised by the Colchesters? Happy and safe, instead of growing up in the public eye? Yes, I think it was for the best. Some might even say it was meant to be. His destiny."

I look up at him. "Why are you telling me all of this?"

Merlin returns my gaze, kind and direct. "Because you

deserve to know where Ash came from. You deserve to know his history because it's about to become his future."

"What does that mean?"

Merlin sighs. "It means a lot of things, I'm afraid, because Luther's lust has sown a lot of seeds that cannot be unsown, but right now, it means that someone has gotten ahold of this story, at least according to my sources, whom I trust. It may be a week before it breaks or it may be a year, but when it does break, it will be incredibly disruptive. And now that you are with Maxen, you must expect to be disrupted too."

I don't ask how he knows I'm with Ash. Whether Ash told him or whether he knows it because he seems to know everything, I always knew, deep down, that Merlin learning about us was unavoidable. I do ask another question though. "When did Ash learn about it himself?"

There's a flash of anger in his eyes, real anger, but I recognize it's not meant for me. "At Jennifer's funeral. Of all the places."

God. Imagine not knowing anything about your birth parents until you're thirty-five. Long after you've given up hope of knowing your real origins. To have your origins be so sordid and so miserable. And then to learn it in the middle of your own personal tragedy…

"Who told him?" I ask.

The anger settles into a hard glitter in Merlin's dark eyes. "His half-sister."

"So she knew."

"Oh yes. Her father made sure of that. Made sure to impress upon her how their lives were ruined by Luther and how her mother was essentially murdered by Luther's lust. Her father nurtured a deep bitterness inside her, the way you might nurture a hothouse flower. With lots of care and attention. Who knows when she finally found the baby that killed her mother, who knows how long she bided her time

184

to confront him about the sins of his father, but she timed her blow with killing accuracy. She couldn't have found a more vulnerable time to tell him."

Jenny's funeral was toward the end of the campaign, only a month or two before the election. "Maybe this sister of his didn't want him to get to the White House?" And then I have another thought. "Is she the one who leaked the story now?"

"I believe so, yes."

"Oh," I say suddenly, sitting up. "My cousin Abilene, she said something to me today. 'You don't get to be that powerful that young without some big skeletons in your closet...' She said there were rumors about Ash—rumors that I might not be able to handle. She must have heard about this somehow. This must be what she meant." *Shows how well she knows me*, I think irritably, *if she thinks something like this would make me feel differently about Ash.*

But Merlin glances away from me when I say this, and an uncomfortable shiver works its way down my spine.

"Merlin?"

"There are...other...things about Maxen that I'm sure will come to light, when it's the right time." Merlin's voice is unreadable, his face is a walled garden of secrecy. "And yes. I imagine they will be difficult to hear."

"Like what? I don't like the idea of everyone knowing things about the man I love that I don't."

At the word *love*, Merlin's face softens. "I know. I'm not trying to be deliberately evasive, Ms. Galloway. If I could, I would tell you right now because I believe that you do love Maxen. I believe that you have a right to know. But these things...well, they aren't my secrets. They aren't my stories to tell."

I run a hand over my eyes. Between Abilene and Merlin, today has been filled with too much information, too much emotion. I just want to be back with Ash again, under his body or sitting at his feet, where things feel right.

*Or with Embry...*a voice whispers in my head.

I ignore it.

"One more thing before I go," Merlin says, standing up and smoothing down his suit jacket. "I owe you an apology."

I stand up to join him, but I don't move to stop him or encourage him, and he continues.

"There are times that I know I must have seemed cruel or dismissive to you. Times that I *was* cruel and dismissive. That was unkind to you, and I'm sorry. I only ever had Maxen's well-being as a priority, and for a long time, I was concerned that you would hurt him."

I'm dumbfounded by this. "*Me* hurt *him*?" I ask, thinking of all those nights I spent longing for him, my heartbreak in Chicago.

"You see yourself and your potential much differently than the rest of us do, I assure you."

"Now you sound like Embry," I mutter, and maybe that was a mistake, because it sends a frown pulling at Merlin's mouth.

"Indeed. Well, it's not so irrational to believe that you had the power to hurt Maxen—one look at his face that night in London, and I knew he was lost to you. And that's why I introduced him to Jennifer Gonzalez and did everything I could to make sure they married."

"You set him up with Jenny to keep him away from me?" I have no idea how to think about this, even though I know exactly how to *feel*. A slow anger creeps up my body. "You wanted me away from him badly enough that you made him marry someone else?"

"I didn't make him do anything," Merlin says mildly. "I introduced him to Jennifer and encouraged their affection as much as possible, but in the end, the choice was his. He chose her."

Why this still stings, I have no idea, but it does. I wrap my arms around my body. "I never understood," I murmur, "why you disliked me so much."

"I told you," he says, walking toward the door, "I worried you would hurt Maxen. I still worry about this, but it's out of my hands now. Perhaps this too is destiny. All of our destinies."

"I won't hurt him," I say, following him to the door.

"You won't mean to. Not the way his sister wants to hurt him. But you will hurt him much worse than she ever could. My only hope is the knowledge that you'll bring him more joy than pain."

"You can't know any of that," I say, and I hate how petulant my voice sounds. "You're not actually a wizard." Then I add, for the sake of the seven-year-old Greer, "Are you?"

Merlin laughs again, the same room-warming laugh, and despite myself, my anger abates a little. "Goodbye, Ms. Galloway. I am sure we will see each other again soon."

I hold open the door as he walks out, and when he steps onto the front stoop, something occurs to me. "You said you wouldn't tell me those rumors about Ash because they weren't your stories to tell. But then why did you feel like you could tell me about Ash's birth parents?"

Merlin turns and smiles. He seems oblivious to the brutal November wind. "Haven't you guessed it yet? That story is my story too."

It's obvious now that he's said it, and I can't believe I didn't guess before. "You were the boy, weren't you? The boy on the estate who showed Luther the way into her room?"

"After Maxen's sister told him the truth, he came to tell me. I'd had no idea, but as soon as I heard the whole tale, I knew. I'd never forgotten that night, the night I met the president. I'd never forgotten how sad he looked, how…

187

gutted…he was with loving someone. But after Maxen told me the story and I put it all together, I realized I should have known he was Luther's son long before then. Because that gutted look? Maxen had been wearing it for years whenever he thought about you."

And with that, Merlin leaves, and my anger leaves with him. Confusion remains, frustration remains, but the anger vanishes, leaving an empty hole in its place. I watch him get into a waiting car and drive off, and then I close the door, my body abuzz with too many different emotions. It's time for the coffee and bourbon I promised myself earlier, except maybe I'll skip the coffee and go right for the bourbon.

And it's as I'm pouring myself a steep glass of Blanton's that I realize Merlin never actually answered my question about being a wizard. I sit back in my kitchen chair, staring at the whiskey, thinking back to the first time I met Merlin. Thinking back to my first kiss with Ash, my night with Embry, and everything that's happened since. I think about Ash's sister and the brightness in Abilene's eyes and the upcoming state dinner and the rumors swirling around the man I love, rumors so dark that everyone seems afraid to speak them out loud.

Lastly, I think about Embry, about the way my heart still aches for him. About the way I still secretly want his heart to ache for me.

I drink the whiskey in four long swallows without coming up for air, and then I pour myself another. Ash and I getting together should have been the end of the story, the happily ever after to our fairy tale. But somehow I have the feeling it's just the beginning.

I throw back the whiskey and pour myself a third glass.

THE QUEEN

CHAPTER 17

THE EGG-BLUE GOWN RUSTLES PRETTILY AS I WALK UP THE stairs to the second floor of the Residence, the silk of the tiered skirt just loud enough to be heard over the gentle strains of music coming from below. The dinner is set to start soon—there's a string quartet playing Chopin as the guests chatter over cocktails and hors d'oeuvres—and while I'll be by Ash's side for most of the evening, I want to find him before the dinner starts. Share a moment that's only the two of us before the cameras start flashing and the gossip kicks in. Before the hungry wolves realize they've just found their next dinner.

I think I hear a sound coming from the living room, and I slip through the open door saying, "Belvedere said I could find you up here—oh."

Ash isn't alone.

Looking like a prince or a movie star in his crisp black tuxedo, he's sitting on the sofa, leaning forward, long legs bent, power coiled in his body. And Embry—also in a tuxedo—is in front of Ash, sitting on the carpet. It's clear

that both of them were engaged in a serious conversation—
there's a furrow in Ash's brow and a cast of unhappiness to
Embry's shoulders—but that's not what stops me in my
tracks. Because Embry isn't just sitting in front of Ash, he's
kneeling. Kneeling in front of Ash the same way I would—
between his outstretched legs, caged in by the shiny black
dress shoes planted on the floor. Kneeling in front of Ash as
if it's the most natural place in the world to be. And Ash isn't
only leaning forward, he's got a hand fisted in the shoulder
of Embry's tuxedo jacket, as if they're getting ready to fight
or to kiss.

A bolt of unthinking desire sizzles straight to my core,
and my chest tightens with an unfamiliar excitement.

Both men both freeze at my entrance, looking over at
me with expressions I can't read right away. Guilt, maybe,
or maybe just guilty surprise, or maybe it's something more
complicated, like relief laced with anger…or anger laced with
relief. And I don't know what my own face betrays because I
don't even know what I'm feeling myself. *They're just talking,
they're best friends, they're the president and the vice president,
it's natural that they would talk together.*

But like this? And I can't help it, I feel a stab of jealousy
at their closeness, at their shared history. How many years
has Embry been able to be close to Ash, how many years has
Ash been able to stare into Embry's ice-blue eyes, while I was
denied both of them? How often do they get to touch each
other and talk together, how many evenings have started this
way when all of my evenings have started with loneliness?

They both unfreeze at the same time. Ash drops his hand
from Embry's shoulder, and Embry eases himself back so he's
lying on his side on the carpet, propped up on one elbow, all
casual elegance and ease. It looks almost illegally decadent of
him, especially in that tuxedo.

"Greer," Ash says, and the only thing I hear in his voice

is affection. Happiness that I'm here. I must have imagined the guilt and the anger; I must have been mistaken in thinking that Embry kneeling in front of Ash means something. And I'm certainly imagining the strange tugs of feeling in my chest at the sight of these two men so serious and intimate with each other. I'm imagining the near painful pull of heat in my belly at the sight of Embry on his knees between Ash's legs.

"You look like a princess," Embry says as I walk over to the couch. His voice and face are teasing and friendly, but his eyes tell a different story. His eyes tell me that he remembers what I look like underneath the dress, that he remembers what I taste like and feel like. Being denied orgasms all this week has made me painfully responsive, my arousal on a hair trigger, and I have to remind myself to breathe normally.

I'm not here with Embry. I'm not here *for* him. I'm here for Ash. Ash, Ash, Ash.

Oh, but why does Embry have to look so good right now? Lounging on his side like a tiger, blue eyes like the inside of glaciers? It's too much to be around him even at the best of times, but now, when I'm so starved for pleasure that I could come from a single touch, it's murder.

I sit next to Ash on the sofa, the motion deliberate and precise. Ash watches me carefully, taking me in, the thoughtful furrow in his brow growing slightly deeper.

"This is a very beautiful dress," he says, reaching out to run a finger along the neckline. It's not scandalously low, but the corseted bodice pushes the swells of my breasts over the top and his finger follows the sloping curves. I let out a shuddering breath, almost a moan, and then I hear Embry scramble to his feet.

"I should leave you two alone," he says, making for the door.

"Embry," Ash calls after him.

But Embry doesn't look back, just tosses a half wave in Ash's direction. "I'll see you downstairs," he says, and then he's gone.

Ash's profile is thoughtful when I turn back to look at him. And I think I should tell him now, explain about Chicago and Embry and all about that night, but I don't know how to start. And I don't know how to finish either, because if I tell that story to Ash, he'll be able to see in an instant that Embry still affects me. That my feelings for him aren't over with. And there would be no way to verbalize that my feelings for Embry don't at all cancel out my feelings for Ash. They are related and intertwined; they are layered on top of one another; they are both and together and all at the same time.

Even I don't understand how there's room for both inside me—how could I expect Ash to?

There's another moment of silence, and then Ash reaches for me. He easily pulls me onto him, until I'm a ball of embroidered silk perched on his lap, and he lays a light kiss on the exposed nape of my neck. One hand is splayed against my stomach, holding me close against him, and the other one is digging in my skirts, skating up past my legs to my thighs.

I part for him with a happy sigh, and I feel the wide pads of his fingers probing my pussy through my lace thong.

He hooks it with one finger so he can investigate further. "Wet," he confirms in a rasp. "You're already wet. Is it for me?"

"Yes," I moan, shivering as his fingers graze my clit. "It's for you."

"Because this pussy is mine. Only mine. It gets wet only for me, is that right?"

It's not a lie when I breathe, "Yes, yes. It's your pussy. It's wet for you." And it's the truth, somehow, because even when I crave Embry, even when my body keens for him, it's bound up with Ash. Even when I gave my virginity to Embry, it was because of Ash. My body can't separate wanting the two.

There's a nip at my neck and a playful smack on my cunt. "Keep yourself wet for me," Ash orders as he withdraws his hand from under my skirt. "And then, after the dinner, I'm going to spend the rest of the night taking care of my pussy. How does that sound?"

I sigh. "Like dinner is going to take too long."

———

The dinner goes much as I expected. Ash and I walk down to the dining room together, and there's a frenzy of cameras and questions, a buzz of interest running through the guests. I feel a little like Cinderella in the blue silk gown, with my thin crystal headband nestled into my updo. Abilene tried to coax me into something a little more daring, saying I needed to maximize my entrance onto the political scene, but once I saw this ball gown, I knew it was the one. And the way Ash steals glances over at me, I know I chose correctly.

After the staircase, Ash presses a kiss to my cheek—to the delight of the crowd—and goes to formally greet the Polish president. I join the other guests, hoping to melt anonymously into the crowd without the president by my side to draw attention.

This fails—magnificently.

First, there are the reporters, and then there are the guests themselves—politicians and their wives, notable Polish Americans, high-ranking military officials. Most of them want to schmooze and make themselves known to me, assess firsthand how important I am to the president and how I might be useful to them in the future. I know how this game is played, so I smile and laugh and shake hands and give them nothing, but do it so sweetly that they don't realize it until they walk away. A few are more daring, more salacious—is it serious with the president? How long have we been together? Wasn't it so lovely of me to comfort this noble, stoic man still reeling from the death of his wife?

Then there are the speeches—one from the Polish president and one from Ash—and Ash's is so rousing that the applause doesn't stop for almost five minutes afterward.

And then there's one more encounter after that, one that leaves me a little shaken. It's during dinner, and even though I'm supposed to be seated next to Ash, he's been waylaid by dignitaries at the other end of the room, leaving me alone with the other guests at the table. I'm fairly adept at the political small talk, but I don't enjoy it, and when the main course of roasted duck in apple appears, I'm grateful for the silence that falls over the table as we eat.

It's then that the woman next to me turns and asks, "So, are you fucking him yet?"

Years of practice keep me from dropping my fork, and those same years of practice make me glance over at her. Raven-black hair. Pale skin. Green eyes. She looks to be in her late thirties—elegant and beautiful and vaguely scornful—and she reminds me of someone, although I can't quite decide why. I look down at her place setting.

Morgan Leffey, Sen.

I've been intentionally avoiding politics since I came to Washington this summer, but after seeing her name, I'm able to dredge up a thin biography of Senator Leffey:

- Republican, but elected in a traditionally blue state.
- A staunch supporter of military action against Carpathia (which could explain why she's invited tonight, to show Poland solidarity in their continued diplomatic tensions with the new, hostile nation).
- Divorced, but now unmarried and unattached.
- No children, no big scandals.

It feels like there's something else that I'm missing about her though, something big. I can't put my finger on it.

All this assessment happens within the blink of an eye. On the next blink, I ask calmly, "Pardon me?"

"I said," she answers with a catlike smile, "have you fucked Maxen?"

I dart a quick glance around us, and she puts a cool hand on my arm. "No one's listening, I promise. Now, have you let the president fuck you yet?"

"That's not your business" I decide is the safest answer.

"That means no," she says, sounding satisfied. "Has he hurt you yet?"

I feel the blood leave my face.

"Has he flogged you? Or tied you up? Fucked your throat? Has he made you cry and then beg for more while the tears are still on your cheeks?"

How can she know this about Ash? About this side of him?

"What he and I have is still very new," I answer carefully. A chess piece answer. A pawn left exposed on the field.

She takes the bait. "Then that's a yes," she says, smug knowledge lacing her words.

I watch her face. *Have you fucked Ash?* I want to demand. *Has he dominated you?* The thought of Ash with *anyone* else sets my palms to itching with envy, but the thought of him with Senator Leffey? Well, that sends daggers of pure, uncut rage straight between my ribs. And the thought of him doing the same things with her as he did with me—the commands, the control, the rough, vulnerable need—it fills me with something deeper than jealousy, a lizard-brain need to defend my territory from invaders, defend it to the death.

As if she knows what's happening inside my mind, she gives me another smile and takes a sip of her champagne. "Don't worry, Greer. Maxen and I are done fucking for now. No need for jealousy."

For now. What a deliberate choice of words. I have the nearly irrepressible urge to dump my own champagne in her lap, but I don't. Instead, I force myself away from my anger, force the jealousy aside, and redouble my focus on her. On the smile curling at the edges of her mouth, her eyebrows quirked in enjoyment. She wants me to flare up and she wants me to be defensive—she's counting on me reacting the way she would in my shoes.

But she's not me, and I'm not her. I give her a small smile that I know looks tentative and shy. "It's hard not to be jealous, Senator. You are a very beautiful person, and like I said a minute ago, what the president and I have is very new. I guess it's hard not to be insecure."

My honesty and intentional sweetness seem to throw her—both the flattery and the truth-telling finding purchase somewhere inside this powerful woman. I follow up, pressing my advantage. "Do you know Maxen very well? Did he hurt you too? I want to please him, but I'm still new to our, um, arrangement."

Every word sings with earnest honesty, sings with submission. *You are so beautiful and worldly,* my words whisper to her. *You know more than I do; you know this man better than I do.*

It works. Her pleased smile remains, but it's no longer shrewd, merely satisfied. "I have to admit, I'm surprised he chose you," she says, glancing at me again. "The young academic, the granddaughter of the famously liberal and feminist Leo Galloway. You seem like the last girl on earth who could handle Maxen Colchester. Not to mention the last girl on earth who would *want* to—surely it will be hard to glad-hand all the Democrats in the Congressional Women's Caucus with belt marks on your ass?"

Her dig falls so short of the mark that I almost laugh, but I resist. She's revealed a profound ignorance about me in just a few sentences, and more importantly, she's revealed the reason she's needling me to begin with. She wants to know why me, why Ash chose *me*, and her barbs reveal that it's about something deeper and fiercer than mere political curiosity.

"I'm actually registered with the president's party," I say mildly. "Not my grandfather's." I changed my affiliation the day Ash announced his intention to run for President as a third-party candidate. Merlin had laid the foundation for a third-party run for years leading up to it, at the state and national level, and when the nation's favorite hero had emerged as the face of the new party, I wasn't the only one turning in my old party card. "And," I continue, keeping my face open and earnest as I move my next chess piece, "I've never found any problem mixing what I want in bed with feminism. Did you? Is that why you and Maxen aren't together?"

Check.

Her lips press together, revealing a flash of irritation, and then she leans in, her voice truly cold for the first time. "Be careful, Greer. You're in over your head with Maxen Colchester. You have no idea the things he's capable of, the things he's done. The secrets he keeps. The lies he tells."

I remember Abilene's warning, Merlin's evasiveness, and there's a shot of ice water running through my veins. How many people know these secrets about Ash? Why am I the only one in the dark?

Morgan sees that she's finally landed a blow, and her voice is both cold and pleased when she says, "And have you ever thought about the reason why you and Maxen haven't had sex yet? Maybe he's told you that he wants to wait, that he wants to take things slow, but no man can take things that slow, trust me. Not unless he's getting it from somewhere else."

Checkmate. And the match is hers.

I can't hear my own thoughts over the roar of the pulse pounding in my ears, the jealousy and the fear—because she's found my real weakness, my real insecurity—and I feel a stupid, ridiculous burning at the backs of my eyelids. *Focus!* I order myself. *Don't let her see you upset!*

I'm saved by a heavy hand on my shoulder, and I look up to see Embry smiling down at me and Morgan. He has a hand on her shoulder too, and she doesn't look confused by it, only irritated in the bored way that familiarity and habit breed. I stare at them both—Morgan in her pale gray Dior gown and Embry in his low-waisted tuxedo—both of them so stylish and elegant, their posture suffused with confidence and privilege. Something finally trickles in from the back of my memory, a wisp of information from years ago, something from a speech Morgan gave in the Senate a few years ago.

Something about a loved one who fought in Carpathia.

"Greer," Embry says. "I see you've finally met my sister."

CHAPTER 18

"*Step*sister," Morgan corrects icily.

"Stepsister," Embry concedes cheerfully. "But we both have the same winning personality, don't we?"

"There's no need for sarcasm," Morgan says, glancing away from us as if bored. "We all know you're here to rescue the princess from the evil witch."

Embry's smile grows wider. "Your words, Sissy, not mine."

Morgan actually looks mortified. "Don't call me that here."

"Did you know," Embry says, as if he didn't hear her, "that Sissy here personally requested to sit next to you once she heard you were attending the dinner? A fun fact I just learned from Belvedere, who learned it from the social secretary. Now, why would that be, Morgan? You weren't planning on causing any trouble, were you?"

"I simply wanted to meet the soon-to-be-famous Greer Galloway for myself." Morgan's eyes sweep back to me, appraisingly. "See the girl that has the president so preoccupied."

Embry's hand curls protectively around my shoulder.

Morgan doesn't miss that, and she raises an eyebrow. "She has you preoccupied too, then? How interesting."

There's a blink of something on Embry's face—worry, maybe—and then it's gone. "They're starting up the dancing, Morgan, so as delightful as this little reunion is, I'm afraid Greer and I must abandon you."

Embry helps me stand, but before we can make our escape, I feel Morgan's cool hand on my wrist. "Don't forget what I said to you," she says quietly, and there's no malice in her voice, only a kind of urgency. "You're in over your head."

"That's enough, Morgan," Embry tells her. "You've done your worst. Now leave us alone."

Morgan sits back with a pretty frown, and I withdraw my wrist and let Embry lead me away, my stomach churning.

"Don't let her upset you," Embry says as we weave through the tables to the far corner of the dining room, where Ash stands with a circle of dignitaries talking and sipping premium vodka. "She's jealous. She and Ash…well, there's a history there. And it's not a pretty one."

"I gathered that much." I take a deep breath. "They used to fuck?"

Embry winces at the word. "I hate such a wonderful word being applied to such a short-lived, stupid thing. They met the first year Ash was deployed, three or four years before Caledonia."

Three or four years before he met me, I think, doing the math.

"And it wasn't anything more than an R-and-R fling. Over in a week. Fourteen years ago."

I'm not often struck by the age difference between Ash and me, but for a moment, I'm stunned by it. Stunned by the fact that he was fucking Morgan Leffey while I was an eleven-year-old skipping around my grandfather's penthouse.

"So there hasn't been anything between them since then?" I ask. "Because that's not the impression I got."

Embry's face has a purposefully open expression, and his voice is so carefully honest and casual. "That's the last time they fucked, I'm certain of it."

He's lying. Or he's not telling the whole truth, but before I can press him further, he tucks my hand in the crook of his elbow and squeezes it. "Let's not talk about my sister now. I just ate like thirteen pierogies in front of the Polish president in order to impress him, and I'm already about to throw up. Besides, we have much more important things to talk about, like how many times are you going to dance with me tonight?"

I smile up at him. "As many times as you'd like."

His eyes glow. "You have to dance with Ash first. But then after that, you're mine."

In his words, I hear the echo of our night together, and my blood stirs to a boil.

You're with me, not him.

That's it. All mine.

He looks away, clearing his throat as if realizing how intense that sounded. "I mean, for dancing, of course. Hey, maybe we can convince the quartet to play Beyoncé—they probably already have the sheet music for that, right?"

I give a small laugh and so does he, but it doesn't dispel the sudden uncomfortable tension between us. It's almost a relief when we reach Ash and the Polish dignitaries.

Embry untucks my fingers from his arm and, with exaggerated ceremony, places them in Ash's outstretched hand. "Your lady, milord."

Ash's fingers tighten around my hand, and he easily pulls me into him, his other hand holding his tumbler of vodka perfectly steady.

"You must trust this man very much to allow him unfettered access to such a beauty," the Polish president says in a thickly accented voice.

I feel Embry's posture stiffen behind me, feel the rush of blood to my cheeks.

"I do," Ash responds. "I trust him with my life."

"Really, it's that I trust the vice president to have such unfettered access to Maxen," I joke to cover over Embry's and my discomfort, but Ash doesn't laugh along with everyone else.

Neither does Embry.

I look to him and then back to Ash, catching them glancing at each other. My heart crashes against my ribs, and for no reason at all, I'm reminded of how tight and hungry my cunt feels right now. How empty.

"Greer, I don't think you've formally met the president of Poland," Ash says, picking up the thread of conservation before our guests could notice the troubled tension hanging between the three of us. "Greer, this is Andrzej Lewandowski. President Lewandowski, this is Greer Galloway, a lecturer at Georgetown and a very important woman to me."

Lewandowski leans in to brush a quick kiss against the back of my hand before releasing it, and it's right then that Belvedere comes up to us. "Mr. President, they're ready for you on the dance floor."

"I suppose that's our cue," Ash says. "President Lewandowski, would you and Mrs. Lewandowski care to join us?"

The foreign leader looks less than thrilled, but nevertheless he finds his wife, and the four of us take to the dance floor. The band strikes up an orchestral version of a famous Polish folk song, and then I'm in Ash's arms, my hand curled around his warm neck and his hand on my waist. We start moving, and I giggle a little at how woodenly Ash dances.

He makes a face at me. "Don't make fun of me. I had to work hard to be this bad; I used to be much worse, you know."

"I don't see how," I laugh as I steer us clear of the Polish couple. "I think I need to have a word with your teacher someday."

"Anytime you want," Ash says, eyes twinkling down at me. "He's right over there."

I glance over to where Ash tilted his head and then laugh even harder. "*Embry* taught you to dance?"

"There's a lot of dead time to fill when you're deployed," Ash says mock defensively. "We had to entertain ourselves somehow."

"So he taught you how to dance?"

"We took turns being the man, if you're wondering." Ash says it jokingly, but I can't help but remember his hand fisted in Embry's tuxedo jacket, Embry's knees on the floor between Ash's shoes.

Ash notices my flushed cheeks before I do, reaching up and brushing my cheek with the backs of his fingers. "You're blushing," he remarks.

"I—" No. There's no way I can tell him the things that are flashing through my mind. "I'm just warm."

He looks at me for a moment, and I see him shelve this away for later. Instead he says in an offhand voice, "You and Embry seem to have become fast friends."

Well, if I was flushed before, I'm sure my face is bloodless now. I can only manage a nod as a voice inside my head screams *tell him the truth, tell him the truth!*

"It makes me happy to see you get along so well," he continues. "You're the two most important people in the world to me, besides my mother and sister, and I want us all to be close."

You have no idea how close Embry and I are, I want to say. I *should* say. But the words stick in my throat.

Embry and I aren't together and we'll never be together now…so what difference does our past make? If I tell Ash about

205

that night in Chicago, it will just add more tension between the three of us, and apparently there's enough of that already.

Stop rationalizing. You know lying is wrong. Tell the truth.

But the moment has passed, and we're spinning across the dance floor and then Ash says, "I heard you also had the pleasure of meeting Senator Leffey."

"Yes," I answer a bit sourly. "She and I are *not* going to be fast friends, in case you were wondering."

He laughs. "No, I didn't think you would be. What did she say to you?"

Here, I decide to be honest. "She told me that you two used to fuck. She told me you're a liar. And she warned me that I was in over my head with you."

Ash blinks in surprise. "Wow. She really dove right in there, didn't she?"

"Yeah."

His face turns pensive. "Morgan doesn't like me very much, I'm afraid."

"Why?"

He sighs. "Lots of reasons. Too many to name. In fact, she has so many reasons to dislike me that it almost feels like fate. We're destined to be enemies."

"I'm guessing those reasons weren't around when you fucked her?"

His hand is suddenly tight and possessive on my waist, pulling me so close that I can feel my dress catching on his legs as we move. "Jealousy looks good on you," he says, leaning his head down to speak into my ear. I shiver at the feeling of his warm breath on my skin.

"But you don't need to be jealous," he finishes, straightening up again. "It was a very long time ago. We haven't had sex in fourteen years."

I'm about to exhale with relief when he admits, "But we have been sexual together since then."

There's that jealousy knifing between my ribs again. "And when was the last time you were 'sexual' together?"

His eyes find mine in the dim light of the dining room, green and intensely apologetic. "A month ago."

"A month ago?" I repeat. I want to rip myself out of his arms, I want to storm away, but I can't, I can't, I can't. There are too many eyes watching, too many reputations at stake, and besides, I don't get to have any claim on Ash's sexual history. Any claim on what he did before we kissed at St. Thomas Becket.

Ash holds me tighter, leaning his head in close. Goddamn him for being so fucking handsome right now, all chiseled planes and full lips. It makes it impossible for me to pull away, to ignore him.

"After Jenny died," he says in a low voice, "I was in a bad place. The cancer came on so fast—she was diagnosed and then two weeks later she was dead—and there was no time to grieve or to process and there was still this campaign to run. This campaign I didn't even want to run any longer. After the funeral, I felt like an imposter in my own life. Like I'd woken up in another man's body. I didn't see myself in the mirror. I couldn't hear my own voice. I would be fastening my cuff links and then realize I didn't recognize my own hands. They felt like puppet hands. Like some sort of clever wooden machine and not flesh and blood."

It's the first time he's really talked about Jenny to me, and my heart is rupturing for him, for that Ash of last year who felt so alien and adrift. I squeeze his neck and he sighs into it, as if the gesture comforts him.

"Morgan and I had encountered each other countless times since that week we were together. She's my best friend's stepsister and a powerful senator on the Armed Services Committee...our worlds collided a lot. And a week after Jenny died, our worlds collided again. Merlin had coaxed me back on the campaign trail, a stump speech in Virginia—it should have been easy. A message I'd been touting for a year in a state that loves the military. And I fucked it up. I stumbled and stuttered, and it was fine that time—everyone was so eager to give me the grieving husband pass—but it wouldn't be fine for long. And I knew it. I knew if I couldn't get my shit together, I would lose, no matter how many pictures were tweeted of me laying roses on Jenny's grave.

"I went home that night planning to get drunk. And I decided the next day I'd call Merlin and tell him it was over. I would withdraw. It had been a pipe dream anyway, to run on a third-party ticket, and there was no way I could win like this. Like…a shell. A ghost."

"But you didn't call him," I murmur. "What changed your mind?"

His eyes are pinned to mine. "Morgan."

Ugh. Knife. Ribs. Ugly, jealous pain.

"She showed up at my door that night. We hadn't exchanged civil words in fourteen years, and yet there she was. 'I know what you need' was all she said. And then she took me to a place she goes to here in town. A sex club."

A sex club?

He pauses his story to smile at my stunned expression. "For a self-admitted submissive, angel, you seem pretty shocked by the idea."

"No, no." I rush to downplay my surprise. "That's totally cool. I'm sure lots of people do that and go places like that and stuff…" I stop babbling, realizing how ridiculous I sound.

A small laugh. "It's easy to forget," he says, "how young you are. How little experience you have. It's okay to be shocked. Just…I want you to understand what I was going through then. Why it all happened the way it did."

He takes a deep breath to continue. "I'd known for a long time that my tastes in bed ran a little…extreme. It had

208

always been there, I suppose, but the war—" He closes his eyes for a moment and then opens them again. "The war made it necessary. It grew and grew and became impossible to ignore, a need that felt like fire in my veins, and I couldn't douse the flames of it. I couldn't cut it out of me, no matter how hard I tried. And I tried. With Jenny, I tried for years. She wasn't like you, Greer, not in the least. She loved me so much and wanted to please me, but I could see her wincing whenever I accidentally got too rough, could see how unresponsive her body was to anything other than tenderness. I loved her, Greer. I gave her tenderness, as best as I could, and then after she fell asleep at night, I'd lie awake and think of you." A shadow crosses his face. "I'm not proud of that. But it was like the more I tried to fight it, the stronger the need became, the more elaborate the fantasies grew. I'd think about venting my frustration on you. All the things I couldn't do to my wife—in my mind, I did a thousand times to you. Bit you, spanked you, ropes, whips, lube. And in my fantasies, you'd thank me. Covered in welts and my cum, with makeup smeared on your face, you'd thank me. And then I'd fuck you again."

"Jesus Christ, Ash," I say, my breath coming fast.

"Too much?" he asks, brow furrowed with concern.

"Can we leave the dinner? I want you to do all that to me right now."

A little pinch at my waist. "Behave. I'm confessing to you what a terrible husband I was to Jenny, and if you're smart, you'll rethink attaching yourself to me."

"Did you ever hurt Jenny or do anything without her consent?"

"No."

"Did you do your best to love her and take care of her?"

He closes his eyes. "Yes."

"Then I'm not rethinking anything," I assure him,

stroking the side of his neck. "You should have been honest with her, and I don't think it's right that you fantasized about me so much while you were married to her. But given the circumstances, it's forgivable, and not something I think will happen between us."

"Fuck no, it won't," Ash says softly, and God, that filthy word on his tongue. My nipples pull into tight buds at the sound of it.

"So what happened when Morgan brought you to this sex club? After years of denying yourself the kind of sex you needed?"

"First things first, Greer. I didn't have sex at the club that night. I haven't had sex with a woman since Jenny died. You'll be my first."

A flutter of relief, of flattered excitement.

"But yes, the club was where I was able to dominate openly for the first time. Morgan introduced me to experienced dominants who showed me how to exert control and inflict pain safely, and then I was able to meet submissives there who wanted control and pain from me. That first night though, I hadn't met anyone else yet. We got to the club, and right there in the open, Morgan stripped naked and put a flogger in my hand."

"What happened then? Did you hit her?"

"Yes, I hit her." He smiles ruefully at me. "I was hard after three strikes. After five, I could remember the sound of my own voice. And after ten, the hands that held the flogger were my own hands again. I was back in my body. Somehow."

"But you didn't have sex?"

A look of fierce distaste, so fast and fleeting I almost wonder if I imagined it. "It was the dominating, not the woman, that got me hard. I didn't touch her, and if I hadn't been so fucked up from Jenny's death, I never would have allowed it to go that far in the first place. I dropped the flogger and called a cab home, left her naked in that room. And when I called her the next day, I told her I wouldn't touch her again, but that I needed to come back. Which suited her well enough—she'd rather be on the other side of the flogger—and since then, I've been to the club many times with her, but never like the first time. We never touched again, via whips or otherwise."

This satisfies me, but only a little. "I don't understand how she can hate you so much but still be willing to be flogged by you. Especially if she's a domme."

"It was a big gesture for her," he concedes, "although all the dominants at that club are required to submit to whippings and beatings at least once or twice as part of their training. But as for the why…Morgan and I are unfortunately connected in unique ways that we can't help or change." Ash shrugs. "I imagine that as much as she hates me, there was a part of her that felt compelled to offer sympathy or relief. And I think it's the way she knew best, and she remembered enough about our time together to know it was what I needed too. We may be enemies here, but on neutral ground, we respect each other. We have a lot in common, after all."

I nod. I think I'm beginning to understand Morgan's place in Ash's story, although the understanding does nothing to dull the jabs of envy I feel thinking about them at a club together, knowing they've had sex.

"So have you been flogged as part of your training?" I ask curiously. It's hard to imagine my tall, muscular soldier bound in place, submitting quietly to whips and paddles.

"I have had everything done to me that I would want to do to someone else. I didn't think it was safe or fair to do something to another person without knowing exactly what it would feel like." He leans close to my ear. "And *everything* was a pretty long list, Greer. I hope you're ready."

"God, yes."

He pulls back with a smile. "I knew you would be."

"And this club—your identity is safe? Morgan can't go to the press and tell them that you were there? There aren't any pictures floating around?"

He laughs. "My little political princess. Of course that's where your mind goes, straight to potential scandal. Yes, my identity was—and is—safe. This club caters to congresspeople, ambassadors, and foreign dignitaries. Their nondisclosure agreements are damning; violate yours and you'll find yourself ruined in every possible way. Trust me—the man who runs this club is more powerful than I am. And I'm not the first president who's been a guest there."

I make a face, thinking about the previous president, a balding, squat Democrat with wild eyebrows and rumpled suits. "Ugh."

"Yeah."

"Mr. President" comes a voice from nearby. We stop dancing and turn to see a tall Black woman walking toward us, a silky emerald dress clinging to her slender curves and fluttering around her ankles. The entire room seems to watch her cross the nearly empty dance floor: partly because she's beautiful—dark brown skin, high cheekbones, curls that bounce as she walks—and partly it's because she's Kay Colchester, Ash's foster sister and his chief of staff. She wouldn't interrupt our dance unless it was for something crucial.

"Kay," Ash says. "What is it?"

"There's been military movement along the Carpathian border with Ukraine. No borders have been crossed, but there's definitely an increase in the number of troops. Our satellite experts only just now picked up on it; it was that well camouflaged, which means this isn't for show. They're planning something and they don't want anyone to know about it."

212

The man I was dancing with disappears, and in his place is someone calm and detached. Coolly powerful. "Where will I be briefed?"

"The Situation Room. It will be short. Twenty minutes at most."

He nods. "After that, I'll need to speak to our people in Ukraine and Poland. Maybe Slovakia too. I'll call from the Residence."

"Yes, sir. I'll get it arranged." Kay's eyes slide over to me, and her businesslike expression opens up. "You must be Greer. I can't tell you how excited I am that my brother is dating someone."

I shake her hand as Ash lets out a huff. "Everyone keeps saying that. It's not like I've been a monster to work with."

"Well, let's just say that I'm glad you have Embry as your whipping boy, or the rest of us would have suffered a lot more."

"I only whip him when he asks for it," Ash says, flashing a smile at me, and I give a shaky smile back, knowing it's a joke but unable to stop myself from biting my lip at the thought.

"Anyway," Kay says with a roll of her eyes at Ash's answer, "my brother here has been a whole new man this last week. You have to understand, he's always polite and respectful, never mean. But definitely not chatty. He's always serious and all about work. However, since last week, I've caught him *smiling*. In front of *other people*. Even *laughing* sometimes. And the thousand-yard stare is gone."

"Ash smiles all the time," I say, looking up at him.

"When I'm with you," he says, his voice warm. He leans in and I expect a kiss on the cheek, but instead he kisses my neck and I have to keep my knees from failing. I hear murmurs around us on the dance floor, and I can only imagine how many cell phone pictures were just snapped of the president with his lips on my neck.

But I can tell he doesn't care. He presses his forehead against mine and speaks quietly so Kay can't hear him. "I have to go to the Situation Room now. And there will be some work to do after that."

"I can leave," I offer. "I know you said we'd spend time together after the dinner, but—"

"Stay," he says. "I want you to stay."

"And wait for you?"

"God, yes." There's something rough around the edges of his voice. "Will you?"

"Yes," I whisper.

"I'll have Belvedere take you back to the Residence, and I'm going to text you instructions. Have your phone ready."

"I will."

"That's my good girl." Another kiss on my neck, and he's already turning away. He and Kay sweep out, and I see Embry's tall frame as he follows them.

I take a deep breath, and with all the dignity I can muster among the crowd of curious onlookers, go to search for Belvedere.

CHAPTER 19

EVEN THOUGH I CAN FIND MY OWN WAY BACK UPSTAIRS, I'm grateful for Belvedere's presence as he wards off guests and journalists and steers me expertly through the crowd.

"So how was your first official event?" Belvedere asks as we finally make it to the stairs.

I think of Morgan Leffey and Ash's story about the club. "It was illuminating."

He seems to know exactly what I'm referring to. "I am sorry about Senator Leffey. If I'd known sooner, I would have had her moved. But the social secretary knows now, and it won't happen again."

I put my hand on his arm as we climb up. "There's no need for that. I can handle her, especially now that I know who she is and how she'll act."

"Just be careful," Belvedere says. His thick hipster glasses do nothing to hide his worried expression. "Senator Leffey is a dangerous enemy to have."

"She's not my enemy," I object. "Just because we are two women with connections to the same man doesn't mean we have to hate each other."

"That's very socially enlightened of you, but it's not only up to you, you know. It's up to Leffey too. And she has a history of cutting down anything or anyone in her path."

"I'm not in her path," I say with a certainty I don't feel. "How could I be? I'm not a political rival. I pose no threat to her."

We reach the top of the stairs, and Belvedere looks at me. "I think you pose more threats than you realize." And it sounds so much like Merlin's curse that I have to remind myself to relax. Why is everyone convinced that I'm dangerous?

"I don't want to pose any threats," I say. "I'm not going to do anything to hurt Senator Leffey. I just want to be with Ash."

His worry softens into affection. "I know. And I'll do everything I can to help." He glances at his watch. "But right now, I should get down there and wait for the president to finish his briefing. Do you have everything you need?"

I wave him away. "I'm a big girl. I'll be fine on my own."

He gives my elbow a squeeze, and then he's trotting down the stairs, taking them two at a time, his floppy brown hair moving with each step. It's then that my phone gives a buzz in my dress pocket. And then another. And then another.

I pull it out as I walk down the hallway. It's Ash, and my stomach flips over when I see the first message.

Get undressed.
You're allowed five minutes to freshen up and prepare yourself however you need
and then I want you wearing nothing but one of my
button-down shirts.

I see the three little dots appear and then disappear, and I wonder where he is right now. In the Situation Room? Looking at satellite photographs of troop movements while he types out exactly how he wants to find me when he gets done?

YOU will kneel on the floor in the middle of the room, hands behind your back, eyes down, and wait for me and when I get there, we are in scene. You are only allowed to refer to me as sir or Mr. President. Understood?

I'm already kicking off my heels as I answer.

Yes, sir.

There's another pause, then:

Good girl.

I have a little trouble unzipping my dress, but I finally manage to peel off the layers of silk and tulle and wriggle out of my thong and strapless bra, laying out the clothes in the dressing room so they're out of sight. And then I brush my teeth and use the restroom, hunt down one of Ash's shirts, and by the time my five minutes are up, I'm kneeling on the carpet, shirt buttoned and sleeves rolled up. I put my hands behind my back, grabbing each forearm with the opposite hand like I've seen submissives do on the internet, and tilt my face to the floor.

It's almost immediately uncomfortable. The carpet presses into my knees with hundreds of fibrous little twists, and the muscles in my arms strain with the ache of holding them in such an unfamiliar position. A thousand million itches spring up on my skin, and every tiny sensation—thirst, the slightly-too-cool air of the room, the faint hunger left over from my half-eaten dinner—is magnified and made all-consuming. I can't use my phone to distract myself; I can't even use my eyes to distract myself—there's nothing between me and being inside my own body. No other person, no other thoughts. No work or family or friends or responsibilities—there's only me and one directive: to wait.

And so I wait, trying not to twitch with the agony of it. I'm used to keeping my mind and body busy, used to filling any empty time with grading or preparing lectures or research for my book, and this is worse torture than anything else I can think of, to keep my body still and *wait*.

Without a clock or my phone, time seems to stretch and warp, and I have no idea how long I've been kneeling in this silent room—minutes or hours or years—and I have the creeping sense of loneliness that comes with silence and stillness. How long would I have to kneel here? Surely, Ash wouldn't expect me to wait longer than a few minutes? Surely he wouldn't want me to ache and itch and come unhinged from the pressure of my own thoughts?

Except I know that's exactly what he does want.

Control. My submission flavored by discomfort, by my desire to please him.

And I do want to please him, so badly.

And with that realization, the position becomes easier to hold, the stillness easier to bear. There's purpose in it now, a reason, and the reason is Ash, the only reason I ever want. I think of him as my knees whine at the press of the carpet, as my mouth gets drier, as goose bumps erupt over my skin at the chilly air of the room. I dismiss each sensation as it arises, my thoughts shrinking down to Ash and the low fire kindling deep in my core, and eventually everything else does fade away, leaving behind a distilled version of myself. A version that waits.

I'm floating in place like this when the door to Ash's bedroom finally, finally opens, and I don't look up, but I do eagerly watch those shiny dress shoes as he walks in. And then stop breathing when a second pair of shoes follows.

That second pair freezes in midstride, as if their owner

is arrested by the sight of me kneeling on the floor with my arms behind my back and my nipples poking through the thin fabric of a man's shirt.

The door shuts and then Ash is squatting down in front of me. "You may lift your head now, angel."

I look up at him, at the man who has changed not at all over the minutes we've been apart even though I feel like an entirely different person. But then my eyes move past him to Embry, and I feel nothing but mindless panic. Panic at being so exposed in front of him. Panic that mirrors the panic on his own face, the speed of his breathing as he looks at me and looks at me and looks at me.

"I hope you trusted me," Ash says. "And I hope you knew that I'd keep you safe while you submitted to me. I made sure no one else came up here while you waited."

I tear my stare away from Embry. "But you brought someone else with you. Sir," I add at the last minute.

Ash nods. "We have a couple phone calls to make, but I can make them from here. I didn't want to leave you alone a second longer, but I also wanted Embry close by while I talked to our people near Carpathia."

"I can leave," I say. I *plead*. "Or I can go wait somewhere else while you call."

Don't make me be like this in front of Embry. I'm too weak to hide how much I'll like it.

"No," Ash says. "I want you to stay."

"Ash…" Embry says from behind him, his face pale. "We can call first thing tomorrow morning. There's no need for me to intrude—" His voice breaks off as Ash runs a finger up my thigh to my pussy and carefully slides it inside of me. Despite the deep unease at Embry's presence, my deprived body responds immediately, and I try to push myself down onto the finger, squirming for more contact and more friction.

"So wet," Ash murmurs.

219

Embry makes a strangled noise from his place by the door.

Ash withdraws his finger and places it in my mouth for me to suck clean, which I do without question, lust overriding my better sense, the better sense that tells me there's no way I can do any of this in front of Embry. It will hurt me and it will hurt him, and then Ash will see why it hurts us, and then *he'll* be hurt.

Ash wipes his hand on his tuxedo jacket and stands up. "Embry, we'll use the phone by the sofa," he says, gesturing to the two small sofas next to the television. "If you want to have a seat."

Embry looks at Ash and then looks to me. I feel the ghost of his hips between my thighs, the slickness of blood on my skin, his passionate kisses that consumed us both with their single-minded want. My body keens for him, just as it's keening for Ash, aching for one or both of them to the point that I can't even identify how I actually feel any longer. There's only the need. The want.

"Embry," Ash says. "The sofa, please."

Embry steps over to Ash, studiously keeping his gaze away from me on the floor. "Are you sure this is what you want?" he asks Ash quietly.

Ash gets closer to him, angling his body so that I can't see Embry any longer, and leans in to speak in his ear. I can't hear what he says, but I see Embry's posture tense up, see his hand flex and clench, as if he's keeping himself from doing something violent. Except when Ash pulls back, the look on Embry's face isn't violence. I don't know what it is, but it makes me shiver and makes the memory of his body against mine all the stronger.

Without another word, Embry goes to the sofa and sits, his face unreadable, his posture strangely easy. As if he's done this before.

Has he?

Have *they*?

Ash watches him, facing away from me with his hands in his pockets. His shoulders are relaxed, and his stride is full of unconscious power as he walks to the opposite sofa and sits, crossing his legs. His long, skillful fingers set to work tugging his bow tie free, and as he's pulling at the fabric, he gives me a dismissive glance. "Crawl to me," he says.

His voice is offhand, his expression coolly indifferent, but all I feel is swelling desperation. This is something I've fantasized about for years, and he *knows* it; he has that letter memorized. So why dangle this in front of me when I obviously can't do it? I can't crawl in front of Embry; the overt submission and humiliation makes the act so undeniably sexual that it feels unfaithful to do it in front of anyone else.

But if Ash is asking me to do it...then does that make it right?

"Crawl, Greer," Ash says, impatiently this time.

I find my voice. "But, sir, Embry is here—"

"He's Mr. Vice President to you right now," Ash interrupts.

"Sir, *Mr. Vice President* is here," I correct myself. "He'll see me."

"And?"

I don't know how to answer that. It is its own explanation; there is no *and*. Embry is here and he'll see me, and I'll see him seeing me, and everything we've tried to keep suppressed the last week will surface.

"Why are you doing this?" I whisper.

Ash locks gazes with me. "Because I want to," he answers simply.

"But—"

"No *buts*, Greer. Do you have something you'd like to say to me?"

The safe word. He means the safe word.

I search his face and find no trace of irritation or anger, and I know that he's giving me the option to end things right now, no questions asked, no wounded feelings or resentment. *He's trusting me*, I think, trusting me to vocalize my needs. To advocate for my boundaries. And that's the heart of this, isn't it? I trust him with control and he trusts me with my voice. I trust him to stop when I ask him to stop, and he trusts me to say *stop* before I'm hurt. His control means nothing without my consent, and my consent is meaningless if I don't trust the man I'm giving it to.

So do I trust him?

And do I feel safe?

Yes.

And yes.

I lower my face from Ash's. "No, sir, there's nothing I'd like to say."

From his couch, Embry exhales—a sound of relief or dread, I don't know.

"Good," Ash says. "Then crawl."

I crawl. Keeping my head down, so I can't see whether Embry is looking at me or not, and doing my best to keep my breathing even, I make my way over to Ash's feet on my hands and knees. I should feel demeaned—it's meant to demean, after all—but knowing that both men are affected by the sight of me slouching across the floor like a cat makes me feel strong. Sensuous. Female. There's the air on my exposed cunt, the shirt riding up over my ass, the stray tendrils of hair hanging down around my face, and I can't help it, it all makes me wetter. Hotter. Hungrier.

Ash's hand comes to rest on my head as I reach him. "Well done," he says warmly, and I feel a flush of pleasure at his praise. "Up here," he commands, patting his thigh.

I manage not to look at Embry as I climb onto the couch,

but I can hear him behind me, restless shifting and rustling fabric, as if he's tugging at his bow tie as well.

Ash takes my hips in his hands and sits me down so that I'm straddling his leg, my bare pussy flat against the hard muscles of his thigh, and I let out a low moan the minute my full weight settles on him. The pressure there is like gasoline to an already burning fire, and I have to force myself not to grind down against him.

"I told you I'd take care of your orgasm tonight," Ash says. "This is me taking care of it."

"Sir?"

"Ride me, rub against me, whatever you need to do to come. But you have to be quiet, since I'll be on the phone."

I can't help it; I look over my shoulder back to Embry. His eyes are on my ass, where it rests against Ash's thigh, and when he realizes I'm staring at him, he lifts his eyes and flushes with shame. I flush with shame too; I wanted to catch him watching me. I look back to Ash, who's watching me closely, those clear green eyes missing nothing. The shame goes deeper than my cheeks, sinking down to my stomach.

"Is this some kind of test?" I ask, my whispering voice trembling on the last word.

"It's not a test," Ash replies. But he says nothing else, merely keeps looking at me with those searing, perceptive eyes.

A ping of real alarm now. He's watching me carefully, and Embry too, and does he suspect? That we have a history? Or only that we're attracted to each other?

"Sir," I whisper. "I don't know if I can do this in front of him. Come in front of him."

Even though I've done it a few times before...

"I think you want to," Ash replies. "Deep down, there's a part of you that wants him to see you all flushed and tousled,

223

that wants him to see how well you can obey me, how pretty that pussy is. Isn't that right?"

The tear is formed and spilling out from underneath my eyelashes before I can stop it. "I don't want to ruin what we have," I mumble, looking down and away from his face. "I don't want to displease you. I don't want you to leave me. Over this."

"Oh, angel," he says, voice soft. "You'll never displease me. If this is too much, tell me. But if it's not too much... then I want you to trust me."

I do trust you.

I hesitate still, but then the phone rings, and Ash holds up a finger, indicating I should be silent. I press my lips together as he reaches over to the phone and presses a button so that it picks up the call on speaker. "Colchester here."

Belvedere's voice comes through. "Mr. President, I have our ambassador in Ukraine on the phone, and she's on a non-secured line. May I put her through?"

"Yes."

There's a click, and then the voice of an older woman comes over the line. "Diana Cotter speaking."

"Hello, Diana," Ash greets her. "I'm sorry for the unexpected call, but I wanted to touch base with you before the next couple days play out. And we have someone here without a Need to Know, so we need to keep it light."

"Of course," she says.

Embry, Ash, and the ambassador start talking, Ash quickly explaining the need to feel out the current political climate around Carpathia. True to his word, Ash doesn't delve into anything requiring high-level security clearance, but it's still fascinating. I'm listening in, my eyes glued to the phone, when I feel a thumb against my clit, hard and rough, rubbing small circles against the swollen bud. In an instant, all the banked desire from the last week is there.

All-consuming, obliterating past and present, obliterating the future, destroying everything that isn't the painful ache in my cunt as I push into Ash's touch.

He pushes back, hard, giving my clit a light pinch that sends my eyes rolling back into my head. He does it again for good measure and I gasp, clapping my hand over my mouth once I realize my mistake, eyes darting back to the phone.

Ash arches an eyebrow at me—a *can you keep quiet* eyebrow—and I nod, a little frantically, desperate for him to keep doing what he's doing. His thumb rubs steadily, the rhythm never breaking as he and Embry talk about border agreements and the UN and the Carpathian president, and I find myself rocking into his touch, squirming down onto his thigh to increase the pressure. His thumb stops as he leans over to end his phone call, but I keep rocking, tilting forward so that I'm rubbing my clit directly against his leg. It's so shameful, so obscene and immodest, to be driven to the point that I don't care that I'm rubbing against Ash's leg like a dog in heat. That I don't care that Embry is watching me debase myself so much, act so mindlessly carnal. There's only the need, and if this is the way I'm allowed to slake the need, then I'm fucking doing it.

Ash sits back, watching me with his elbow on the arm of the sofa and his head braced against his forefinger and his thumb. The erection tenting his slacks is massive, all the more erotic for the expensive tuxedo that frames it, but Ash's face is perfectly controlled. Only the pulse beating at the side of his neck betrays his excitement. "Does that feel good?" he asks calmly as I grind against him.

"Yes," I pant.

A sharp slap on my ass. I jolt and moan.

"Yes, *sir*," I try again.

"Good. My thigh is all you get right now. If you behave, you can earn more. My mouth maybe. Would you like that?"

My shudder is all the answer he needs. He looks past me to Embry. "She's a good girl, isn't she, Embry?"

His friend's voice is hoarse when he answers. "Yes."

Ash looks at his friend, his finger rubbing at his forehead. "Do you still want to go, Embry?"

Once again, Embry takes a long time to answer, but when he does, it's definitive. "No. I want to stay."

A smile curls Ash's mouth. "I thought so. Would you like to see more of her? Maybe without the shirt?"

There's a pause, a pause that seems to last forever, and in that pause I hear five years' worth of agony.

"Yes," Embry finally replies.

Ash looks back to me, and while there's not satisfaction in his face necessarily, there is something else. Confirmation, maybe. Like it wasn't what Embry said but how he said it that told Ash what he needed to know. "You heard the vice president," Ash says, running a finger down the placket of the shirt. "Take it off."

Even in my need-to-come haze, I hesitate. "Can…can you take it off, please?"

"No."

He's going to make me do it. Just like the crawling. Each step of tonight is a crossroads—past what, I don't know— but Ash is making sure that *I'm* the one taking each step. That I'm acutely aware of my own role in this.

I meet his eyes, every pleading, angry thought written on my face, and I feel his hand slide up my thigh and give it a reassuring squeeze. His eyes are so clear and so green, his pupils dilated into huge black pools of hunger. He doesn't say anything, doesn't push, but keeps his eyes on mine, his hand gentle and sweet on my thigh.

He's giving me a chance to safe out. One word, and I could end this misery for all three of us.

But oh God, I can't bear to. Sometimes misery is

better. Sometimes the forbidden fruit is just too sweet not to bite.

I lift my hands and begin unbuttoning the shirt, and both men exhale simultaneously. I should hate the rush of power that gives me, the rush of lust, but I don't. It feels right. As right as kneeling, as right as crawling. As right as standing before a class or thumbing through books older than the college I teach at. Like I was born for it.

I take my time, not to be intentionally seductive, but because my hands are shaking so much that each button is a struggle. It's worth it, though, when I finally tug the shirt free from my shoulders and I see Ash's control almost break. He shifts underneath me, his hand squeezing my thigh so hard I know I'll bruise, and he bites his lower lip.

"Touch your tits," he orders after he regains his composure. "Slide your hands over them and then pull on your nipples. Yes, like that. Fuck."

He shifts again, that erection looking so mouthwatering even inside his pants, and I want it. I want it in my mouth, I want it in my pussy. I want to ride it until my legs shake, I want it so deep inside me that I can't feel anything else. When will we have sex? Surely tonight. Surely he can't bear to wait any longer, because I know I can't. I started birth control the moment we started seeing each other so we wouldn't have to wait a moment longer than we had to.

"What is it, angel?" he asks, eyes lifting from where my hands are on my breasts to my face.

I don't answer right away, and he gives me a light pinch on the ass. "You can always answer me honestly, Greer. I won't ask if I don't want to know."

"I want your cock," I blurt. "I want to be fucked by it. Please. Please fuck me. Please, sir."

His eyes glow with something like amusement, but his voice returns to the nonchalance of earlier. "My cock is a

227

privilege, angel. Being fucked is a privilege. And all privileges have to be earned."

I must visibly deflate at this because he strokes my arm. "When I take your pussy, it's going to be special. We only get one first time together, and I know exactly when I want that to be."

"What's wrong with right now?" I whine.

That earns me another swift smack on the ass. "Turn around and face Embry. He wants to see those gorgeous tits of yours. He wants to see your face when you come."

I'm past protesting, past hesitating. I can blame it on the lust, blame it on Ash and my submission, but the real reason is both simpler and more complicated than either of those. The answer is I want to. I want Embry to see me. And whether it's a test or a gift, Ash is giving it to us.

When I flip myself around so I'm facing Embry, a change comes over the room. It's no longer Embry as the outsider. Now Embry and I are looking at each other, my breasts and my cunt on display for him, my pleasure a performance for his pleasure. And underneath me, I feel waves of power and desire rolling off Ash, as if controlling Embry as well as me arouses a different side of his dominance. As if watching me perform for Embry is more erotic than when I perform for him alone.

The phone rings again, and Ash tells me, "Get to work," before he answers the phone. And then he picks up, and he's talking and Embry is talking too—albeit in a choked, forced voice—and I start grinding against Ash's leg, my eyes on Ash's friend the entire time. As he watches and attempts to talk along with Ash, I slide my hands up my stomach to my breasts, squeezing them hard, the way he squeezed them that night in Chicago. The way he touched me like he'd never get to touch a woman again. His eyes follow my hands, his teeth digging deep into his lip, and when I start fucking Ash's thigh again, his hand curls into a fist on his knee.

I imagine I'm fucking him, I imagine I'm fucking Ash, I imagine I'm fucking both of them. I imagine them fucking each other, I imagine all three of us in a tangle of sweat and thrusting, all barriers stripped away, every hot inch and sweet hole available without question.

And it's this final image that sets the gears of my climax whirring, spinning tighter and tighter until I can feel it poised in front of my womb, a ticking thing ready to explode. My hands drop down to Ash's knee for balance as I lean forward, drop my head, and chase the orgasm I've been waiting for all week. I hear the phone call end, and through the tendrils of hair hanging down around my face, I see Embry sitting on the edge of the sofa, that fist unclenching and clenching over and over again.

"Give it to me," Ash says. "To *us*."

And so I do. I press hard against Ash and ride the swell as I rub against him, crying out as I feel the wick light and the bomb detonate deep inside my womb. Shudders radiate out, pulsing quakes as I tremble on top of Ash's thigh, as I pant and gasp and continue rubbing myself against him to milk every last ounce of pleasure out of this. It goes on and on, all the pent-up longing from this week, all the angst over Embry just adding fuel to the fire. And when I do finally stop moving, my body wrung out, I become aware of Ash's hands in my hair, tugging my head back.

"That was beautiful, angel, but we're not done yet," he informs me. With his hands moving to my waist, he lifts me and sets me on the ground, so that I'm kneeling in front of him. There's a large wet stain on his tuxedo pants where I sat. A stain that I left.

"Look at what you did."

I cast my eyes around for something to clean him with, but he stops me with a hand fisted in my hair. He guides my mouth to his leg. "Lick it clean."

I close my eyes for a moment, overwhelmed by the deliberate humiliation, the dehumanization of it, overwhelmed by the way I respond to it like it's a warm blanket on a cold night. I want to wrap myself in it, burrow into it and never leave. Nothing is more natural than this, nothing has ever been as close to what I dreamed about as a teenage girl. Whatever happens between Embry, Ash, and me after tonight will just have to happen because I don't want to stop.

I open my eyes and begin licking at his pants, feeling like a cat and even more like one when Ash puts a firm hand between my shoulder blades and presses me down so that I'm on all fours. The air is cool on my swollen cunt, revealing every single fold and curve where I'm wet, and with a tremor, I realize Ash has posed me like this so Embry can see my sex on display. I wish I could see his face or hear his voice. I wish I could tell if he liked what he saw, if he also remembers that night in Chicago when he crawled down the bed and ate me like a starving man at a feast.

As I'm licking up the traces of myself, Ash says to Embry, "You're hard."

Embry doesn't speak, but he must nod, because then Ash says, "Pull it out. Show Greer what she's done to you."

Ash doesn't have to tell me to look or force me to turn my head. My heart pounds a beat so strong I feel it in my cunt as I turn to see Embry with his shaking hands on his fly. I recognize the misery in his face immediately. The misery of wanting something so badly even though you know it's wrong. Even though you think it might be a trap. Yet here we are, unwilling to stop, however dangerous it might be.

There's a furrow in Embry's elegant forehead, as if he's concentrating as he slowly unfastens his pants and reaches inside. Then I see the tip of him—the dusky, flared cap with a bead of moisture at the slit—and I lick my lips, thinking of

230

Chicago. Remembering the way that cock invaded me and claimed me. Tore me and fucked me.

Embry sees me lick my lips, and his head drops back against the sofa with a moan.

"All of it, Embry," Ash admonishes. "You show us all of it."

With a couple of quick, jerky movements, Embry shoves his pants farther down his hips so that all eight hard inches are exposed. His balls are high and tight, like he's already close to losing it, and when he puts his thumb at his root and slowly pushes his cock toward us so that it points straight to the ceiling, I see the muscles tensing in his stomach and thighs.

He's breathing fast, his eyes on Ash as he keeps himself displayed for us. "Like that?"

I'm surprised at the huskiness in Ash's voice as he answers. "Yeah. Just like that."

But by the time I've swiveled my head back to Ash to study his face, his control has returned and his attention is on me again. He looks at my face as he addresses Embry. "Wasn't I so nice to let Greer come like that?"

"Yes," Embry responds after a pained second.

"Shouldn't she thank me?" Ash runs a finger along my jaw as he stares at me. I shiver under his caress. "Wouldn't that be polite?"

A breath. "Yes."

"How should she thank me, Embry? With her mouth? With her hands?"

"I—" A heavy breath. "With her mouth. She should thank you with her mouth."

"I like that idea very much," Ash agrees. "Put my dick inside your mouth, angel. Show me your gratitude."

Oh, thank God. I attack his groin with so much enthusiasm that he chuckles, but the laughter dies in his throat the minute I get my hands on the erection I've been craving all night. I waste no time in sucking him; I pull him into my mouth right away, taking him as deep as I can go, swallowing against his crown as it brushes the back of my throat.

"Oh, fuck me," Ash groans, his large hand sliding through my hair and resting on the back of my head. "Yes, angel, just like that. Holy shit."

"What…what does it feel like?" Embry asks.

"Hot. Wet. Her lipstick is smearing around my base. *Shit*," he swears as I start sucking up and down as fast as I can. "She's so fucking eager. Look at this."

"I am," Embry answers softly.

I brace my hands on Ash's thighs, loving the hard feel of the muscle under my hands, the tensing and straining that reveals what his stoic face doesn't. I'm oblivious to everything—my tits bouncing and my hair coming undone—as I focus on my one goal: thanking Ash. I go back to the deep, long pulls, letting him fuck my throat, and that unravels him. Within only two or three minutes, he's taken control from me, gripping my head with both his hands and fucking up into my mouth, letting me breathe on every other thrust. I'm gasping, tears smudging my cheeks, and there's drool, but Ash doesn't care.

"That's right," he hisses, his head falling back once more. "Drain me. Take it, take it all. Oh fuck, angel. Here it comes."

Hot spurts hit the back of my throat, thick and long pulses of him, a deep animal grunt leaving his mouth at the apex of his climax. He holds my head over him as he thrusts through the rest of his orgasm, making sure I've had every last drop of his milk, before he finally loosens his grip and lets me go. Without being asked, I lick him from root to tip, cleaning his satisfied flesh, until I feel a finger under my chin. I lift my face to his, and his face is filled with so much warmth and pride that fresh tears prick at my eyelids.

"Well done, my little princess," the president says. "I'm so proud of you."

Only in this world, only in this context, only with this man, does this wreck me. I have my own life and my own goals and my own power, and yet here in this room, none of that applies. Tonight *was* hard, tonight *did* seem impossible, and so Ash's praise and the emotional fallout of having a scene in front of my former lover triggers a wave of tears I can't fight off. I bury my face in Ash's lap so the men won't see me cry.

I want Ash to be proud of me in these scenes. So much.

He strokes my hair but then abruptly stops, gently but quickly moving me aside so he can jump to his feet. I look up, confused and vision blurred, and I realize that Embry has stood up and is walking to the door, fumbling his fly closed as he does. Ash strides across the room and slams his hand against the door as Embry tries to open it, closing the door again and effectively pinning Embry between his body and the wood.

Embry turns to face Ash. "Please let me go," he says wretchedly. "Please."

"You're still hard," Ash tells him. "Aren't you?"

"I can't stay here."

"I'll let you leave if you can show me you're not erect," Ash says, and I've never heard anything so soft and menacing and filthy. "Pull it out and show me. Prove to me you don't want this and you can go."

Embry's handsome face is twisted with delicious torment, his stubbled jaw tense with suffering. "I know what game you're playing, and I know that I'm going to lose."

Does he know because he's played a game like this with Ash before? What history do the two of them share?

Embry asks again, his suffering turning into anger. "Please, Ash."

"You and I don't have a safe word," Ash says. "And if we did, it wouldn't be *please*. Do I need to have Greer come over here and help?"

233

"No!" Embry bursts out. "No. I…okay."

There's complete silence in the room as Embry bends to Ash's will and unfastens his pants and slowly withdraws his penis. It's harder than ever, swollen and dark and angry, throbbing with every beat of his heart. Even though I just came moments earlier, my pussy gives a whiny little throb of its own.

"Happy?" Embry demands.

Ash doesn't answer him but turns to me. "Go get your dress. The one you wore tonight. Bring it to me."

I scurry up from the floor to obey, hurrying into the dressing room and returning with the pile of blue silk. Embry and Ash haven't moved, but there's so much pre-cum at the tip of Embry's cock that it glistens in the ambient light of the bedroom, and Ash has kept his hand against the door, splayed against the wood right next to Embry's head. The posture is intimate somehow, even though they aren't touching, and the way they're looking at each other is suffused with the kind of violence that only comes from real anger.

I hand the dress to Ash and he hands it to Embry. "Relieve yourself."

"What?" Embry's voice is a study in breathless incredulity.

Ash nods toward the dress. "It's soft, isn't it? The dress? And Greer looked so beautiful in it, didn't she? Like a fucking princess, you said when you saw her. Did you think about fucking her in it tonight?"

I freeze. Embry's blue eyes flare with torment.

Ash goes on. "Did you think about what it would be like to rub your bare cock against all that silk before you finally shoved inside her little pussy? About how the silk would feel fisted in your hands while you pinned her to the ground and fucked her?"

"Ash," I choke out.

He ignores me. "She would have liked it, I think. Watching you defile that expensive dress as you defiled her.

And it would have felt so good, wouldn't it? All that blue silk and that sweet pussy. The most beautiful woman in the room a thrall to your cock."

Embry stares at him. "I know why you're doing this."

"I know."

And that's all there is to it. There are no explanations, no defenses, no logic. It's what Ash wants, and therefore in this scene, it's law.

"Now wrap that dress around your cock and relieve yourself." Ash's voice turns seductive. Dark and tempting. "I bet it would only take a couple of pulls, don't you? And it will feel so good, fucking that dress you've been obsessed with all night. Marking it. It will feel so good to have Greer see how big your cock gets as you pretend to fuck her, how much cum you could fill her with if she'd only let you."

"Jesus," Embry pants, the muscle in his arm bunching as he slowly fists his erection with the skirt of my dress. The silk slides easily over his straining flesh, whispering softly on his cock. "Oh, Jesus." The last word breaks into a moan. His head falls back against the door as he's lost to himself, but he can't resist seeing his cock on my dress, and he looks back down. All three of us watch as it moves in and out of the silk, rude and male against the pretty blue flutters of fabric.

Ash was right—it doesn't take long, and with a shuddering exhale, Embry releases. Thick ropes of cum spray my dress, spurt after spurt after thick spurt, each pulse accompanied by a crude jerk of his hips and a ragged groan. My nipples are so tight it hurts, same with my cunt, and oh God, how I wish Embry's cock were inside me now. That those crude jerks were plowing into me. That all that cum was mine.

After a few more thrusts into the silk, he slows, slumping back against the door, dropping the dress to the floor.

"Don't you feel better now?" Ash asks. "Didn't it feel good to get rid of that ache?"

Embry nods wordlessly, eyes still closed, pulse still hammering in his throat.

"Greer liked it too. Didn't you, Greer?"

My cheeks flush red with shame but I answer honestly. "Yes, sir."

Embry tucks himself into his pants and fastens them up, running a hand over his jaw. He looks dazed, as if he's just woken from a long sleep, his blue eyes unfocused and his voice uncertain when he says, "I'm going home now."

"Good night, then."

Embry looks at me and then looks at Ash, that dazed expression more pronounced than ever. "Good night."

Ash moves his hand so Embry can open the door, and then Embry leaves, closing the door behind him. Ash stares at the door for a minute and then faces me, his face apologetic. "I'm sorry, angel. But I need your mouth again." His hand is already on my head, forcing me to my knees, and his other hand digging out his cock, and he's so hard already, viciously, violently hard.

Watching Embry made him hard, I realize. And the jolt of jealousy comes concurrent with the jolt of arousal.

Ash doesn't go easy on my mouth, but before he comes, he pulls out and reaches down for me, picking me up easily in his arms and carrying me to the bed. He spreads my legs and drapes them over his shoulders, pressing his hot, skillful mouth against my pussy and devouring me. I come with his dark head and wide shoulders between my thighs, and then he's straddling my chest, fucking my mouth to get his cock wet and then fucking my tits. When he finally comes, his hands mean and bruising as he pushes my breasts around his cock, it's with something almost like a roar, like the orgasm is torn from him.

And later that night, I wake out of a deep sleep to find Ash wrapping my small hand around his throbbing erection.

He closes his large hand over mine, guiding me to jack him off with short, hard pulls, the way men do it to themselves. The way men do it to other men. He comes with a quiet grunt, and after I clean him with a warm washcloth from the bathroom, he folds me into his arms and drifts off to sleep immediately, whatever monster he awoke within himself tonight finally, finally sated.

CHAPTER 20

SIX WEEKS LATER

THE SNOW IS FALLING THICK AND FAST OUTSIDE AS EMBRY walks into the room with a bowl of fresh popcorn. "Can you explain this to me again?" he asks, setting the bowl down on the coffee table in front of Ash and me. "Is this like a Martha Stewart thing? Is this because cranberries are disgusting and serve no other purpose?"

Ash looks up from the cranberry and popcorn garland spilling out of his lap and around his feet, a needle poised in one hand. "Did your family really never do this?" he asks skeptically.

Embry arches an eyebrow at the mess of popcorn and cranberries and thread. "No."

Ash goes back to his work, reaching into the bowl of warm popcorn to thread another piece onto his garland. "I suppose you and Morgan had servants to decorate your family Christmas tree."

"Actually," Embry says, "we did. The trees were too big

for us to put up ourselves, and the one in the main hall had to be decorated using scaffolding."

"Sounds like it would have taken a lot of popcorn," I comment, not looking up from my own garland.

"The hidden costs of wealth," Ash remarks drily.

"We did have the mistletoe, though," Embry says. I glance up at the doorway where our own bunch of mistletoe hangs; Ash insisted on putting it up there the minute we got to the lodge, and then kissed me for several long, sweet minutes underneath it as Embry watched with a troubled expression and his hands in his pockets.

"We need someone to kiss you under the mistletoe, Embry," I say.

"I agree," he replies. "Maybe one of the Secret Service agents will be lonely later tonight."

We all laugh, but a wave of sadness goes through me for Embry. The perennial third wheel.

I'd kiss you if I could, I wish I could say. Maybe he already knows.

Embry grabs a handful of popcorn for himself and throws his body onto a low sofa nearby, and for a few minutes, there's only the sound of the fire in the fireplace and the snow against the windows and the rustle of popcorn in the bowl. Then I ask Ash, "Have you heard from Kay about the Carpathian treaty yet?"

He shakes his head. "I told her to give it a rest tonight. There's no point in her spending her holiday chasing down senators who are ready to enjoy theirs."

It's Christmas Eve, and Ash, Embry, and I are at Camp David. Kay and Ash's mother are coming for Christmas dinner tomorrow night, but for now, it's just us and the Secret Service. Even the nation is quiet right now—there have only been a handful of texts from Kay and Belvedere since we got here this morning. Ash and his staff have been working hard to get senatorial advice and consent for the new Carpathian treaty, in the hopes of having it inked and signed before spring comes and a land offensive from the Carpathians becomes possible.

Other than the work on the treaty, though, it's been a quiet December. Quiet for the three of us as well—six weeks have passed without a repeat of what happened between us the night of the state dinner. We haven't even talked about it.

But even without talking about it, something seems to have shifted. Embry—widely famous for having a different date for every event—still has a new woman on his arm almost every night, and there are times he comes into the Oval Office or the Residence with swollen lips and tousled hair, smelling like sex. Knowing he's fucking other women—and lots of them—hurts a secret corner of me that I refuse to let anyone see, but it's a secret corner that's used to it. During the campaign especially, Embry's playboy status was a running joke among pundits, and unlike Ash, he's never brought up his sexual history to me, never made me any promises, and he doesn't have to, because we aren't together. I have no claim to his sex life, and I've accepted that, even though it stings.

Embry's fucking his way through the Beltway elite aside, he's seemed more attached to Ash and me than ever since the state dinner. At night, he'll leave whatever party or gala he's at and join us at the Residence, freshly fucked and still wearing a rumpled suit or tuxedo, and watch television with us or help me sort through medieval research. On Sunday mornings, he's there next to us in church, and on Sunday afternoons, he's stretched out on the sofa in the Residence living room, yelling about football with Ash and teasing me about Nathaniel Hawthorne or whichever American writer we've decided to hate that day. In the mornings, when I'm getting ready to sneak out of the Residence without being seen, Embry is there with coffee and a newspaper, and the three of us share a quiet breakfast before the sun breaks over the horizon, sipping coffee and waking up for the day. Embry's sewn himself into the rhythms of our days, so much so that whenever he's gone, it feels like something's unraveled.

And through all that, Ash and I still haven't slept together. Something that bothers me more and more every day.

No man can take things that slow, trust me. Not unless he's getting it from somewhere else.

Ugh.

I push Morgan's words out of my head and try to focus on my popcorn-and-cranberry garland. Try to focus on how happy I am to be here, snowbound and as alone with Ash and Embry as I've ever been. I get to have them both to myself for an entire day and night, and I mean to enjoy every minute of it.

"Anyway," Ash says after a minute, going back to our conversation about the treaty, "I think I mostly convinced the senators we need."

"Convinced is a kind word for it," I tease. He's spent the last five weeks meeting personally with every senator on his list, wooing, cajoling, threatening, leveraging—you name it, Ash has done it in order to keep the United States from going back to war. "I hear some congressmen are actually physically frightened of you right now."

Ash shrugs, but he smiles down at his garland. "Whatever works."

"No work talk," Embry complains, flinging an arm over his face. His voice is muffled when he speaks again. "I hate work."

"Says the man who read my daily briefing out loud to us in the car."

"I did it to stop you from playing more of that awful music," Embry says from under his arm.

"Christmas music?"

A stifled groan. "Yesssss."

"Bah humbug," Ash says, leaning down to bite off the string with his teeth. He makes a knot at the end of the garland and then puts his needle on the table. "Are you going to help us hang these up or what?"

"What do you think?"

But then he heaves himself off the couch and helps us anyway, criticizing our garland placement before pushing us out of the way and doing it himself. Ash laughs and pulls me back, standing behind me and wrapping his arms around my stomach. He rests his chin on my shoulder. "This should be every Christmas."

Embry scoffs, long fingers plucking at the garland to make it drape evenly along the boughs. "Shitty decorations and the three of us bickering?"

I feel Ash smile, feel the genuine longing in his voice when he answers, "Yes."

————

That afternoon, as the snow lets up and the December sunlight begins to wane over the woods, Ash asks me to go on a walk. Embry is stretched out on the floor, asleep after a lazy afternoon watching *A Christmas Story* and drinking scotch; there's a white puff stuck in his hair from when I threw popcorn kernels at him to try and wake him up.

"He'll be fine," Ash says, handing me my coat. "He never gets to nap since I forced him to run for office with me. We should let him sleep."

I pull the coat on and wind a scarf around my neck, which Ash uses to tug me close enough to kiss. "You're beautiful," he murmurs. "Even all bundled up."

I press my lips to his, letting him part my lips with his own. I taste him—all mint and scotch and a hint of popcorn—and sigh happily. But when we pull apart, there's something resigned in his face.

"Ash?" I ask. "Is something wrong?"

He looks at me for a long moment, his brow creased and that gorgeous mouth turned down at the corners. He doesn't answer my question. Instead, he says, "Let's go on that walk."

After a brief word to Luc, the lead agent on duty, we head out to the woods, following a narrow trail into the trees. The snow is deep and thick, untouched, and walking through it soon has our breath coming out in huge puffs of smoke. Ash looks like a model in his scarf and wool coat, belted jeans and boots. For a moment, I stop walking and just look at him as he continues ahead, long legs making easy work of the snow.

How is this my life? Stringing garlands with the president, watching the vice president fall asleep like a teenaged boy on the floor? It feels so surreal, dreamlike, like I fell asleep in my office at Georgetown and conjured this new life for myself.

Ash notices I'm not with him and turns to me. "What is it, little princess?"

"Nothing." I shake my head and smile. "Just thinking about how blessed I am."

This should make Ash smile in return, make him happy, but instead there's a new shadow in his eyes. He walks back to me and takes my hand, the leather of our gloves creaking together in the cold. "This way," he says, pointing to an opening through the trees. "There's a spot I like right through there."

We move in that direction and come upon a sweet little rill, lined with ice but still running, tracing a silver path through the woods. There's a massive stump next to it, which Ash brushes the snow off of, and then we sit together, pink noses and frosty breath, listening to the narrow stream trickle past.

Ash doesn't speak for a long time, and I don't push him, even though his uncharacteristic unhappiness has me worried.

Is he going to end things between us?

The thought slams into me like a meteor, sending buried fears and insecurities flying like debris. Is this about Embry? About the glances we can't help but exchange in the hallways or those mostly accidental brushes of the shoulder in the elevator?

Or was Morgan right? Is he sleeping with someone else? Oh God, what if it's her?

I knew this was too good to be true. I *knew* it. And I chose to believe anyway because I wanted it so badly.

I'm curling my fingers against my palms, trying to control the panic racing through me, when Ash finally speaks. "Do you believe we're responsible for the sins of our fathers?"

I'm startled by the unexpected topic. "No, not at all."

"Original sin?"

"As much as I like Saint Augustine, no."

He smiles at me, small lines crinkling around his eyes. "You're a bad Catholic."

"I love the Church, but it's hard to convince me that two words can sum up human nature. Especially since Jesus himself never mentioned it."

The crinkles go deeper. "Hippie."

I put my hand on his leg, squeezing the firm muscle. "What's wrong?"

The smile fades and he looks away from me, stretching out his legs, making it impossible for me to keep my hand there. As if he doesn't want to be touched. By me. That meteor is still glowing hot and destructive in my chest, and my cheeks flush red with embarrassment and fear.

"I wanted this to be a happy getaway. Just the three of us, no work or stress. No papers for you to grade. Just us and popcorn garlands and the snow."

"It is happy," I say, trying to search his face for answers. "*I'm* happy. Are you not?"

He lets out a long breath. "No. I'm not."

I'm being burned alive with fear now. There's no way this conversation will end happily, no way he brought me out here to tell me something good. I reach for him. "Ash, if this is about—"

He holds up a hand. "I guarantee you that whatever you think this is about, it's not."

"I don't know," I reply slowly. "I'm thinking a lot of things right now."

He pauses and then speaks. "It's about Morgan Leffey."

My hand freezes in midair. "What?"

"I know. I know."

I drop my hand, and my voice trembles when I ask, "Are you…are you sleeping with her?"

His head snaps to mine. "Excuse me?"

"Is that why we haven't slept together? Because you're sleeping with her? Because you go to the club with her, and maybe you secretly want someone less submissive in bed and—"

In an instant he's straddling the stump so he can frame my face with his hands. "Angel," he says. "I haven't been to the club since I saw you that Sunday in church. And I certainly haven't slept with Morgan again—and I can vow to you right now that I *never* will. You'll understand why in a few minutes, but I just want you to know right now that you are perfect for me in every way. In bed and out of it."

"Then why are we talking about this?" I whisper.

"We're not. We're talking about the sins of our fathers. Well, just my father, actually."

His father. Penley Luther.

"Merlin told me he explained the whole story to you, except I think…well, I know he didn't tell you the whole story."

245

I wrinkle my forehead. "There's more?"

He blows out a big breath. "Yeah. One thing more. The name of my birth mother. Do you know it?"

I shake my head. Presidents live on in history books and vice presidents live on in crossword clues, but senior advisors certainly don't live on anywhere. Much less a senior advisor that died before I was born.

"Her name was Imogen." He closes his eyes. "Imogen Leffey."

"Leffey," I repeat.

"Yes." He opens his eyes. "Leffey. She was also Morgan Leffey's mother."

There it is. The rumors Abilene and Merlin alluded to. The crucial fact I had forgotten about Morgan at the state dinner. The fact that her dead mother used to work in the presidential cabinet. And that indescribable something I saw in her that reminded me of someone else...it hadn't been Embry at all. It was Ash I saw in her face, Ash's green eyes and black hair and high cheekbones and sensual mouth.

Ash, Ash, *Ash*.

Her *brother*.

"You and Morgan had the same mother?" I ask slowly, numbly. "You're...you're brother and sister?"

"Half-brother and half-sister, yes."

"And you...*you*..."

All the disgust I could ever feel, all the horror and revulsion and judgment, all that and more is in his voice when he answers. "Yes. I fucked her. I fucked my own sister."

He looks up to my eyes, and in those green depths, I see wells of self-hatred and guilt so deep they scare me. "I didn't know the truth at the time. I still don't know if she did. What is it that T.H. White says in *The Once and Future King*? 'It seems in tragedy that innocence is not enough'? Well, it's true. She came to visit Embry while we took an R and R in

246

Prague, the first woman out of uniform I'd actually talked to in months, and I pursued her. Fucked her against an alley wall with the Prague castle looking down over us. Took her back to my hotel room and we barely left it the whole week. She was the first woman who ever let me dominate her. Who encouraged it. And I took that encouragement and spent the week using her every way she'd let me."

He chews on his lip, the guilt practically slicing up from under his skin. "So you see, it doesn't matter that I didn't know. I still did it. I *chose* it. I *enjoyed* it. I even had fond memories of it until Jenny's funeral."

I remember Merlin's story. "That's when she told you."

He smiles bitterly. "Yes. The perfect time for her, I suppose. A way to gut me and try to ruin my campaign. But then why take me to the club and try to help me the very next week? Sometimes I think she herself doesn't know how she really feels about me."

"Merlin said her father raised her to hate you."

Ash shrugs, looking down to where the gold of my hair spills out from underneath my hat. He twines the ends around his leather-clad fingers. "That's true. I don't doubt that in the least, but"—a pause—"she hates me because of something else. Something I did in Carpathia."

"To her? But I'm sure you didn't mean to. You helped so many people there, saved so many lives."

He swallows. "I'm not a hero, Greer. I hate it when people say that. I did the best I could, I tried to win battles and save my fellow soldiers and as many civilians as I could, but I did bad things there. All those men I killed...so many... and God, I wish I'd shot them all. *I wish.* But so many of the battles were in villages and towns; we were clearing out places building by building, room by room. I stabbed them. Strangled them. Beat them to death. At the end of the war, they'd resorted to using teenagers, just barely tall enough to fit into their uniforms, and not just boys but girls too. Do you know what it's like to be attacked in the dark, to stab or punch or choke and then get out your flashlight and realize you've just killed a teenage girl?"

"Ash," I say softly. "I had no idea."

A joyless laugh. "Now you know why I can't sleep."

"So what happened with Morgan?"

He keeps his gaze studiously on my hair. "She came to visit the base a few months after that week in Prague. It was a little outside official channels, but the Leffeys are a powerful family, the kind that can pull strings whenever and wherever they want. And it was a secure base—we thought—before war was declared, before we knew there would be a real war.

"One day…well, there was a town famous for its medieval church nearby, next to a little lake. Morgan went that morning to tour the church, and we didn't think anything of it. Except that evening, we got word that the separatists were getting close, and we had to evacuate the civilians in the town. But we were too late. The separatists got there first. It ended up being the first real battle of what would become the war. *My* first real battle.

"They'd locked up all the men and women they could find in the church while they looted the homes. All the children they'd put on a boat. For security, I think. To keep the adults of the town compliant while they pillaged it, to force the men to join their militia. But maybe there was a miscommunication. Or maybe it was never just for security. By the time we got to the village, the boat was on fire."

My hand flies to my mouth. "With the children?"

Ash nods grimly. "That's all we knew at first. Hostiles present, civilians locked in the church, children on a burning boat."

"What did you do?"

"I was only barely in command then. Just a second

248

lieutenant. I was so young, and I..." He looks hopeless. "I chose the children. I sent four men to the church. But the rest of us went to the docks. We were dodging enemy fire the whole time, trying to find a couple boats to steal, going across the lake. But we made it. We got to the boat and found an older child fighting off the fire with an extinguisher. We got all seventeen children off safely."

I breathe a sigh of relief. "Oh, thank God."

"But the adults in the church..." His voice is tight, tormented. "I should have known better. I should have realized it was a trap. I should have sent more men. All four killed, and all of the civilians, the church lit on fire. We fought our way to the church, chased off the separatists, and opened the doors to complete carnage and flames. Almost forty men and women shot. Only one survived."

"Morgan?" I guess.

"I knew she was there. I knew the odds of her being in the church were high. But the boat..." Ash spreads his hands out, palms up, as if pleading with me to understand.

"She survived, though. She lived."

Ash slumps those powerful shoulders. "Barely. Shot in the shoulder. She played dead. When we found her, she was underneath two other bodies, unconscious from blood loss and surrounded by fire. When she woke up, the story she heard from the army doctors was that we'd chosen to rescue another group of civilians, even though we knew she was in the church. I don't think any other circumstances mattered to her after that."

"But that's so unfair!" I explode. "Anyone would have chosen the children!"

"Greer, she almost died. It was mere luck that the bullet missed anything vital, and even more luck that we managed to pull her out before the church burned down around her. She would have died because I didn't properly allocate my men, because I didn't think about the situation critically enough. Yes, I had to choose those children, but there was a way I could have saved everyone, and I didn't see it. I was too panicked and inexperienced, and it almost cost her life. Of course she hates me. I knew she was in danger and I chose not to come after her."

"I still think it's unfair," I maintain. "You did the best you could."

"You've been in politics long enough to know that sometimes our best isn't good enough."

I turn so that I'm straddling the stump as well, scooting forward so that I can slide my legs over Ash's legs and wrap them around his waist. I put my arms around him and press my face against his neck. "It's good enough for me," I say against his skin. "*You* are good enough for me. Always, always, always."

He pulls back to look at me, brow furrowed. "I'm telling you that I fucked my sister and almost killed her, and you're comforting *me*? I thought you'd want to run away. I told you this so that you could...escape."

I press my hand against his jaw, my thumb touching his lower lip. It's so soft and firm all at once, just like Ash. Strength and beauty and determination combined into one heady mix. "Is this why you were so unhappy earlier? Because you thought telling me about Morgan would make me leave you?"

He nods miserably. "I'd deserve it, Greer. And I couldn't let us move forward without you knowing the worst of me. It wouldn't be fair to you."

"Even if it wasn't fair, I'd still stay. I'd endure anything to stay. But I don't see this as the worst of you. These sins are the sins of a good man, not the sins of a cursed one."

"I feel cursed sometimes." His lips move against my thumb. "Only when I'm with you and Embry do I feel some

250

sort of sanity. Like there can be good things in life for me, even after all the evil I've done."

"Oh, Ash." I look up into his eyes. "War may be evil, but you're not, and if it took killing all those people to bring you here to me, then I won't allow you to torment yourself with these things any longer. I don't care what you've done; I care what you *do* and that you're here with me now."

He sucks in a breath and searches my face. I see the faint sheen of unshed tears in his eyes, hear the swallow of his throat. "Do you really mean that?" he whispers.

"Yes." It comes out clear, honest.

The truth of my answer hits him like a bullet to a Kevlar vest. Blunt force, ragged exhale, fractured man. He collapses into me, his arms pulling me so close that I can feel him even through the heavy wool of our coats, and he buries his face into my hair. "What did I do to deserve you?" he mumbles.

I'll always love the other versions of Ash—the cool-headed politician, the beloved hero-president, the fierce dominant—but this version? This broken-down, vulnerable man? There isn't a word strong enough. There's this vibrating in my bones, in my blood, somewhere on the cellular level, a vibration like every single one of my atoms wants to fly away and fuse to his atoms. This is more than wanting to bleed or bruise or kneel; this is more than listening to the same speech over and over, sacrificing sleep and time to go over policies and strategies. This is wanting to come apart for him, literally. This is wanting to burrow so deeply inside of him that he has to carry me with him forever. This is being flayed open, bleeding, whipped, scourged, just wounds on top of wounds on top of wounds, each wound a whisper of promise.

you can own me
because now I know I own you
give me more
and I'll give you everything

And that's when I find the courage to finally say it. "I love you."

"God, those words from your mouth," he says with feeling, moving his mouth from my hair to my lips. "I don't deserve it, but *fuck*, I'll take it."

He kisses me, that trembling honesty heating into a molten urgency. "I love you," he breathes into my mouth. "Surely you already know that. You must know."

"I do now," I pant in between kisses, cursing all the leather and wool that keeps our bodies from pressing together the way I need. But the moment I start rocking my hips against his, he straightens up and smiles.

"I have something for you," he says, biting his lip like a shy child.

"A Christmas present?"

"Yes. I wanted to wait until after I told you about Morgan to give it to you... I didn't want you to think I was trying to manipulate your reaction."

I roll my eyes at his incessant chivalry. "You are so circumspect for a man who spends his nights spanking me until I can't breathe."

"That's precisely why I'm circumspect," he says and slides off the stump, and I immediately miss his warmth. Then I realize what he's doing, and my entire body flushes with hot, happy disbelief.

He's kneeling.

In two feet of snow, he's kneeling.

Behind him, the stream is a twisted silver wire, the trees are leafless sentinels, the snow is a never-ending cloak of glittering fleece. There's color high in his cheeks—from the cold or emotion, I don't know—and he's still boyishly chewing on his lip, nervous and excited. Between his leather-clad fingers is a ring, platinum and diamond, glittering in the fading light.

"I wanted to do this later tonight, but I can't wait," he says. "Greer Galloway, will you marry me?"

My heart thuds painfully against my chest, like it's trying to punch its way out, and I feel my molecules leaving my body, blowing away like leaves before a storm to seek out Ash. Our breath, our life, it's already tangled, and finally, finally, finally I understand what people mean when they talk about destiny. What they mean when they talk about *meant to be*. Why the fairy tales didn't waste time explaining how the prince and the princess fell in love, because all along it was as natural and inevitable as breathing.

I join him in the snow, ignoring the cold, wet bite of it through my jeans. I cup the hand holding the ring with both of my own, and then drop kisses along the exposed line of flesh between his sleeve and his glove. I lift my head, dizzy with happiness.

"Yes."

CHAPTER 21

EMBRY'S NOWHERE TO BE SEEN WHEN WE GET BACK TO THE lodge, and after we shuck our coats and unwind our scarves, Ash puts a finger to my lips. I nod to show that I understand, and then he's leading me by the hand through the lodge, back to our bedroom. It feels like sneaking, like we're cheating on Embry somehow by creeping so quietly back to our room, but I have no idea why I feel like this. Ash and I have every right to go to bed together, and maybe hiding it from Embry is the kindest thing to do…given the circumstances.

Oh God.

The circumstances.

I have to tell Ash about Embry and me now. After his confession about Morgan, after his firm insistence that we move forward without secrets, it would be shamefully dishonest of me not to tell him. But if I'm truthful with myself, I recognize that I'm afraid. Afraid Ash will be angry…and maybe I'm a little afraid that he won't be angry enough. I'm afraid Embry will feel betrayed that I told our secret without asking him. I'm afraid that if I admit what happened in Chicago, Ash will suspect I still have feelings for Embry and that will be the end of any real trust between us. Because really, how can the three of us ever trust each other once the truth is laid bare?

Trust without truth isn't actually trust, I remind myself. And if there's any time to rectify that, it's right now. With a ring on my finger and Ash's confessions still echoing in my thoughts.

But when I walk into our room and Ash shuts the door behind me, he presses his finger to my lips again.

"I've wanted to do this since the first time we met," he speaks, pushing close to me. His erection presses into my belly. "I've been fantasizing about it for ten years."

I take a short, stilted breath beneath his finger. Is he saying what I think he's saying?

His other hand drops down to find mine, to play idly with the new ring on my finger. "It's not going to be easy, being my wife. There will be so much scrutiny and so much sacrifice, and I'll forever be asking you to step between public and private roles—sometimes with no transition or warning. But right now...right now, it's just the two of us. Right now those things are far away. And right now, I'm going to make you completely mine."

I look up into his eyes. "Is it... Are we..." I feel like I can't catch my breath.

He grins down at me. "Yes, my impatient angel. I'm not going to torture us any longer."

I drop to my knees. Not because he's going to fuck me—although that's part of it too—but because I love him so much. Because I'm so grateful. Because he's Ash and I'm Greer, and when we're alone, I belong on my knees.

It's as simple and as complicated as that.

He strokes my hair, tangled and messy from the hat I wore outside, and allows me to rub my cheek against his thigh. "My beautiful angel," he murmurs down at me. "My little princess. How have I lived so long without you?"

I don't know, God, *I don't know*, but now that we're together, I don't know how I lived this long either. Survived, yes. But *living*—how did that ever happen before I was able to sit at Ash's feet?

Reluctantly I pull back, bowing my head and placing my palms flat on my thighs. He lets out a long breath, and his hands leave my hair. And then he kneels down in front of me, his hands covering mine, his head ducking so he can meet my eyes.

"Greer, I want to give you what you want. This first time, I want you to let me serve you, and I want you to let me take care of you. There's no need for our first time to be...well. You know."

I'm shaking my head before he even finishes. So fucking chivalrous. So fucking wary of himself. It's both commendable and painfully exasperating—especially now, with my nipples pulled into aching beads and my pussy already swelling with the thought of Ash inside of me. Part of me distantly recognizes that this is a first for him too—he's been married and he's dominated in a club setting, but this is the first time he's ever mingled love with kink, and he wants to make sure that I get both in equal balance.

But still.

"I want what *you* want. You know that you aren't forcing me, right? You know that I'm not merely playing along? I *choose* this. I choose you. Every time I kneel, I know that I can stand back up, and every time you push me, I know I can say your name and make it all stop. And when you do things to me, I have just as much power over them as if I were doing them myself, because I can stop you at any time. I'm choosing what I want, and what I want is you how you are."

He's peering deep into my eyes now, and I hope he can see

the truth there, just like he always can. A tiny flume of anger courses through me, and I give it passage through my words.

"You want to know what else I want? I want what I dreamed about ten years ago too. I want to be dragged to the edge of shame and fear and darkness, I want to not recognize myself, and I want you to be the glorious, demanding beast that you are. You want to take care of me? Then fucking own me. Wreck me. Tear me up and sew me back together the way that only you know how."

His lips crash into mine, a kiss not meant to convey love but a kind of deep gratitude, a sort of hot joy. "You perfect thing," he says huskily, his voice already melting into his Other Voice, the one that haunts my sweetest dreams. "You unimaginably perfect thing."

And with the ease and grace that comes with strength, he rises fluidly to his feet. "Take off my shoes."

Relief, happiness, *right*ness, it all twines around the arousal, making it sharper and brighter.

I do as he asks, trying to hide my happy smile behind my curtain of hair as I tug at the laces, but he sees the smile anyway.

"Are you a happy angel?" he asks. "Serving me?"

"Yes, Mr. President."

"I'm happy when you serve me. It pleases me to see you on your knees." He resumes his idle caresses of my hair as I carefully lever one shoe off and start on the other. After I finish with that, he bids me to stand up and he starts undressing me, his fingers sliding between fabric and skin and lingering there before he peels the clothes from my body, his eyes hot on every new inch exposed. He strips me like you'd strip old wallpaper or faded carpet to get to the antique house underneath, utilitarian and anticipatory and disdainful and reverent all at the same time. And soon I'm completely naked, shivering in the cold room.

His fingers brush against my nipples and I squeak, my body starving for real stimulation.

He gives a chuckle. "Eager, are we?"

I don't dare answer. Every time I play this game with Ash, it feels like the first time, like I'm peeling back a new layer of myself with every humiliation I endure, revealing a woman pink-skinned and raw and glowing underneath.

"Hands on the footboard of the bed. Legs spread."

I obey, swallowing. I know what's coming next, and sure enough I feel a large hand between my shoulder blades. It runs a gentle, almost exploratory, path down my spine, and then rubs circles on my ass and flanks.

"Breathe, angel."

Crack.

The first one is never that bad. No, the first one is fun in a way, like being scared at a haunted house or jumping into a cold pool on a hot day. Startling, bracing, sending sensation sparking down your legs.

Crack.

Crack.

Crack.

"Breathe," my master repeats.

I breathe in.

Crack, crack, crack.

I breathe out.

"Again."

I breathe again.

Ash deliberately disrupts the rhythm, making sure I relax before he strikes, or that he strikes several times in quick succession so that my body has no choice but to yield to his dominance. Pain shimmers behind my sternum like a living entity, pulling at my lungs and stomach, and my hands shake as they try to grip the footboard. My whole body shakes, and there's heat glowing in my eyes. I'll be crying soon. Very soon.

My feet scrabble at the floor as Ash continues his assault, a leg involuntarily kicking up and trying to cover my ass with my foot. Ash pushes it back down with a noise that can only be described as evil delight, and spanks me all the harder for my resistance. *Crack* goes his hand, and there's the heavy panting of his breath, and the pain in my chest like a familiar houseguest, rifling through my feelings like a pantry, tossing out fear and anger and humiliation and leaving behind a deep mindlessness that feels almost like bliss. There's only the pain and Ash, and everything else shrinks to a pinpoint and vanishes.

Crack, crack, crack.

And then Ash is folding his body over top of mine, his jeans scratching painfully at my raw ass, his thick cock hard as steel against my flesh. He fists my hair and yanks my head back so he can kiss my cheeks.

No…so he can kiss the *tears* on my cheeks. The visible and undeniable proof of my submission.

In a wrenching instant, his body is gone over mine, and I actually moan a little at the loss. Only to moan again as I feel his mouth somewhere other than my cheek, somewhere much, much better.

It starts with a kiss on my pussy, an almost chaste one, if such a thing can exist. Then it blossoms into wet, warm caresses, his tongue tracing up from my clit to my entrance, firm on one stroke, flat and wide on the next. The pain where I was spanked flares around the hot point of his mouth like the corona of a sun, like the halo around a saint, the golden thing that highlights the beauty within its circle.

He rubs my back as he tongues me, pets my thighs as if I were a horse that needed gentling, and God help me, I love it. I buck into his touch, practically purring as he runs his warm hands over my abused flesh, and occasionally I hear him chuckle to himself as I get especially eager. The pain subsides, but the bliss stays, and all that nibbling and licking and sucking is stirring a twisting pressure in the cradle of my pelvis. I'm going to come soon, the delicious kind of orgasm that can only happen after pain and pain-triggered endorphins, but then something unexpected happens. Ash's hands come to rest on my ass, and slowly, ever so slowly, they spread my cheeks apart so that I have no secrets from him. I'm completely exposed.

The twisting pressure freezes mid-twist, discomfort and embarrassment managing to gouge their way past the bliss.

"Ash, I've never—"

He silences me with one lick. One brush of his tongue against my darkest secret. The sensation is like nothing I've ever felt, too shallow, too slick, too dirty, too *everything*, and I squirm frantically away from him. A hundred what-ifs run through my mind, only to be chased away by a fingertip and Ash's stern voice.

"This is *mine*, little princess. My hole. Yes?"

The fingertip is probing. Pushing. Gradually and almost lazily breaching my most elemental barrier.

His other hand comes up to slap my ass, right on top of the spots still raw from the spanking. My leg kicks up and he impatiently pushes it back down. "I asked you a question. Is this mine?"

Oh, the invasion. How small it must look and yet how big it feels. "Yes, sir," I answer, my voice cracking on the last word.

"That's right," he says arrogantly. "This one and this one"—a finger enters my pussy—"and your mouth. Every hole belongs to me, doesn't it?"

"Y-yes, sir."

The finger finally tunnels past the first ring of muscle, sinking up to a knuckle. I sputter and pant and kick my legs, and all I get for my pains are more spanks.

"And this ass—this is mine to bite or to spank. And the hole there, that's mine to lick. Mine to play with. Mine to fuck. Isn't that right?"

"That's right," I gasp.

"Mine to show off, mine to display. I could order you to display yourself in the middle of the Oval Office, to pull down whatever pretty pencil skirt you're wearing and have you bend over for inspection, like a prize animal at a show. Would you like that?"

The thought is so degrading, so awful, that of course it triggers a wave of submissive lust.

"You don't have to answer, Greer. Your pussy just answered for me."

I press my face into the bed, humiliated, shaking, on the precipice of orgasm. The finger leaves, replaced by his tongue again, but this time he doesn't stop at licking. This time he pushes the tip of his tongue into the pleated rosebud, sending a frisson of filthy electricity straight to my clit.

The pleasure is undeniable and immediate, but so is the shame, the reflexive resistance. My hands fly back instinctively to push him away, my legs trying to close, and that earns me an angry growl. Ash wrestles my wrists away from myself and kicks my legs back open with a grunt.

"I could fuck you like this," he hisses. "Holding you down. Is that what you want?"

My answering moan fills the room.

His arm wraps around my waist like an iron bar and then I'm lifted bodily from my feet and tossed onto the bed, as if I weighed nothing more than a sack of flour. "On your stomach. Show me your face."

Moving my limbs takes a strange kind of effort, as if the leashed-up orgasm inside my body is weighing me down, but I manage, and there's a moment of unfiltered tenderness when I feel Ash's fingers gently brushing my hair away from my forehead, sweeping it over my head so it won't tickle my face. He drops a light kiss onto my jaw. "Doing okay?"

"I'd do better if you'd fuck me."

He laughs. "I love it when you get desperate. What's your safe word?"

"Maxen."

"Keep it close at hand. We're going to try something new."

He straightens up, and from my vantage, I see his strong and certain fingers as they work his belt open and slide it from the loops. I swallow as I watch him double up the belt and run it through his palm.

My mouth parts, protests rise to my lips. I've never been belted before, never had anything more intense than a hairbrush, but before I can run through my options, before I can rationalize this or ask him to stop or to pause, he lets fly with the belt and a leather stripe of pain hits my upper thighs.

It's agony. It's unbearable. The breath leaves my body as I arch backward and my mind goes blank. There's nothing but pain, nothing but the sparking static of it, and when I finally draw in a breath, it comes in and back out as a choked sob.

Maxen.

For the first time ever, my safe word is there on my tongue, ready to be spoken.

"Too much?"

He asks right as a shot of endorphins hits my bloodstream, right as a pulse of swollen arousal hits my cunt.

"Don't you dare stop."

The belt flies again, slicing through the air with a whistle, higher up on my thighs this time, on the crease between my legs and ass. A real sob comes out, an actual cry, and I'm writhing and burying my face in the bed.

"Angel."

I sense rather than see his arm pull back, and I know—I

just *know*—this one will be on my ass, on the skin already inflamed and welted from his hand. The moment hangs in the air like the belt, and as I draw in another shuddering breath, I realize this is my chance to say his name. My chance to end this.

But I won't.

I press my lips closed, sucking in my crying breaths through my nose. The belt falls, and my lips open right back up in a scream.

All across my ass there's fire—not just where the belt's hit but *everywhere*, as if the skin ignited under the leather and the flames spread instantly everywhere else. My scream dies into a sobbing groan, the blanket underneath my face is wet with tears, and I'm rubbing my face against it without even knowing it.

I hear the belt drop to the floor. "Oh, Greer."

His voice is as broken as I feel, as flayed raw.

"My little princess," he murmurs, crawling onto the bed over me. His hand slides between my stomach and the bed, and then I'm turned over as gently as child so that I'm on my back. "Such a good angel. Such a sweet, obedient princess."

Through my tears, I see his eyes like green fires in the dark.

"Ash," I choke out.

His head bows and then his mouth is at my cunt, eating me like a man possessed. Wildly, with noises coming from his throat as he tastes me, with the passion of worship. And somehow, magically, my orgasm is fusing itself back together, ten thousand times stronger for all the pain, as if all the nerve endings singing along my skin have now all joined together to sing in pleasure.

My groans turn into moans, moans into whimpers, and I hear Ash say with his lips against my clit, "Come on, angel, take it. Take it from me."

He slides a finger into my vagina, and then another, and then a third probes at the tight hole underneath, and I explode. Into a tornado of misery and shame and pain and sensation, into a storm of bliss and pleasure so raw and fierce that my womb cramps hard as it contracts. I think I'm screaming again, and I'm definitely crying as this climax tears through me, punches a hole straight through me like a hammer through Sheetrock. I can barely see, barely hear— it's just feel, feel, *feel*, as I come with my skin on fire and my muscles sizzling.

I'm not finished orgasming when Ash moves up over me, one hand working his fly open. He doesn't bother to undress all the way, just yanks his pants down far enough to expose his cock and then finds my still-clenching hole and presses his tip to it. I'm so wet that he's able to notch himself at my entrance with no effort, and then he pushes into my swollen pussy with a grunt that curls my toes.

Or maybe it's his giant cock curling my toes. It's hard to tell.

He pulls back and shoves back in—it's a tight, tight fit—and I whimper at the stretching feeling as he buries himself to the hilt.

"Fuck, I'm so hard for this," he pants. "Feel how hard I am. Feel how big."

I can, I *do*. I'm impaled on his bigness, speared on eight throbbing inches, and I might as well be a virgin again. It's the same kind of perfect discomfort that I felt with Embry, a pain that seems to scratch a deep, deep itch on the inside of my body, the kind of pain that draws me toward pleasure almost against my will because it's so very, very right.

He's still wearing his sweater over a button-down shirt, and the fabric brushes against my erect nipples every time he thrusts and moves over me, reminding me that I'm naked and he's not, I'm vulnerable and he's in control. Sex with

Embry was wildfire, uncontrollable lust, two storm fronts colliding in an eruption of electricity and noise. But sex with Ash is different—harder and deeper, more intense and more controlled and more spiritual and more everything else possible, and it feels as though he's everywhere inside of me, all over me. His hard body covers mine, his marks burn my ass and thighs, his mouth is hot and biting at my neck and jaw and breasts as his cock possesses me from the inside out.

"Am I bigger than him?" he rasps in my ear. "Do I make you come harder than him?"

I forget for a minute that he doesn't know it's Embry, that to my sir, *him* is just a mysterious male-shaped silhouette from my past, and I'm nodding. I'm gasping yes. Yes, yes, it's all true, because in this moment, there's no man bigger or harder than Ash. There is no man other than Ash, and he makes me feel like there's no other woman, as if his entire life and purpose is to hold me down and fuck the life out of me.

He keeps talking; he tells me how beautiful I am, how precious, how good I make him feel. How tight my sweet cunt is, how it squeezes him, how much he likes making my tits move with each shove of his hips, how he's going to fill me up so full that I'm dripping for days.

I reach for him, for his sweater or for his hips, but my hands are wrestled back down over my head, and Ash pins both forearms there with one hand. The submissive pose unleashes something dark in him, some animal intent on ravaging and marking, a monster that saws its perfect dick in and out of me so fast and so hard that a stream of words escape my mouth, nonsense words mixed with uncontrolled noises and grunts, *yes* and *no* and *oh oh oh* and *please more please sir please please*.

I'm being hammered, I'm completely at his mercy, and he's so big, it *hurts*, it hurts. Even I can't tell if the whine from my throat is pain or pleasure, and then he changes the angle of his hips, and the entire world flips over. Suddenly, like before but even stronger, the pain joins forces with the building orgasm, rendering me senseless. Speechless. I'm nothing, I'm everything. I'm the light and the dark and the air and the void. Strong force, weak force, gravity, electricity, magnetism are all pinning me underneath this violent, tragic soldier, and as he fucks the literal breath out of me and as I see stars and as I squirm in abject pleasure, I know everything is true. String theory, magic, multiple lives, miracles, God, parallel universes, it's all true and it's all real and it's all happening inside me right now at this very instant as my climax detonates like a dying star inside me.

It's not a gratification, this orgasm—it's gospel. It's good news. It's revelation and apocalypse. It's joy and judgment and the answer to every question I've ever asked. Everything in my life has led to this one moment, this one exchange, this one feeling of my body shuddering uncontrollably under Ash's.

"Take it," he's saying into my ear. "Take your pleasure. Take *me*." And I do, I do, I take my pleasure and I take him and I take me, and then like the most poignant sacrifice, like the most tender death, Ash pulls me close and, his body rigid and frozen over mine, erupts inside me. He's got one hand cradling my head and the other holding my hip down, and his mouth hovers above my mouth, so every soft grunt and needy pant is warm against my lips. I feel every throb and every pulse, every hot spurt of him, and there's so much that he's spilling out of me.

He keeps himself buried to the hilt until he's finished, and then he kneels up without pulling out, stroking himself slowly with his tip still inside me, eyes locked on mine.

The act is so biological, so possessive, that my cunt gives an involuntary clench, ready to come again. He shakes his head at that and pulls out, leaning down to give my pussy a reverent kiss before he climbs off the bed.

And then…and then I'm not sure what happens. He turns on a light and somehow he ends up undressed and in bed cuddling me and crooning to me, stroking my arms and hair and back, and murmuring words of gratitude and pleasure—*he's pleased with me*, I think somewhere deep inside myself and the thought makes me happy. But I can't speak. My hearing feels fuzzy, like I'm hearing everything through earmuffs, and my thoughts are nonexistent. Like I'm floating, blank and warm, but I'm also shaking, trembling like a leaf in the wind.

Bit by bit, layer by layer, I swim up toward consciousness.

"You," I murmur to Ash. It was supposed to be *I love you*, but the words are so fleeting and so hard to form.

"You," he says back to me in a voice so filled with love that I ache. He wraps his body more securely around me and pulls the blankets tighter around us. My shivering slowly, slowly stills, but I become aware of the wet pillow underneath me, my cheeks cool against the air, and realize I've been crying.

Ash holds me as my tears leak out, like a slow, dripping rain. "I love you," he whispers over and over again. "I love you."

Eventually, after a few minutes or a few hours, my tears stop and I feel warm again. I roll over so that I can nestle into him, and he lets out a satisfied growl, as if it made him happy that I sought his comfort. "My princess," he says, holding me tight. My world is this. My world is him. "My angel."

I nuzzle my face against his chest. "Will you hold me for a while longer?"

He kisses my hair. "As long as you want. I could hold you for the rest of my life." He lets out a small laugh. "And anyway, I've never seen someone drop that far and that hard into subspace before. I'm not letting you out of my sight until you've got both feet back here on planet Earth."

Subspace. It's happened a few times after Ash and I have scened together at the Residence, but never like this. Never like a waking blackout, never to where I cry and shiver without feeling either.

But as my mind returns to my body, it also returns to my worries from earlier.

Namely to Embry.

I should have told Ash as he was proposing, before we had sex. I should have told him six weeks ago. I should have told him that day at St. Thomas Becket. I should tell him now.

"Ash," I say, keeping my face away from his. "There's something I need to say."

"Yes?"

"You're not going to like it."

"Try me."

I have no choice. It has to be done. "You know the man who I slept with before? My first time?"

He stiffens around me. "Yes."

"It was Embry."

The world seems to freeze, time ticking on as everything waits in bated stillness. And then Ash says in a wooden voice, "I know."

He knows.

He knows.

Shit.

Fuck.

He kicks the blankets off his legs to climb out of bed. I feel his warmth pull away from me, watch his naked form as he pads into the en suite bathroom and flips on the light. I hear the sink running.

Panic squeezes my throat like a sadist is choking off enough air that I feel dizzy but keeping me conscious enough to witness the almost-certain end of my relationship with Ash.

Ash comes back out of the bathroom with a glass of cold water, which he hands to me. "Drink."

Even though we just had the raunchiest, roughest sex imaginable, I still cover my body with a sheet as I sit up. I drink and he sits on the side of the bed, watching me with his President eyes, the ones that miss nothing. His war eyes. I can't read his face.

I finish drinking and move to set the glass down on the end table, but he reaches forward and takes it from me. For a moment, he looks at the imprint of my lips on the rim of the glass, a muscle ticking in his jaw.

"You know?" I finally ask, my fingers knotting in the sheet.

"I guessed," Ash admits softly.

"How did you guess?"

He pulls his lower lip into his mouth and then releases it. "Let's start at the beginning and work our way up to that. When?"

"Chicago," I answer.

He nods, as if this is confirmation for something he already knows. Maybe it is. Maybe Embry did tell Ash about us, and I just didn't know about it. He rotates the glass in his hands a few times and then sets it down on the table himself.

"It didn't mean anything," I start, but he holds up a hand.

"Don't lie to me. Please."

His tone is guarded, but there's something starkly exposed in his words. As if he wants to beg me for something but doesn't know how or what or even why he needs it.

I take a deep breath and start over. "It meant something to me. How could it not? It was my first time, and it was so good—" I stop and pivot, realizing Ash probably doesn't want to hear about how good that night was. "But Ash, he never even called me after. I left my number and everything,

269

and I heard nothing for years, not until you sent him to me. It must have been the worst lay of his life," I try to joke.

The joke falls flat because Ash is already frowning. "It wasn't."

"Well, that's kind of you to say—"

"I'm not being kind," he snaps. "I know it for a fact."

I stare at him. "How?"

He runs a hand through his raven hair. "Embry called me that morning, wanted to grab coffee. He wanted to tell me all about this…*angel*…he had in his bed. He thought he was in love, even though it'd only been one night. If I had known that his angel was *my* angel, that it was you, I would have thrown myself in front of a train."

"But you didn't know?"

He presses his palms together, fingertips pointing down to the floor, and stares at his hands. "Before he could tell me about his night, I told him about mine. About how this girl I'd met four years before had shown back up in my life. About how I'd been too much of a coward to tell her about Jenny right away, and then she'd discovered it in the worst way possible. I told Embry that this was Email Girl, that those letters I'd kept in my breast pocket all those years in Carpathia had been from her, the letters he caught me reading time and time again. I told him this girl's name."

My mind spins. Embry had known my name too. Which meant…

"And after I finished and tried to be a good friend and ask him about his angel, he changed the subject. And he never mentioned that night again."

"That's why he didn't call, didn't try to find me…" I trail off.

"How selfless of him."

"Back to you guessing. How? We've never…we haven't done anything other than what you wanted us to do that night of the state dinner. We haven't kissed, haven't even hugged."

"I know," Ash says. He crawls forward on the bed and slowly pulls the sheet down, baring my breasts to him. My nipples harden the minute they touch the cool air. "It was that night that helped me see it. He was obviously attracted to you, but…well, there was something else there. Something deeper. And after that, you two were so careful around each other. Never getting too close, never talking too long. Never alone. That's what people do when they're in love with someone they shouldn't be, Greer."

"I'm not in love with Embry."

"I told you not to lie to me." The sheet is all the way pulled down now, and then his hand slides up my sternum to circle my throat. He doesn't squeeze or press, but he makes a collar of his fingers, a collar not of leather or metal but flesh and blood. *You're mine*, the hand says. *You're mine and not his.*

I'm fiddling with my new engagement ring without realizing it, and then his other hand comes down on top of both of mine. "Stop," he says. "You're not giving that back to me. You're not taking it off. As long as you still want it, I will be your husband."

"Yes, sir," I say, relief pricking at my eyelids. He doesn't hate me now; he doesn't want to end our relationship. If nothing else, I can live with that.

His hand presses at my throat, forcing me to lie back.

"How did he do it?"

"Do what?"

"How did he fuck you that night?" Ash is kneeling over me right now, his cock rock-hard and angry looking. "Did he flip you over so he could see your ass? Take you up against the wall because he couldn't wait?"

Maybe I shouldn't answer that. But I do. "It was…like this. Him on top."

Quick as lightning, Ash is stretching his body over mine,

271

his cock pressed against my clit. I can't stop the moan that I let out.

"What else?" Ash asks. His voice is rough. Rougher than I've ever heard it. And his eyes are so dark, no longer green but black.

"He, um, he sucked on my breasts. Bit them. Like he was nursing, but hard and kind of desperate."

Ash lowers his head and nips at the tender curves of my breasts, sucking and teething and kissing, and within half a minute, I'm panting.

"What else?" Ash growls against my tits. "What else did he do?"

"I didn't tell him I was a virgin until he was trying to get inside. And when I did tell him, he got…*mean*. Like it turned him on too much for him to control himself."

In the here and now, there's a wide cock pushing against my folds and then Ash stabs inside so hard I gasp. "Mean like this?" he asks, punctuating his question with several vicious thrusts.

"Yes," I cry out. "There was blood. He liked it. I liked it."

Ash stills, his cock quivering. "There was blood?"

"A lot. It hurt. I came so hard."

"I bet you did," Ash says, jabbing in again. "It should have been me, my cock. That blood and pain should have been mine."

"Everything can be yours now, Mr. President."

"Yes, it can," he growls, rolling his hips and grinding against my clit. I make a low keening noise. "How did he come—on you? Inside you?"

"Inside me," I say, my voice breathless. "He wrapped his arms behind me and put his weight on me. Oh God, yes, just like that."

Ash feels entirely different than Embry—wider, stronger, more deliberate—but in this position, I can so easily summon the memory of Embry's body over mine. I can so easily pretend.

"I want to feel what he felt," Ash tells me, his lips against the place where my jaw and my neck meet. "I want to pretend I'm him. Are you pretending, angel?"

"I…I don't know." And I don't. One moment it's Ash over me, the next moment it's Embry, and the moment after that it's both of them, and I'm the center of a hurricane of hands and mouths and eager flesh.

"I believe you," he says, his hips rolling so perfectly in and out. This third orgasm is like a key turning in a lock; there's an abrupt shift and suddenly everything in me is open and ready, and the climax rushes in, vicious and cruel, each pull so painful and bright that I can't catch my breath. It's my orgasm that sends Ash over the edge, and he gives a rough grunt and releases, this time fucking his way through the orgasm with those slow rolls, his entire body shaking.

And then he moves off me, disappearing into the bathroom and returning with a washcloth. He cleans me carefully, meeting my eyes.

"Are you okay?"

I nod. "Are you?"

"I don't know."

He returns the washcloth, and to my great relief, joins me back in bed, wrapping me in his arms. "Are you mad at me? At Embry?" I ask.

He lets out a long breath, his chin resting against my head. "No."

"But you're feeling something."

"Oh yes," he answers. "Definitely that."

"Jealousy? Because you don't need to be jealous, I swear to you."

"I know you believe that." A hand sweeps up my back and strokes along my spine. "Jealousy is such a limiting word,

273

isn't it? Because there are so many kinds of jealousy. There's feeling possessive, which I do of you…but then again, I also feel possessive of Embry. There's insecurity—that maybe Embry was able to give you something I can't, and that you're able to give Embry something that will change his relationship with me. And then there's this strange kind of desire—thinking about you with him makes me hard. I don't know why. It just does. And I know desire doesn't always make logical sense, that it's inherently politically *in*correct, that sometimes we crave depraved things."

The hand moves to my hair, loving and lazy and indulgent. "But even knowing all that, I couldn't have predicted how I would actually feel knowing that he fucked you. Desperate and a little angry and scared and…excited. Jealousy on its own can't hold all of those feelings, but I don't know what other word can. So I suppose it's good enough for now to say that yes, I am jealous. Of both of you."

I know how that feels, don't I? To be jealous of Embry and Ash at the same time, jealous of them having each other in a way that I'll never have, with their war history and fraternity and close working relationship. It's a circle I'll never be inside of, and it stings, stings, *stings*.

"Go to sleep, Greer. We have all the time in the world to think about this."

I want to protest, want to resist him, because there's no way I can fall asleep after our first time having sex, after he learned about Embry and me. No way at all, no matter how languid my limbs are, how thoroughly and utterly wrecked my body is, no matter how warm Ash's arms are and how steady and reassuring his breathing is…

———

I wake up alone, the bed cool next to me. Ash must have gotten up to work—is it morning already? I blink at the clock

274

on the nightstand for a moment, waiting for the numbers to make sense. 11:13 p.m. I've been asleep for three or four hours, and my stomach reminds me that I didn't eat before that. I sit up and stretch, and then hunt through the room for pajamas and slippers.

I won't bother Ash if he's working, but I plan on bothering the shit out of some crackers and cheese. I open the door and head out toward the living area, seeing the twinkly-gold light of the Christmas tree spilling out around the corner. There's nothing better than that light on cold winter nights. Cozy and quiet and joyful.

I turn the corner with a smile on my face and then freeze.

Ash is standing underneath the mistletoe.

Kissing someone.

My blood pounds in my ears and my throat is immediately tight with pain, but I can't look away and I can't interrupt. I'm as useless as a pillar of salt, doomed by my inability to look away.

Ash is wearing a thin T-shirt and low-slung pajama bottoms that highlight his flat stomach and narrow hips. His hair is tousled, and even from here, with only the light of the Christmas tree, I can see the stubbled outline of a day-old beard. His hand is fisted tight in the shirt of the person he's kissing, yanking that person close and holding them there.

And when they turn I see that the person is—inevitably, fatefully, tragically, wonderfully—Embry. Still in his sweater and jeans, barefoot and rumpled, with his hands underneath Ash's shirt and digging into the small of his back.

The kiss is so slow and lingering and deep. They meet and explore, and then their lips pull apart and there's fluttering eyelashes and long breaths, and then they're kissing again. There's both a familiarity and a hesitation there, as if they're relearning something they used to know. Ash will come in, his lips a breath away from Embry's, his body and face painted with longing, and then Embry will press forward, all passion and no thought, kissing hungrily until Ash slows him down, his hand going flat on Embry's chest and his mouth pulling back just the tiniest bit until Embry cools off. And then Ash moves in again, these soft, gorgeous noises coming from his throat.

After a few minutes of this, Embry's hand finds the waistband of Ash's pajama pants and moves down. I can't hear what he says to Ash, but I hear a small groan and I can guess.

And with that groan, my brain sputters back to life like a neglected engine, and I wish I could turn it back off because there's too many thoughts, too many questions, all contradicting each other, all fighting each other.

I'm aroused.

I'm angry.

I'm curious.

I'm betrayed.

I don't ever want this moment to stop.

And seeing this now, in this way, I realize I already knew. Not consciously maybe, but the knowledge was there like a shipwreck waiting for the sands to shift, waiting for me to finally turn my head and see what part of me has suspected from the beginning.

Suddenly what Ash said back in the bedroom makes sense. *Jealousy* is a word with too many meanings. It's a TARDIS of a word, bigger on the inside, a small, mean thing on the surface, but a complicated dance of emotions and negotiations within. I'm suffering with every single meaning of the word *jealous*.

I'm relieved that now I'm not the only one in this engagement that kept an important secret. I'm terrified of what happens next. Because really. What could possibly happen next? This was supposed to be my fairy tale, with me as the princess and Ash as the prince, but there's a third person here, a person we both want and who wants both of us.

None of the fairy tales I read as a girl had three people.

My thoughts are interrupted by another groan from Ash, but he's stepping back and adjusting himself inside his pants. Both men have bee-stung lips and wide, dark eyes, both men seem a little thunderstruck with each other, awed and incredulous and as yet unsatisfied.

"Merry Christmas, Embry," Ash says in a roughened voice.

Embry's voice is husky too. "Merry Christmas."

Ash turns away, his thumb at his forehead and then touching his lips, and Embry stands stock-still under the mistletoe as Ash leaves and walks toward the office. He stands there for several long minutes, his eyes on the hallway where Ash disappeared, and then he finally turns around and goes to his bedroom, his hands scrubbing through his hair.

And me, I'm left alone in the cold hallway. Confused, wanting, hurt.

Jealous.

In love.

CHAPTER 22

THE COLCHESTERS ARRIVE CHRISTMAS MORNING, BRINGING presents (and bags of groceries since Ash's mother refused to let anyone else prepare Christmas dinner). She and I spend the day in the kitchen while Kay, Embry, and Ash huddle around the table and work. I'm hopeless with cooking— Grandpa had a full-time chef when I was a girl and my meal prep in college consisted of eggs and instant noodles—but even so, she gives me a big hug after dinner and proclaims me "one of the family." And when she learns that my mother died when I was seven, she holds me tight, smelling like the piecrust she just rolled out and Elizabeth Taylor perfume, and tells me to call her Mama. I almost cry.

The day is so busy from start to finish that I never have time to bring up last night to either Embry or Ash, even though I can feel a kind of fracture in me, a fissure across the surface of my soul, and wisping from that fissure are all sorts of questions. Was that their first kiss? Do they kiss often?

Do they do more than kiss?

Have they fucked before, and are they fucking now?

It's like I woke up and the world was sideways, but I'm the only one who notices. I'm dizzy and fragile and uncertain, while everyone else is as steady and normal as ever. Because the men don't know that I know. And Embry doesn't know that Ash knows about us. And probably there's something else I don't know, and what if it *is* that Ash and Embry are cheating on me with each other?

Is a kiss cheating?

Is it cheating if they haven't fucked each other but want to?

And there go all the different jealousies again, flying like an evil witch's monkeys to swarm my mind, filling my head with memories of the kiss and also images of them fucking. Fucking naked, fucking in their tuxedos, fucking in their army uniforms…

And at one point, that train of thought sent me to my bedroom with the excuse of a headache, although really I had to relieve another kind of ache, rucking up my sweater dress and pulling my panties aside the moment the door closed, coming in less than a minute to the image of those two strong bodies grinding together.

(And of course Ash knew—*somehow*—that I came without him, and I spend that night biting his belt while he switches my ass with nettles he found growing next to one of the lodges.)

The day after Christmas, the world explodes. There's a pipeline leak in central Wyoming, and the day after that, a terrorist attack in Germany. Colombia falls apart, the VA reform bill needs to be reworked, and Ash is set to give an important speech on sex trafficking in front of the United Nations. And suddenly I go from having Ash and Embry all to myself to not seeing them at all. Both are hopping all over the country, both are working nonstop, and the one night I get to spend with Ash, he wraps his arms around me and falls asleep immediately, even before I've had a chance to turn off the light.

Two weeks mostly without him, and I'm a fidgeting, daydreaming wreck, twirling my ring on my finger, sighing at the snow, sleeping in a shirt of his I borrowed and never returned. So when Ash invites me to join him and a few others—Merlin and Embry and the secretary of state—at a public meeting between the United States and Carpathia in Geneva, I jump at the chance. Maybe I'll finally find a way to extract the answers to all my questions.

At the very least, I can steal another shirt.

"Thank you for letting me bring Abilene."

Ash looks up from his desk, a surprised smile lighting up his face. "You're awake."

Air Force One thrums around us, and I'm constitutionally unable to resist white noise and soothing vibrations. Once the plane took off, Ash insisted on tucking me in for a nap in the Executive Suite, a nap that lasted almost as long as the flight itself. I'm currently standing in the doorway holding my briefcase with one hand while the other tries to untangle my messy blond waves.

"I am, and I'm going to get some work done, but I thought I would tell you thank you first."

"Of course." He leans back in his chair. "I'll probably be busy most of the trip. It seemed like it would be more fun for you to have your friend nearby. Speaking of…any chance you'll reconsider the sleeping arrangements?"

I grin at him. "God, I wish. But Merlin said absolutely under no circumstance could we room together."

Ash drops his head back against the chair. "You would think being engaged would be enough for propriety's sake."

"Apparently not."

His eyes slide to my briefcase. "What work do you need to do?"

Sigh. What work don't I need to do? "I'm finalizing the syllabi for my three classes this semester and pulling together their initial assignments. Plus I told myself I'd work a little more on the book before the semester kicks in. *Oh*, and your social secretary won't stop emailing me."

"About the wedding?" His eyes are soft when he says the word, and it drains the annoyance right out of me.

"Yes. She wants it to be as big as the royal wedding. Bigger, if she can manage it."

"And what do you think?"

"That I don't care as long as my dress is pretty and I have time to teach."

Ash looks thoughtful when I say the word *teach*, but he doesn't say anything. I didn't ask for his input about me continuing to teach because it felt too much like asking for permission, and I would have done it no matter what he said anyway. I know Ash supports my decision, but I don't know about everybody else…especially the American public.

Merlin certainly doesn't like the perception it sends out, but while I'm willing to wait to move into the White House and willing to sleep in different hotel rooms, my career is not up for discussion. And as far as perception goes, who would have more respect for the White House than Leo Galloway's granddaughter?

"What do *you* think about the wedding?" I ask.

"Come here and I'll tell you."

"I'm not falling for that old trick," I say, and yet I'm crossing the office to his desk anyway. He spins in his chair so that he's sideways to his desk, and he pats his knee. I climb up there, all my stress about the work and the wedding dissolving away in the strength of his arms.

"When it comes to the wedding, I want two things," he tells me, his tone unusually serious. "If you're not attached to having it in a particular place, I want it to be at the church

I grew up going to in Kansas City. And I don't want to see you the day of the wedding. I know it's parochial and a little superstitious, but I want that moment where I see you for the first time at the foot of the aisle."

"Okay," I agree, entranced by his solemn mouth. "Whatever you want."

The solemn mouth breaks into a smile. "Those words are so delicious on your lips, angel. Can I have whatever I want all the time?"

"Of course," I say, fluttering my eyelashes at him.

"You flirt. What about right now?"

"Yes, sir."

His breath hitches as I smooth his tie down his chest. "Go close the door, little princess. I have an idea about what I want at the moment."

———

Abilene is polished as always in knee-high boots and a cut-out blue dress that only a willowy redhead can pull off, her pretty features arranged into an expression of cool boredom. But I see her blasé facade thin as we're ushered around by the Secret Service, when we're surrounded by the most powerful people in the world arguing over who gets the last clementine on Air Force One. She's eager and girlish, even though she's trying to rein it in, and nowhere is it more apparent than when she is around Ash.

I'm almost grateful we are taking a different car than him to the hotel; watching her around him is difficult. She clearly lied earlier when she said her crush on him was over, and I've clearly been lying to myself that I'm not still insecure around Abilene. She's so beautiful and so vivacious compared to me, and especially with the mistletoe kiss in the back of my mind, it's hard not to worry about what Ash really wants, ring or no ring.

We pull up to our hotel, an agent opening the door for us and helping us out of the car, and Abilene looks up at the marquee with a puzzled frown. "I thought we were staying at the Four Seasons?"

I shrug, tipping the doorman as we walk through the front doors. "Merlin asked the Secret Service to float a few different hotel names and go through the process of vetting each one, so that it was impossible to tell which would be picked. He was worried about the Carpathians trying to infiltrate the hotel staff."

"So you don't know where you're staying in a city until you get there?"

"I think this is rare. But Merlin and Ash both worry about the Carpathian president, and they thought this was safer."

Abilene makes a noise of understanding, and it's the last time she brings it up.

That night, strung out from jet lag, we get ready for the diplomatic dinner with the Carpathians. The next few days will be filled with negotiations and bickering and barely veiled acrimony, but tonight we're all supposed to play nice, give the world lots of pretty pictures, maybe a nicely framed shot of Ash shaking Melwas Kocur's hand. I know how important peace is to Ash and how tormented he is by the years he spent fighting in Carpathia, so if the one way I can help make this treaty happen is to attend a dinner by his side, then I'm more than happy to do it. But I have no illusions about how congenial or enjoyable the evening will be; I've been to enough "bipartisan" events with Grandpa Leo to know that people very rarely lay their swords down for the sake of Italian wine and banana flambé.

"Is that what you're wearing?" Abilene asks, stepping out of the bathroom as she fastens her earrings. She's wearing a skin-tight gold dress with a plunging neckline, her scarlet hair cascading down in sultry waves, and for a moment, the old fear hits me hard. That she'll always be the sexy one, the lovely one, while I'm stuck as her shadow.

I look down at my dress, a one-shouldered flowing thing, gauzy and with thick bands of intricate detailing around the neckline and hem. It's a color between white and silver, and I liked the way it set off my naturally golden skin and hair when I tried it on.

But now I'm having doubts. "What's wrong with it?"

"Nothing," Abilene says in that voice that means there's definitely something wrong with it.

I squeeze past her to go into the bathroom to look in the full-length mirror. I mean, compared to Abilene's long red curls, my updo does look a little modest. And yes, my dress isn't form-fitting like hers, but I like the way it flows as it moves, the heavy hem and soft chiffon layers giving the occasional hint of my waist and breasts underneath, not to mention the sheerness of the fabric, which can only be seen in the right light or when the dress moves just so. There's a very short shift underneath all the layers of chiffon to keep things from getting too scandalous, but overall it's very sensual, in a muted, diplomatic dinner kind of way.

"It just seems a little flat," Abilene says. "Did you bring another gown?"

"No," I say, suddenly having doubts.

"Greer Galloway! You always have a backup gown! Always, always!" There's a knock at the door, and Abilene sighs. "I'll get it."

I'm still turning and frowning into the mirror when I hear the door open and Ash's gravelly voice say, "Hello. May I come in?"

I step out of the bathroom to see Abilene standing in front of Ash, staring at him. She's breathing hard, frozen in place, and for a moment, I have the strangest feeling that she's going to take a step forward and touch him. That she's going to try to kiss him.

But she doesn't. After a few seconds, she steps back and lets him walk inside. When he sees me, he stops, his mouth parted as if he was about to speak and then forgot the words.

"What's wrong?" I ask, paranoid that his expression means he has all the same doubts about the dress that I now do.

"What's wrong is that you're fucking perfect, and I want to have you all to myself tonight," he growls, stepping forward and caging me against the wall with his arms. I'm acutely aware of Abilene standing right behind him, watching, and I'm also acutely aware that I almost don't care. "That color makes your eyes look silver. And your skin looks so fucking edible…" He leans down and bites my exposed collarbone, and agonized pleasure spreads through me like a toxin, hijacking my nerve endings and my capacity for higher thought.

But I still manage to put my hands on his chest and give a meaningful glance in Abilene's direction. She's turned away, pretending to go through her clutch, but I know she's as painfully aware of us as my body is of Ash.

Ash looks very much like he doesn't give a fuck about Abilene being there, but he still drops his arms and takes a step back. "I suppose we should get going," he says reluctantly.

"We should," I say, ducking past him to grab my heels and clutch, and as I do, he turns to Abilene.

"You know Embry doesn't have anyone to walk in with," he says kindly. "Would you like to walk in with him?"

"Like his date?" Abilene asks. I think I'm the only one who can hear that note of flat panic in her voice, that tug-of-war between pleasing Ash and having to spend the evening with a different man.

"Embry is an excellent date, I promise. Greer can attest to that."

I send him a sharp look, and he returns it with a mild look of his own.

"Which definition of jealousy did that come from?" I mutter as he opens the hotel door for me.

"All of them."

————

When we arrive at the ballroom where the dinner's being held, we meet Embry at the door looking cold and resigned in his white tuxedo. But when he sees me, he straightens up and presses his lips together, as if to keep from licking them.

Ash surprises me by spinning me into a little twirl in front of Embry, as if to show me off. "Doesn't she look divine, Mr. Moore?"

I can tell by the way Embry's eyes follow me that he's able to see my body through the dress. "Good enough to eat, Mr. Colchester."

And my answering shiver has nothing to do with the cold.

"And Abilene is doing a year's worth of charity and consenting to be your date," Ash adds. "So you see, we'll each have a granddaughter of Leo Galloway on our arm tonight."

Embry smiles, but it doesn't reach his eyes. "Wonderful." He extends an arm to Abilene, who takes it gracefully, although she looks equally miserable. "Shall we begin?"

Ash and I walk behind them, and Ash leans in to whisper, "You're cruel to wear this in front of Embry, you know."

"Abilene thought I should change."

"You look like a goddess. It's pure torment to be around you in that thing."

I stroke my fingers up his bicep. "And what would you do if we didn't have to be here?"

286

He flashes a wicked smile. "I've always wanted to fuck a goddess in the ass."

I blush so hard that he laughs. "Stop," I mumble, embarrassed and hot between the legs. "Someone might hear you."

"You're the one who started it. And do you really think I'd be the first world leader to fuck someone's ass? There's at least two or three English kings who've beaten me to it."

I slap his arm, trying to get him to lower his voice. "Well, they didn't do it to their wives. And they *definitely* didn't talk about it in public."

Ash's eyes sparkle but there's a husky catch in his voice when he says, "We really need to raise your comfort level with sodomy. And I can think of a few ways we could start."

"Also," I continue in a low voice, making sure my voice doesn't carry down the long candelabra-lit hallway, "you're not allowed to stir me up. Because I'm not wearing anything under my dress."

Ash stops walking, right there in the middle of the hallway. His entire body is a study in masculine interest. "What?"

"It's for dress-logistic reasons, you pervert. But it does mean I need my body to behave."

In the blink of an eye, I'm crushed against him, a large hand between my shoulder blades and the other on my ass, pressing my pelvis against his. With my heels, I'm tall enough to feel his swelling erection right against my mound, and it's enough to make my knees weaken.

"What's your safe word?" he asks, his breath hot against my ear. I feel the faint scratch of his jaw against mine—even only an hour after shaving, he has a five o'clock shadow.

"Maxen," I swallow.

"That's right. It's yours to say, yours to use."

I nod, feeling his face against mine, melting into his searing certainty, his undeniable lust. We're alone in the hallway save for the Secret Service agents who are staring studiously at the entrances and exits and not at us.

"Good. Now that's out of the way, know this: your body is mine, and when your body behaves? That means it's obeying me. If I want your nipples so hard I can see them through your dress or your pussy so wet that you leave a mark on your seat, then you'll do it. Got it?"

"And what if I don't?" I murmur in a teasing voice.

He pulls back a little to search my eyes and then squeezes me when he sees that I'm kidding and not trying to express a limit. "Then maybe we'll revisit our sodomy conversation earlier than planned."

"You can't punish me with something I want."

"Oh," he breathes in my ear, "but isn't that what makes it fun?"

He presses his lips to the sensitive spot behind my ear and then straightens up, taking my hand into the crook of his elbow and starting us down the hallway again. "Just wait until I tell Embry that you aren't wearing anything underneath that dress."

"What?"

Ash smirks. "You didn't really think I'd keep that kind of amazing information away from him, did you?"

I stare at him, puzzled and horrified and—I know, isn't this always the case?—turned on. "Ash...do you really think that's fair?"

"Fair to whom?"

"Goddammit, fair to any of us. We still haven't talked about—"

"And we're not going to here. We will talk, I promise, and we will navigate all this history between us. But for now, don't make Embry suffer for loving you. I'm not."

"He doesn't love me," I protest. (A little weakly because, oh, how the thought of him loving me makes my heart beat faster.) And then I remember the men kissing under the mistletoe. Is that included in the history Ash is referencing?

I open my mouth to ask him, to tell him I know, but then we're at the door to the ballroom and the moment is lost.

CHAPTER 23

MELWAS KOCUR AND HIS WIFE, LENKA, ARE THE LAST TO arrive. They sweep in grandly, like movie stars, and even I have to admit, they look the part. Melwas has dark blond hair and a square jaw, his wide face offset by a strong nose and arrestingly dark eyes, and Lenka is a human doll, bird-boned and delicate with a little pointed chin and bow-shaped lips. But also like a doll, she has glassy, vacant eyes, and when they come up to Ash and me for formal introductions, I see that she's been crying.

I look back to Melwas and the way his fingers dig into her skinny upper arm, and I see all I need to know.

The introductions are tedious and time-consuming, because there are advisors and vice presidents and cabinet members, and only a few of us speak Ukrainian and only a few of them speak English, and so almost everything has to go through translation. But I was raised to smile and pretend and find common ground and shake hands and quietly spy, and so that's what I do.

And finally, thankfully, it's time to sit down and eat. I'm

seated next to Lenka, with Melwas on my other side, and Ash next to him. The idea, I suppose, was to give Melwas and Ash ample time to informally converse, but the effect is that I'm sandwiched between a human shell and a man I suspect is a monster.

It's not pleasant, but again, I was raised for moments like this. I take a drink of wine to preemptively reward myself and then I turn toward Lenka. "Do you speak any English?" I ask.

Her eyes dart up to me, then back down to her plate. She's barely touched her salad, and a soft roll lies buttered on her plate but uneaten. This makes me profoundly sad for some reason. No matter how dark my life has gotten, I've always seen carbs as one of life's few real gifts.

She finally shakes her head. "No English," she manages.

"I don't speak Ukrainian," I apologize. Dammit, why wasn't my boarding school education more useful? All those hours translating Cicero and Rousseau, and not a single one focused on any language in the Slavic family tree. "And I suppose you also don't speak Old English or Middle English then. But maybe…Francais? Deutsch? Latin?"

Lenka's head snaps up and the faintest pulse of life shows in her eyes. "*Ich spreche Deutsch.*"

I give her a big smile. "*Wunderbar!*" Another sip of wine and a decision to forgive Cadbury Academy a little. "My German is very rusty," I explain to Lenka in German. "I haven't used it much since college, when I transitioned to medieval languages."

"I haven't spoken it in many years either," Lenka says softly, also in German. I recognize instantly that her accent and pronunciation is much stronger than mine.

"You must have learned it very young. You sound almost like a native speaker."

Lenka picks up her fork and pokes at her salad. "My

291

grandmother was German. She looked after me while my mother worked, and I grew up speaking both Ukrainian and the language of my mother's family. But"—she shoots a glance across me to where Melwas and Ash are talking in a mix of Ukrainian and English—"my husband does not like for me to speak in German because he doesn't understand it."

"Will it bother him to know we're speaking in it now?" I ask as gently as I can.

She gives a small nod, swallowing. The action looks almost painful given how slender her neck is.

"But surely he would be proud to know that his wife was performing her diplomatic duties so well," I say.

She looks confused.

"Think of it. Here you are, charming the soon-to-be First Lady, who will go back to the president of the United States tonight and tell him how kind and intelligent the Carpathians are," I explain. "You are proving what an asset you are, what special gifts you bring to his position."

"I did not think of it like that." She chews her lip for a moment. "But perhaps my husband would not like you to be charmed. He might think that I have undercut his power, his wish to make the Americans afraid of him."

"Do you want me to act intimidated instead?" I ask honestly. "I can. No one will know but you and I."

"You'd do that for me?" she asks, those doll-blue eyes disbelieving. "But why?"

"Even if our countries are barely at peace, I think loving a president puts us in a very small club. I think that makes us friends. Don't you?"

"I don't know," she says uncertainly. "I don't have very many friends."

I reach under the table and squeeze her small hand. "You have one more tonight."

And for the first time, I see a tentative smile on her face.

It's gone almost immediately, but it was most definitely there and I reward myself with more wine.

After dinner, there are a few requisite speeches and polite applause, and then the dancing is set to begin. I'm to dance with Melwas and Lenka with Ash, and she's shaking as we stand up.

"I'm not sure what you've heard about my fiancé," I tell her in German, "but he is very kind. Unfortunately he is a miserable dancer and you will have to protect your feet."

This wins me another smile. "I will try." But the smile quickly fades. "My husband...he can be unkind. I am sorry in advance if he's unkind to you."

"It's not your fault if he's unkind. Nothing he does is your responsibility," I tell her seriously, searching for precisely the right words in German to express this. "And I promise when it comes to your husband, I can take care of myself."

"You may think that now," she says sadly, "but he has a way of getting what he wants when it comes to hurting people."

And at first, I think she's wrong. Melwas leads me out on the floor as Ash and Lenka take their positions, and there's nothing but charm on his face as he takes me in his arms and we begin dancing. In fact, he's a very good dancer, and for a minute or two, we are so focused on dancing and maintaining smiles for the photographers that we don't converse. But just as I'm beginning to relax, he speaks.

"You are a very beautiful woman," he remarks. His English is remarkably clear. "Your President Colchester is a very lucky man."

"Thank you," I answer politely. "But I consider myself equally lucky."

"Do you now?" His wide forehead wrinkles in mock puzzlement. "But of course! The great American hero, the soldier no one could defeat. They say that America never lost a battle when he was there on the battlefield. Is that true?"

I don't like where this conversation is going. "You tell me if it's true," I say, pleasantly enough to mask the challenge in the words.

"You know, he and I once fought face-to-face," Melwas says, steering me expertly into an elaborate spin. There's impressed applause around us as he guides me back into place. "A small village called Glein. And he was willing to let a church full of civilians burn that day. That doesn't sound very heroic to me, but then again, maybe you Americans care more about winning than how you win."

I can't help the itchy hot indignation that prickles across my skin, and frankly, I don't want to help it. "Are you saying their deaths are on President Colchester's hands and not on the men who shot them? On the men who lit a boat full of children on fire?"

To my surprise, Melwas smiles widely. "You've got spirit in you. I like that in a woman."

I think of Lenka and seriously doubt that.

"So if you were there," I continue, "were you the one who gave the order? Did you personally shoot any of the civilians? Set fire to that boat?"

"Do you think I'm such a monster?"

I think of Lenka. I think of the treaty. I think of the mental chessboard my grandfather taught me to hold in my mind as I spied for him, and yet I throw it all out in favor of honesty. "Yes. Only monsters try to kill children, President Kocur, and a real man wouldn't pass the blame onto someone else."

Anger flashes quick on his face at the dig at his masculinity, and his shoulder tenses under my hand. "You test me, Miss Galloway," he says, and his hold on me tightens. "Do you also test your hero in this manner?"

I lift my chin. "I don't need to."

"You know, if you were my wife, I'd make sure you never

talked this way to me again." He yanks me close to him and I stumble with a small gasp. "And I would enjoy giving you that lesson very much."

Another yank and I feel him. Feel *it*. He's hard.

If I ever wanted to know if there was something wrong with me, if I ever felt confused by the dynamic between me and Ash, all of that blurriness is wiped away. I see it clearly now, the difference between consensual power exchange and the actual violence men can do to women. I know immediately what Melwas means by *teaching a lesson* and it wouldn't be playful spankings bounded by a safe word and affection. All I feel at Melwas's words is nausea and the urge to run.

I try to pull back, but he doesn't let me, making sure I feel exactly how much stronger he is than me. "I didn't mean to be ugly," he apologizes suddenly, as if struck with a sudden mood swing. "Not to such a beautiful woman. Perhaps you could visit me tonight, and I could make amends."

I refuse to struggle against his hold, even though the erection pressing into my stomach is triggering all sorts of instinctual alarms. I look him in the eye. "You know that won't happen."

He gives a shrug that is so very Slavic. "Maybe not tonight. But someday I'll see what the great hero gets to enjoy every night."

He's jealous of Ash. It's so obvious that I'm surprised I missed it, but it makes so much sense. Melwas fought in the same war, emerged as his fledgling country's ruler, and yet outside of Carpathian borders, Ash is the one venerated like a saint.

"And your wife?" I ask, looking over to Ash and Lenka. Lenka is leading Ash through the steps, and they're both laughing—the smile and color in her cheeks doing wonders for Lenka's beauty.

I feel rather than see the irritation run through Melwas's

body, although I'm not sure if it's at Lenka's happiness or the fact that Ash is the one giving her the happiness.

"She has no say in these things. I've made that very clear to her."

Poor Lenka. Does she pretend not to see Melwas with other women? Or is she secretly relieved that she alone doesn't have to bear the brunt of his lust?

And then for no reason at all, I think of Embry and Ash under the mistletoe, Ash's fist in Embry's shirt and my heart pounding in the dark. Am I like Lenka? Standing passively by while my partner cheats on me?

The thought is like a tuning fork, humming along my bones, deep into my teeth, and all of my priorities fall right back into order, and I'm Greer Galloway again, the professor, the spy, the political princess.

"I suppose you have made that clear to her. And I will make it clear to you—I'm not interested. Tonight or ever."

"A challenge," he says, his accent growing thick. "I have not had a challenge in a very long time."

"You will lose," I say, and I say it with such certainty and calmness that it throws him. His grip on me loosens.

"May I cut in?"

I look up to see Embry next to us, unsmiling and warlike, all of the meanings of his interruption obvious.

Get away from her.

She belongs to someone else.

I'm not afraid of you, and I don't give a shit about diplomacy.

I don't think Melwas really gives a shit about diplomacy either, which he makes apparent by stepping forward and pointedly adjusting his tuxedo jacket to cover his erection. Embry sees this, his face contorting into an expression of wolfish rage, and for a minute, I wonder if he's going to take a swing at the Carpathian leader. But then Ash and Lenka are coming up to us, and Ash is saying something in Ukrainian as he bows and kisses Lenka's hand and then gestures to Melwas.

Lenka giggles. *Giggles*. And the sound jars Melwas out of his locked stare with Embry. He says something brusque and demanding in Ukrainian and then stalks off the dance floor, Lenka scurrying after him.

"I'm going to kill him," Embry says quietly once they're gone, his hands curling into fists.

Elsewhere, I see other couples spilling onto the dance floor, more or less oblivious to the crisis that was just averted by a giggle. Adrenaline is pumping through me like I've been fighting, like I've been attacked, and Ash steps to me and takes my head in his hands.

"Are you okay?" he asks seriously, searching my face. "I came over as soon as I saw something was wrong. I'm sorry I wasn't there to help you when you needed me."

"I'm okay." I take a deep breath and realize my hands are shaking. "He… It doesn't matter. I'm fine, and I didn't need help."

"You're not fine though," Embry hisses, turning to Ash. "Did you see how he was holding her? Touching her? We can't let him near her again."

Ash looks at me thoughtfully, on the surface all cool analysis while Embry seethes and mumbles threats next to him. But when I meet his eyes, there's nothing cool or composed in their deep, clear depths. In them, I see the soldier. I see lead and fire and blood.

"He wants you," Ash says finally. "That much is clear. I'm doubling your security for the duration of your stay, and you tell me the moment he says or does something untoward again. Understood?"

"I can take care of myself," I say a little snappishly. "I don't need you to rescue me."

Ash looks impatient. "This isn't a game, Greer. You were

just sexually assaulted by the leader of a country hostile to ours. Like it or not, you are an extension of my office now—your safety and the safety of our country are intertwined, and aside from all that, you are the most precious possession of my heart. I will do everything in my power to keep you safe."

I don't even know why I'm so riled up right now, so peevish, because none of this is Ash's fault, but I bite off a caustic "I'm not anyone's possession" and glare at him.

And then he's leaning into my ear, his hand on the small of my back. "That's right, you're not my possession. You're going to be my *wife*. My wife who kneels at my feet, who presents her cunt to me without question when I demand it, who trusts me with her heart and soul and future. You think it's *either/or* that you belong to yourself or belong to me, but I'm telling you right now that it's *both/and*. You belong to yourself *and* you belong to me, and I don't fucking care that it seems like a contradiction because we both know it isn't. Now if you can't accept that, then say my name right now and we will step back and renegotiate our relationship. But if you are willing to submit to the fact that I will move fucking heaven and earth to keep you from harm, then say *yes, sir*."

My irritation leaves instantly, my emotions taking a crash as the adrenaline in my blood begins to plummet down to pre-Melwas levels. "Yes, sir," I say, feeling instantly guilty for taking out my fear and anger on him. "I'm sorry, Ash. I'm not angry with you. I'm just shaken up."

"I know." He gives me a lingering kiss on the lips, parting them with his own and sliding his tongue inside my mouth. I taste mint and whiskey and Ash. "I love you," he whispers, pulling back. "I have to go talk to Merlin, though. This... complicates things."

"Please don't let me undo all the work you've done for the treaty," I say, instantly filled with unease.

"You haven't done anything wrong," he says flatly. "This is on Melwas. The treaty must go forward, but I think more precautions need to be put in place immediately. Stay with Embry—you don't leave his side, got it?"

The irrational desire to pick a fight with him has disappeared. "Got it."

He gives me another quick kiss and then he's off to find Merlin.

CHAPTER 24

"SHALL WE DANCE?" I ASK EMBRY, TAKING ONE OF HIS STILL-fisted hands in both of mine. He still looks like he's squaring off for a duel, and people are going to notice soon if he doesn't stop.

"Dance?" he asks blankly, like I've just asked him to donate a kidney.

"We are still on a dance floor," I point out. "And we still have to pretend that we're here for diplomacy."

"I guess," he scowls.

"Come on," I coax, sliding a hand up his shoulder to his neck. I did it to make him dance, but the second my hand touches his neck, I realize what a mistake it was. It's the first time I've really touched him since he came to my office at Georgetown. Firm, deliberate touch.

And it's the first time he and I have been mostly alone together, without Ash.

His lips part and his pupils dilate into black pools of lust. I make to drop my hand, but his hand covers mine, and he moves it back up to his neck as we slowly start dancing.

Both of us are good enough dancers that we don't need to pay attention to the steps or the music. "That feels good," he murmurs. "Having your hand on me."

I want my hand to be everywhere on him—his flat abs and curved ass and thick penis—I want him trembling underneath my touch as sweat springs up on his forehead, I want him so desperate for me that he can't form words, I want to sit on his face and have him eat me while he reflexively tries to fuck the air.

The brief fantasy is so vivid and so unlike me that I have trouble catching my breath. Is it possible to be a different person with two different lovers? For a woman to be different with one man than she is with another? With Ash, I never want anything other than what we have. But for some reason when I think of Embry, I think of him moving beneath me, of feral passion without negotiation, him sometimes rough and fast and me sometimes cruel and teasing. Not a power exchange, but a power dance, back and forth, side to side, mindless and spontaneous.

"You okay?" Embry asks, eyebrows slanting together, and I snap back to reality, my cheeks warm.

"Yes," I say, and then add quickly, to steer us away from more dangerous topics, "Where's Abilene?"

Embry sounds weary, not sarcastic, when he answers. "You mean my date?" He tilts his head to the side, and I follow the gesture, seeing her dancing with one of the men from the Carpathian delegation. He can't stop staring down her dress, and there's a certain satisfaction on her face that I can't quite read. "I hope she's having fun," I say. "I hope they hit it off. But I am sorry she wasn't a very good date."

Embry looks down at me. "I'm afraid I wasn't a very good date either. The whole time I was wishing I were with someone else."

My throat tightens. Does he mean me? Or Ash?

Does it matter?

"I told Ash about us," I blurt out for no reason. Well, no reason other than the thought of him longing for Ash's touch across the ballroom sends electricity skating across my skin, almost more than the thought of him longing for me does. Electricity quickly followed by betrayed anger.

God, what the fuck is wrong with me that I'm turned on and jealous at the same time?

Embry sighs. "I know."

"Have you guys talked about it?" I ask. "I feel like it's this big thing looming over us, the fact that I've slept with both of you."

He looks miserable. "I feel like that too. And no, we haven't talked about it much. He told me on Christmas Eve. He told me that he knew and that he was jealous and that…" He stops, his vision growing hazy and his skin hot under my touch, and I realize he's remembering the kiss. My skin also gets hot as I remember it. "Anyway, we haven't had a chance to talk since then. So I don't know where we stand."

"Neither do I," I say.

"And sometimes he'll say things—like he's trying to needle me or test me. Or maybe torture me."

"Like what?" I ask, puzzled.

Embry's eyes close, his skin still impossibly hot. "Like that you're not wearing anything underneath your dress tonight."

My breath stutters and he opens his eyes.

"Do you know what it's like," he says in a hollow voice, "to have him tell me things like that? Or to be in the same building and know that, at that very moment, he's inside you? Or to remember what you taste like and not even be able to hold your hand?"

"Embry," I whisper.

"I couldn't go back to you in Chicago, not after he told

302

me about seeing you. You know he read those emails every day? Rain or snow, hot or cold, on base or sleeping on rocks and pine branches. I'd find him with his miniature flashlight in his teeth and his hand on his belt. I'd hear him grunting in the shower stall next to me and know he was thinking of you. That went on for years…and then to find out this mysterious email girl was *you*. The girl I'd decided to marry after less than eight hours together."

The girl I'd decided to marry…

His words sink like anchors, finding my most vulnerable depths, but I push them aside as typical Embry hyperbole. I have to. The alternative is taking them seriously, and if I take those words seriously, I might fly apart.

"I thought you didn't want me," I say slowly. "It…well, it hurt a lot. For a long time. Because I gave you something, and I don't mean my virginity necessarily, but myself; you were the first person I allowed myself to be vulnerable with. That I exposed my heart to. And then you just vanished, like it had meant nothing to you."

He gives an empty laugh. "You thought I didn't want you… Greer, I burned with wanting you."

My stomach flips over.

And then his lashes lower. "I still burn with wanting you."

"Don't do this," I beg. Because if he says the words out loud, if we drag this out into the open—

"I can't pretend anymore," he croaks. "I thought it was just an infatuation—who wouldn't be infatuated after a night like we had? But all the time I've spent with you these past few months has made me realize it's worse than that. I'm in love with you. I'm consumed with you. And I'm in hell watching you with Ash."

I look away, fighting the pain in my throat. He's in love with me. And I think I might still be in love with him. Which puts us both in hell.

"But all the women…all those dates…" I can't keep the pain and jealousy out of my voice, even though I'm desperate to. I keep my eyes on the other dancers, trying to distract my mind from the endless rotation of longing and betrayal. I see Belvedere dancing with Lenka, Melwas talking with our secretary of state, no trace of Abilene, who must be off grabbing a drink with her new acquaintance. But even an entire ballroom of political leaders can't keep my eyes from sliding back to Embry. His sharp jaw and high forehead and invitingly wicked mouth, which is currently tight with emotion. "I just didn't think you could want me if you were fucking all those other women."

He looks at me helplessly. "I *ache* with wanting you. All the time. And at the end of the day, you two get to go fuck, and I have to know about it." His voice grows frustrated. "Don't I get something to take the edge off?"

A childish part of me wants to stamp my foot and yell *No!* Which is ridiculous and selfish for every reason under the sun, especially if he loves Ash too, if he's aching for two people instead of only one. I don't answer him because I can't answer with the thing I should say, which is *do what you want.*

"I won't anymore," he breathes suddenly, "if that's what you want. I won't see anyone else. I won't fuck anyone else. I'll be completely celibate so that you can know exactly how fucking lost I am to you. Oh, Greer, please. Please just tell me if you feel the same way. Tell me this is eating you alive too and that I'm not alone."

I should lie. I should lie and tell him that I don't love him, that I don't want him, that being around him isn't torture. Because I see in the flutter of those long eyelashes and the agony written on his Darcy-esque brow that despite the carefully applied veneer he's adopted as vice president, he's still no more in control of his emotions than he was five years ago. His passions and urges master him, drown him, and I see now that Ash has been trying to protect him. That he tells Embry things about me not to torment him, but to share what he can of me. To help soothe the constant storm contained inside this beautiful, vulnerable soul.

Don't make him suffer for loving you. I don't.

Ash knew all along. Ash always knows. And instead of reacting in any number of fair or understandable ways—with demands or denial or coldness—his reaction instead has been to be honest about his feelings. To share. To stay and not pull back. To remain in a relationship with a best friend and a fiancée who secretly love each other.

All of a sudden, my heart hurts for Ash most of all. As if it weren't enough to be president, to have to shoulder the burden of us, Embry and me, and still remain loving and honest as he did so?

Well, honest about everything except whatever exists between him and Embry.

I feel impaled with all these contradictory feelings, and I can't fight it anymore.

"Yes, I love you," I admit brokenly. "I fell in love that night in Chicago and I couldn't stop being in love, even after you abandoned me. I couldn't stop being in love with you even when I started seeing Ash. Yes, I want you. All the time. I want you both, I want you and Ash, and I can't stop myself from all this wanting, even though it'll damn me to hell. And I almost like it when you fuck all those other women because it gives me a reason to hate you, to feel like, just for a moment, I'm free from loving you. But I'm lying to myself. I'm never really free. You could walk in smelling like another woman—*tasting* like her—and if I could, I'd still throw myself at your feet."

I can see that I'm hurting him, every word a slice across that beautiful face as we whirl across the dance floor.

"It makes me desolate, Embry, hollow and hurting and I hate myself sometimes but I can't stop wishing for you. I feel like a liar. Like a snake or a…I don't know, a man eater or something."

That coaxes a faint smile to that perfect mouth. "I don't think you can be a man eater if you only eat two men."

I look up at him and at that smile, and my courage finds me.

Now.

Tonight.

It can't wait any longer.

"I saw you and Ash on Christmas Eve."

He actually stumbles as we dance, missing a step and quickly correcting himself. "What?"

"Under the mistletoe. I had been asleep, but I woke up and decided to go find something to eat…and instead I found you kissing him."

He lets out a breath. "Greer. Wait. It's not…"

"It's not what I think?" I look up into those blue eyes. "The two men I love aren't also in love with each other?"

Eyelashes down and then back up. "I don't know if he loves me," Embry says, as if that's a real answer. "And it hasn't happened since. Or before. I mean, before like when you and Ash were dating."

"So it was the first time since Ash and I started dating. But you have kissed before that?"

"This really should be something you and Ash talk about," Embry says, and there's a wild discomfort in his voice, the repressed panic of a cornered animal.

"But it's your story too," I point out. "And now it's mine. I deserve to know, Embry. We haven't so much as talked about the weather without Ash in the room, but you think it's okay for you two to sneak off and make out in the dark?"

The words are angry. Hell, I'm angry all over again.

"No," he says wretchedly. "It's not okay."

"Then tell me the truth! Don't I at least deserve that?"

He gives a ragged sigh. "What do you want to know?"

"All of it. Everything. Why you kissed that night. Your first kiss. If you've fucked. If you still want to fuck."

The expression on his face is a mangle of panic and apology and lust, and on him, it looks beautiful. Sensual and haunted. Before I can stop myself, I slide my hand up to his face, my fingertips ghosting across his perfect cheekbones and chiseled jaw. He swallows.

"It started in Carpathia," he says. "In the village of Caledonia. Do you remember it?"

"The battle where he saved you."

"It wasn't a battle. Not like you'd normally think of. It was almost a massacre, a complete ambush. The village was evacuated, and we thought it was empty. Our plan was to establish a presence there and then begin moving up the valley, to where we thought the Carpathians were encamped."

"But they were there."

"They were there," Embry confirms, his face shadowed with the memory. "They waited until we were doing a building check, this apartment tower, and then they started picking us off. We sheltered inside to fight back, which had been their plan all along. You couldn't walk through this place without tripping claymores left and right, and they'd taken out the windows on the lower floors so they could shoot in grenades."

"Jesus Christ," I say, shaken. It's one thing to watch war on television, to listen to the generals testify in Congress, to read articles from embedded journalists. But to hear a soldier speak about it is such a stark reminder that all those explosions and fires, all that rubble and broken glass—that happened around people. *To* people. Real men and women, dead or injured, exposed to the most depraved barbarity imaginable.

The music changes to a slow waltz, and Embry unconsciously changes his steps to match the music. I follow suit, and he keeps talking. "Ash saved us. He was the only one to think of the elevator shafts. Everyone wanted to go up to the roof, wait for a helicopter, but Ash insisted it was too dangerous. What if a Carpathian helicopter came first? He sent everyone down to the service floor and told them to go out the basement windows, but only if they faced the forest and only once he said so."

"What happened?" I ask, as caught up as I would be if I didn't know the end of the story.

"I got shot," Embry says with an unhappy shrug. "Ash wanted to be the last one down the shaft, and I refused to let him wait alone, and then the Carpathians began shooting their way into the building. Ash called for the troops downstairs to take their chance and escape into the forest and then told me to get down there. I wouldn't, not without him, and then the Carpathians appeared. I got a bullet to the calf and another in the shoulder—which meant no climbing down the elevator shaft. Ash pushed me behind him and fought off the Carpathians until I could crawl to the stairwell. And then...well, I suppose you know the rest. While I was a useless pile on the floor, Ash managed to keep the Carpathians off of us long enough to discover an outside exit on the ground floor. He carried me out and we managed to get to the forest."

I relax a little and then remember my original question. "But what does this have to do with you and Ash being together?"

Embry glances away from me, not out of avoidance or embarrassment, but as if he's searching for the right words to explain something. "There's kind of a...high...from fighting like that. Cheating death. It's the adrenaline, I think. For some people, it slows them down, makes them dazed. Other people get amped up, like they can't stop talking or laughing or moving around. But not Ash. It makes him restless in a different kind of way. It—it makes his blood hot."

Dark spots of color appear high on Embry's cheekbones, and I realize that he's *blushing*. He's also gone someplace deep inside himself, remembering something that makes him tremble a little under my hands. "Embry?"

His gaze snaps back to mine, his eyes going clear again but his cheeks still flushed. "He saved my life. I wanted to show him how grateful I was."

"Oh," I say softly, feeling my own cheeks warm as I imagine the scene. Blood and torn fabric and Ash's hard body pressing Embry's into the ground. "Did you fuck each other?"

"He fucked *me*. A few times. Once wasn't enough to calm him down." A harsh laugh, but the harshness isn't only bitterness; it's need and sarcasm and regret. "He screwed Morgan a few years before that and then he screwed me. Like *Brideshead Revisited* in reverse. Except we make the Marchmains look like the fucking Brady Bunch."

"Did you like it?" I ask a little breathlessly. I don't know why I need to ask, why I need to know, but I do, I do. "Did you come?"

"Would you believe I came as many times as he did? With a bullet in my shoulder and morphine burning through my blood? The first time I came almost immediately, rubbing against the rucksack he'd bent me over. And when we got to base…it kept going for a while. A couple years. And then he met Jenny…" A long breath. "And then after Jenny died…"

My mouth goes dry. "You fucked after Jenny died?"

"Several times. Until this fall. That's when we stopped again."

"But he told me…" Tears burn at my eyelids "He lied to me. He said that he hadn't been with anyone since Jenny died."

"Did he say that, or"—Embry's voice is careful—"did he say that he hadn't been with any *women*?"

I try to find my breath again, but it's somewhere down at my feet. "Yes. That. No women."

Embry searches my eyes. "Are you upset?"

"That you slept together? Or that you guys have been on and off again for nearly a decade and I had no idea?"

"Either. Both."

"I'm angry that you and Ash haven't told me about your history. I'm torn apart with jealousy to think you two have been wanting each other while I've been here." I lower my voice. "And I'm shaking with how hot it makes me to think about the two of you together. I wish I could have seen it. I wish I could have been there, taking you in my mouth while he fucked you. I wish I could have seen his face as he came."

"Jesus, Greer."

The stark arousal in Embry's voice is ragged and hungry, and I'm trying to fight off my own hungry reaction. But I can't—not entirely. I make sure to press against Embry as the dance brings us closer, confirming what I suspected: he's rock hard.

He gives a soft, surprised grunt as my body grazes his erection, and his eyes are hazy once more. "You guys do that to me and it's so confusing."

"Do what?"

"You—you mix up my feelings for you and Ash. I get hard thinking about him, and then you touch me. Or I'm aching at Camp David listening to you scream for him, but then he's the one who comes out and kisses me. I can't keep track of what or whom I want anymore. I just...*want*."

I grip his tuxedo lapel, both excited and a little frightened that he's just articulated something I haven't been able to articulate for myself. "That's what's happened to me."

Those aristocratic eyebrows rise in happy astonishment. "Really?"

"Really. From the beginning, even, I couldn't separate wanting you from wanting him. When we had sex in Chicago...well, part of the reason I did it was because I was hurting so much about Ash."

"Me too," he confesses.

I look at him in confusion, and then I remember that night on the Ferris wheel, his broken voice.

They aren't my someone. No matter how much I plead, no matter how much—how much I give of myself.

"Do you think he knows?" I ask. "That we both love him so much that we ended up falling in love with each other?"

Embry sighs. "Would it change anything if he did?"

We move again for the dance, my hip brushing past his penis again—accidentally this time—and he hisses.

"Sorry," I say, knowing I don't sound sorry at all.

He shakes his head. "I'm just as bad as Melwas. Hard for you at a fucking diplomatic event."

"Yes, you're both incurably prurient, but there's a key difference."

"What's that?"

I lean up to his ear, using his lapel to pull myself higher. "I like it when you're incurably prurient."

He grins down at me, the guilt and torment vanishing for a moment and leaving behind the rich playboy who'd charmed me on a Chicago sidewalk.

But as we finish our dance, as we find new partners to dance with and the night grinds unbearably on, as my own betrayals and post-confessing-forbidden-love-shock wears off, something heartbreaking occurs to me.

Ash sent Embry to get me. Ash sent Embry to get me even though he and Embry had been fucking right up until then. How cruel must that have felt to Embry? Like he was

311

good enough to secretly fuck, at least until the right fuckable woman came along, but then he wasn't wanted anymore? I haven't ever thought of Ash as homophobic, as brutal in a way that went past the bedroom, but now I feel a righteous sense of anger on Embry's behalf. All those years together, and Ash just tossed him aside for Jenny. And then picked him back up and tossed him right back aside for me.

No wonder Embry is tormented. Ash has been merciless to him. Unforgivably dismissive.

And as I perform all the duties I came to do—charming and chatting and almost absentmindedly gathering tidbits and gossip for Ash—I slowly decide to confront him. About all those carefully worded not-lies, about his cruelty to Embry, about the three of us.

About what the fuck happens next.

CHAPTER 25

ASH HASN'T RETURNED TO THE DINNER BY THE TIME IT comes to a close, so Embry and I are the ones to make the formal goodbyes and excuses for Ash's absence, even though we have no idea where the hell he is. In my current mood, that makes me angrier than ever, so angry that I barely nod at Luc when he informs me that both Abilene and the president are back at the hotel and I'll be riding there alone.

And when I get to the hotel, Luc says, "The president has requested that you grab your things from your room and join him in his."

I stop right there in the lobby and glare up at the giant Quebecois man. "And what if I don't want to sleep in his room tonight?"

Luc looks uncomfortable. "I understand that he and Merlin are concerned that you'll be a target for Melwas. They both feel better with you in the president's room."

"And my cousin? If Melwas decides to attack my room—which won't happen—he'd still find her. It's okay to let her stay there but not me?"

The agent looks like he really, really doesn't want to have this conversation, and I sigh, taking pity on him. It's not his fault that Ash is a controlling asshole and I mean to confront him about it. "Fine, fine. Let's get my things."

When I get to my room and open the door, Abilene jolts off the bed, as if she's been electrocuted. "Greer!" she says, her voice far too bright. "You're back."

I give her a strange look, and she gives me a toothy smile—the one she learned from watching the Duchess of Cambridge tour the Commonwealth in heels with a baby on her hip.

"Ash wants me to change rooms," I say, a little peevishly, and start tossing things into my suitcase.

She shifts on the bed. "Did he, uh, did he say why?"

"Something about security and Melwas, but the reason doesn't matter because it's rude to just order people around like their feelings don't matter." I seal my mouth closed, realizing I'm perilously close to yelling or crying, and then the whole mess about Embry and Ash will spill out, the whole sordid fucking triangle.

"Oh, just the security then? That's not a big deal."

She still sounds strange, and part of me thinks I should ask her what's wrong, that I should sit down on the bed and put my arms around her shoulders and coax her into opening up. It wouldn't take long because Abi always wants to open up. All she needs is the faintest invitation inside your attention and then she's wailing in your lap, like some sort of emotional vampire.

But I'm my own emotional vampire right now, and I have to go drain Ash's blood before I burn everything down. I zip my suitcase closed. "I'll see you in the morning, Abi."

"Right," she says faintly. "In the morning."

Luc holds the door for me as I give her a little wave and wheel the suitcase back out into the hallway, and then he takes it from me without asking, lifting it as effortlessly as I'd lift a bag of bread. "This way," he says, and we walk down the hallway to the elevator to take it one floor up to Ash's room.

After walking past legions of Secret Service agents, Luc swipes the hotel key card to access the presidential suite, and then we're inside, Luc trundling off with my suitcase and me walking straight for the large armchair where Ash is sitting. I'm still in my gown, and it flutters and glints in the low golden light of the room as I stride toward him.

I'm ready to draw blood, but then I see how tired he looks. His jacket is off and thrown carelessly over the table, his bow tie unknotted. He's balancing a tumbler of scotch on his knee, and something about the color in his cheeks tells me that it isn't his first. And the weariness in his face is so profound, so deeply etched, that I can't bear to add to it, which irritates me. How dare he be tired when I need him to be strong? When I need him calm enough to weather the storm I want to scream into existence?

He looks up at me, green eyes nearly liquid with exhaustion. "You're angry about something," he comments.

I don't ask how he guessed, because even if it weren't written all over my face, he'd still know. "Yes."

"We have a few things to talk about then." He takes a sip of his scotch and then waves over toward the bar. "You want something to drink?"

"Actually, I think I do."

As Luc leaves and we're left alone, I make myself a small glass of single malt, walk over to the chair across from him, and sit down. I don't choose to sit at his feet, a choice he notices but doesn't remark on.

A choice that hurts me more than it hurts him, I think.

But still, stubborn and cranky, I stay perched on the chair, refusing to give him anything until he gives me some answers.

"I think you should go first," he says, twirling the glass

on his knee. Even slumped back in his chair, he looks power-ful. Even exhausted, he looks in charge. It's both marvelous and terribly unfair.

"Fine," I say. "Okay."

And then realize I have no segue into the things we need to talk about, no warm-up. I just have to dive in. I take a deep breath and look Ash square in the face.

"Embry told me he loves me tonight."

"I believe I told you he loves you tonight as well, only you didn't believe me."

"I told him I love him too."

Ash takes this like a blow he knew was coming but still wasn't entirely prepared for. A look of hurt—real, awful hurt—crosses his face, and he lifts his glass to his lips and drains the entire thing in a few practiced swallows. When he's finished, he sets the glass on the table next to him and looks at me with eyes the color of pain. "So you did," he says softly. "And then what did he say?"

"Not much of anything, because right after I told him that, I told him that I saw you two kissing on Christmas Eve."

The blood drains from Ash's face. This he hadn't expected, he hadn't seen coming. "Oh my God, Greer," he says in a horrified voice, "why didn't you say anything?"

I nearly explode. I shoot straight to my feet, tower-ing over him in my stupidly tall heels. "Why didn't *I* say anything? Why didn't *I* say anything about my fiancé cheat-ing on me? Why didn't *I* say anything about the only men I've ever been with, the two men I love, being in a secret relationship for ten *fucking years*?"

I don't know what I expected Ash to do, but it wasn't to grab my hips and yank me down onto his lap. His arm is an iron bar around my back, his hand implacable and heedless of my carefully styled updo as he fists my hair to make sure I'm looking at his face.

But his face isn't angry. It's hurt and regretful and tired, but not at all angry, and for some reason, this unlocks my own hurt and tiredness, my own regret. My anger ebbs away like the tide, leaving behind a dirty residue of confused betrayal.

"When I saw you two under the mistletoe," I whisper, "I thought my heart was literally breaking. Like my aorta had twisted and my valves had clamped shut. I couldn't breathe. I couldn't think."

"You have every reason to hate me," he says, his eyes locked on mine. "Every reason to be angry. I have asked you to trust me, and then I betrayed that trust in the worst way possible. I'm sorry, Greer. I'm so very, very sorry. If this... changes...things between us, I completely understand. I'm at fault, and I deserve whatever you want to do to me."

Normally, I'd applaud a man who apologized without excuses, without desperate defenses of himself, but right now? Tonight? I want to know what Ash was thinking that night under the mistletoe, what he was feeling. I want him to fight and rage, argue and plead, so that my own tangle of emotions won't feel so alone and outsized compared to this graceful defeat.

"No," I say. "I want more. You're not supposed to give up. You're not supposed to submit. You're supposed to fight for me! You're supposed to explain all this away and make me feel better!"

His eyes search mine. "But I can't explain it away. I *did* kiss Embry. I kissed him, and I enjoyed it. I kissed him because I'd just learned about you two sleeping together, and when I saw him that night, all rumpled and lost-looking under the mistletoe, I just..." He stops and shakes his head. "I'm not going to try to justify what I've done. It was wrong to kiss him that night, and it was wrong not to tell you. I'm so, so sorry."

317

I want to hit him. I want to scream at him. I settle for glaring. "Stop saying you're sorry. I don't want your *sorry*."

His eyebrows pull together. "Then what do you want?"

"You. Him. Us. I want it all to make sense. Do you love him?"

He blinks, the act making him look younger, more vulnerable. "Greer…"

"I saw you that night, Ash. You weren't kissing him like he was a friend or an old fuck; you were kissing him like you needed it. Like you'd been waiting months for it. You were *trembling*, and you looked at him like…like you look at me sometimes. Like you can't decide whether you want to kiss me or make me cry."

He's still blinking, those eyelashes long and dark, those bottle-green eyes bright and aching behind them. "Greer, this doesn't need to be… What good will it do—"

"I'm not the fucking public," I say, narrowing my eyes. "I'm not a poll. I'm not a key demographic. Stop trying to spare my feelings and just tell me." I pause, and then add, because I think Ash needs to hear it, "Embry loves *you*, you know. He told me that too. He told me about the first time you were together, he told me that you were together after Jenny's death. He thinks that you don't love him back, and why wouldn't he? With the awful way you've treated him?"

Ash freezes, his hand still fisting my hair, his arm still anchoring me down against him. "What?"

I'm simmering again, biting off words and not caring how they land. "You know what I'm talking about. He's good enough until you meet a woman, right? You could fuck him until you met Jenny, and then you dropped him, and then after Jenny, you were back to using him again. Until you had me. Until *you sent him* to fetch me for you. How do you think that makes him feel? How could you?"

Ash's lips part and close and then part again. "Greer, I asked Embry to marry me. Twice."

I was all ready to continue with my excoriation on Embry's behalf, but Ash's words filter their way into my consciousness and stun me. "What?" I whisper.

"I asked him to be my husband. Twice. And do you know how many times he said no?"

I shake my head mutely.

"Twice," Ash says.

"He—he didn't say anything about that."

Ash makes a noise that could be called derisive—if it wasn't so wounded. "No. I suppose he didn't."

"When did you propose?"

Ash loosens his grip in my hair, and unconsciously I reach back to make him tighten it again. This draws the first smile I've seen from him since I came in the room. But he stays on topic and answers my question.

"The first time was in Carpathia. We'd been dating for two years. He insisted we not tell anyone, and I agreed because I loved him. But I thought maybe if he saw how serious I was about him, how much I wanted to be with him, he wouldn't be so intent on having a secret relationship. I had a buddy of mine buy a ring in Rome when he went there for leave and bring it back. I planned it so just the two of us would be out in Embry's favorite valley by that base—you could stand at the top of this ridge and see for miles. I got down on one knee while we both had guns slung over our shoulders."

Ash smiles at the memory, but then his smile falters. "Embry said no. It wasn't legal then, you see, and I think—I don't know. Maybe he was worried about our careers or maybe what his family wanted. He didn't give me a reason. He just said no and told me we should stop seeing each other."

Even now, seven or eight years later, I can hear the bitter heartache in his voice.

"Merlin introduced me to Jenny not long after, and we gradually fell in love. She wasn't at all like Embry, she wasn't at all like you, and maybe that felt safe to me. She wasn't the strange girl who coaxed my darkest self to the surface, she wasn't the man who'd faced death with me. She was... easy. Uncomplicated. She loved like normal people loved, she desired like normal people desired. With her, I was a different kind of man, a kind that didn't have such twisted feelings inside. After I'd been wrapped up in you so long, only to have my first real relationship end like that...well, I guess I'm just trying to explain why I fell in love with Jenny when I was still in love with both of you."

I turn that over in my mind for a minute. So many networks of love and heartbreak, so many deep folds and layers to a person's heart. But it made a strange kind of sense to me, that he could love me and Embry and Jenny all at the same time. Not very many people love like Ash loves, as fiercely and fully, and maybe one person alone could never have held all that he needs to give.

"And then you proposed to him again?" I ask, trying to figure out what happened next.

Ash lets go of my waist and rubs his forehead with his thumb. "After Jenny died. That night Morgan took me to the club and had me flog her, I left and I went straight to Embry. He gave me so much that night, more than any person should have to give another, because I unleashed it all on him. My grief, my pain, this new sister that was also his sister whom I'd also fucked... I was a tornado. And he welcomed me."

I pull his hand away from his forehead so I can see his eyes. My touch stirs him; he shifts in the chair and meets my stare again. "He wanted to keep us secret again. Merlin wanted it to be secret. But it was legal now and I didn't fucking care about the election—but I did care about him. Five months ago, I asked him to marry me again. I thought for sure this time…" He trails off and gives me a watery smile. "Well. The best-laid plans and all that. And then I saw you in that church a few weeks later and it felt like fate. I wanted to see you, and the moment I told Embry about it, he volunteered to help me. I thought he wanted to make amends for rejecting my ring a second time…of course, now I know better. He wanted to see you."

"Oh God, Ash," I say, my chest hurting for him. This incredible man who'd been rejected twice by the person he loves.

"Greer, I'm—I'm not telling you this so that you feel like you were in any way a second choice. You know that I love you, that I've been obsessed with you for years. But I just want you to know that what I had with Embry was serious to me. It was the realest thing I'd ever felt until I finally had you. I didn't kiss him because I wanted to hurt you. I kissed him because even though he's broken my heart twice in ten years, I still think he looks beautiful in the winter moonlight. Because sometimes I think I might literally die from wanting to feel his lips on mine."

A few heavy minutes pass as snow blows against the window next to us.

"Okay," I say in a whisper after I can't stand the quiet any longer.

"Okay what?"

"I think I understand now. You and him. Us."

His hand leaves my hair and traces a warm trail from behind my ear to my shoulder. "I deserve the worst, Greer, but I don't want it. I don't want you to leave me."

I startle. "Who said anything about leaving?"

He frowns. "You were so angry—and with good reason—I just thought—"

321

"That I'd leave you? Like Embry did?"

"Yes," he confesses.

I squeeze his hand. "I'm angry. I need to be able to be angry sometimes. I need to be able to demand answers. But that doesn't mean I don't love you. It doesn't mean I don't want to stay." A deep breath with the next admission. "Especially because I love Embry too. He and I haven't… please believe me, Ash, we haven't touched since that night in Chicago."

"Oh, I believe you," Ash says in a voice I feel down into the pit of my stomach. "That's something neither of you could hide from me."

And there's something about the way he says that, possessive and omnipotent and maybe a little cruel, that sends cold bolts of fearful desire through me.

"So what happens now?" I ask. "Where do we go from here?"

"I don't know," he admits.

"Where do you want to go from here?"

He looks up at me, and then all of a sudden he's standing with me in his arms and we're walking toward the bed. He lays me on my back and crawls over me, brushing the hair out of my face as his hips settle into the cradle of mine. I try to stifle my moan at the feeling, but it doesn't work.

"What else were you feeling that night?" he asks.

"What?"

"On Christmas Eve. You said your heart was breaking, but what else did you feel when you watched Embry and me? Did you feel"—his fingers dance down from my face to my breast, where my nipple hardens instantly through the soft chiffon—"curious? Did you wonder what it might feel like to be in between us? Did you wonder what it would look like to see Embry's mouth wrapped around my dick?"

I don't know how to answer. I don't know which answer

322

is best for our future or what he wants to hear, so I tell him the truth. "Yes. Yes, I was curious. I was—" Ash's fingers are moving down to my hip now, burning warm trails through the fabric, and it's hard to concentrate. "I was turned on."

"Did it make you wet?"

"Yes," I whimper.

"Are you wet right now?"

But he doesn't wait for me to answer. He finds out for himself, and I can tell by his pleased grunt that he likes what he's found. I spread my legs wider for him, and within a few heartbeats, he's got his flushed erection in his fist, stroking it and kneeling up over me.

"On your stomach," he orders. I flip over, shivering when I feel my dress dragged up over my ass, and shivering even more when I feel the fat tip of his cock against my folds. He pushes in, just the right amount of rough, and I practically purr with the sensation of his thick shaft spearing me.

He brings his body down over mine, his lips near my ear and his arm under my breasts so he can grab and squeeze all he likes. Only his hips move, deep and powerful, all muscle and deliberate, unhurried strokes.

"I don't know what the future looks like," he says, his breathing still calm and even, as if he were sitting on a couch and not shoving eight inches of hungry flesh inside me. "I don't know what we're supposed to do next. The three of us are never going to stop loving each other and we're never going to stop being jealous. But at least we all know now."

He shifts the angle of his hips and I gasp, and then the hand that was plumping my breast slides down to my clit and starts rubbing. I bury my face in the covers and moan.

"Would you like it if Embry were here right now?" Ash asks. I can hear the smallest ragged edge in his voice, as if he's aroused by his own words. "Underneath you while I'm on top? The two of us pressing against you, demanding

323

satisfaction and attention? And when we've taken every-thing we can from you, would you like to watch us fuck each other? You should see how fast Embry comes when he's being fucked, Greer, it's really quite something."

I'm moaning almost nonstop now, squirming into the blanket, the image of the three of us fucking too much for me to bear. The image of Ash buried in Embry's ass light-ing me on fire. I come suddenly and hard, clenching around Ash's cock as my hands claw at the blankets.

"Oh, so you do like that" comes Ash's voice in my ear. I can tell by the erratic thrusts of his hips that he's getting close himself. "I like it too. The thought of you two together makes me so fucking hot—" He breaks off and pulls out, and the bed shakes as he strokes himself to a hard, furious finish.

He lets out a rough groan, and wet heat shoots onto my ass and the small of my back, and I realize I'm smiling into the blankets. I don't know if it's the catharsis of Ash and I coming clean with each other or the mild display of dominance or just the good old-fashioned sex hormones, but all the feelings from earlier tonight are washed clean and hung out to dry. Still there, not vanished, but no longer so dirty and unsettling, no longer secret.

Something cool and silken dabs at the semen on my skin, and I turn my head to look up at Ash. "What are you using to do that?" I ask scoldingly. "It better not be your bow tie."

Ash gives me a sweetly sheepish look and tosses the stained bow tie onto the ground. "Oops."

"Oops?"

"Shh." He crawls up next to me, sliding a hand under my stomach and turning me so that I'm facing into his chest and his strong arms are wrapped around me. "Stay here with me a moment."

"My shoes are still on," I protest. "And we're sideways on the bed."

"Don't be so conformist. And about the shoes…" I hear a clunk followed by a second clunk as he toes off his dress shoes, and then he tugs off my high heels with his feet. "Better?"

I flex my toes. "Much better."

"Good." He pulls me tight, kissing my hair, and for a few moments we just hold each other and listen to the wind blowing off Lac Léman.

I press my lips to the exposed slice of skin near his collarbone. "What are we going to do?" I ask again, my whisper barely audible over the wind.

Ash's hands rub my back, and when he speaks, he speaks slowly, like he's still figuring it out for himself. "I don't think we can decide that without Embry. Whatever happens next, it should be a decision between the three of us, something that the three of us can agree on and live with. If you're still going to have me as a husband and I'm still going to have him as my vice president, then we're stuck together. And I think until this conversation happens, we should make sure there's nothing physical or even verbally sexual transacting between anyone other than the two of us. Embry is off-limits until we sort this out."

I nod against him. He's right. He's almost always right.

"Also—until we can find a time for all three of us to talk, I want the two of us to be honest with each other. I made the mistake of hiding and lying before, and I don't want to do that again."

"Honest like…?"

"Like when we're thinking of him, we tell each other. No more hiding our feelings for him, even if it feels wrong to admit them out loud. Because really, who would understand better than me how you feel?"

I sigh-laugh. "I guess that is true."

"I know it is."

"Okay," I agree. "I trust you, and I think you're right. You and I will be honest and we'll only be sexual with each other until we talk with Embry." I chew on my lip. "Does that mean...after we talk, you want to be sexual with him?"

"Honestly? I want the three of us together. But I also want you all to myself. And I want him all to myself. My feelings are very intense and wildly inconsistent about this. All I know is that it's not only up to me. And not only up to you or Embry. It has to be together or not at all."

Tiredness hits my body all at once. There's been so much to unpack tonight, so much that I'll still be processing it for weeks to come, and there is so much work ahead. But if that work means the three of us could—

No. I refuse to entertain fantasies about it or about Embry until things are settled. I'm engaged to Ash, and even if we have a nontraditional dynamic beginning to flourish, I'm still determined to remain emotionally dedicated to him until we openly decide otherwise.

I yawn and Ash starts stroking my back again. "There's one more thing," he says, and he sounds as tired as I feel.

"What is it?" I ask over another yawn.

"I want you to be careful around Abilene."

I definitely wasn't expecting that. "Abilene?"

I can feel Ash hesitate next to me, his body going still as he searches for the right words. "She accosted me tonight at the dinner, after I'd spoken to Merlin. She...well, this is uncomfortable and awkward to say, but I think she has feelings for me. She tried to kiss me and she told me—it's not important what she told me, actually, but it gave me the impression that she's not going to look out for your best interests."

Oh, Abilene. No wonder she seemed so nervous when I went to pick up my suitcase.

"What did she say?"

"Greer—"

"Please, Ash. She's my cousin and my best friend and if she's harassing you or disparaging me, I need to know."

He relents with a sigh. "She said she'd make a better wife to me than you would. That she could make me happier. And I told her that simply wasn't possible. You are the perfect woman, objectively speaking, and also the perfect woman for me, and I told Abilene that. She was understandably upset, and I'm guessing humiliated. She left me without another word."

"Oh my God." I roll away from Ash to stare up at the ceiling. "I'm so mortified. And I'm so sorry."

"You had nothing to do with it." Ash is still on his side, and he twirls a tendril of my hair around his finger. "And I am endeavoring to forget about it. But I thought you should know that she seems to harbor some deep resentment of you. I tried to make it unequivocally clear that I loved you and nothing would change that, but I don't know if it will be enough."

"I don't know either," I say, thinking of the way Abi has nursed her obsession with Ash through the years. "She can be quite determined when she wants to be."

Ash's lips are on my hair now, and then on my face, and then on my lips. "She's not more determined than I am. Rest assured, she holds no allure for me."

That does ease my mind a little, although I'm still uneasy about this latest development. It almost seems unhinged, unstable, especially for a woman who's spent years trying to perfect the most charming, put-together personality imaginable.

But then Ash's hands are back under my dress, his stiffening cock warm against my hip, and everything else slowly bleeds away.

CHAPTER 26

IT TURNS OUT THAT FINDING A TIME FOR THE THREE OF US to talk is harder than it sounds. The rest of our stay in Geneva is busy, with Ash and Embry gone from six in the morning to one o'clock the next morning, and all the hours between are filled with helping Kay put out fires back home.

Abilene avoids me so expertly that I don't see her until we fly home, and when we board the plane, she apologizes for her absence, blaming it on the Carpathian man she spent her days with. I watch her eyes as she tells me about him, as she asks me how much I've seen or talked to Ash since the dinner, and I realize she doesn't know I know.

It's dishonest, but I feed that belief, telling her everything she wants to hear. I act innocent, I act like I have no idea she's still in love with Ash or that she tried to kiss him at the dinner, and it makes me a little sad to see how easily she swallows what I say. I think about the way she acted when I first told her about Ash and me, about the way she lied about something as trivial as how I looked in a dress.

Maybe Ash is right to say I shouldn't trust her.

But once we get back home and settle into the fast-paced rhythm of work and life, I also settle back into loving her. She's just Abilene—passionate and fierce and impulsive. And I'm the last woman to judge another for making mistakes because of a man like Ash. I forgive her, go on loving her and having weekly lunch and sometimes grabbing cocktails after work on Thursdays, although I try not to bring Ash up around her any more than I have to, which seems to work for her just fine. She even acts happy when I ask her to be my maid of honor, though I can see the brittle displeasure in her face when she thinks I'm not looking.

But what can I do?

The wedding consumes every waking minute. There's the planning, of course, but then there's the endless rounds of interviews and photo shoots that Merlin and Trieste—the press secretary—keep signing me up for. Overnight, I'm transformed into America's sweetheart, the granddaughter of a former vice president marrying the youngest president in history. My face is everywhere in print and online, to the point where I'm recognized on the street and where students I don't know stop me on campus for Snapchat selfies. It's flattering the first few times, but slowly it becomes a nuisance and then a real burden. All the work I did, all the choices I made to build a life of quiet solitude, it's all undone in a matter of a few weeks. Even Grandpa Leo calls me to warn me about the dangers of constant press attention.

Both Embry and Ash are incredibly busy too, and it's only once or twice a week that I get to sneak into Ash's bed, and it's only on Sundays that all three of us are together for church and sometimes football. But I'm usually grading papers or working on the book, and Belvedere and Kay and Trieste and Merlin are constantly in and out, and the moment just never comes, that moment where the three of us are alone and have unlimited time to just *talk*.

At first it's agony, every missed day that turns into a missed week that turns into a missed month. Ash and I keep our word to each other and we both act carefully around Embry. He acts carefully around us in return, especially after Ash informs him of our decision to have an agreement created by all three of us. Ash tells me that Embry agrees to that, and I smile at the irony that we have all talked about talking but still haven't *talked*.

I wonder if Embry knows how often we bring him up when we're alone, sometimes as we're having sex, but other times as we're falling asleep or even as we're simply working in silence together. Ash will set down his pen and rub his forehead and say my name in the kind of pained, quiet voice I know means that right now he's missing Embry. And I'll crawl onto his lap and whisper *me too me too me too*, and kiss him until we both feel better again.

And so the days pass, interminable and yet dizzying in how quickly they fly by, until I find myself holding Ash's hand as Air Force One touches down in Kansas City the day before our wedding, a warm day in May. Ash's mother greets us with a big hug on the tarmac, and then we begin the painstakingly photographed dance of the rehearsal and the rehearsal dinner. All the while being achingly aware of Embry watching us, of Embry there like the unseen shadow of our future marriage.

He said it was hell watching Ash and me. Was watching us walk through the ceremony worse than hell? *Is* there anything worse than hell?

Yes, I decide as we make our toasts and speeches at the rehearsal dinner. Loving two men but only marrying one—that's worse than hell. Watching Embry quietly die is worse than hell. Watching Ash watch Embry, and wondering if he wishes he were walking down the aisle with him instead of me—that is much, much worse than hell.

Ash and I part that night with a chaste kiss. And I go to bed in my own room, staring up at the ceiling and wondering what new hell tomorrow will bring.

CHAPTER 27

THE WEDDING DAY

ABILENE WENT TO FIND THE VEIL AND SOME LUNCH, AND SO for the moment, I'm alone. I stand in my hotel suite, which also serves as my bridal dressing room, so silent and calm after all the rustling of tissue paper and the chatter of women and the noisy comings and goings of every single female relative Ash or I have. I turn to the mirror for the thousandth time, and for the thousandth time, a cold dagger slices through my heart, slicing it right in two.

One side, still red and healthy, pulses with joy. The other side, black and frozen, feels nothing but icy despair.

It's really happening.

It's really happening.

The one thing I want most in the world—to marry Ash—and the one thing I want least in the world—to be separated from Embry.

I can't cry—I spent too many long hours in the makeup chair for that—so instead I smooth my hands along the expensive fabric of the dress and turn away, the huge skirt of my wedding dress turning with me.

Don't look in the mirror, I tell myself. *You'll only want to cry again.*

Most women wouldn't cry to see themselves as I look right now. Custom gown embroidered with Swarovski crystals and silver thread. My white-gold hair coiled into a sleek ballet knot at the nape of my neck. Diamonds glittering at my ears and throat. There is a princess in that mirror… and I can't bear to look at her.

I walk over to the window and press my hands to the glass. The hotel room looks out on an unfamiliar skyline, a healthy and contained cluster of skyscrapers, old brick warehouses, and architectural oddities. Kansas City's skyline. Ash's skyline.

Ash.

Has any woman loved a man like I love my Ash? If he ceased to love me or I ceased to love him, my entire world would shrink to a singularity and then explode. I need him like I need air, like I need the sun or like I need God.

I can't *not* marry him. Every cell in my body cries out for his presence, pines for the slightest brush of his hands or words or eyes; I am as destined to marry Ash as much as I am destined to have my gray eyes or my blond hair.

So why the tears, Greer?

But of course I know why. Ash would know why too if he could see me right now. Because I can't help loving Embry, because neither can Ash, because the three of us have some sort of twisted, fucked-up love that no church would agree to sanctify, much less the American electorate.

I'll marry Ash as Embry watches, as Embry hands Ash the ring that will seal our vows, and the three of us will quietly ache together, quietly die together, even as Ash and I are quietly born anew as man and wife.

There's no way around this, nothing that can be done, at least nothing that I can see. I can't not marry Ash. I can't stop craving Embry. Both of them love me, and both of them love each other. Whichever way we move, there will be heartbreak, and Embry knows—has always known maybe—that if he forces me to choose, if he drags my choice into the open air and says *me or him*, then it would be Ash.

It would always be Ash.

And maybe that's why I want to cry, because my heart is breaking for Embry just as much as it's breaking for me.

A knock sounds at the door, and I shake off my thoughts, expecting Abilene and the veil. "Come in," I call, blinking a few times to rid myself of the lingering tears.

I hear a key card snick in the lock, and the heavy door opens. I step away from the window, prepared to fake a smile and a laugh for Abi, prepared to take the veil from her and pin it to the delicate tiara set in my hair.

But it isn't Abilene who walks through the door.

It's the best man.

"Embry," I whisper. I breathe his name like it's the last breath I'll ever take.

He walks in and turns to close the door behind him, shutting it and carefully swinging the deadbolt closed.

We haven't been alone together for so long, weeks and weeks and months and months, but now here we are, alone at last. But I'm dolled up to be the American Bride of the Century and he's in his tuxedo, and so the wedding hovers in the air like its own entity, a third presence in the room.

I train my eyes on the floor, not trusting myself to look in his face, not wanting to see the torment I know will be written there. Not wanting him to see the torment written on my own face. Isn't this hard enough as it is? Why is he here? Why come and force this moment between us when we could have simply gone on as we always did—ignoring, denying, avoiding? Silently dying?

Embry steps deliberately toward me—so unlike him, so unlike the turbulent, impulsive man he is. He stops just out of reach, his dress shoes black and gleaming against the carpet.

"Greer," he says quietly.

I force my eyes up to his, trailing up his long legs, up that perfectly fitted tuxedo jacket which highlights the lean, hard lines of his waist and shoulders, and then finally up to his face, where pain is stamped onto every handsome feature.

The moment my eyes lock with his, I know it doesn't matter that we aren't touching. The electric heat in his eyes is desperate, and I know he can see the same in mine, and in that instant, in my mind, we share a thousand scorching kisses, he trails caresses over every inch of my skin, I come a thousand times under his slender, muscled body.

Those ice-blue eyes blaze with heat and I shiver. "What are you doing here?" I ask in a whisper.

"I wanted to see you. You know…before…" He trails off.

He steps closer, lifting a hand. I shouldn't let him touch me, not on my wedding day, not in my wedding dress, but my chest is filled with that tight ache, and so I close my eyes and hold my breath as he reaches forward.

The backs of his knuckles graze against my cheek, sending shivers chasing down my back, and every brush of his fingers over my skin makes me want to scream, makes me want to cry.

My eyes flutter open to find him staring intently at me, those blue eyes glacial with pain. My gaze drops down to his mouth, where his lips are parted ever so slightly, as if he has to catch his breath.

I can't stop staring at them, those firm, straight lips with their barely there tilt at the corners, the tilt that can turn from a smirk to a sneer to a smile, depending on his moods. I want those lips. I want them against my mouth; I want them pressed to my throat; I want them between my legs. I want his lips and his hands and his cock, and I want him to rip off my wedding dress and do what his searing stare promises and fuck me. Ash be damned.

Except…

Except I love Ash. Except I promised him I wouldn't touch Embry until the three of us had finally talked.

I suck in a breath and take a step back. It's too dangerous, Embry here and my heart so twisted in knots. Embry notices my step back, and his eyebrows draw together the tiniest amount, confusion and hurt simmering under the surface of his expression. I hate hurting him, and I hate myself for doing it, but what's the alternative? How can there be any other way?

"You have to go," I choke out, turning away from him, unable to look at his wounded face any longer. "You can't—and I can't—just. Please."

"I can't go yet," Embry says, and his voice has lost its earlier husky uncertainty. In its place is the dispassionately icy tone he usually uses with recalcitrant senators or the puerile hordes of reporters and paparazzi that follow his every move. It's his Vice President voice, and it makes me shiver. "Ash asked me to deliver a present to you. I made sure Abilene would be occupied so I'd have enough time to give it to you personally."

I let out a long breath, wondering if this is how it will always be. Alone together only when there's a pretext, forever divided by the one man we love more than each other or ourselves.

"Greer." The ice in Embry's voice thaws the tiniest amount when he speaks my name. "Please let me give you your present. You know how Ash was about seeing you today, so he asked me to deliver it."

I finally turn back to him and he holds out his phone, indicating that I should take it. Confused, I reach for it, and then the screen lights up with Ash's name.

My heart soars at the same time that it sinks. I grab the phone and touch the *accept* button, pressing the phone eagerly to my ear as if it has been weeks since we last spoke instead of hours.

"Ash," I say, my voice hiding nothing. I know he can discern every doubt, every guilty thought, every needy pang I've felt in the last six hours and he can do it all just from that one syllable. What's more, I welcome it. With Ash, I never need to be shriven. He knows each sin the moment he hears my voice or looks at my face, and then all is immediately forgiven.

"Greer," he says, his voice soothing and sure. "I wish I were with you right now. I miss you."

"I miss you too," I say, ignoring the way Embry's eyes are pinned on me as I speak.

"I know you look beautiful right now," Ash says, his voice going a shade deeper, a shade rougher. "I won't be able to keep my hands off you after you walk down the aisle to me."

"Can't you come see me before then?"

A warm laugh. "You don't care for this particular tradition?"

"What point does it serve, other than to keep our guests waiting longer while we take pictures?"

"It serves the point of marking the moment I first see you. When I first lay eyes on my bride, I will be surrounded by our family and friends and watched over by God. I want the first moment I see you to be special and apart from any other moment, just like today is special and apart from any other day. Greer, today is the most important day of my life."

My throat tightens. "Oh, Ash."

"And," he adds in a voice heavy with promise, "patience is always rewarded, my little princess. Always."

His voice—and the murmured *little princess*—makes my cunt ache and my pulse pound, and when I think about tonight after the wedding, when I think about Ash's broad, muscled body pinning mine to the bed, I can barely breathe.

"I miss you so much," I say. I'm repeating myself at this point, but I don't care.

"Greer, I want to give you your present now."

"The phone call isn't my present?"

That warm laugh again. "I'm not that stingy. No, it's not your present. I want you to hand the phone to Embry for a moment."

I obey, as I always do with Ash, and Embry takes the phone. He paces away from me, back toward the suite's sitting room, so that I can't hear what he's saying to Ash. They speak for a few minutes together and when Embry returns, his face reveals nothing, although I think I detect a hint of a frown on that perfectly shaped mouth.

He hands the phone back to me, and I hold it up to my ear. "Ash? What does this have to do—" I break off my words.

Embry is getting to his knees. In front of me.

"Greer" comes Ash's voice through the receiver. "I want to be there so badly right now. I want to touch you and taste you and tell you how beautiful you are. I want to make you feel good."

While Ash speaks, Embry tilts his face up to mine. Something pulls at the edges of his calm mask now, but I can't tell if it's pleasure or pain, joy or contrition. And then his elegant hands with their long fingers reach for the skirt of my wedding dress.

I freeze.

"Embry…?" My voice is no louder than a raindrop

coursing down a window, but both men hear it. Embry bites his lip but starts lifting the hem of my dress.

Ash, on the other hand, says, "Stand still, Greer. Are you standing still?"

"Yes," I say, unable to tear my eyes away from Embry's, unable to move away from this terrible, terrible, delicious thing. I tremble with a molten heat low in my belly as Embry's able hands slowly gather up all of the layers of petticoat under my dress.

Ash continues talking. "I kept thinking about what I wanted to give you today, and honestly, Greer, there isn't really anything I couldn't give you. Jewelry or exotic vacations or rare editions of the books you love, anything I could have dreamed of, I could get for you—but they were just *things*. I didn't want to get you a thing for a curio cabinet or a jewelry box. I wanted to give you something that you could carry with you through our new life together. Something that would make you a promise."

Embry's hand brushes up against my stocking-covered ankle and I gasp.

"What is it, princess?" Ash asks in a low voice.

"Embry... I mean, Ash, I—" I can't find the words just then because Embry's hand slides up my calf and everything stops. My thoughts, my feelings, my guilt—my world shrinks to Ash's voice on the phone and the fingers moving past my knee and Embry's face, so controlled. But lust and anger and determination are fissuring across that control, and I can see his wide pupils and the pulse pounding in his neck and the trembling of his lips.

What is happening? I think distantly to myself. What am I letting happen...and all while I'm on the phone with my soon-to-be husband?

And then the world slams back into motion, and I make a strangled noise, stumbling backward, away from

339

Embry. He starts to stand and come toward me, and I hold out one of my hands, moving backward until my back is pressed against the floor-to-ceiling window overlooking the skyline.

Embry looks down at my shaking hand and then back up to me, those fissures in his control now full-on fractures, and he says, "Greer…"

"Don't test me," I whisper, not sure if I'm whispering to the groom or the best man. "Don't test me like this."

Ash's voice comes into my ear. "Relax, Greer. I want to give you this. I want to give you something you want… something you deserve."

This isn't happening. I missed a connection somewhere, misunderstood something vital, because there is no way, *no fucking way*, that Ash is offering his best friend to me as some sort of wedding present, not when we agreed that Embry was off-limits until we figured everything out. This is my wishful thinking turned toxic, this is my darkest fantasies turning into delusion—

"I want you to let Embry give you my gift," Ash tells me. "While I listen. That's what you'll give me in exchange: every single moan, pant, and cry will be for me."

"You can't be saying what I think you're saying," I say. "We agreed…you know what we agreed to. This isn't it!"

"I know, but I can't wait any longer," Ash says with a growl. "Today is hard enough without denying ourselves."

"But what about you—"

"Oh, don't worry, angel. I'll have something out of this for me too."

I hear the dark roughness in his voice and I realize I'm so very, very wet.

As if he knows, Ash asks, "Are you wet right now? Are you wet from Embry reaching under your dress?"

I lick my lips. I can't lie—Ash would know. But how can

I admit the truth? Yes, I am wet. Yes, I want Embry's mouth on me. Yes, yes, yes to all of it.

"Close your eyes," Ash orders.

I do, my panting somehow louder in my head when I can't see anything. The glass window against my back is cool and strong, just like Ash's words in my ear.

"I know you're wet. I know it like I know Embry is hard right now, just from the mere thought of touching you. You want it, don't you? You want it so much that you're shaking with the effort it's taking to hold yourself back."

I feel the hem of my skirt lift again. Embry is back in front of me, but this time I don't try to move away. I keep my eyes shut, wishing I had the strength to open them and tell Embry to stop. The strength to flee temptation.

"Answer me," Ash demands. "Are you wet right now? Do you want it?"

"Yes." The word comes out strangled and hopeless.

"I knew you did," Ash says. "I knew you wanted it. Spread your legs, sweetheart, and let Embry make you feel good."

"But I don't want to hurt you." It's my final plea, my final argument, my final grasp at some semblance of sanity. My skirts are almost up at my waist now, and I know the moment Embry catches sight of my delicate, hand-embroidered French panties because he takes in a sharp breath, as if punched in the gut.

"It all hurts," Ash says. "It hurts watching you two watching each other. It hurts watching him with other people. It hurts knowing that I've asked him to walk down the aisle to me twice and he's refused me both times. There's no part about this that doesn't hurt, but what's the alternative? Living without the pain means living without each other."

My eyelids burn with unshed tears, and it takes all my willpower to keep them from falling.

"At least this way," Ash says, "I can have some control over it. At least this way, I can make it feel good just as much as it hurts."

You're breaking my heart, I want to say, but that's a lie because my heart is already broken. Instead, I just say, "I can't bear to hurt you any more than you already are, please. Please don't do this."

"No." The word is final. "I want this. God, Greer, I'm so fucking hard right now, it hurts. If I were there—" He stops and I hear one long sigh. "Tonight," he says instead of finishing his thought. "Tonight."

It is a promise. A gift and a curse, because tonight when my cravings are relieved by Ash, it will be in our wedding bed, and Embry will be somewhere else, alone.

Or worse, not alone.

My chest tightens with unreasonable jealousy at the thought.

Embry transfers the heavy material of my skirt to one strong hand, and then I feel his other hand run up the inside of my thigh.

I let out a soft whimper. My skin cries out for Embry, just as the rest of me cries out for Ash. What I wouldn't give to have Ash here, ready to take all my pent-up lust and mold it into something that won't kill me with guilt.

Because I will die with guilt.

But somehow it doesn't stop me from squirming with want as Embry's hand runs up my other thigh. And then it happens. With one deliberate, grazing touch, Embry's fingertips skate across the lace covering my folds, and I gasp. Embry looks up at me with hooded eyes, and I stare back.

"I can smell you," he says, his voice cracking a little at the end. "It smells so good."

I shiver. A thousand voices, a choir of warnings, seem to sing in my mind. *Stop this. Stop this. Stop this.*

But his words, the way his voice roughened, as if being able to smell my need is the one thing that can break him…

I don't stop him. In fact, I reach down and gather my skirt into my arms so that Embry's hands can be free, something he immediately takes advantage of by sliding his palms to my ass and squeezing. The groan he lets out when he does goes straight to my clit.

His fingers once again graze over my folds, tickling the lace, and it feels as if everything has become electric. The air, his skin, my skin—everything hums with insatiable need.

Embry leans forward so that the only thing I can see below the heavy bunches of fabric is his light brown hair, and then he kisses the tops of my thighs, lingering soft kisses that trace the lines of my stockings and the clips of my garter belts. I'm already panting by the time his lips brush against my mound.

"Oh my God," I breathe. "Oh my God."

"Tell me what's happening," Ash demands. "Tell me everything."

"I shouldn't be doing this," I mumble. "I have to stop."

"Don't you fucking dare," Ash says.

"Ash…"

This time, Embry doesn't stop after hearing my hesitation. He keeps going, kissing the line of my panties, kissing along the swirling lace patterns, nuzzling into me. The nuzzles turn aggressive, rough and hard, punctuated with sharp nips at my flesh through the lace. Each bite pulls a noise out of me, and each noise pulls an intake of breath from Ash.

"Tell me, Greer." It's a command that doesn't brook argument.

"I—he's biting and kissing me through my panties." *I should stop him. I should push him away. We will all regret this after it's over, me most of all.*

And I even get as far as putting my hand on Embry's head, thinking I would push his mouth away from me, but right at that moment, he licks me right through the lace and I practically dissolve. My fingers instead wind into his thick hair and tug sharply, making Embry groan so loudly that Ash can hear it.

"Fuck," Ash breathes, hearing Embry's noise. "What's happening now?"

"He's licking me," I say. "He's licking me through the lace. His mouth is so warm and *oh*—"

My fingers tighten in his hair as Embry begins sucking my clit through the lace. I squirm against him, holding his mouth fast to where I want it, feeling the licking flames deep in my core.

"He's sucking my clit now," I say, barely recognizing my own voice. Who am I, so brazenly telling my future husband about what his best friend is doing under my wedding dress? Who is this woman who leaned against a window and opened her legs for this? But I'm too far over the edge now, too wet, too sensitive, too sinful to let this end. Regret seems like a distant thing on the horizon, fuzzy and irrelevant, and with every lap of his tongue and kiss of his lips, Embry wipes the guilt from my body.

And then his deft fingers are at the clasps of my garters, easily unhooking them, and memories of another night, years and years ago, surfaces in my mind.

And like that night, Embry looks up at me as he pulls my underwear to the side, exposing my wet, pink cunt.

"I need," he says quietly to me, and the déjà vu hits me so hard that my knees almost buckle, because of course that's what he said to me the night he took my virginity too. And the way his eyes blaze, the way he slowly licks his lower lip tells me that he remembers exactly what he said that night too.

That he hasn't forgotten.

"He's pulled aside my panties now," I tell Ash. "He's looking at me there."

Not just looking. *Looking*. Devouring with his eyes. Making plans, marking possession with his stare, as if by memorizing every curve and glistening fold of my pussy, he can claim ownership somehow. *This* is the male gaze that academics always talk about, *this* is what they meant. Because in this moment, I feel objectified, branded, almost dehumanized.

Fuck if it doesn't make me wetter than ever.

"He's taking off my panties now," I say, the soft scrape of the lace on my thighs almost more than I can bear. And then Embry helps me step free of them, afterward putting one warm hand on each thigh and parting my legs so that I stand in a wider stance.

Embry groans at the sight of my exposed pussy.

"He's looking at me again. He can see that I'm all the way bare. And I'm so wet, Ash. Do you remember the time I rode your thigh in front of him?"

"God, yes," Ash says, and I think I can hear the rustle of fabric, as if he were parting the fly of his tuxedo pants to palm his cock.

"I'm wet like that. *Oh*. Oh God."

"Tell me, princess."

"He…" I swallow, my fingers finding Embry's hair once more. "He put his finger inside me. And another one. They're sliding in so easy, Ash, I'm so wet, but I'm swollen and it's so tight."

Ash rumbles in response, and I hear more movement, the sound of skin moving over skin. The mental vision of Ash rubbing himself to my narration of being finger-fucked by his best friend makes the flames at my core lick higher and higher.

Embry curls his fingers, pressing against the sensitive

nerve endings clustered near the front and I moan. He leans forward and sucks my clit into his mouth again, this time without the barrier of the lace, and the hot, wet contact is almost shocking in its intensity.

"Sling your leg over his shoulder," Ash tells me. "And push his face against your cunt. Grind into his mouth."

I do as he commands, and the moment I begin fucking myself against Embry's mouth, his control shears away. One hand grips my ass, his fingers digging into my flesh, while the other hand continues to fuck me mercilessly. And his mouth…

"It's like he's starving," I breathe into the phone, watching his head move below my skirts. "Like he's trying to eat me alive. His fingers are so deep in me, so fucking deep. I can feel them in my belly."

"God, I wish I were there," Ash growl. "I'd watch you come while he shoved his fingers in you. I'd make him kiss you while his mouth still tasted like your cunt. And then I'd make you kiss me."

Ash's words are like curtains catching fire, sending the clenching burn of my cunt streaking upward toward my chest. I'm going to orgasm, I know it, but I won't be able to stand, my knees are about to buckle as it is, and as if Embry can sense this, I'm all of a sudden being tugged down by my waist. Tugged down to the floor as he lies back, and then his fingers are digging into my hips, planting my pussy firmly over his mouth. I'm straddling him, riding his face, and the minute his tongue slides into my hole, I know it'll be mere moments before I lose it.

"Embry pulled me down to the floor," I manage to say into the phone. "I'm riding his face, my knees are on either side of his head. His hands are groping my ass."

Ash's voice sounds scraped and scratched, as if he can barely talk. I imagine his massive hand moving up and down

346

on his long, thick erection as he speaks. "You're going to come this way, aren't you? Like a queen, riding what's yours. Fuck his face hard, baby, that's what he wants. He'll have your smell and taste still on his lips when he watches me put my ring on your finger. He'll remember the feeling of your thighs cradling his jaw when he watches us dance our first dance at the reception."

"Jesus," I half moan, half pray, burning up from the inside. I happen to look up right at that moment and catch our reflection in the floor-length mirror on the wall. Me, flushed and panting, necklace and tiara flashing in the light, kneeling in a cloud of white silk and tulle. The fabric almost completely hides the strong, tall man beneath me, except the wandering hands that are now roaming up to my corseted breasts to squeeze and grab. The bride riding the best man's face. The groom, alone as he rubs himself listening.

The fairy tale, gone up in flames.

I am gone up in flames too. There's nothing left but a burning silhouette of need, and I forget everything but the hot mouth I'm fucking and the thick breaths of my fiancé at my ear, peppered with his murmured commands—*ride him hard* and *grind, sweetie, grind till it feels good* and *push your clit in, make him suck it.*

Heat crackles, flames rise, buildings and civilizations collapse into blistering beds of coals as, at last, release snaps free from my womb.

"I'm—" I can't finish, can't speak, can't breathe, contractions so fierce they make my eyes water centering in my pussy.

"I know, angel," Ash rasps. "You don't have to tell me."

And then everything explodes outward. The contractions multiply, the walls of my cunt pulse, my clit throbs against Embry's tongue. I cry out and cry out again because

347

it feels like a living thing has a hold of me, puncturing me in the best ways, sending tingling heat to the roots of my hair and the tips of my toes. My cries slowly turn into whimpers, and beneath me, Embry's mouth goes from ravenous to tender, gently sucking and kissing my pussy.

"My cock wants you," Ash says raggedly. "It's getting thick now. Dark and shiny. It wants to be in that wet pussy, but I can't have it right now. So I'm using one of your silk blouses to jack myself off with."

I moan at his words, aftershocks still traveling through me.

"I'm going to come," he tells me, "and when I do, I'm going to pretend I'm standing over you right now, while you look all messy and flushed and ashamed. I'm going to pretend you're looking at me with those big, gray eyes, looking guilty and scared, as I shove my cock down your throat. I'm going to pretend that you're licking me clean after I come."

"Oh God," I whisper. The image sends my cunt fluttering again, a second, milder climax now chasing through me as I imagine Ash, his tall frame looming over me, his face implacable and angry as he fucks my mouth. As he punishes me for accepting his own gift.

And maybe that's the most fucked-up part of all, that I find that follow-up scenario just as arousing as what just happened.

Ash grunts, an unashamed, male sound, and I know he's coming right now. Know long spurts of cum are erupting into the soft silk of my blouse, probably ruining it, but I don't care. The mental image of him defiling my clothes, all because he's so aroused by listening to Embry and me, is worth it.

A thousand times worth it.

But as his breathing returns to normal, as my orgasm subsides but I still allow Embry to kiss my cunt, I look up in the mirror at myself and panic.

What the hell will happen next? What will happen to the wedding and marriage that the press has already dubbed the second Camelot? Ash calls me his princess, and maybe I looked like one before I let the best man under my skirt, but this is no fairy tale.

Or if it is, it's the most fucked-up fairy tale I've ever heard of.

CHAPTER 28

THE WEDDING DAY

LOVE ENDURES ALL THINGS.

I marry Ash with Embry's bite marks on my thighs, and Ash marries me with his bite marks on Embry's neck. There's something kind of beautiful about that, I think dazedly as the priest recites our wedding mass. Something kind of beautiful and fucked up. Who needs a ring when you have bite marks? Who needs vows when you've literally bled for one another?

Then there comes the moment where the priest asks for Embry to furnish the ring—*my* ring—the one that will mark me as Ash's wife and bind me to him for the rest of my life, and my tears threaten to return. I'm not sad. I'm not afraid or overjoyed or angry or guilty or excited or jealous or suspicious—it's that I'm *all* of them. Every single feeling, all at once, a carnival of flashing thoughts and emotional noise inside my head. And that it has to be Embry to hand Ash that dainty platinum band…

Embry pats his pockets dramatically, and the crowd

ripples with laughter at the "best man lost the ring" gag. Father Jordan Brady—a handsome young blond with that unmistakable Christian hipster vibe—is too polite to roll his eyes, but I sense he goes somewhere deep inside himself to escape the threadbare frivolity of the old joke.

Embry finally removes the ring from his pocket and starts to hand it to Ash. And instead of holding out his palm to take it, Ash turns to Embry and slowly uncurls Embry's fingers from the ring. To everyone else, it looks like Ash is simply being careful with the small piece of jewelry, but I see both the promise and the apology in the gentle way Ash touches Embry's skin. What does it feel like to take a ring from a man who refused yours? And for Embry, what does it feel like to still be in love with a man you couldn't bring yourself to marry?

Despite the circus of whirling questions and emotions, the moment Ash takes my hand, I feel everything go quiet and slow and right. His hand is warm and certain around my own, his fingers sure and careful as he slides the ring onto my finger, and when I look up to his eyes, I know beyond a shadow of a doubt that he will do everything in his considerable power to keep me safe and loved.

And I know with the same certainty that I will do the same for him.

We exchange vows, we take communion, we sing the hymns and chant the chants. And at the end, when Ash lifts my veil and kisses me firmly on the lips, I feel the faintest flickering of the one emotion I haven't been able to muster yet today:

Hope.

———

"Congratulations."

Ash and I look up from the bridal table to see Embry in

front of us. He's already given his speech, but there's still cake and dancing to be had in the massive reception pavilion. It's set high up in the river bluffs, overlooking the dun ribbon of water below, and less than a mile off, the skyline twinkles merrily. All around us are nearly seven hundred guests laughing and eating and drinking while the press hovers nearby like moths near light.

But Embry looks pale. Tired. He's still in his tuxedo jacket, even though Ash has long since ditched his, and I can tell that he hasn't had anything to eat or drink.

"Embry," Ash says warmly. "Pull up a chair and eat with us."

"Actually, I think I'm going to head back to the hotel," Embry says, not looking at either of us. "I'm not feeling well. A bug, I think."

"Stay," I say, reaching for his hand. "Please. Drink with us. Dance with us."

He glances at me and then at Ash, at us together at the bridal table with our rings glinting in the twinkling lights. "I can't. Congratulations again. I wish you both all the happiness in the world."

And with those hollow words, he leaves.

I stand up, about to chase after him, but Ash takes my hand and stops me. "Greer. The press."

"Fuck the press," I grumble, but I allow him to tug me back down to my chair anyway.

"And besides," Ash continues, "it would be cruel to ask him to stay and endure his pain so publicly."

Love endures all things. The Bible verse from the church floats into my mind. But perhaps love shouldn't have to endure all things. Perhaps it would be cruel to make Embry stay.

"Angel," Ash says, taking both my hands into his. His fingers find my ring, and I smile at the possessive way he rubs it with his fingertips. "*Wife.* What's your safe word?"

"Am I going to be belted in order to earn my piece of cake?"

A small smile but he doesn't take the bait. "Say it so I know that you have it close. That you know it's yours to use for any limit. *Any* limit."

I look down to where his fingers are playing with my ring. "Maxen."

"Good." He leans down to kiss the ring, letting his lips linger at the junction of metal and flesh. "Tonight's our wedding night, Greer."

"I know," I sigh. "Can't we just leave these people and start it now?"

He hesitates, his lips still on my hand.

"What is it? Were you planning on doing something extreme tonight? I'll try it. You know I'll try anything you ask me to."

"That's what I'm afraid of. You have to agree to this because you want it, not just because you think I want it."

He straightens and takes a deep breath. "I want Embry to join us tonight."

I don't answer. I can't answer, actually, because I've forgotten how to breathe.

"Today was perfect," he says in a low voice. "Listening to you on the phone while he touched you was…electrifying. And marrying you, Greer, saying those words to you was the happiest moment of my life. Today feels like magic—*tonight* feels like magic—and I want more of it. I want us, all three of us, to feel it together. If today was about the two of us making vows, then tonight should be about the three of us taking the next step together."

I finally find my voice. It's dry, threatening to crack. "And what's the next step?"

"I don't know," he says, giving me a smile so beautiful it breaks my heart. "But I'm ready to find out."

The evening passes in a blur. We dance, my grandfather cries, Abilene flirts. There are too many senators and heads of state and businesspeople and celebrities to keep straight, and it's impossible to keep track of time or the number of people who wish us congratulations. When I glance at Ash's watch, I'm shocked to see it's past eleven p.m.

"It's late," I say to Ash, squeezing his hand.

He squeezes back. "I'm having a hard time being patient too. Just a little while longer, angel."

Finally, Ash waves Belvedere over, who passes word to the wedding planner that we're ready to leave. The party is still in full swing, the band having packed up and a DJ having come in, and any other time, I would have wanted to stay. But tonight, Ash's bed waits for me.

And maybe Embry will be in that bed too.

Ash and I hold hands and leave the pavilion as people line up and wave sparklers, glittering fire spitting and dancing around us, hissing down into the soft green grass below. We wave, kisses are blown, and then we're packed into the Beast, the black Cadillac designed specifically for the president.

My dress surrounds us in clouds of silk and tulle, and Ash is laughing as we try to smash it down so Luc can close the door. The door closes and then I'm being dragged into Ash's lap, tulle and all, and we're surrounded by walls of wedding dress.

"We're supposed to wave goodbye through the window," I whisper, although I like the sudden, if ridiculous, privacy we have right now.

Ash groans but nevertheless wrestles the gown out of the way so that we can wave some more as we pull away and drive toward our hotel. The minute we're away from the crowd, Ash lets the dress swallow us again.

"This reminds me of playing with a parachute in kindergarten," he says, glancing at the fabric.

"A parachute?"

He raises an eyebrow. "Did you not do that at your fancy boarding schools? Is my plebeian public school background showing?"

"I went to a Montessori school outside of Portland. We used parachutes more than most kids use pencils. But we sat underneath them rather than drag them inside a Cadillac."

Those dark eyebrows slant together as I get a wicked smile. "I'm happy to sit underneath your skirt, if that's what you're asking."

I'm sideways on his lap, with my legs slung over the large wooden hump in the middle of the seat that houses Ash's communications systems, and he takes advantage of my position, reaching for my legs under my dress and then following the lines of my stockings until he reaches my bare cunt.

"You never put on more panties?" he asks huskily. "Your pussy was bare this whole time?"

"Why do you think I had you pull the garter from my knee instead of my thigh? I was trying to make sure the essentials stayed covered."

His fingers probe the soft skin of my lower lips. "Did it bother you that I had your panties in my tuxedo pocket?"

I lean my head back against the window, parting my legs to give him better access, though he stays away from the flesh that wants him the most, opting instead for the soft creases between my vulva and my thighs. "I thought it was unbearably hot."

"Me too."

"Did you and Embry…" I look for the right words and can't find them. English has more words than any other Western language and yet I can't find the ones that convey curiosity and arousal and permission and jealousy all at the same time.

All the same, Ash seems to know what I'm asking. "We kissed. In the groom's dressing room at the church. He walked in and I took one look at him, and then I had him up against the wall." Ash leans his head back against the headrest of the seat. "We kissed for a very long time, until I made sure that I had tasted every trace of your cunt on his mouth, and then I marked his neck. Did you see? I wanted you to see. I can't decide if that was cruel of me or kind."

"I can't decide either," I whisper.

Ash's fingertip lightly runs up my seam, exposing how very, very wet I am. "Maybe it doesn't matter."

"Or it does matter, but I don't care."

But we're interrupted by our arrival at the hotel, a modern construction with a coldly fashionable decor. As we walk through the back entrance, my phone buzzes inside my small purse and I pull it out.

> Abilene: tell me when u get to ur hotel safely so I don't worry about u
> Me: just got here! It's so pretty!
> Abilene: which hotel did u end up at?

Just like in Geneva, the security team vetted a few hotels before picking a final one only hours before we left the venue. It's an inconvenience and a lot of extra work and not part of the normal protocol, but Merlin with all his mysterious sources of information advised Ash and his security team to go to the effort since it was such a high-profile event.

I don't think twice about it as I text back:

> we're at the Raphael.
> Abilene: sounds amazing, I'm so jealous! Enjoy ur wedding nite!

"Who are you talking to?" Ash asks. We're in the elevator now, riding up to the presidential suite, alone at Ash's insistence and at Luc's obvious displeasure.

"Abilene." I notice he's sliding his own phone into his tuxedo pants. "Who were *you* talking to?"

"Embry. I invited him up to our room to talk."

"Ash…"

I step into him, tilting my head back so I can peer up into those stunning green eyes. "No matter what happens tonight, I want you to know that I will never regret marrying you. If I had to choose, it would be you. Every time."

"You don't know how much I wanted to hear those words," he says roughly, sliding his hands through my hair. "Oh, Greer. What have I dragged you into?"

His lips on mine are hungry and searching, and I let him take my mouth like I've let him take everything of mine, the simple surrender of the act clearing my mind and stirring my blood. We're still kissing as the elevator doors open, and Ash kisses me all the way down the hallway to our room, past the agents pretending to not see us making out like teenagers. Luc opens the door to the suite, Ash kicks it closed behind us, and then we're alone.

"Do we wait for Embry?" I ask as soon as Ash lets me up for air.

"I'm not waiting to do what I've wanted to do all day, which is this." And then he lowers his mouth to my neck. The scooped neck of my dress—modest enough to pass Merlin and Trieste's "America's sweetheart" test—still dips low enough to give Ash access to my collarbone and the tops of my breasts, which he bites and sucks with pleasure. And then he's back to my neck, kissing and nibbling and sucking until my knees are weak and he's supporting all of my weight in his arms.

"This dress," he murmurs. "I've been staring at this perfect neck all day. It's been driving me wild."

My hands fist his lapels as he continues taking his pleasure, appreciative noises coming from the back of his throat as he tastes my skin. He's coming back up to my lips for a proper kiss when we hear a soft, tentative rap at the door.

We look at each other, and then I let go of Ash's jacket and go to the door, not even bothering to check through the peephole before I open it.

It's Embry.

He gives a quick look over his shoulder at the Secret Service agent standing nearby. "May I come in?"

"Please do," Ash says from behind me, and Embry steps inside. He's lost the tuxedo jacket and vest, although his bow tie still hangs loose around his neck. His sleeves are rolled up to his elbows, exposing strong, sinewed forearms that flex and harden as he closes the door behind himself and then shoves his hands in his pockets.

"You wanted to see me?" he asks. There's something almost defensive in his posture, in the way his shoulders are ever so slightly hunched, in the way he squares off to face Ash.

"Yes," Ash says. "We did."

And then he walks right over and kisses his friend, cupping a hand around the back of Embry's neck to hold him there.

Embry's eyelashes flutter and a small breath leaves him, but he doesn't pull his hands out of his pockets, he doesn't relax. "What are you doing?" he asks as Ash pulls away. "I thought today was to get it out of our systems before the wedding ceremony. Not...more."

"I told you the last time I asked you to marry me," Ash says softly, "that I don't want you out of my system. No matter how many times you want me out of yours."

Embry looks away, emotion ticking in the muscles of his cheek and jaw. "It was for the best I said no. You know that."

"Greer says you told her that you loved me. Is there a reason you can't tell me that?"

Embry doesn't speak, doesn't look at Ash.

"Because I love you," Ash confesses in a torn-up voice. "I'm sorry if I didn't say it enough before. I'm sorry if I made you feel like I only wanted to use you, to fuck you like I owned you. I do want to use you and own you, but because I love you."

"Stop it," Embry whispers, squeezing his eyes closed. "Just—*stop it*."

Ash takes a step forward, changing tactics. "The three of us—we all love each other. We've all tried to live without each other. It obviously didn't work." A rueful smile. "So we need to try something different."

"Like what?" Embry asks, still turned away from us.

"We need to find a way to be together."

"What the fuck does that mean?" Embry asks, turning back to Ash. There's a scowl on his face, but his eyes are wet. "You and Greer are married now. There is no *together* for us three."

"Says who?" Ash responds. "We know what happens when two people fall in love. It's happened between each of us. We have to find out what happens when three people fall in love. All together, all at once."

"This is fucked up." And then Embry frowns. "And I don't want to be the third wheel in your marriage. A guest who gets kicked out when he wears out his welcome."

"You're not and you won't be." I speak up, and Embry turns toward me. It's the first I've spoken since he walked in. "It's supposed to be the three of us, can't you see that? Can't you *feel* it? Today in my dressing room or the night of the Polish state dinner—couldn't you feel what was happening between us all? God, Embry, don't you want us? Don't you want to fuck me again? Have Ash inside you again?"

His cheeks flush red against his fair skin. "Of course I fucking do," he says. "Of course I fucking want it. That doesn't mean it's right."

"Just because it's not common doesn't mean it's wrong," I say, pleading almost. I walk up to him and take his hand in mine. "I can't live the rest of my life like this. Torn between the two of you. Watching Ash watching you. It will rip my soul in half."

Embry exhales.

"But we can't do anything without you wanting it too," I say. "If you can't be one of three, then you have to be one alone. We have to decide the boundaries here and now, because when Ash and I get back from our honeymoon, we will need to know exactly where we stand with you."

"This can't work," Embry says, looking down to where I'm holding his hand. "You understand that, right? There's no possible way the three of us could make this work."

"It will be hard," Ash says, coming up next to us. "It won't be easy at all."

"People will suspect. They'll learn the truth. If it ever gets out, all three of us will be ruined. Forever."

"That's right," Ash says, and he takes Embry's other hand. "We'll have to be extremely careful."

"And we'd have to have boundaries of our own. For the sake of your marriage and my sanity, everything would have to be crystal-clear about what's okay and what's off-limits."

"Yes," I agree, looking at Ash. "We would have to figure that out too."

"And the minute it hurts too much, the minute it stops working, we have to be honest about it," Embry says, and his tone has shifted from resistant to something quiet, begging. "We have to be able to stop it if it ends up wounding us."

Ash and I are holding hands now too, the three of us standing joined in a circle. It feels very solemn, very surreal, with the low sconces throwing off patterns of gold light and the patter of May rain sounding on the window.

"Yes," Ash affirms. "But we have to promise each other that we'll try to make it work. That we won't run away when it gets hard. That we will love each other as best as we can in all the ways we can for as long as we can."

His words hang in the air, serious and spiritual.

I take a deep breath and go first. "I promise."

"Me too," Ash says.

Embry looks at us, our faces, our wedding outfits, our joined hands. He looks down to where we hold his hands too. He takes a deep breath and a tear spills over and races down his cheek so fast that I barely see it before it falls to the floor.

"I promise too," he says finally, heavily.

The moment is almost more sacred than the actual marriage vows I recited earlier, almost like God knows that this is the real promise that needs to be made.

This is the real wedding that will happen, not with incense and boutonnieres but with words and skin and sweat.

CHAPTER 29

THE WEDDING NIGHT

ASH IS THE FIRST TO MOVE, AND HE LETS GO OF EMBRY'S hand, gesturing toward the large bed at the end of the room. Embry nods wordlessly, and they both lead me back to the bed, each one holding one of my hands. I have to remind myself to breathe, seeing both of these powerful men in front of me, muscled arms straining against their shirts as they tug me to the bed. Together.

We reach the bed, and Ash turns me to face Embry.

"Kiss her," he orders his friend softly.

And Embry, looking like a sinner already in hell, cups my face in his hands and does as the president asks. When his lips brush against mine, I taste scotch and need, but he's too eager to stay on the surface for long, parting my lips with his own and licking into my mouth with searing intensity, making me stumble back.

Ash catches me, positioning me so I can rest against his chest as Embry kisses me like he'll never be able to kiss me again. I feel a tugging in my hair and I understand why Ash had me face Embry: he wanted to pull the elegant ballet bun loose and have my hair down and available for him. It spills over my shoulders in silky waves as Embry continues to ravish my mouth, his tongue firm and seeking, his breaths in between kisses fast and desperate.

We didn't kiss earlier today, I realize. *This is our first kiss since Chicago.*

I've waited five years for this man, and he kisses me like he's waited one hundred and five years to kiss me.

There must be a signal I don't see because then Embry pulls away and Ash is coaxing me onto the bed, onto my back. The men lie on either side of me, propped up on their elbows, stretched out in long lines of muscle and expensive fabric.

And I forget to breathe again.

Ash reaches over me and takes Embry's hand, and Embry lets out a low groan as Ash guides his hand to my leg and presses it against my calf. Slowly—so slowly that I think I might perish—Ash moves Embry's hand higher and higher and higher, lingering at the lacy tops of my stockings, and then moving up to the sensitive skin of my inner thigh. The sight of both of them reaching under my skirt, my husband forcing his best friend to touch my pussy, threatens to rip the breath right from me, and when I feel the tangle of warm, blunt fingertips against my quivering flesh, I come to life, gasping in a breath and spreading my legs.

Ash smiles down at me. "What do you want, angel?"

"We'll give it to you," Embry whispers. "We'll give you anything you want."

I chew on my lip a moment, hoping he means that. Because I want to be finger-fucked and eaten, I really do, but there's something I want even more than that. Something I haven't had before. "I want to see what happens when you two do more than kiss."

"Oh really?" Ash asks, and two thick fingers slide inside me. I sigh happily. "Would that turn you on?"

"You have no idea."

"I might have some idea. Feel how wet she is, Embry. Feel it." A third finger, this one from a different hand, slides in and my hips lift off the bed at the sensation.

Embry nuzzles his face into my neck, I think at first to kiss me. But as the seconds pass with his lips lingering on my neck, I begin to wonder if it's because he's nervous about kissing Ash.

"Embry," I murmur. "Let me see you and Ash together. Let me have that."

And when he lifts his head, I see his eyes are glassy again, like melting glacier ice. His hand leaves me and he gets to a kneeling position. Ash mirrors him, and I'm the luckiest woman in the whole goddamn world to be witnessing the president of the United States deliberately palming his cock through his pants as the vice president watches with his lip between his teeth.

"I'm sorry," Embry finally says. His voice is throttled, his eyes glazed with unshed tears. "I'm sorry I said no. I never stopped loving you. I just wanted to do the right thing."

"You're here now," Ash answers gruffly, one hand still on his erection as his other reaches for Embry's shirt. "You're here now."

I think they're going to kiss, that they're going to come crashing together over me in a tangle of muscle and long-stifled desire, but they don't. Instead, Embry traces Ash's mouth with his forefinger—the finger that was just inside me. And then he pushes it past Ash's lips.

Ash sucks on the finger, shoving two of his own in Embry's mouth, the two that he felt my wetness with, and I watch them as they lick the taste of my cunt from each other's fingers the same way I'd lick melted chocolate from my own. Ash's eyelids are hooded as Embry takes his fingers deep into his mouth, and Embry is breathing hard at the sight of his own finger between Ash's lips. He lets his hand fall free, and then suddenly the kiss happens, fast and hard like a clap of lightning.

"Ash," Embry breathes. "Oh, Ash."

Ash grunts in response, leaning into Embry's neck and biting the mark he made earlier. Embry practically buckles in response, and then Ash is off the bed and hauling Embry off too. Ash kisses him again, this time pressing the length of his body against Embry's. They are thigh to thigh, stomach to stomach, chest to chest, and I can tell the moment their cocks brush against each other's because they both let out identical noises, twin *unf*s of helpless pleasure. Embry's hands are all over Ash—fumbling with his vest buttons and shirt buttons—while Ash is the one holding Embry's neck, his other hand running possessive lines up and down Embry's back that make Embry shiver.

Ash moves his attention to Embry's throat again, and Embry's eyes close. And then fly open in near-agony as Ash presses his wide palm to Embry's cock.

"Jesus," Embry moans, pushing against Ash's hand. "Jesus, that feels good."

"You like that?" growls Ash. "You like having my hand on you?"

Embry nods, his mouth opening to make words, but they don't come out. And I've gone from lying on the bed to kneeling, fighting the urge to run my fingers over my clit as I watch. I want to spend all my orgasms on their bodies, not waste one on my own. But *fuck* it's hard to hold back, especially with the rough way Ash rubs Embry, rougher than I would ever dare to be with a man.

And Ash is different with Embry than he is with me, not just rougher but faster and more demanding, like he's less afraid of hurting Embry than he is of hurting me. He fists a hand in his best friend's hair and yanks him down to his knees, while his other hand undoes his fly in a few jerky, feral motions. Embry and I exhale in unison as he draws out his erection, which is so hard that the skin on his shaft looks shiny. There's already pre-cum beaded at the top of the swollen, fat tip. His cock is so obscene like this, framed by his tuxedo pants, dark and hungry as it bobs in front of another man's mouth.

And that other man opens his mouth obediently, training his eyes on Ash's. Ash waits a moment, one hand in Embry's hair, the other on his own cock, looking like some sort of vengeful king meting out the most humiliating justice possible. And then he shoves his penis down Embry's throat without warning, without mercy, drawing out only when he feels like it and pushing in as hard and as fast as he likes.

"Pull yours out," Ash tells Embry. "Pull it out and rub it while you suck me."

Embry does as he's told, unfastening his pants and tugging them down far enough past his hips that he can expose himself. His dick is hard and shiny like Ash's, slightly more slender with a slightly less flared helmet, but just as long and veined and hungry.

My mouth waters, and I slide one leg off the bed to move closer, to see how Embry would taste, but Ash's voice stops me in my tracks. "Stay there, little princess."

"But—"

"This little show is for you, remember?" He turns his gaze away from Embry's handsome lips wrapped around his dick and looks at me. "I *will* tie you to that bed if you can't follow directions. Understood?"

I pout. "Yes, sir."

"Good girls get rewarded, Greer. And bad girls get what's coming to them. Just remember that."

"And what exactly do the bad girls have coming to them?" I ask a little coyly, fluttering my eyelashes.

Embry laughs around Ash's cock, and it must feel good because Ash swears violently and then narrows his eyes at both of us. "*Behave.*"

Reluctantly, I obey, sitting back on my heels in a pile of lace and silk and watching Embry stroke himself as Ash mercilessly fucks his mouth. And as abruptly as he pulled Embry to his knees, he forces him back to his feet and pulls him into a wet, searching kiss.

And then he wraps both of their cocks in his huge hand and squeezes them together.

"Holy shit," Embry mumbles, breaking away from the kiss and dropping his head onto Ash's shoulder. "Fuck."

Ash says nothing, but his jaw is clenched tight as he begins to work his hand up and down their dicks, the undersides and heads slippery and rubbing against each other with each punishing pull of Ash's hand.

Embry is mumbling feverishly into Ash's neck and Ash is nodding at his words, but his hand doesn't let up, doesn't slow or slacken its grip. He jacks off those two cocks as easily as if it were just his own, and more and more pre-cum comes out as he works, making things slippy. Messy.

Neither of them mind the messy, the slippy, the bare biology of stimulation and compression and release. Instead, Embry is rocking into Ash's grip, moaning into his shoulder, and Ash is staring down at the two cocks in his hand like he's never seen anything like it, like he's awed and humbled at the same time.

And me? I'm as tight as a snare drum, my cunt so hot and aching that it feels like a wound between my legs. It's beyond *sexy* or *sexual*—those words are for a different woman in a different place. This is pure physiological need, this is body instead of mind, this is feeling without thinking.

"I'm gonna come," Embry says, his voice muffled by Ash's neck. "I'm gonna come."

"Me too, little prince," Ash says, almost soothingly. "It's okay. Just let it happen. Just give it to me."

God. Does it get any fucking better than this?

Also, it's the first time I've ever heard him call Embry that, *little prince*, and it makes me wonder about all the times he calls me *little princess*. Which of us got our name first, I wonder, and where did the nicknames even come from? And then I decide I don't care. I like that Embry and I are the little prince and little princess, the king's matched set of consorts. I like that we belong to Ash, that our names belong to Ash, that he considers us special and royal and apart from everyone else, but still miles below him, at least in the bedroom.

And Embry must like it too because Ash murmurs, *it's okay, little prince, you don't have to be strong anymore*, and Embry erupts with a pained cry, shooting thick, pulsing spurts over Ash's fist. Ash strokes up once, strokes down once, goes up one more time, and then he gives a soft grunt and ejaculates onto his semen-covered fist, his other hand reaching for Embry's hair and pinning Embry's face against his neck as he shudders his release all over his hand and Embry's flesh. And then he pulls Embry's face to his, rewarding his little prince with soft, sweet kisses even as their cocks still twitch in his hand.

Embry moans into the kisses, clutching his fingers into Ash's shirt, and it's such a moment of extreme vulnerability, these men with their sticky, softening flesh and open, history-laden eyes, that I almost feel guilty watching this moment, more so than any other moment that led up to it.

I don't stop watching, though.

When they pull apart, they both look at me, pupils wide and lips parted. I crawl up to the edge of the bed, and Ash says in a voice so even and calm you'd think nothing had even happened, "It's up to you, little princess. What happens next?"

I run my tongue along my teeth as I think. "Can you take off your clothes and then come back to bed?"

Embry nods dazedly while Ash smiles. "Your wish is our command, angel."

They both head into the bathroom, and I hear the sound of clothes hitting the floor and the sink running, and then they both come back out, cleaned off and completely naked. Even with their recently sated cocks swinging heavily between their legs, they're still deliciously hard and male otherwise. Wide shoulders and tapered waists, notched lines of muscle along their stomachs. Both men have that perfect trail of hair leading from their flat navels to their dicks, Embry's a dark brown and Ash's a jet black, and they both have long legs that look carved from stone.

I watch happily as they stalk toward the bed, their eyes on me, and when they reach me, I press a hand to each of their chests, feeling powerful and powerless all at once.

"I should tell you that I've never done this before," I joke.

"Neither have I," Ash says, and though he's smiling back at me, his voice is serious.

I look between the two of them. "You two never…shared a woman before?"

"We've never shared a woman, and I've never been in bed with more than one person," Ash says. He glances over at Embry, who still seems slightly come-drunk from his release at Ash's hand.

"I have, um, been in bed with more than one person," Embry admits a little sheepishly.

But I'm not jealous—at least for now. I'm curious. I let my hand drift down from his chest to circle his navel. "And was it ever like this? Two men and one woman?"

Embry's beginning to breathe faster, his blue eyes cloudy. "Yes."

"Hmm." My hand drifts lower, following that trail of hair all the way down to the thick root of his penis. He shudders as my playful fingers walk their way around him, stroke along his testicles and probe the sensitive skin of his perineum. "Did you like it?"

His breath catches as I press a gentle knuckle into the soft patch of skin below his scrotum. "Yes."

"Did you make her come?"

My hand moves back to his shaft, which is thickening and growing once again. Embry's head drops back. "*Fuck.* Yes, I made her come."

"You made it feel good?"

"So good," he chokes out. I'm squeezing his crown now, feeling him stiffen and fatten in my hand. "So fucking good."

"Are you going to make me feel good?"

"Shit *yes*, I am," he growls.

Ash's hand circles behind me, sliding down my back and rucking up my skirt to grab my ass. "What do you want, Greer?" he asks gruffly. "What do you want us to do?"

I look up at him, at the tension lining his shoulders and neck, at the semi-hard cock slowly growing between his legs, and I know that it's taking everything he has not to take charge. Not to simply throw his little princess and his little prince down and do whatever he likes with them.

As if he knows what I'm thinking, he pulls me closer, pressing me into his chest. "This is a big step," he murmurs. "I'm asking a lot of you tonight, and I want you to feel safe, if not comfortable."

Just like our first time.

But unlike our first time, I realize there are a couple things that I genuinely wouldn't be ready for if they happened, along with a couple things I really need.

"I want you to take charge," I tell him. I'm still stroking Embry's cock as Ash and I talk, and I can tell Embry's struggling to focus on the conversation happening in front of him instead of on the small hand fisting his length. "But I want…"

I bite my lip. I've never had to set boundaries with Ash before. I've always been able to fling myself right into his depraved claws and know that my safe word was enough, and I find that it's hard to actually say the words out loud.

"You have limits," he finishes for me softly. "Of course, angel. What do you need?"

I feel shy as I say this, although that's fucking ridiculous given the circumstances—these men have seen every part of me there is to see. What can I possibly have to feel shy about? "We haven't done anal yet. And I don't know if I can do my first time with two men…" I blush. "…you know. *Inside.*"

"That's a good idea," Embry agrees hazily. He raises his arm to slide around my back, and then he's grabbing my ass along with Ash. I feel his fingertip graze the small rosette between my cheeks and I shiver. "No one's been inside here?"

I shiver again as he presses against it. "Ash…Ash licked me there. And his finger…*oh*—" Embry's finger breaches me as I talk. "But he hasn't fucked it."

"Yet," Ash adds in a voice full of dark desire.

"*Fuck*," Embry says, pushing his finger in to the knuckle. I arch in pleasure-pain. "I can't fucking wait. But if we're going to make it feel good for your first time, we'll have to do it right. Just one inside at a time. And then"—the finger goes deeper, and I have to let go of his cock and put a hand on his chest so I don't fall over—"we can work you up to taking us both at once. Would you like that?"

"Yes," I gasp, and then his finger is gone, swatted away by Ash.

"No playing while she sets her limits," he scolds and then turns back to me. "What else, little princess?"

I look back at him and then to Embry, and my voice is very small when I say, "I want you both to hold me and kiss me. I know there will be times when we're rough with each other, when we're fast and dirty and there's nothing romantic about it at all. But it's my wedding night tonight, and I just want...I don't know. I want to feel like a bride. I want to feel cherished."

There was nothing else I could have said that would have had such an impact. Ash seizes my waist and yanks me close, burying his face in my hair as Embry drops his head on my shoulder with a noise that sounds ripped from his chest.

"Oh, princess," Ash says roughly. "I vow to God that we will make you feel cherished. We'll make our bride feel loved and perfect."

Embry makes another helpless noise at *our bride*, and so do I, the idea of being a bride to both of these men heart-breakingly joyful and arousing.

"My sweet angel," Ash murmurs in my hair, still holding me tight. He almost sounds near tears. "Without a second thought, I would have given you half my kingdom had you asked. But you asked for the one thing I most desperately want to give you." His lips press into my hair and then he steps back, scrubbing a hand through his hair and chewing on his lip. I see the moment he goes from vulnerable to strong, from gutted by my honest request to taking charge to see my wishes carried out.

He snaps his fingers and I scramble off the bed to kneel at his feet. "Stay here," he orders, his eyes twinkling even though his face is serious. "I have to take a meeting with the expert."

He and Embry step away toward the window and begin talking together in low voices. I only catch a few words, but it seems like he's asking Embry questions and Embry is answering. I hear the words *both* and *comes first to get her as wet as possible* and *it should be you, you know it should be.*

And then Ash turns and walks over to the large armchair on the other side of the room, taking a seat with his bare feet planted firmly on the floor and his thighs spread wide. Even naked, he looks regal and kingly, his hard cock reaching up to his navel and resting against his belly, the sack below his penis large and heavy-looking.

"Crawl," he instructs.

I crawl.

In my wedding dress, with Embry trailing like some sort of palace knight behind me, I crawl to my lord and master, hyperaware of every sensation. The diamonds still heavy in my ears, the sound of lace and tulle rustling along the carpet, the prickling awareness of Embry stalking along behind me, as if to make sure I don't escape.

Like this, it's easy to pretend that I am some sort of captured princess being hauled before her captor-king, or the bride in an arranged marriage facing the tyrant she now belongs to. A frisson of excited fear shoots down my spine at the thought.

Leave it to Ash to cherish me by making me crawl.

When I reach his feet, I know better than to look up at him. Instead, I gracefully settle back onto my knees, my toes tucked together underneath my dress and my arms behind my back in a box position. I keep my eyes down, even though I know the slightest flick upward would reward me with the sight of that thick, delicious cock and those hard, hair-dusted thighs.

I stare at the carpet.

"She's well-trained," Embry remarks.

"Well, she wanted to be trained, unlike other people I know." The words are pointed. Then I feel his finger on my chin. I look up and meet his eyes, the color of sharp bottle glass. "On your feet, princess."

I rise, feeling the expensive skirts of the dress unfold around me as I do.

"Beautiful" is all he says. And then his gaze moves to Embry. "Undress her for me."

Embry obeys, his fingers easily working through the buttons and laces at the back of my gown, plucking them loose and freeing them. The dress opens up in back, and habit causes me to put my hands on the bodice to keep it from falling. Embry forces them both down and then roughly tugs the dress down past the petticoat underneath, tossing the gown carelessly aside. The petticoat comes next and then I'm standing there wearing only my corset, my stockings, and my garter belt.

"The corset too," Ash says. "I want to see her breasts."

Embry unlaces the corset as easily as he did my dress, making me wonder how much practice he's had getting women out of outfits like this. And then I decide I don't want to know.

The corset loosens and is peeled away, revealing my breasts, which are high and firm and aching. My nipples, already tight little furls, grow even tighter in the cool air, under the gaze of both these men.

Ash's cock jumps at the sight, but he seems otherwise unaffected, and his voice is casual when he says, "Turn around, princess. Just like that. You really are so beautiful."

When I'm facing him again, he lifts a finger and gestures to Embry. "Show me her pussy."

I shiver as I feel Embry press against me, his cock so hot against my hip it feels like it could brand my skin. He hooks a hand behind one knee, lifting it up and then spreading me wide, so that I'm balanced on the ball of my foot while Ash leans forward to inspect my cunt. He doesn't say anything, just looks and probes with two indifferent fingers.

"Hold still," Embry whispers in my ear. "Because if he likes what he sees, he'll put his cock in you. Would you like that?"

I nod, whimpering as Ash continues his nonchalant inspection of my cunt. His fingers make a wide V and separate my folds while he reaches up with his other hand to pull back the skin of my clitoral hood, exposing the swollen bud underneath. He presses a thumb against it—doesn't rub it or strum it, just presses—and I practically collapse. Embry keeps me upright.

"Responsive," Ash comments, removing his thumb and fingers. I moan at the loss.

"Would you like me to see if she's wet inside?" Embry asks.

Ash leans back and gives an indifferent nod. Only the painful-looking throb of his cock and the heat in his eyes tell me that he's only playing a game, setting a scene, pushing all of my buttons in exactly the way only he knows how.

Embry reaches around from behind me, still keeping my leg slung over his other arm, and slides his hand over my mound. The moment he makes contact with my pubic bone, I whimper. The moment he pushes two fingers inside me, I cry out, reaching back and grabbing at his neck for balance.

"Oh yes," Embry rasps. "She's wet."

"Wet enough for my cock?"

"Most certainly."

Ash purses his lips and thinks for a moment, then says, "You have ten seconds to get her dripping."

"Show me your wedding ring," he commands. "Show it to me."

I slide my left hand over the top of Embry's head so Ash can see the ring.

"Whom do you belong to?"

"You, Mr. President."

"You're fucking right about that. Ten seconds are up," Ash says. "She better be soaking wet."

Embry pulls back with a reluctant groan. "She is. I made sure of it."

"Good." Ash spreads his legs a little wider. "Put her on top of me. And then put my cock inside her."

The color is back on Embry's cheeks, color that I know is mirrored on my own cheeks, and I feel his hands shaking as he tentatively brackets my waist.

Ash makes an impatient noise. "*Now.* I'm not accustomed to waiting."

Embry's hands tighten on me and then I'm being lifted onto Ash's lap, as easily as if I were a doll. He arranges me so that I'm straddling Ash's hips, and even raised up like this, I can feel the heat rolling off Ash's erection. It takes everything I have not to reach down and impale myself on the perfect member right now.

Embry goes down to one knee, biting his lip as he keeps one hand on my waist and drops the other to fist Ash's girth. With a shuddering breath, he brushes the tip of Ash's cock against the lips of my pussy until he finds the wet, inflamed flesh of my entrance. And with no warning, I'm shoved down onto the huge cock, the invasion so sudden and so big that sparks of pain fly through my chest, stealing my breath.

"Oh, now that is some good pussy," Ash says with a groan, his hips shifting underneath me. "Make her come on me," he tells Embry. "I want to feel what it's like when she comes."

Embry's trembling hands return, this time to my hips, and he slowly moves me back and forth on top of Ash. "Lean forward," he says in a ragged voice. "It will rub your clit against his body."

I do as Embry says, glancing back over my shoulder to see him. His normally perfect hair is tousled and messy from my hands and Ash's hands, and there's sweat gathering along the lines of his clavicle and in the furrowed lines of his stomach. His face is like it was that night in Chicago—gone. Lost. Swallowed up by his own lust. I can tell that following Ash's commands takes all of his focus, and Ash must be able to tell too because he says, "You're doing such a good job, my little prince. You're making me so proud."

Embry's hands tremble even more, but he keeps at his task, moving my hips and fucking Ash's cock with my pussy. I feel like a toy or a sex doll, a tool, an extension of Embry's body, and the feeling is deeply, awfully thrilling. To be just a thing to these men, just a tight pussy, the thing they use to relieve their needs—the thought sends knots of lust pulling deep in my belly, right where Ash's thick cock rubs mercilessly against my womb.

"Does it hurt, Embry?" Ash asks softly. He looks meaningfully down at where Embry's dark red cock is leaking in long drops. "Do you wish you could touch it? Just once?"

Embry drops his head against his chest. A single nod.

"She feels so good," Ash says, with just a hint of cruelty in his face as he does. "You did such a good job making her wet for me. You're moving her so good on top of me. It's too bad you can't feel it too."

"You're mean," Embry whispers. "I forgot how mean you could be without even raising a hand." But he doesn't sound hurt. He sounds like Ash's meanness is water in a desert, like he can't get enough.

"You better make her come fast, Embry. It would be embarrassing if you came without even being touched, wouldn't it? You want to save your seed for her pussy, don't you?"

"Jesus," Embry grinds out. "Jesus, Ash."

But then he's moving my hips harder, helping me fuck Ash while Ash tucks his hands behind his head and watches the two of us work my cunt on his cock like he's watching the evening news.

Embry knows instinctively what I need, not a fast up-and-down but a rolling grind back and forth, and between Ash's hard cock against my womb and the grind of my clit and seeing Ash so aloof and detached and in complete dominant mode, it doesn't take long before that lust finally knots itself so tightly that it breaks.

"You're getting tighter," Ash remarks, a flicker of interest in his eyes as he looks down at where we're joined. "Are you going to come on me?"

I nod, unable to find words, unable to find the strength to do anything but grab onto the arms of the chair as the climax tears loose inside of me. I grind myself down as far as I can go, feeling Ash's testicles against the cradle of my ass, desperate for that hard presence inside of me, that hard spear piercing right through the epicenter of my need. And Ash, who can read my body better than I can read my own, leans forward and wraps his arms around me, pulling me down onto him as he thrusts up.

Both Embry and Ash are holding me in place as I shudder and quake uncontrollably, holding me pinned against Ash so that there's no escaping the overwhelming pleasure, the vicious waves of heat racing down to my toes and up to the top of my scalp. "Ash," I gasp. "Embry. Oh God. Oh my God."

It's there on Ash's cock, it's everywhere that I have nerve endings, and it holds me tighter even than my men are holding me. And as I come down, I see that Ash's jaw is clenched tight and his eyes bright, and then Embry is reaching underneath us, and I feel him circle Ash's testicles and tug them down.

"Shit," Ash hisses. "Fuck."

But slowly, agonizingly, I feel him relax underneath me, his stomach unknotting and his face losing that taut expression of pain.

"Ouch," he finally says, with a laugh, his laugh jabbing his cock into my still tender cunt. "Thanks for that."

"You deserved it after teasing me about coming early," Embry sniffs.

And then I'm pulled off Ash's cock and swept into his arms. He carries me so easily, his strong arms like steel underneath me. "You aren't going to come?" I ask fuzzily, still dazed from my orgasm.

"Oh, I am, doll. All three of us are going to come again. But that was to warm you up for the real show."

"The real show?" I ask, confused, as he lays me carefully on the bed. And then he climbs in next to me and I feel Embry on my other side, two hot-blooded parentheses surrounding my naked body. "*Oh*," I say, breathing hard. "I see."

"Yes," Embry says, turning me so that I'm facing Ash. Embry nuzzles the back of my neck. "I told Ash you'd need to come first. We both thought that little scene might set you off nicely."

I blush.

Ash moves closer to me, running a hand from the nip of my waist to the curve of my hip. "Don't be embarrassed, angel. I know exactly how you need to be cherished." And then he pulls my leg up to his hip, opening up my wet pussy. He doesn't enter me though. Instead, he uses my leg to pull me so close that our bodies are completely pressed together, his erection crushed against my belly, my breasts crushed against his chest, and then our lips meet in a scorching kiss.

"My wife," he murmurs against my lips. "My little princess."

His mouth is demanding, needy, and as soon as I think I've adjusted to the sensation of his firm tongue sliding against mine, I feel Embry's mouth on my neck. His cock is pressed against my ass, his hips grinding it into the peach-like skin there, and his hands are everywhere—forcing their way between Ash and me to roughly palm my breast or reaching over my leg to pluck at my clit or spanking my ass with hard, sporadic spanks that made me gasp and grunt into Ash's mouth.

And then the two of them show me the meaning of the word *cherish*. My hair is coiled around hands and kissed from the ends to the roots. My stomach is caressed and my back is rubbed, my thighs are chafed while my feet and hands are massaged. My lips are gently bitten and kissed by one male mouth while another mouth marks love behind my knees and on the small of my back and behind my ear. My nipples are sucked, both at once, by mouths so soft and warm, and those mouths move to my inner thighs, biting and kissing and nibbling. Those same inner thighs are chafed and teasingly scratched with stubble as the men fight over my pussy, both of them taking turns suckling my clit and tongue-fucking my channel and tracing letters of love across all the wet, swollen flesh. The sight of those heads wrestling for space and impatiently nudging each other out of the way sends my toes curling.

Time disappears, becomes nothing, and there's only them. My men. My husband and his best friend, the president and the vice president, two ex-soldiers who couldn't help falling in love with each other.

Who couldn't help falling in love with the same woman.

Twice they bring me to the brink of orgasm, and twice they back off, their hands and mouths suddenly preoccupied with sucking my fingers or tugging my hair, and by the time they move back up to their original positions—Embry behind me and Ash in front—I'm squirming and bothered and mindless with need. You could have asked me any question, and I wouldn't have known the answer. The only word I can remember is *more*.

More

and *more*

and *more*…

More hands. More stubble. More quiet grunts and insatiable mouths. I need it all, want it all, will die without it, and it's at that moment that Ash slings my leg back over his hip and brushes his lips across mine.

"Okay," he says, his eyes on me but his voice directed at Embry. "It's time, little prince."

"Thank you," Embry breathes. He presses so close behind me that I can feel the rough hair of his thigh against the back of mine. And then he reaches down, and with a groan that I can feel all the way down to my toes, he guides himself to my pussy, all eight straight inches sliding in with one thick thrust.

I come immediately. I'm so on edge, so wound up from the last however many minutes and hours of their attention, that the second I feel Embry inside of me after all these years, I release.

"Oh fuck, Greer," Embry groans in my ear as I convulse around him. Ash is chuckling to himself as he kisses my face and neck. Embry thrusts in deeper, my ass smashed against his hips, and he holds himself still so he can feel each flutter and wave of my walls. "I've been waiting so long," he says breathlessly. "So long to feel you come around my cock again. So long to fuck you. And oh God, it's so much better than I remembered."

The pulses eventually stop, and then Ash kisses my forehead. "I'm going to finger you while Embry is inside of you, okay?"

"Okay," I say, so languid and limp after my climax that I'll agree to anything.

"It will be uncomfortable at first," Embry warns in my ear. "But we'll go slow and we'll make it good for you."

"I'll be checking in with you," Ash says. "This is…new. For everyone except Embry at least."

I feel Ash's fingers against my clit, rubbing past the too-sensitive flesh and making me jolt as he finds the place where Embry's flesh meets my own. Embry grunts and I know that Ash is doing something to him that I can't see, something that makes the man behind me stiffen and growl. "If you want me to last," he grits out, "you're going to have to stop that."

Ash gives a dark little laugh and returns his attention to me, pushing one finger inside of me. "That's not so—*oh fuck*." Ash added two more fingers in the middle of my sentence, and now my back is arching, my body bucking automatically to get away from the foreign pressure.

"Talk to me, angel," Ash says calmly. "Open your eyes and talk to me."

I didn't even realize my eyes were closed. I open them and try to find the breath to speak, reaching past the pain swirling behind my sternum. "It's uncomfortable," I manage. "Embry was right."

"It will get better," Embry assures me. "But if you need to stop or take a breather, just say the word."

But I don't want to say the word. I want to have both of them inside of me, I want to have a moment where all three of us are completely joined. Ash presses his forehead to mine, looking at me through his long, dark eyelashes. "Breathe with me," he coaches quietly. "Follow my breathing."

It's nearly impossible, but I manage it. I manage to bring a breath deep into my stomach and slowly let it out, mimicking Ash's exaggerated breaths. And as I breathe and the pain gradually turns into something else, Ash moves his hand so that his thumb can rub against my clit while his fingers massage the spongy front wall of my channel.

"Oh," I exhale. "Oh *God*."

"There you go," Embry croons. "That's not so bad now, is it?"

"No." I shake my head a bunch of times and both men laugh. "Not so bad at all."

"I'm adding my last finger now," Ash warns me. "Keep breathing into your stomach and try to hold still."

It's to the point where I can't discern what flesh is finger and what flesh is cock, there's only the pressure and the pain and the orgasm lurking out of sight, feeding off of both. But I keep breathing and I hold still, and as Embry nuzzles the nape of my neck and Ash keeps his forehead against mine, the sharp pain fades away, leaving behind the pleasure, now stronger than ever.

Embry drops a kiss on my shoulder. "Greer, it's going to be tighter when he puts his cock inside of you, but not that much tighter. It will be just like this, where the pain is followed by pleasure, but it's easiest if you hold still. Do you think you can do that?"

I feel drunk. Or drugged. Or maybe this is just what joy feels like, a thick cock and an extra four fingers. "I don't know," I reply shakily.

"Okay," Embry says soothingly. "That's okay. We can help you hold still. Would you like that?"

"I—I think so."

"Okay, sweetheart. We're right here with you, okay? You just keep talking to us, and tell us if you need to pause for a moment. We're right here with you and"—his voice gets thicker, rougher—"and we love you. We're going to take care of you."

I give a dazed nod, and both of them move to wrap their arms around me, Embry's arms tight around my waist and Ash's wrapped around Embry's shoulders, pinning me fast between them. My face is in Ash's neck and Embry's face is in the back of mine, and there's nowhere to move, nowhere to go. I dredge up my safe word from the depths of my mind, but I won't use it. No matter the pain, I won't use it because I *want* this pain.

I'll die without it.

"Breathe, Greer," Ash reminds me as he takes himself in hand and guides himself to my pussy. "There you go. Just like that. Good girl."

"The first part is the hardest part," Embry promises, his mouth moving against my skin. "Once his crown is inside, the rest gets easier."

Embry is right. Ash presses his cock against Embry's cock and my entrance, and I have this sudden moment of cold fear when I realize this won't be the gentle pushing and sliding of normal sex; Ash is going to have to wedge himself in; Ash is going to have to shove and thrust and punish.

I don't breathe.

And then he stabs inside of me with a merciless grunt.

I think I scream. I *know* I buck and thrash against them, my body trying to drag itself away from the brutal invasion, but their huge arms are clamped tight around me and my body is held still for their cocks to fuck.

"Greer, Greer," Embry soothes, and Ash does the same, his handsome face in front of mine crooning meaningless words to me, like I'm a skittish horse—*stay* and *good girl, there's a good girl* and *it will be over in just a minute, just another minute, baby.*

It's impossible. It's unlivable. I'm being split apart like an atom and my pain will burn down the world.

"You're forgetting to breathe," Ash says gently.

I'm still trying to move away from the pain, still straining against their iron arms, and all of us are sweaty with the effort of it.

"Hurts," I manage to get out. "It hurts."

"I know, baby," Embry says lovingly from behind me. "I know. But it won't in a minute, I promise."

"Breathe," Ash repeats sternly, and his President voice

reaches me where his gentle voice can't. I suck in a sudden deep breath, and the rush of oxygen clears my head.

I burst into tears.

The men kiss me and murmur to me, their teeth and lips and words making up for all the pain their bodies are causing, and I don't know how long the minutes pass like this, with me sobbing and sweaty between them, and them hard and brutal inside of me, repeating over and over again how much they love me, how beautiful I am, how good they'll make me feel.

I surrender. Completely. I lose myself to the pain, sobbing against Ash's throat. I stop struggling against it, stop fighting it, and let it become me. Not for them, not even for my sir, my president—not this time.

This time, the surrender is mine and my own. My choice, my need. My destiny.

"Breathe," Ash reminds me over and over again, and over and over again I do, each breath a gift, a chemical, astonishing gift. Each breath anchors me to myself, to this moment, to the two men I love, to the matching metal on Ash's and my fingers, to the rain outside. Each breath anchors me to the pain, and the moment I allow that fusion to happen, the pain disappears. Bit by bit, as if dissolved by my surrender, the pain is swallowed up by the swell of building pleasure, mere raindrops swallowed by a vast and endless sea.

"There she is," Embry says wonderingly. "There she is."

At some point their grip on me has loosened, freeing their hands to rub soothing paths along my thighs and my waist, and I realize that I'm staying there completely on my own, opening myself to their bodies not because they are forcing me but because I want it. Because it's starting to feel like more than pain, more than the sharp pressure of being so viciously stretched. It's starting to feel *good*—good like earlier.

Good like a different way to be cherished.

"Oh, angel," Ash says roughly, pulling back enough to see my tear-lined face. "You are too fucking beautiful like this." He kisses my hair, my cheeks, my lips. "You are amazing," he murmurs in an awed voice. "My amazing princess."

I can't speak. I can only nod.

"I want to fuck you now," my husband says with a yearning look down at my body. "But I need to know you're ready."

I nod again and he smiles. "Words, princess. I need to *hear* you say you're ready."

It's so hard to find the right words, like catching fireflies in the velvet dark that's become my mind. "Yes," I finally manage. "I'm ready."

They begin.

Ash goes first, pumping his hips experimentally, sliding the length of his cock against the length of Embry's, and I feel Embry shudder behind me and mumble something unintelligible.

"Fuck, that feels good," Ash grunts, thrusting in again. "It's like I'm fucking you and her at the same time."

I feel Embry nod against my neck, as if he's as lost in the sensation as I am.

Because I am.

Lost.

And then both men begin moving, going slow to find the rhythm that suits us all best, because of course it's not about finding the best way for two people, but for *three*, and then they find it, that perfect tempo, their two cocks rubbing together inside my pussy the same way they rubbed together inside Ash's fist earlier tonight. Underneath me, I feel the way their sacks press and rub against each other's, the tangle of my legs with theirs, the slippery wet way our skin moves against each other's—so wet I know we might have to call housekeeping for new sheets after this is all done.

I'm shaking now, shaking from fullness, shaking from

endorphins and adrenaline, and I feel feverish—hot and cold and sweaty and covered in goose bumps, and the men are the same way, just long, lean expanses of sweaty, shivering muscles, and when Ash finds my hand and drags it to his mouth to kiss my wedding ring, I know it's almost all over for me. I know that the feverish pleasure is about to surge past every lingering ache and doubt and drown me as I lie.

"Ash," Embry groans. "God, Ash, your cock. And she's so tight, Jesus *fuck*, so fucking tight…"

"I know," Ash grunts, shoving into me, sweat dripping from his face. "Believe me, I know."

"I'm—" I can't find my breath or my words or my thoughts. All there is inside me is the wave, the shuddering, tangy, metallic threat of an orgasm too strong to withstand.

"I know, princess," Ash says. "We'll follow you. Be brave and go first, and we'll follow you."

I want to respond, I should respond, but I can't because I don't exist any longer. I'm nothing but electricity and chemicals and fuel, I'm nothing but a barely held together collection of molecules about to fly apart. Embry is sweating and desperate behind me, Ash all forceful grace and strength in front, and then both of them shove up at the same time, both perfect, flared tips kissing against my womb at the same time, and once again I'm being split apart like an atom, once again I burn down the world, but this time when I cry out, it's from pure, helpless joy, it's from pleasure and love and perfection and eternity and marriage—this very real marriage happening between the three of us.

They keep their word and they follow me, Embry first with a series of grunts that send my bones vibrating with an aftershock orgasm, and Ash with a pant and a moan that hits me square in the chest, cracking my ribs and puncturing my heart with the heavenly music of it. They keep fucking through their orgasms, masculine grunts and curse words as their semen spills inside of me, as everything inside of me is slippery and warm and intimate.

Minutes pass, minutes where it's just the rain and the pounding of our pulses, and everything is wet and sticky but we just can't bear to unspool this moment, to pull apart what we've just shared, to separate what we've just joined together.

I stare up into Ash's eyes, which are clearer and happier than I've ever seen them, and then I start laughing, not because there's anything funny, but because I'm so happy that I'll cry if I don't laugh, except I've already started to cry again too.

My laughing forces both softening cocks to slip out and Embry groans, but he's laughing too, and Ash joins in as warmth spills out of me.

"We need a shower," I say in between laughs.

"We need a *nap*," Embry says, rolling onto his back and yawning boyishly.

"Shower first," Ash insists. "Our poor princess needs a little aftercare."

Except that once we get into the shower, the aftercare somehow turns into more sex, Ash and Embry together, and then me and Embry, and then the three of us again, and Ash makes me swallow double the recommended dose of Advil for my poor cunt before we strip the bed of the ruined sheets and curl up together on the bare mattress, my prince on one side of me, and my king on the other.

Embry falls asleep immediately, and I turn to face Ash, who's blinking slowly and worshipfully at me. "Happy getting married day," I tell him.

"Happy getting married day," he says back.

"What happens next?" I ask, knowing he has to be sick of that question from me, but he just smiles.

"I was wondering when you were going to ask that."

"I don't know why I ask…you always say you don't know."

"Except I do know this time." Ash wraps his arms around both me and the sleeping Embry, gathering us close to him. I press my face against his neck and hear the gentle rumble of his throat as he speaks. "What happens next is we all live happily ever after."

CHAPTER 30

I WAKE UP SORE, SWEATY, AND HAPPY.

Embry has flopped over onto his stomach, one leg bent, snoring loudly, and Ash is still wrapped around me, although his arms are slack and he's flung a leg out to the side to cool off. His breathing is even and steady, and I know if I could see his face in the dark, it would be that rare expression of vulnerability that squeezes my chest every time I see it.

I blink in the dark for a few minutes, content and safe and transformed. I feel like a different person. A realer person. Like a fairy-tale princess awakened from slumber. But this fairy tale also comes with an aching pussy and a powerful thirst, so I carefully wriggle out of bed to go find some more Advil and a glass of water.

It's only been a couple of hours since we collapsed onto the bed, and it's a deep dark outside the windows, even with the city glowing around us. *Plenty of time to snuggle back in*, I think as I use the restroom and swallow the pills. *A perfect way to end a perfect night.*

My phone buzzes on the nightstand, and since I'm up, I go check it.

> Abilene: I know it's the middle of the nite but I need to talk. can u come down to the lobby? It's important.

I'm already grabbing my robe and putting it on, searching for hotel slippers to go with it.

> Me: omg, are you okay? I'm coming down now.
> Abilene: I'm okay, I just need to see u.

With my hand on the door, I think about waking up one of the men and telling them I'm going downstairs, but they both look so perfect and boyish stretched out on the bed that I hate to wake them. I'll tell Luc or one of the other agents waiting in the hallway, I decide. And if Ash wakes up, then he'll be able to find me right away.

But when I open the door and step out into the hallway, I don't see Luc. Or any of the other agents. I slip my phone into my robe pocket and walk farther down the hallway, puzzled. Even while we sleep, there's usually perimeters of agents guarding the room. We're never really alone.

I turn the corner to the see the elevator, and again—no one. Even though I know for sure there's always an agent at the elevator.

Something's wrong, I think, and the moment I think that, I know I need to get back to the room, back to Ash. It was stupid of me to come this far down the hallway in the first place, but the best thing to do now would be to—

Oh shit.

There's a man standing in front of me wearing a hotel employee uniform and blue latex gloves, a cleaning cart at rest behind him. His uniform says *Daryl*, but I know he's not a hotel employee. Because I've seen him before.

At the Carpathian diplomatic dinner.

I take a deep breath, preparing to run. And he steps toward me with a cold smile.

Ready for Embry's Story?

I've been many things.

I've been a son and a stepbrother. An army captain and a vice president.

But only with *him* am I a prince. His little prince.

Only with Maxen and Greer does my world make sense, only between them can I find peace from the demons that haunt me. But men like me aren't made to be happy. We don't deserve it. And I should have known a love as sharp as ours could cut both ways.

My name is Embry Moore and I serve at the pleasure of the president of the United States...for now.

This is the story of an American Prince.

Read on for a sneak peek at
American Prince, the next in the New
Camelot series from Sierra Simone

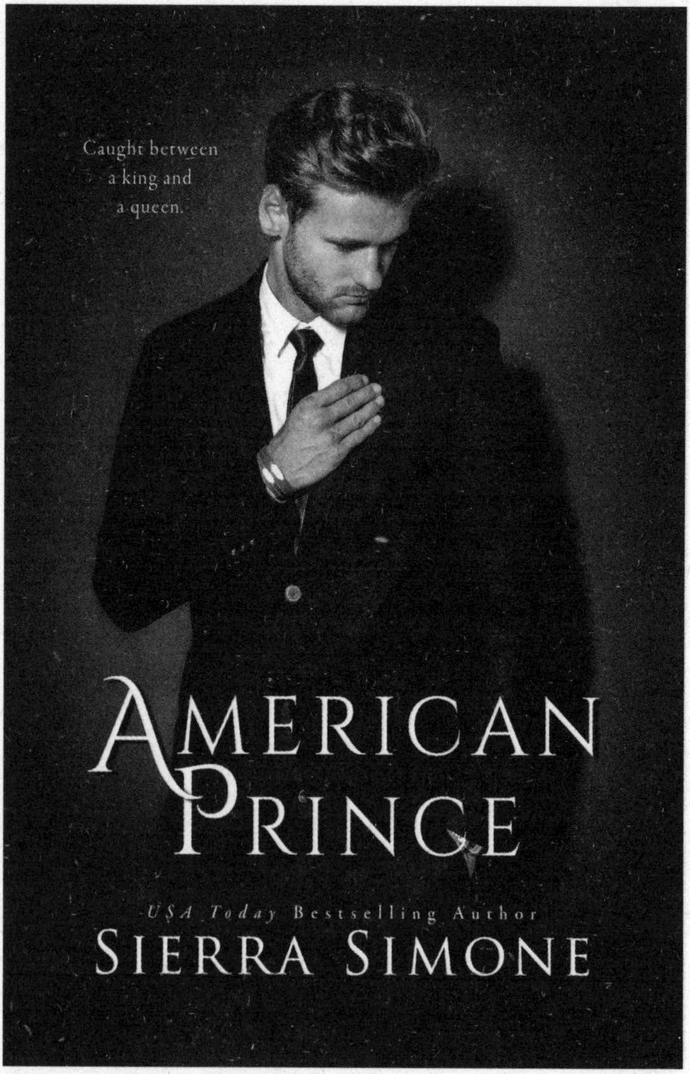
Caught between
a king and
a queen.
AMERICAN
PRINCE
USA Today Bestselling Author
SIERRA SIMONE

CHAPTER 1
EMBRY

BEFORE

I MET A KING WHEN I WAS TWENTY-ONE YEARS OLD.

But that's getting ahead of the story.

First, about me, Embry Moore, son of the terrifying Lieutenant Governor Vivienne Moore. To the outside world, I must have looked like a prince. I grew up with horses and boats and my own fucking lake, went to the most exclusive schools, graduated college early, and went off to play war because it sounded like fun.

It was before the war had actually started, back when people thought the Carpathian separatists would settle down like they always had, and it seemed like the best kind of adventure to have: spend some time in the mountains, play soldier for a while, build a résumé toward my inevitable future in politics.

Princes do it all the time.

Easy.

And it *was* easy…until my second month on base.

I wanted cigarettes, I think. That's why I missed the beginning of the fight. Evening had fallen, a rosy gloaming that masked the squat ugliness of the base, and as I grabbed the silver cigarette case off my bed and trotted back down to the yard, I remember thinking that the world couldn't get more beautiful than it was in that moment. The smears of orange and red and purple off to the west, the dark spurs of the mountains to the east, the brisk, clean air, and the promise of stars twinkling overhead. What could be lovelier than this? What else could stop my thoughts, stop my breathing, stop everything that wasn't simply awe and unbelieving gratitude?

It shows how differently I used to think then, asking *what* instead of *who*.

I turned the corner into the yard, already pulling out a cigarette to light, when a blur of gray-brown-green crashed past me, making contact with another blur of gray-brown-green. I jumped back, the cigarette knocked from my hand and trampled underfoot, and I narrowly missed getting sucked into the tornado of fists and boots that was now drawing a crowd from everywhere nearby.

"That was my last cigarette, asshole," I said to no one in particular.

A big guy called Dag—everyone had forgotten his real name by that point—was staring at the fight with his arms crossed and a keen expression of disgust. "Dipshit."

I grunted in agreement. The commissary had recently stopped carrying cigarettes as part of some new health initiative, and I really, *really* didn't want to have to walk the mile down to the little Ukrainian village to get a new pack of smokes tonight. But now it looked like I had to.

"You going to step in?" Dag asked me, tilting his head toward the fracas in front of us.

"After they made me drop my cigarette? They deserve a few black eyes." I said it jokingly, but Dag didn't crack a smile. I added, "They're not my guys anyway." It was a big fucking base, after all, and I wasn't about to exert all my energy for two jackasses fighting over God knew what.

"You *are* the only officer around though," Dag pointed out.

"Like you care one way or the other." But I glanced around the yard, and sure enough, I was the highest-ranking soldier there.

With a long-suffering sigh for Dag's benefit and after muttering something about not being a fucking babysitter, I walked forward to break up the boys and make it clear that one of them owed me a new cigarette.

But someone beat me to it.

A wide-shouldered man strode into the center of the fight, as calmly as you might walk along a beach, grabbed one soldier by the back of his shirt, and yanked him back. He moved fast to restrain the other fighter, so fast that my mind only registered slivers of him. Flashing eyes, a full mouth. Dark hair. The kind of olive skin you were born with, the kind that stayed warm and bronze through the winter. Italian maybe, or Greek.

"Holy shit," Dag said. He sounded impressed. Or maybe not. Sometimes it was hard to tell with Dag.

Percival Wu, one of our translators for the locals, came up behind us from the barracks. "That's Colchester," he told Dag and me in a low voice. "He just got here yesterday."

In that moment, I didn't care who he was. I was just relieved I didn't have to step in. To be honest, I'd only left OCS a few months ago, and it still felt strange to be in charge of other people.

I grew up around power, around the kind of people who exercised authority with effortless ease, but I myself had spent most of my life dodging any and all responsibility. Consequences were something to be charmed and flirted out of, other people were worth only how much fun they could give me. I had next to no practice taking care of other people… I could barely keep myself out of trouble.

In fact, I rarely bothered to—why would I, when trouble was usually so much fun for everyone involved?

I know this all makes me sound selfish, and I was. I was a bad, selfish child who grew into a bad, selfish man…but don't mistake selfishness for obliviousness. I knew how bad I was. I knew how sinful, even though I told myself I didn't believe in sin. In the late hours of the night, after I'd drank or fucked or fought, depending on the circumstances, I'd lie in bed and watch the stars wheel through the sky outside and know—just *know*—that I was unnatural somehow. That some people were born wrong, born all warped and empty inside, that I was born without the parts that made people brave or pure or good. I knew that I was born without a conscience, or maybe a heart or a soul. I would think about this, then I would twist my body into the sheets and shove my face into the pillow. And as the air left my body, I would think about every awful thing I'd done that day. Every awful thing I'd ever done. And I'd hate myself for all of it. Hate myself for how selfish I could be, how thoughtless. I knew better than to chase anger or lust or escapism to their inevitable bleeding, sticky, intoxicated ends, but every single time, I did it anyway.

Every. Single. Time.

But it was only dusk then, and night hadn't come yet and neither had the self-loathing. In that moment, I only felt relief and a vague kind of gratitude, and the desire to go find another cigarette.

"Show's over, I guess," I told Dag as I turned away to go down to the village. And then I felt a presence behind me. A presence that wasn't the slender form of Wu or the hulking, stone-faced Dag, and I stopped walking. But I didn't turn.

Not at first.

"You want to tell me why your cigarette was more important than your men, Lieutenant?"

The voice was the kind that made you pause. It was deep, yes, and held this interesting mix of husk and melody, like a song whose notes had been burned around the edges.

But it wasn't the sound itself that stopped you—it was its purity. The strength of it. And not the kind of strength men my age pretended to have, all unearned swagger, but actual strength.

Calm, clear, honest.

Unequivocal.

It was the voice of someone who didn't lie in bed at night and wish he'd never been born.

I turned to face him, already thrown by the sound of that voice, and then I felt completely knocked down by the sight of his face. Dark eyebrows above eyes such a complicated shade of green that I couldn't decide if they were truly pale or truly dark. A serious mouth and high cheekbones, and a square jaw shadowed by stubble. Given his hyper-fucking-regulation haircut and gleaming boots, I guessed that Colchester was not the kind of man to miss his morning shave. Just the kind of man who couldn't keep a smooth face for more than a few hours.

But it was more than his features that struck you. It was his expression, his gaze. He looked to be my age, and yet there was something in his face that seemed older than his years. It wasn't even about age, now that I think about it. It was about *time*. He looked like a man from a different era, a man who should have been riding horses through thick forests, rescuing damsels and slaying dragons.

Noble.

Heroic.

Kingly.

All of this I thought in an instant. And in the next instant I had the sudden, uncomfortable feeling that he had just seen all he needed to know about *me*, that he'd seen my selfishness and my empty carnality and my dissolute laziness. That he'd seen every night I'd pressed a pillow over my face and wished I had the courage to snuff out my own worthless existence.

And I felt a sudden flush of shame. For being me. For being Embry Moore—Second Fucking Worthless Lieutenant Embry Moore—and that pissed me off. Who was this pretty asshole to make me feel ashamed of myself? Only *I* got to make myself feel that way.

I took a step closer to him, squaring off so that our chests were only a hand's span apart. With some satisfaction, I realized I had an inch or so on him, although he probably had a good thirty pounds of pure muscle on me. And with even more satisfaction, I realized his uniform had a gold bar on it. A second lieutenant like me.

I found my voice. "They weren't my men, *Lieutenant.*"

"So you were just going to let them beat the shit out of each other?"

I rolled my eyes. "They're big boys. They can take care of themselves."

Colchester's face didn't change. "It's our job to look out for them."

"I don't even know who the fuck they are."

"So when you're out there, fighting the Carpathians, that's how it's going to be? You're only going to look out for the men directly underneath you?"

"Oh, trust me, Lieutenant Colchester, I always keep both eyes on a man directly underneath me. Both hands too."

Dag and Wu laughed, and I grinned, but in the blink of an eye I was backed against the metal wall of the barracks with Colchester's warm forearm pressed against my throat.

"Is this all a joke to you?" he asked quietly, so quietly that the others couldn't hear. "Are those fake mountains over there? Fake bullets in your gun? Because it's not a joke to the Carpathians. They don't have fake bullets, Lieutenant Moore, and it won't be fake IEDs they plant in the roads either. You're going to be asking these men to follow you, even when they doubt you, even when you doubt yourself, and so you better believe it matters that you take care of them. Here, there, every-fucking-where. And if you can't accept that, I suggest you march over to the captain's office and ask for a transfer back home."

"Fuck you," I growled.

He pressed his arm tighter against the side of my throat, cutting off most—but not all—of my blood flow, and his eyes swept across my face and then down my body, which he had caged against the wall with his own. His eyes looked darker in the shadow of the wall, like the cold depths of a lake, but there was nothing else cold about him right now. His body was warm against mine and I could see the pulse thrumming in his neck, and for the briefest second, his lips parted and those long eyelashes fluttered, like he meant to close his eyes but forgot how.

"Fuck you," I repeated, but weakly this time, weak from his arm against my neck and something else I didn't care to examine.

He leaned in close and whispered in my ear, "I'd rather it was the other way around." And he stepped back, dropping his arm. I sucked in a ragged breath, the fresh oxygen cutting through my blood like ice.

By the time my vision cleared, Lieutenant Colchester was gone.

ACKNOWLEDGMENTS

To every author who wrote a book about King Arthur, to my mother for giving me a copy of *The Once and Future King* when I was only eight, and to my AP English teacher, who let me make my senior project a book about how sexy Mordred was.

To Laurelin Paige, who held my hand, read countless drafts, quoted Rob Bell to me, and finally got me back for that time I made her change the beginning of *Fixed on You*. You were right about the beginning; you were right about everything. Of course.

To Nancy Smay of Evident Ink, the Editor From Heaven, who corrected my tenses and patiently explained to me exactly why a president can't talk about drone strikes in front of his new girlfriend. I don't deserve you. NEVER LEAVE ME.

To the No Shadow Bitches, I won't out you here, and I solemnly swear not to get *one* of you worked up about biting necks again.

To Melanie Harlow and Kayti McGee, my sNAtches, my confidantes. And at Target prices!

To Ashley Lindemann, who pets my head and keeps the lights on while I transmogrify into a hermit crab. Everyone should know by now we're a package deal.

To Jenn Watson, who tells me what to do and has zillions of great ideas and has never once complained about the lecherous way I look at her.

To Rebecca Friedman, you are possibly the smartest, most energetic woman I know, and sometimes when you're trying to talk to me about agent stuff, I space out and just think about how pretty you are.

To my Lambs—you guys are the best readers a girl could ask for, and I promise to keep writing the most depraved smut possible for all you very depraved ladies. And especially you sexy ladies I met in Birmingham and LA and Virginia Beach, let's just all go on vacation together someday, k?

To the bloggers, all you amazing wizard women who read faster than I can shoot a glass of whiskey and still find the time to be online and cheerful and helpful. As always, the Dirty Laundry girls and Literary Gossip girls make my days brighter. Amie and Martha, there are some times where your kindnesses have been the things that gave me the strength to keep wrestling with this book. Candi, you are the oil in my engine (yes I want that to sound dirty) and Ang Oh, someday I want to come canvassing with you and your wife and learn all your secrets to having such pretty hair.

To my fellow authors who have propped me up with a drink or a hug or have let me chug champagne in their backyard while I had hand, foot, and mouth disease (it's a long story), thank you. Especially CD Reiss, Becca Hensley Mysoor, JR Gray, Stacy Kestwick, Sarah MacLean, and a bunch of young adult authors who I won't embarrass by putting their names in the back of a book about double vaginal penetration, but you know who you are. Or at

403

least you remember drinking with me in Illinois or in Texas or at the Lake of the Ozarks or in Fort Morgan or in Tennessee.

And finally to Josh, my once and future king. You'll always be my King Arthur (and scotch will always be my Lancelot. Or Tom Hiddleston if he's free. I love you!).

About the Author

Sierra Simone is a *USA Today* bestselling author and former librarian who spent too much time reading romance novels at the information desk. She lives with her husband and family in Kansas City.

Sign up for her newsletter to be notified of releases, books going on sale, events, and other news!

thesierrasimone.com

thesierrasimone@gmail.com